KATY REGAN

The Story of You

HARPER

Harper
An imprint of HarperCollins*Publishers*
77–85 Fulham Palace Road,
Hammersmith, London W6 8JB

www.harpercollins.co.uk

A Paperback Original 2014
1

Copyright © Katy Regan 2014

Katy Regan asserts the moral right to
be identified as the author of this work

A catalogue record for this book
is available from the British Library

ISBN: 9780007237456

Set in Sabon LT Std by Palimpsest Book Production Limited,
Falkirk, Stirlingshire

Printed and bound in Great Britain by
Clays Ltd, St Ives plc

MIX
Paper from
responsible sources
FSC **FSC™ C007454**
www.fsc.org

FSC™ is a non-profit international organisation established to promote
the responsible management of the world's forests. Products carrying the
FSC label are independently certified to assure consumers that they come
from forests that are managed to meet the social, economic and
ecological needs of present and future generations,
and other controlled sources.

Find out more about HarperCollins and the environment at
www.harpercollins.co.uk/green

THE STORY OF YOU

Katy Regan was Features Writer and Commissioning Editor of *Marie Claire* before leaving to concentrate on writing fiction in 2007. Whilst there, she wrote a column *And then there were three . . . sort of* about her experience of having a baby with her best friend (who just remained a friend). This proved so successful it ran for two years and now, ten years ᵗ ᵗ people still remember it.

When she's not writing fiction, Katy writes features for the likes of *Stella* magazine, *Psychologies* and *Marie Claire*. She is also blogging about her experience ᴏᴛ writing her fifth novel on her website, www.katyregan.com. She lives in Hertfordshire with her son. *The Story of You* is her fourth novel.

Also by Katy Regan

In loving memory of Nanna R and Grandad F

ACKNOWLEDGEMENTS

Well, this one was a beast! And without the skill, talent and, above all, patience of so many people, it definitely wouldn't have seen the light of day. Huge thanks then go to my editor, Kim Young, who stuck with me, the book, and more moving deadlines than you could shake a stick at. Also to Lizzy Kremer, whose unwavering belief, support and creative input never cease to amaze me. Harriet Moore, the restructuring of this book was basically down to you and your belief in it truly kept me going when I was flailing. How can one so young be so clever?

I want to thank, as always, all the team at HarperCollins: Kate, Claire, Thalia, Heike (for yet another gorgeous cover), the Sales team, Art, Marketing and of course, the lovely Louise Swannell, plus anyone I've forgotten for all your hard work and creativity. Also, thank you to everyone at David Higham Associates.

This book was more research-heavy than any other book I have written and many people gave their time to help me make things authentic and factually correct (give or take poetic licence where appropriate). However, *very* special thanks go to Katie Wiblin, (a *real* psychiatric nurse) who was on the end of the phone and email throughout the entire long, drawn-out process and who put up with and answered my constant, ridiculous questions with amazing diligence and patience. I couldn't have written this without you Katie! Also, in no particular order, thank you to the following people who helped me with specifics (I apologise in advance for anyone I have forgotten): Nigel Simpson, Laurie Armantrading, John Spector, Kiran Ramani, Tom Hocknell, Kellie Smith, Nathan Filer, Angela Drinnan, Mandy Carey and everyone at Buckinghamshire MIND, Sam Afhim and RETHINK, Claire Townend, Philip Hodson, John Maynard, Andrew Marshall, Chris Flood, Thomas Patel, Lynne Jordan, Melissa Sanchez, Debbie Thomson and Michael Heard.

Huge thanks to Helen Nesbitt and Louis Quail for reading and giving invaluable feedback and HELP! And to Sue Kite for long discussions in her kitchen. Also, to all my lovely author friends, online and in the flesh. A girl could not wish for more support and love with this book and I am forever indebted.

FINALLY, thank you, as ever, to friends and family for putting up with me. I promise I won't make such a meal about the next one. (And yes, I do know I say that every time.)

PART ONE

PROLOGUE

Mid-May 2013

The first time it happens, I'm on the Tube; coming back from a Depression Alliance coffee morning with Levi, which would be about as much fun as it sounds if Levi wasn't one of my favourite patients (I know you're not supposed to have favourites in this job, but sometimes you can't help it).

It's Friday, rush hour, in the middle of a May heat wave, so you can imagine the fun and games. I'm sardined in at all sides, about halfway down the aisle, right hand gripping the bar above, really wishing I'd shaved my armpits.

'Everyone move down the aisle,' the driver shouts through the Tannoy. 'This train's not moving until everyone moves down.'

Most people just tut and stand there. It annoys me when people do that. There's a time for rebellion, I think, and rush hour on a Friday is not it. I want to get back,

3

jump in the shower, then pop into the Turkish bakery for some of those pastries my sister Leah likes, and get to her house before 7.30 p.m. to catch the kids before we talk. If you get to my sister's house at 7.33 p.m., forget it. Toys packed away, entire house wiped down. It's like she never had kids.

I nudge the person next to me to get her to budge up. She staggers slightly and I murmur an apology. She's trying to eat a prawn-cocktail salad standing up and I think: that's dedication, that is. That's hungry.

Eventually, the doors close and we jolt into action; soon I'm hurtling through the dark.

I crane my neck to look at the Tube map above: fifteen stops to Archway, which is home, but only four till Leicester Square, when all the tourists will pile out. It's not so bad when you break it down like that. A poster grabs my attention: something about match.com and 'making love happen' and, just below it, a woman wearing a badge in the design of a Tube stop that says BABY ON BOARD. My eyes drift automatically to her midriff: there's no sign of a bump yet beneath her white, broderie-anglaise blouse. Probably in those first vulnerable months, I think. Maybe just found out, giddy with excitement. I watch her, imagining her life. I like this game – it comes with the territory of the job, I suppose. I think, here's a woman who knows how to do pregnancy; this is no martyr, soldiering on. I imagine she will get home tonight to her Victorian conversion, where husband (Steve, thirty-four, civil servant) will be waiting with a vast shepherd's pie and give her strict instructions not to lift a finger.

There will be a pile of pristine baby-grows already in the drawer; a basket filling daily with talcs and wipes

4

and cotton-wool buds. I was obsessed with the baby basket when Mum was pregnant with Niamh. I would pull it from under her bed and pore over the baby-scented goods; count what new items she'd got that week, grilling her about names: Niamh or Sadie if it's a girl, Richie if it's a boy. (Richie King! What a name! He'd have got the ladies, if he'd ever made it into the world.)

I imagine this woman will call her baby Ben; Ben or Holly – something safe that will never go out of fashion. The train stops at Embankment and many get off, but the hordes get on. A woman listening to Daft Punk next to me disappears and is replaced by a man wearing white, stained overalls. He's sweating and smells as if he's had a few after work – as well as of something else, something heady, which hits you immediately between the eyes. Turps. Takes me a while to put a name to it. Must be a decorator, I think.

The train hisses on to Charing Cross. It's becoming like a furnace in here now; I can feel the hand that's gripping the bar above is clammy with sweat, and the straps of my rucksack are rubbing on my shoulders. The carriage sways and shudders along, the man who smells of turps accidentally puts his hand over mine and we exchange a shy smile. I can see the pearls of perspiration form on his shiny head, and then, before he can stop them with the handkerchief he is struggling to take from his pocket, run down to his ears and onto his eyebrows. I feel sorry for him; I think, I bet he can't wait to get out of here.

Woman with the prawn-cocktail salad is hanging on with one arm in front of us now, wilting with the heat. She suddenly yawns, a huge, wide, doggy yawn, revealing bits of iceberg lettuce. When she eventually clamps her mouth shut, a gust of fishy breath envelops us. Man who smells of turps and I exchange an eyebrow raise. *What a relief, someone else who has surpassed me in the bad-Tube-etiquette stakes.* I love the nonverbal communication that goes on in the Tube, the humanness of it all, the fact we're so often thinking the same.

It comes as I catch my reflection in the window: dark hair pulled back and badly in need of a wash; eyes always more smiley (and crinkled at the sides) than I expect. It starts, deep and penetrating, a heart-burn in my chest, then, travelling at speed, spreads down my limbs, up my neck, my face, into the palms of my hands, until I feel something has to happen to release me from this heat, or else I will combust, surely? I will pass out.

I cough, then swallow, or try to, but it feels like a bunch of dried leaves has been shoved in my mouth. God, I'm going to be sick, I think; I'm actually going to puke. And I panic – I think, I don't have a bag. But then, as suddenly as the heat struck, an icy wave descends – the chills – and I gag, but nothing comes out. I am sweating buckets now. If I raise my shaking hand to my forehead, an actual droplet comes off on my finger. My heart pounds hard and fast, like a spray of bullets. I can't get my breath and I think, my God, I am having a heart attack.

I blink back the sweat and open my eyes, but the Tube map in front of me is swerving so much that I have to close my eyes again in case I pass out. We stop at two, maybe three more stops and I tighten my fingers around the bar above me; reach out to a vertical pole in front of me, but my palms are so wet that it slides right off and I stumble, accidently standing on the man-who-smells-of-turps's foot. I shake my head by way of apology, but I don't look at him, although I am aware of him looking at me. It feels like a bag of wet sand is sitting on my ribs. No matter how much I try to expand my chest, I can't get enough air, and I am consumed – overwhelmed – with a wave of terror that this is it: I am dying. But I've been lied to, cheated. Everyone said Mum died peacefully, that death is peaceful; but it isn't, it's horror.

The last thing I am aware of, someone is touching my arm. I say, 'I think I am having a heart attack,' and then there's a screeching sound, the wail of an alarm. Then I am sitting on a bench on the Tube platform; the man in the white overalls who smells of turps is holding my hand. Another man in green overalls is asking, 'Are you a diabetic?'

'No,' I say. 'I'm not diabetic. But I've just found out I'm pregnant.'

Chapter One

Three months earlier
February 2013

Dear Lily

I'm going to end it with Andy. I've decided.

I'm sitting here, alone at a restaurant table for the second time this week, whilst he's outside arguing with the Ex, and I've decided enough is enough. There's only so much sitting alone in restaurants picking at olives a girl can take. I don't even like olives!!

Andy's a nice man and it's been great to have the company, but I've realized that's it: it's just company, someone to watch telly with and go out for dinner with and cook with (though even that's started to grate: How many hours has that man spent with a pestle and mortar? What's wrong with a shop-bought curry sauce now and again?). I've started to wonder, what's in it for me, you know? How did I ever think I could have a successful relationship with a man going through a messy divorce? He needs too much himself. He's broken. And, as you and I know, I spend enough time with broken people in the day job. I can't be the therapist outside of it too.

Oh, Lily, but I've started to wonder if *I'm* the broken one, if I'm the one who needs therapy. Am I to keep doing this? Is this to be the pattern my relationships take? Long periods of celibacy followed by unsuitable, emotionally unavailable men? It's like I pick them out or something.

I worry that what happened all those years ago has scarred me forever, that I'm too scared to fall in love with anyone – because look what happened when I fell in love with Joe, look at the fallout then! Maybe going out with people like Andy, who I'm never going to fall in love with, let's face it, is my way of dipping my toe in relationships, playing at having a boyfriend but never actually diving in with both feet. And that's a bit tragic, isn't it? That I might never fall in love again? That at thirty-two that's it, game over?

I sneaked my notepad underneath some work notes and pretended to read them whilst really watching Andy arguing on the phone to his Ex, outside yet another Modern European brasserie in central London. It was something I'd grown very accustomed to during the past year.

From a purely psychological point of view, it made fascinating viewing. Andy was a confident man, very male in his behaviour and attitude, and yet he looked so weak when he was on the phone to Belinda (or Belinda Ballbreaker as I call her, since she means WAR in this divorce. She means war in life, generally, as far as I can tell . . .)

He had his back to me and was flexing alternate bum cheeks, running a hand, anxiously, through his salt-and-pepper curls. Andy was a very handsome man, yet it struck me at that moment that his hair was not dissimilar to Russell Grant's. Maybe this was the self-protection kicking in, the physical attraction waning to make The End more bearable.

'Sorry, sorry, *so* sorry, honey.'

Eventually, Andy came back inside the restaurant, red faced and apologizing profusely. I looked studiously at my notes, as if I'd been doing this all the time. 'She hung up on me,' he said, palms in the air, as if this had never happened before. 'She actually put the phone down.'

I made a sympathetic face but I didn't say anything. I wanted to know what would happen if I didn't offer advice or thoughts like I usually did; if I didn't allow him to offload on me.

Andy stood there for a few seconds, as if needing to physically recover from the latest bashing from his Ex. It was no good – he really was good-looking, with his piercing blue eyes and his dusky skin tones. No matter if his hair had a touch of the 'Russell Grant' about it . . He looked like an architect, I thought, and I'd always fancied dating an architect: that mix of practical and creative.

I picked up the menu and pretended to read. Eventually, when he realized he was getting nothing from me, he came round the back of my chair and wrapped his arms around my neck.

'I'm sorry,' he said, nuzzling into me. He smelt of soap and the outside. 'You've been here all this time, sitting patiently.'

'That's all right.' I shrugged. 'I always know to bring a book with me to dinner now.'

'Or your notes, you have here I see . . .' he said, indicating the work file I'd got out.

(Sarcasm is generally wasted on Andy.) 'Why can't everyone be as lovely as you, Robyn? Tell me. Why do I always go for the feisty ones?'

I bit my lip. Robyn wasn't about to be lovely Robyn any more.

He sat back down again. I knew he was waiting for me to ask him about the conversation with Belinda, how unfair it all was, what a bitch she was, but I resisted.

'So how was your day at work, beauts?' he said, finally, after we'd ordered – me the ham-hock terrine, him the goat's cheese and beetroot. 'How are the certified mental as opposed to my ex-wife who's yet to be diagnosed?'

I took some bread from the basket and tore at it. 'Oh, you know, just a day like any other, really. Two sectioned, one attempted suicide.'

I knew that throwing a word like 'suicide' into the conversation this early on in the evening would be seen as provocative by Andy, but to be honest, he'd annoyed me. I felt like being provocative.

'Oh dear. Liam again?'

'Levi, it's Levi.'

'Sorry, Levi. Cry for help, I imagine?'

12

'Yes, most probably,' I said. This was Andy's line for everything.

I wondered when I should break the news to him: now, or after the meal? In between courses? I felt like giving my own little cry for help: 'Argh! Get me out of this!' Maybe I wouldn't tell him at all. Maybe I'd give him one more chance.

Andy picked up the wine menu. I could tell he wanted to get back to him and the phone call, but I was determined to carry on.

'Anyway, I also went to Lidl with a sixty-three-year-old woman dressed in hot pants and a Stetson today,' I said.

'Bloody hell, is that all she was wearing?' said Andy.

'Pretty much . . .'

'Poor woman . . .' he added. He had a look on his face like I'd told her to put on the hat and hot pants as some sick and twisted joke. 'I mean, can you imagine the humiliation, how embarrassed you'd be?'

'Andy, she's manic, she couldn't give a toss,' I said, laying my napkin on my knee. 'She's so disinhibited, it's a miracle I got her to put on any clothes at all.'

'Ah, but this is the issue, isn't it?' he said, leaning back into the chair and lacing his fingers. Andy likes to do this – try to have some philosophical debate, when actually, I doubt he's genuinely that interested. I *know* he doesn't know what he's talking about.

'What's the issue?'

'That's the job of the psychiatric nurse, isn't it? To make sure she knows when she should be inhibited and when she shouldn't.'

I tried really hard not to look irritated.

13

'Well, I don't think . . .'

'I mean, can you imagine how awful that would be?' he said, leaning forward, lowering his voice. 'How demeaning, being allowed to walk into a supermarket in hot pants when you're drawing your pension?'

I started laughing. Sometimes I think Andy thinks I am much more earnest about my job than I actually am.

'Yeah. It'd be brilliant. Sixty-odd, waltzing around Dulwich Sainsbury's in your hot pants, all the yummy mummies running out of there screaming, "Aaaaagghhh!"'

Andy pulled his chin into his neck.

'Robyn, please.'

'*Well,* honestly.'

He went back to the menu.

'Let's order wine, shall we?' He smiled, determined not to make this into an argument, even though I was up for one now. An argument would make this whole thing easier, of course.

I waited. I counted.

'Do you know what Belinda said to me?' he said.

Eight seconds. Impressive.

'No, what did she say to you?'

'That I was selfish – I mean, of all the things . . . That she wasn't surprised the girls didn't want to spend much time with me because I didn't know how to talk to them, that I didn't understand them. She said I don't listen to them properly when they call and . . .'

The starters came, and he was *still* going on about it. Then, suddenly, mouth stuffed full, he started waving his hand in front of my face.

'Oh, my God, I completely forgot to tell you! I've got a surprise!'

'A *surprise*?' My stomach lurched. I'd psyched myself up now. Don't start being perfect boyfriend now.

'Yep,' he leaned forward and put his hand on mine. 'I haven't got the girls next weekend – their mum's taking them on some sort of girly shopping extravaganza; my idea of a living hell, as you know – so I thought we could go away together.' He patted my hand and grinned at me. He did have a lovely smile, the most unusually blue eyes. 'Well, actually, I just thought *to hell with it* and I've booked somewhere.'

I forced a mouthful of food down my throat. 'Oh,' was all I could manage.

'Well, aren't you pleased?' he said, disappointed. 'Robyn, come on, you could look a *bit* more excited.'

But I wasn't excited, I was irritated: irritated by his having delayed our dinner by twenty minutes to have an argument with the Ex; irritated by him talking about nothing but his ex-wife; irritated and bored to tears with the whole divorce saga. No, I'd made my decision. The fact I didn't feel even a smidgen of excitement about the prospect of a mini-break (and I'd been hankering after a mini-break for absolutely ages) cemented it.

I sighed. 'Oh, Andy, I'm just a bit bored of it, that's all.'

'Of what?'

'Of always talking about you and Belinda and the girls and the divorce.'

He looked genuinely hurt and shocked and, for a second, I felt bad.

'But it's the biggest thing that's ever happened to me, Robyn, you know that. I can't just switch my emotions off when I see you. Like a tap!'

15

'Really?' I tried not to say it unkindly. 'Because I'd like you to try, Andy, just a little bit.'

He frowned, his shoulders slumping, genuinely deflated. 'But you're so good at listening.' The innocence with which he said it killed me. 'I thought you were interested.'

'Andy, I *am* interested, to a point. All I'm saying is, just, it would be nice to be asked how *I* am, occasionally, and to be allowed to reply in more than one sentence before you start talking about you again.'

'But you don't like talking about yourself.'

I kind of laughed. This was true. I had said that.

'But, I didn't mean like never, ever, ever!'

Andy searched my face. It was at times like this that I worried he might be on the spectrum. He just really did not get it.

'Your relationship with Belinda and the girls, it's becoming like a chronic ailment,' I said. 'Like a boil on your bum, or sinusitis. It never goes away, and yet, I get a daily update, whether I like it or not. And whenever I suggest anything that might help, you're not interested. Sometimes I feel like you just want to moan.'

'Oh,' he said, 'I see. Well, can I make it up to you? Will you come away? I've booked a lovely hotel in Watford.'

'*Watford?*'

'That's the nearest town – it's actually on the outskirts of Watford. It has a spa, a golf course. I could play a round whilst you get pampered. Have a facial or a massage – one of those treatments all you girls like to have?'

'Andy,' I said, and as the words left my mouth, I did feel reassuringly sad. 'I don't think it would be a good idea to go away together. In fact, I think we should break up. I'm really sorry, but I just think this isn't working any more.'

Chapter Two

March

Robyn,

I hate to do this on Facebook, but I haven't got
your number and the email address I tried doesn't
work any more. I've got some really bad news: my
mum died suddenly on Tuesday. She was fine,
went out for a curry with Dad, then came home
and had a heart attack. I can't believe it. I know
what people mean now when they say, 'I keep
expecting her to walk through the door.'

I've never seen my dad like this. I know this
won't have rocked his faith in the long run, but he's
struggling. I think he realizes it's different when it
happens to you, you know?

Personally, I am enraged: I mean, fifty-nine? WTF.
Thirty years of service and that's how he repays
my dad? If one more person tells me he works in
mysterious ways, I'll punch them. I remember you

17

saying that to me once, after your mum died. I remember exactly where we were, too – down the cricket ground. I probably gave you a cuddle, then tried to slip my hand up your top . . . *God*, I'm sorry, Robbie. Going through all that at sixteen, with only a sixteen-year-old me to talk to. I had no idea. Now I do.

The first person I thought of calling was you, because I knew you'd understand but, like I say, I had no number, so here I am telling about the death of my mother on f**ing Facebook!

The funeral's a week tomorrow (1 April) at 3 p.m. at St Bart's, Kilterdale obviously. (Dad says he's giving it, but I'll believe that when I see it. He's a mess.) I'd love you to be there. I know Mum would too. She was talking about you just days before she died, about that time we all went on a barge holiday to the Norfolk Broads and she had one too many Dubonnet and lemonades and fell in. Hey, she wasn't a typical vicar's wife, was she?

Anyway, my number's below. Hopefully see you there.

Hope you're well, darl X love Joe X

I smiled as the memory floodgates opened . . . The barge holiday and the night of Marion's 'Dubonnet Splash'. My God, I'd completely forgotten about all that. Joe and I had only been seeing one another a month and were still in the unhealthily obsessed stage when, against their better judgement, Marion and the Reverend Clifford Sawyer (Joe's dad) decided to take us with them. A rev he may have been, but Cliff loved a tipple, as did Marion, and a major plus point of a barge holiday, they soon found, was the number of pub stops one could make along the way.

We'd all been in the pub this one afternoon, but Joe and I had offered to go back to the barge to make a start on the carbonara for tea. But we hadn't made a start on tea, we'd just made out. Marion had come back tipsy and, seeing us suckered against one another (thank *God*, fully clothed), surrounded by chopped raw bacon, because that's as far as we had got, she'd dashed off in desperation for fish and chips, falling, as she did, in between the canal bank and the boat. She'd done this *Carry On*-style dramatic scream. Oh, how we'd laughed . . .

'Robyn, if you could tear yourself away from Facebook and whatever is so funny just for a second, then perhaps you could fill us in on last night? By all accounts, it was an eventful one?' (It was only then that I realised, I was still laughing sixteen years later.)

I'd got Joe's Facebook message on the night shift. By now – 8 a.m. at handover – I could think of nothing else. I knew it off by heart. I'd read it so many times.

I turned away from my computer to find the whole office waiting for me to start and Jeremy – our team Manager, perched on the edge of a desk, wearing one of his 'five for a tenner' shirts.

'Yes, it was eventful,' I stuttered. 'Really, really busy actually.'

In fact, there must have been something in the planets – something in the full moon, which hung like a mint imperial over south London – because, as well as receiving Joe's Facebook message, the first contact I'd had from him in five years, it had been one of the busiest night shifts I'd ever done. Everyone was going mad.

John Urwin – one of Kingsbridge Mental Health Trust's most notorious clients – had been arrested after being caught having sex in Burgess Park.

'And all you need to know about that,' I said, when I finally got myself together enough to join in handover 'is that he was butt naked when arrested but *still* wearing his Dennis the Menace wig, and I think you have to love John for that.'

Kaye, Parv and Leon, also CPNs (community psychiatric nurses), had an affectionate giggle, but Jeremy was not amused. 'If you could just stick to what actually *happened*, Robyn.'

And so I told them how John was a little 'agitated' when I arrived at Walworth Police Station. (This was a distinct downplay of events. I'd been able to hear him shouting as soon as I got there.)

'WHY CAN'T A MAN HAVE SEX WITH HIS GIRLFRIEND IF HE WANTS TO? IT'S AN ABUSE OF MY HUMAN RIGHTS, DOCTOR! MY HUMAN RIGHTS!'

But Dr Manoor and I had managed to calm him down. Dr Manoor has been John's psychiatrist for years, and thankfully knows him as well as I do.

John is perhaps one of the more extreme clients I work with (although there's not really such a thing as 'extreme' in this job) and institutionalized now. I find people like him the absolute saddest. It's as if they had their breakdown aged 18 and stayed that age – arrested development. John has been sectioned more times than most people have had hot dinners. Still, if you talked to John when he was well, he talked a lot of sense. He was a bright man – he could tell you every single species of butterfly – and he was in a relationship.

Because the night shift had been so full on, handover ran over. As well as John Urwin baring all in Burgess Park, Levi Holden was admitted with an overdose. I really don't mean to sound glib when I say this happens quite often.

Of the thirty people on my caseload, Levi is probably my favourite: six feet of utter gorgeousness for a start. He's also hilarious, when he's not suicidal. And even when he is suicidal, he's probably funnier than the average person. He has a little job washing cars in the Dulwich Sainsbury's car park. The other day, he was making me laugh so much, slagging off all the Dulwich mums in their four-by-fours and their two-hundred-pound weekly shops.

'Those mo-fo dull witches wid der massive wagons and their whining dollies in the back and enough food to feed the whole of Peckham. It's a wonder they're not more mo-fo wide, the amount of money they spend on food!'

I laugh a lot in my job. I guess, with darkness has to come light, and you'd be amazed how gallows the humour can get. 'You don't have to be mad to do this job, but it helps,' they say. But I wonder if we're not all a bit mad already, and it's just a question of when, not if, the lid comes off.

I find it hard at the best of times going home and straight to sleep after a night shift. Your body is exhausted but your mind is on overdrive: Will Levi take another overdose? Will John be on the psychiatric ward, yelling for his Dennis the Menace wig? These are usually the things I am thinking as I leave the office for my bed. Today, however, it was Joe's Facebook message.

We were having one of those freak, early spring warm spells – Peckham's teens had already stripped to their Primark hot pants – and so I decided to walk to Oval rather than get the bus. Camberwell was alive and kicking: African ladies in tropical-shade headdresses, stalls piled high with okra and plantain, spilling onto the street. A watermelon rolled onto the pavement. As I put it back, I could just make out the wiry form of Dmitri, the owner of the shop, sitting like a drying chilli on his deckchair at the back. I passed Chicken Cottage and the launderette, where the aroma of fried chicken turned into the heavy, bluebell notes of Lenor. Across the road, in the park, a group of teenagers were dancing to some rapper blasting from a pimped-up beatbox. The heart of South London couldn't have been beating harder if it tried, and yet, amidst all of this life, I was thinking about death – of Joe's mum, and my mum, and everything that happened in Kilterdale, and how I really didn't want to go back there, for a funeral of all things. The question now, of course, was how the hell was I going to get out of it?

Eventually, I caved, and went into Interflora in Camberwell. The woman behind the counter was eyeing me up over her half-moon glasses, as if she knew my game.

'Can I help you, madam?' she said eventually.

I smiled at her. 'No, I'm just looking, thanks,' and continued pretending to browse around the shop, which didn't take long since you couldn't swing a cat in there.

'Okay, well if you need any help . . .' she said, going back to her book, but I could feel her eyes on me; they were following me round the shop. Eventually, I felt compelled to speak.

'Uh, actually, could you recommend flowers to send to a funeral, please?'

She perked up at this and took off her glasses.

'Well, the classic of course is the lily,' she said, getting up from her seat behind the counter and coming round to the front. She had a matronly bosom and was wearing a lilac, pussy-bow blouse. 'But you can have bouquets arranged with carnations, roses; anything you like.'

I nodded, remembering the carpet of bouquets left outside the crematorium at Mum's funeral. The messages that all started, 'Dearest Lil . . .' and finished, 'Always in our thoughts.' I remember being so depressed that Mum had now become merely a thought in people's heads. How long before she wasn't even that?

'May I ask who it's for?' asked the woman. She was much more friendly now. 'Is it a close family member? Do you know what sort of flowers they liked?'

'Roses,' I said, 'peach ones.'

I must have spent more time with Marion up at the vicarage that summer than I remembered.

'We do a lovely wreath with peach roses,' she said. 'Some irises, green foliage . . . When is the funeral?'

'A week on Friday.'

'In London?'

'No, up North. A little village near the Lake District.'

She let out a little gasp. 'Which one? My son and daughter-in-law live up there.'

23

I hesitated. Nobody had ever heard of it. 'Kilterdale,' I said.

'No . . . my son lives in Yarn!'

I was genuinely shocked. In fifteen years of living in London, I could count on one hand the number of people I'd met from anywhere near my home village, it was so back of beyond.

She said, 'It's glorious up there. Always fascinates me how anyone would move from somewhere like that to here.'

There was a long pause. It was only when she spoke again that I realized she'd wanted an answer to that question. 'Anyway,' she looked a bit embarrassed that her foray into conversation hadn't been more productive, 'that needn't be a problem. You can have a look at what the wreath might look like here – I have some in the back – and then we can contact an Interflora branch near where the funeral is being held.'

I felt my shoulders relax. 'That would be great, thank you.' Then, as I watched her bustle into the back of the shop, the nagging guilt crept in.

'*I had no idea, I'm sorry. Now I do.*' Joe had said in his message. But he did have an idea, even at sixteen. Whilst other lads in his year were worrying about popping cherries, getting it on with Tania Richardson, Joe was dealing with me, *posing* as his sane-and-together girl-friend but who, inside, was collapsing with grief. Now here I was, copping out of his mother's funeral.

I was kicking myself for even joining Facebook, because if I hadn't, I wouldn't be in this position, and Joe would never have found me. I only have fifteen Facebook friends, as it is, most of whom are work colleagues. I say things to my sister, Niamh, like: 'Why does this person I did swimming with twenty years ago want to be my friend?' Which she thinks is hilarious. Niamh is nine years younger than me, the accidental result of a drunken, food-themed fancy-dress party for my parents' fifteenth wedding anniversary – yep, my sister was conceived whilst my parents were dressed as a 'prawn cocktail': Mum as the prawn and Dad as Tom Cruise in *Cocktail* – and therefore thinks I am geriatric. 'It's a social-networking site, dumb-ass. You social-network on it,' she says. I don't think I'll ever like it, though: I don't want blasts-from-my-past being able to find me, or to see pictures of the sorts of drunken states my sister gets herself into. I worry about her. She turned twenty-three in January and I still worry about her.

I picked up some freesias and inhaled their lovely scent, wondering how long you could leave a message like Joe's before you answered it, and decided two days was already too long.

'Here we are . . .' The lady clattered through the plastic strips of curtain separating the shop from the back, carrying a peach-flowered wreath. 'It's pretty, isn't it?' she said, holding it up. 'They'll be able to make you one up like this in no time.'

I sniffed it.

'Yes, it's lovely. How much?'

'They start at seventy-five pounds and go up to a hundred.'

'Seventy-five *pounds*?' It flew out of my mouth before I could stop it.

'It is expensive, but then when you think of what it's for . . . what those flowers say. Your personal goodbye.'

As if I didn't feel guilty enough already.

Going in person would say a hell of a lot more, I knew that. I knew that for much less, fifty quid perhaps, I could get a train ticket up to Kilterdale, or fill up my car with petrol. So, I wouldn't even be able to plead poverty if I sent the flowers.

'I'll have a think about it,' I said, having decided to do nothing of the sort.

'Okay, well don't leave it too late to order.' She went a bit frosty after that. 'They need time to make it up.'

I made a swift exit out of there.

Chapter Three

Honestly, sometimes I wonder if Eva – my Polish, hoarding next-door neighbour – lies in wait for me. I'd made it into the lobby of my block. I'd even got so far as leaning across the mound of bin bags that block her entrance and, as each day passes, mine, to put my key in the lock, when she swung open her door.

'Ah, Missus King . . .' She was wearing a mustard-yellow sun dress, which clung to her form like clingfilm around an enormous block of cheese. 'I very happy I sin you, I bin worried sick of you. I not seen you for *days.*'

Behind her, an avalanche of more bin bags stretched back and up, indefinitely.

'Eva, you saw me yesterday, remember?' I said, peering past her shoulder. I was always fascinated about how she might sleep: wedged between shelves like you saw on those Channel 4 documentaries about chronic hoarders? Up against an ironing board? 'We were discussing when you might ring the council for someone to help you come and move this stuff so I can get to my front door without straining a muscle.'

I just gave it to her straight these days. I was over being subtle, even polite.

She looked me up and down through those dark, hooded eyes then: 'You look thin,' she sniffed, ignoring me. 'You still pining for zis, zis little man?'

I laughed. 'Andy, you mean? No, Eva, I'm fine, it was for the best, but thanks for asking,' I said, pushing the bags aside with my foot.

'He no good enough for you,' she said, as I managed to get close enough to my door to open it. 'He too old. He no give you enough attention . . .!'

'Don't worry, Eva, I'm really okay,' I said, then, before I closed the door, 'Now promise me you'll ring the council about those bags!'

I locked the door and leaned against it for a second, just closing my eyes. Silence. The thing was, Eva was right: I was pining for Andy – not pining so much as missing him; I was in an 'Andy mood'. Joe's message had caught me off guard and I suddenly craved the familiarity of him.

I went into the living room and turned on the TV for company – since Andy and I finished last month, I've done this every day – then I ran a bath. I'm also the cleanest I've ever been.

It's funny; when I bought this place – a slightly shabby, ground-floor, two-bed in a small, 1930s block – four years ago with the money Mum left me, I relished coming home to an empty flat. After spending all day talking to people – often about their suicide plans: how they had the vodka and the Temazepam at the ready – I relished having a place to myself; a sanctuary from all the madness. I'd often just sit there when I got in, in silence, take the phone off the hook, read a book, eat sweetcorn straight from the can. Then, a year ago, along came Andy and changed all that. For the first time in four years, I had a boyfriend; and, what's more, I liked it.

I made sure the bath was as hot as it could be without actually scalding me, then I got in. It was 6 p.m. – 6 p.m.! What the hell was I supposed to fill the rest of the evening with? There's only so much lying in a bath and exfoliating you can do, after all. I thought about poor Joe – about those awful few days of bereavement, the shock, the need for people around you. Then I thought about the reality of going back to Kilterdale and seeing him after all this time, the feelings it might unearth, the memories I'd boxed up for sixteen years now. It made me so anxious.

I thought about Andy – familiar, benign Andy, who was so wrapped up in himself it made it impossible for you to think about anything else – about calling him and inviting him over, just to 'veg', as he put it. I imagined sitting next to him on the sofa, watching *Dragon's Den*, and sharing a kedgeree (Yes, Andy was a big fan of a smoked-fish item, I thought fondly). What harm could it do?

I met Andy on a speed-dating night. I'd gone with Kaye from work – God, I love Kaye. She always says to me, 'Kingy, never settle. There's far too much fun to be had with a packet of Oreos and BBC iPlayer.' (Kaye is thirty-seven and still refuses to settle. She watches a lot of TV and eats a lot of Oreos.) He was the older man – forty-two to my thirty-one – and I liked that, the idea of being looked after for a change. We chatted easily for

29

the allotted three minutes. Afterwards, he made a beeline for me at the bar.

'I like you, Robyn. You're different. In fact, I'd say you're marriage material,' he said, and from there, 'we' just sort of happened. I gathered he felt free to throw around phrases like 'you're marriage material' because he was going through a horrid divorce and therefore never likely to marry anyone ever again. And we had a lot of fun for a while, Andy and I. I even liked the fact he'd been married and had two kids, at first: it made him seem 'normal', as in, what you'd expect a normal, functioning bloke to have done at forty-two, I guess . .

Before Andy, I'd given up on any kind of normal. I'd realized normal – as in marriage and kids – was not the way it was going for me. And that was fine, I'd made my peace with that. Kaye and I had decided that, if all else failed, we'd join a hippy commune and grow our armpit hair and eat biscuits all day like we did at work. But then Andy came along and he made me believe in normal again. He made me want it.

I topped the bath up with more hot water and lay back, staring despairingly at the damp patch on the bathroom ceiling, which was encroaching like an oily tide.

Finishing with Andy had probably been the most amicable ending of a relationship I'd ever known, perhaps because I'd never been more than someone nice to fill a space for him, and that was fine. It was as though he'd swooped in, post-separation, for some respite care at the Hospice of St Kindness (i.e. me, or anyone else who would listen to him) and was now recharged, ready to take on the world again. When I'd told him it was over, he'd looked disappointed and taken aback, but not hurt,

I noted. It was the sort of expression you might wear if you'd just been told there was no more carrot soup on the menu and you'd have to have leek and potato.

After leaving the restaurant, we'd walked to the Tube together, even chatted as we glided down the escalator. As would be the case, a busker was singing Adele's 'Someone Like You' with accompanying pan-pipe backing track when we got to the bottom. He'd taken hold of my elbows and we'd gazed at one another with sad smiles as the busker sang how sometimes it lasts in love, and sometimes it hurts instead. Then Andy said, 'I'll be in touch.'

And I'd smiled, because he couldn't help himself, he couldn't help but promise, even at the end, something he couldn't deliver.

'It's okay,' I said. 'You don't have to.'

'At least let's have a cuddle, then?' he'd said, opening his arms; and we did, and it was nice. Andy's a good hugger. It's the one thing we'd both done well probably because there's no pressure in a hug, is there?

'Okay, bye then,' I'd said.

'Yeah, I will call though, yeah?'

'Yeah,' I'd said.

'Take care of yourself, honey.'

Then we'd turned and gone our separate ways. Two minutes later, I was gliding up the escalator when, out of the corner of my eye, I saw him coming down the other way.

'Sorry, I went the wrong way,' he said, and I laughed to myself all the way home because, was there ever the end of a relationship that so exactly replicated the relationship itself? Hit-and-miss, half-baked, stop-start. Just a little bit of a shambles, basically, with some farce thrown in.

No, finishing with Andy Cullen was the right thing to do, I decided, lying there until the bath water grew cool. I didn't want to see him, I was just scared and putting off getting back to Joe.

I decided to ring my sister, Leah, instead. It's practically impossible to have a normal conversation on the phone with her these days because she's always so busy with the kids, so it's a numbers game: if you ring her ten times, you might just get lucky once. Jack, my five-year-old nephew answered. We had a short discussion about peregrine falcons – I totally dig the conversations I have with my nephew – then I said, 'Is Mummy there?'

There was some high-pitched squealing in the background, which could have been Leah or Eden, my three-year-old niece – it was difficult to tell.

'She's cleaning up Eden's poo,' said Jack.

'Oh,' I said, darkly.

'She needed the toilet but didn't make it. A poo fell out of her skirt in the kitchen.'

I laughed. Then stopped. Jack wasn't laughing. This is because Jack knew that a poo in the kitchen was on a par with the apocalypse for his mother.

'Okay, well, don't worry. Tell Mummy—' I was about to tell him I'd call back later when Jack shouted:

'Mummy! Aunty Robyn's on the phone!'

I could hear Leah's sigh, literally metres away in the kitchen.

'Well, tell Aunty Robyn that I am knee-deep in your sister's crap at the moment and that her beautiful, adorable, butter-wouldn't-melt niece's bum has exploded all over my new kitchen floor.'

'Oh.' Jack came back on the phone. 'Mummy said the C word.'

'Mm,' I said, 'she did. That must mean she is very stressed. Tell her I'll call her later, okay?'

'She'll call you later, Mummy!'

'Ha! Well, she can try, but I'll be doing bedtime then . . .'

I reasoned that I may not have got to speak to my sister, but at least any yearnings for Andy, and/or a boyfriend or family life had been very successfully abated.

That evening, I sat on the sofa, nursing a bottle of wine, writing fantasy replies to Joe, hoping that, the drunker I got, the more likely I'd be just to press 'Send'.

Dear Joe,

I'm so sorry to hear about your mum and ordinarily I'd love to come to the funeral, but unfortunately I am on holiday . . .

Dear Joe,

I can hardly believe it's taken me three days . . . the reason is, I was trying to think of a way of telling you . . .

Dear Joe,

Oh, my God, what must you think of me?! I rarely log onto Facebook so . . .

In the end, three days, in fact, after Joe sent me the message, and mainly because I ran out of different ways to apologize, I wrote:

Dear Joe,
I'll be there. See you at 3 p.m.
Robyn x

Chapter Four

Dear Lily

I was thinking today that of all the things I've told you so far, I haven't told you how I got together with your father. He says it's typical of me, that the day we should get together is the day I save him, when what he doesn't know is that he saved me.

The date was 18 May 1997 – almost sixteen years ago! It was the end of the summer term, of high school, and we were signing one another's shirts: SHINE ON, YOU CRAZY DIAMOND! Although, personally, I was doing nothing of the sort . . .

Picture your mother: I am sixteen, I have thick dark hair with a fringe, and very recently I've committed trichological suicide by trying to dye it peroxide blonde. Your granddad didn't notice for a fortnight, which gives a very good indication of how he was at that time. The barnet is an atrocity; every time I get it wet, it goes green for some reason, and so my sister Leah gives me a 'body perm' in the kitchen one Saturday, in the hope this will distract the eye (it doesn't).

It's been six months since we lost Mum and I'm blown apart. There seem to be bits of me everywhere; some shrapnel is still inside. I don't know who I am, or who to be, and so I try different guises: 'arty', 'rebel', 'one of the crowd'. Mostly, I am just all over the shop. But you have to at least believe it's going to be okay, don't you? And even though Mum is gone, I still believe in life. I think, if I can get past this bit, it will get better. Your grandma always said I was the strong one, and I'm determined to prove her right.

So here I am, this mad, sad, determined girl with green hair on the day I save your dad's life at Black Horse Quarry. On the day he saves mine.

In those days, the quarry was a glittering lagoon to us; our little piece of paradise. Now, I realize, it's a death trap, surrounded with dog-turd-laden scrubland (funny how what you remember and what actually *was* are often two different things). The wayward among us would bunk off and go down there in those last weeks of term. That day, I was there with my best friend, Beth, as usual. Your father was there with Voz and other members of 'The Farmers'. There were also some 'Townies' (named because they went to school in the town, rather than in Kilterdale – the back of beyond – like us 'Farmers'); all that strange, male, tribal rivalry. Saul Butler was ringleader of the Townies. Your dad had a love – hate friendship with him (i.e., he knew he was an idiot but that it was wise to keep on the right side of him too).

So there was I, sucking my stomach in, in my new tie-dyed bikini. Beth and I were discussing losing our virginity. Beth had lost hers the week before to Gary Trott. It had been quite the spiritual experience and, apparently, she'd 'cried uncontrollably'.

I said to myself then: Robyn, you are not 'crying uncontrollably' with any old person. You will wait for the right person – for Joe.

The quarry had almost mythical status in the area back then. There were cars and old shopping trolleys down there for us to get our legs tangled in and our parents had forbidden us to go anywhere near it – which obviously heightened its appeal.

It was surrounded by cliffs of varying heights that we called the 'forty-footer', 'sixty-footer' and 'hundred-footer'. (Only those with a death wish attempted that.) It was a scorching day, this 18 May 1997. My skin was sizzling away in Factor zilch coconut oil. Beth was jabbering about Gary Trott. I was looking at your father, admiring his muscular legs in his Speedo swimming trunks. All the boys were running to and from the edge of the hundred-footer now; your dad was pretty wild back then – all this energy and none of it channelled, trying to be the big man in front of the Townies. There were several big splashes as the Farmer lot jumped in. Then there was just Saul Butler and your dad, standing on the edge, sizing each other up.

'Come on!' Voz was shouting from the water. 'Sawyer, jump!'

Butler looked at Joe, then took a few steps back as if to run in – which is why I think Joe jumped the way he did, suddenly and awkwardly and not far enough out. But Butler didn't jump, just Joe.

Beth was still talking. Your father hit the water. There was a lot of screeching, but the sun was blinding my vision. I got onto my knees to get a proper look. Then I realized that it wasn't your dad who was screeching, because he was still under water.

There was a huge commotion and I felt this monumental surge of determination. I'd seen someone die (Mum) before my very eyes, and I wasn't seeing it again. I ran round to that side of the quarry; your dad was surfacing on and off now, gasping for breath. Voz was trying to keep him afloat but he was struggling, shouting out. 'He's got his foot stuck!' I didn't even think this would be the first and last time I would jump off the hundred-footer, I just did it. It seemed to take forever to hit the water. I remember feeling overcome with gratitude that it was at least the water, rather than a crane or a trolley. I swam with all my might to Joe. All those years swimming for Kilterdale paid off, because I was a demon out there! Your dad was trying to keep his head up. There was wild terror in his eyes – it reminded me of a panicked horse. I dived down below. I could see his foot flailing in the murky water. He had it wrapped round some tubing – it looked like the inner of a tyre, but I couldn't be sure. It didn't take me long to set his foot free, then I pushed him up, me following, until we got to the sun.

It was ages till he could breathe properly again, once Voz and I had pulled him onto the rocks. He must have belly-flopped because he'd really winded himself. When I looked up, Butler was still standing at the top of the cliff, white as a sheet.

Everyone was hugging me, calling me a hero, but all I could think was: Great, the first time I get to have skin-to-skin contact with Joe Sawyer, I look like this. Do you know the first thing your father said to me, after, 'I think you just saved my life'?

It was, 'Did you know your hair was green?'

So, that was how I met your father. That was the start of the summer that changed everything.

As soon as I'd heard that whooshing sound that told me my message telling Joe I was coming to the funeral had gone, I'd wanted to reach inside the computer and take it back again. Now there was the four-hour journey up to Kilterdale to worry about. So much time to sit and mull.

Thankfully, the train was so packed that I spent most of the journey sitting on my bag by the Ladies', too busy moving every time someone needed the loo to think about where I was going. I eventually got a seat at Crewe; halfway, I always think, between London and Kilterdale. The tall sash-windowed houses of London are far behind, we've passed the Midlands plains, and now the wet mist of the North has descended; there's the red-brick steeples, the people with their nasal, stretchy vowels. Soon, there will be the hard towns with their hard names – Wigan Warrington – before the factories thin out into fields and sheep, and then that crescent of water, surrounded by cliffs and mossy caves. The grey-stone houses stretching back, higgledy-piggledy. The whole thing looking as if it's about to crumble into the North Sea at any moment. Kilterdale: my home town. It's the place I used to love like nowhere else, and now it was the place, save for the odd guilt-provoked trip, I avoided at all costs; where life for me began, and life, as I knew it, had ended, too.

I closed my eyes. At least there was one benefit of going back: I'd get to ask Dad about Mum's ashes. Since the day we'd got them back from the crematorium, delivered to our door and so much heavier than I'd ever imagined, we'd kept them on the mantelpiece in a blue urn. Denise (evil stepmother, although not so much evil, perhaps, as hugely insecure) had gradually colonized the area: replaced the photos of us with ones of her own daughter, but the ashes had never moved. Last time I'd been home, however, they hadn't been there. I'd asked Dad about it then and several times since but he'd always shirked an answer. This time, I decided, I couldn't let it go.

An old man got on at Lancaster and sat next to me. He was eating his homemade sandwiches out of tin foil. I secretly watched him as he munched away, then as he brought something rustling out of the plastic bag beside him. It was a DVD. When I craned my neck, I saw it was *The Texas Chainsaw Massacre*.

'I love horror films,' he said, when he caught me looking – a really naughty glint in his eyes he had, too.

'Me too,' I told him. 'And *Texas* is definitely in my top five, although I'd argue that *Halloween* is your ultimate classic horror. Have you seen that?'

Stan and I chatted the rest of the way home. He told me he was eighty-three and used to be a cinema usher. He'd lost his wife four months ago and slasher-horror got him through the long, lonely nights (Stan seemed completely unaware of the irony of this). He also told me he'd been a bit depressed since she'd died and was just coming back from a hospital appointment about the blackouts he'd been having.

'I think it's when I've had enough,' he said, 'when I miss her too much. Part of my brain just shuts down.'

Stan had a squiffy eye, so you weren't quite sure which way he was looking, but as I looked at his good one, I said, 'I think you put that beautifully.'

Stan was also a blessing: since I was enjoying our conversation so much, I didn't even notice we were pulling into Kilterdale.

There was the familiar tug of guilt when I saw my dad at the end of the platform. I know he wonders why I don't come home more. Last Christmas was special, however. Denise's sister invited her to spend it with her in France, and so just Dad and Niamh came down to London. Niamh and I hatched this plan to go swimming in the Serpentine on Christmas morning, just as we used to go in the sea at home on Christmas Day when Mum was alive, all and sundry looking on: *There they go, the nutty Kings!* Amazingly, Dad said, yes – must have been still drunk from the night before – and I saw a little of my old dad that day, the hairy hulk emerging from the water, his teeth yellow against the icy blue hue of everything else, and yet the best sight ever: Bruce King and his big, wonky, yellow teeth. My dad laughing.

He wasn't laughing now, however, standing at the other end of the platform. He looked sheepish. He often looked sheepish these days, as if he was perpetually in the doghouse, which he probably was, for leaving Denise home alone for half an hour. I'd asked him specifically to come on his own, though. There were things I wanted to talk to him about that I didn't want to discuss once we'd set foot in Deniseville (a twisted world on a par with some of my patients' psychotic delusions) and we were going to Mildred's Café, like old times, for some 'Dad and Daughter' time.

As I walked towards him, I could see that his thick, strawberry-blond hair was combed neatly in a way he never had it when Mum was alive; when he would regularly pick us up from Brownies wearing leathers and smelling of beer. Now he was wearing red chinos, pulled slightly too high, and a linen blazer. He looked like Boris Johnson.

'All right, Dad,' I said. Despite the fact I spent a lot of my time disappointed with him, I couldn't stop the rush of love I felt when I saw my dad: the pure, blood kind, not based on any kind of spiritual connection.

'Hiya, Bobby,' he said, and we hugged briefly as he brushed his whiskery jowl next to my cheek. 'Journey all right?'

'Yeah, grand.'

We walked to the car in the evening sunshine. Dad doesn't do standing on the platform and chatting. Mum would have told you half her news before you even got to the car. 'I see you've brought the weather with you, like your sister,' he said.

'Oh, is Niamh here?' I said, helping Dad lift my case into the boot. This would have been a big improvement to matters. Niamh has grown up with Denise. She understands her; the atmosphere improves.

'No, but she was, she was here with Mary last night, but they've gone off on one of their expeditions for the weekend. You know how those two are attached at the bloody hip,' Dad said, slamming the boot shut. He turned to me and studied my face for a second, as if about to say something profound, then changing his mind.

'She'll never find herself a boyfriend, the rate she's carrying on.'

I pictured my sister and Mary, cuddling up under the stars in their clandestine tent, and I felt like crying. I wished she'd just tell Dad. It must be a huge burden for her to carry around.

Dad patted the pockets of that beige jacket for his car keys. I stepped back to give him the once-over.

'We might have to have a word about this little ensemble, Dad,' I said.

He raised his bushy blond eyebrows. 'You're a cheeky bugger, now get in that car,' he said. When I looked in the rear-view mirror, I saw he was smiling.

The car was spotless.

'Just had a valet, Dad?'

'Every Monday. Without fail,' he said, as we turned out of the station. 'You know how Denise likes things spick and span.'

Oh, I knew.

Dad used to drive a pick-up truck. He used to bomb

around the lanes like a nutter, one tanned arm hanging out of the window, thick gold chain around his neck, smoking a café crème, us three rattling around in the back – with no seat belts – amongst the timber and the old car parts, and the paraphernalia of whatever project Dad had up his sleeve at the time. I used to hate it when people asked when I was younger: What does your dad do? Because, genuinely, I didn't know. I longed for him to have a normal job like my friends' dads – on the railway, or with the Gas Board, but my dad had various jobs which changed all the time, so I could never keep track. He rented boats out to fishermen in Morecambe Bay, he mended people's cars in our back garden, he did up houses (just not our own). He had a stint as an ice-cream van driver one summer, but used to swear all the time at kids who annoyed him. 'Oh, piss off, Johnny, you little pillock.' Mum used to tell him off, whilst finding it hilarious. I didn't laugh at it then, but I do now. My dad's funny. Just not always funny ha-ha.

It's only a five-minute drive from the station to Mildred's Café, near the shore, but you have to go the whole length of Kilterdale, and it's like passing through a museum of my life; where at every turn there's a relic from my past. We pass the swimming baths, where just the whiff of chlorine means I'm ten again, flat-chested and streamlined as a dolphin – through the muffle of the water, I can hear the cheers of my parents, (in particular, my mother and her foghorn voice, which Niamh inherited): 'C'mon, Bobby!' as I pound towards the finish line, another medal for Kilterdale Carps.

There's the tiny cinema where, when Niamh was a baby, Mum would drop Leah and I off for the Saturday matinee, where they'd play old films. I loved those little snippets of freedom, the times alone with my big sister. The building is dilapidated today, but I can still smell the popcorn, the fusty velvet of the seats; I can still feel the ache in my throat as I tried not to cry at *E.T.* in front of Leah, and the feel of my hand in her bigger one on the walk through the fields back home. I miss Leah, I think. I miss us being children together.

We pass The Fry Up, Kilterdale's chippy, where every Friday we'd go, all five of us, Mum letting us have cans of Dr Pepper and her always having a battered sausage: 'It's not as if I eat like this every day of the week, is it, girls?' she'd say, grease dripping from her chin. In the summer, we'd sit on the little bench outside, Niamh being fed chips in her pushchair – the same bench on which, years later, I'd sit with Joe eating chips, and we'd talk about our lives that were yet to unfurl, no idea of what was to become of us, what lay ahead. I savour those summers, these memories. In my mind's eye, they're like sunbursts, sparkling on the sea. But then, like a current dragging me under, I always come back to the summer of '97. Those memories feel like the cool, dark waters that run beneath the sunburst-covered sea, beneath everything I do.

We had to go down Friars Lanes. Due to the early warm weather, the hedgerows were high and bursting with green shoots; the fields, brown and cloggy with mud in the winter, were speckled with green. If you looked up, the trees were smudged with birds' nests. They looked like masses of black thread.

I could feel Dad looking at me. 'So,' he said, eventually. 'Why are you going to this funeral?'

He rarely spoke so directly and I started, found myself feeling defensive.

'I don't know, 'cause it's his mum and it would be nice to support him. Because Marion was so good to me when my mum died?'

Dad nodded slowly and looked at me with this sad smile.

'What?' I said.

'Nothing, it's just . . .' He paused for what seemed ages. 'I thought you'd left all that behind, Robyn . .'

'I have.'

'So . . .'

I tried to look at the fields, the copses beyond, not at the lanes unfolding in front of us.

'So, what?'

'So, I'm worried about you, that's all. I'm just being concerned Dad.'

I was touched he was being concerned Dad.

'It's just the service and a few sandwiches back at the vicarage,' I said. 'And anyway, it was an excuse to see *you*.' I reached over and touched him on his shoulder. He flinched, just ever so slightly, but he did, I felt it.

'Okay, well that's all right then.'

'Dad, I'm thirty-two,' I said. 'I'll be fine.'

He patted my knee and smiled. 'And you're still my little girl,' he said.

Silence descended. It was thick and sticky and I didn't know how to move it.

Dad spoke, eventually, changing the subject: 'Look at them fields, eh, Robyn? Absolutely marvellous. I bet you miss all this in London, don't you?'

I wish I did. I wish coming back was like therapy

for me, like going back home was therapy for other people.

'Yeah, not many cow-pats in Archway,' I said. I kept looking out of the window, so he couldn't see my eyes water.

I was glad once we'd got to Mildred's. There was something about travelling in a car with Dad these days that was intense, what with the elephant squeezed in there with us.

We sat at our usual table at the back and ordered the same thing we ordered when Mum was alive: me a cappuccino and a millionaire's shortbread, Dad a cup of tea and a teacake. Mum used to have a banana milkshake with cream on top and a herbal tea. She thought the latter cancelled out the former. She was a bit deluded like that. It's probably why she thought three Rothmans a day couldn't hurt anyone, and maybe they didn't, who knows? Maybe the Rothmans had nothing to do with it.

Dad pulled up his red trousers, sat down and searched my face.

'Bloody Nora, you look more like your mother every time I see you. Same beautiful smile.' His eyes still welled up when he mentioned her.

'Thank God, eh, Dad? I lucked out, gene-wise.'

'Yep, you got your mother's looks. Niamh is more of a King, I think, and Leah, well . . .'

The teacake had arrived.

'Have you spoken to her, Dad?'

Dad made sure every millimetre of that teacake had butter on.

47

'No, I haven't managed to yet.'

'But you know how upset Mum would be if she knew you two hardly spoke.'

'She's never in, I've tried lots of times.' I was kind of disappointed he felt he could just lie like that.

'Dad, Leah hardly ever goes out in the evenings any more, you know what she's like about leaving the kids.' He looked up. 'Okay, you don't, but I'm telling you, she's paranoid, especially about Jack and his asthma. She had to take him to A&E the other night.'

Dad had picked up the teacake but put it down again. His whole face sort of slid.

'Did she?'

'Yes.'

A blackbird appeared at the window. It sounds ridiculous, but I sometimes liked to imagine it was Mum when things like that happened, checking in on us. I felt like she was urging me to get to the point.

'Dad, also, about the ashes,' I said. 'Please can I have them? I've been asking for over a year now.'

'Well, it'd help if we saw more of you. There's only Niamh that comes to see us.'

Thank God for Niamh, I thought. I hated what had happened, but most of all I hated what it had done to my relationship with my father, with my home town. As a family, we used to be so close.

'Anyway, I've got some news,' he said, changing the subject. Dad never had news. 'Denise and I – well, I . . . am selling the house. We're going to move to somewhere smaller. It's too much for Denise to clean.'

That blackbird flew off then, presumably to have a good snigger.

48

Weirdly, I didn't feel emotional about them moving out of the house we all grew up in; it hasn't been 'our' house since Denise moved in, four months after Mum died, anyway, and magnolia-d the living daylights out of it.

'That's great news, Dad,' I said. 'So when might this be?'

'We've put an offer in on a place in Saltmarsh, so all being well . . . a couple of months?'

I smiled. 'I'm pleased for you, Dad,' I said, and I was. Staying in that house with all the memories of Mum had affected him more than he let on, and whatever I felt about Denise, I couldn't bear Dad to feel sad. 'It'll be good, a new start.' He looked pleased I'd taken the news so well.

'So, Mum's ashes then,' I continued – he wasn't changing the subject that easily. 'All the more reason for me to have them. Mum would hate to be in any house but that one. She loved that house.'

I tried to imagine Mum being happy in a dormer bungalow in Saltmarsh when she was alive, and struggled.

'I know, I know.'

'Even if she never got her new kitchen.'

Dad laughed, then sniffed, his eyes misting over again.

'Also, when are you going to call Leah?' I said, patting his hand. 'Because surely this is the perfect opportunity for you two to stop being so ridiculous? The funeral was sixteen years ago.'

He sighed. *You conned me into thinking this was a nice cup of tea with my daughter and you planned this all along.*

'I will, okay? Just don't bloody hassle me, Robyn,' he said. 'You know how I hate to be hassled.'

'Yeah, I know, I'm sorry.'

I feared I'd overstepped the mark; rocked what was turning into the first proper, one-to-one chat with my dad for over a year, and was eager to rein things back, but then Dad looked up and his whole face lit up. 'Oh, here she is,' he said, smiling at someone behind me. The scent of Elnett reached me before I even turned around, to see Denise walking towards us – her jet-black hair sprayed stiff, the lashings of silver eye shadow right up to her brows, and that look in her eyes already: *This IS a competition and I shall win.*

I looked back to Dad. I wanted him to see my face, how annoyed I was that he'd clearly invited her, but he'd already got up and was getting his wallet out. 'What do you want, love? I'll get it.'

Chapter Five

I timed my arrival at the church to avoid the bit where everyone mingles outside before they go in. I've never liked that part. I can still remember to this day, outside this same church, the humiliation of having to face my six-foot, surf-dude cousin, Nathan, whilst I was a blotchy, snotty wreck at my own mother's funeral. All the embarrassing hugs from people I didn't know. I was glad Joe was spared that part too, because he was carrying the coffin. I walked up the path of St Bart's, just as they were taking it out of the hearse. It was pale oak against the vivid blue sky, with a waterfall of peach roses on top (I was right about those).

There was the crunch of shoes on gravel. Someone cried 'one, two, three' as it was lifted onto the shoulders of six men. I recognized Joe straight away, of course; at the back, one trouser leg stuck in his sock, a look of such gritty determination on his face, as if he were about to charge through the stained-glass window of the church and deliver her to the gates of heaven himself. I recognized every single one of the five other pallbearers too: Joe's uncle Fred at the front. Peg-leg Uncle Fred, Joe used to call him, Joe being one of those people who could get away with insulting people to their face. On the other side of him was Mr Potts, still with his extraordinary eyebrows. Mr Potts would often be sitting at the vicarage kitchen table when you went round, talking *really* animatedly as his caterpillar eyebrows did Mexican waves across his forehead. Joe and I used to debate how differently Potty's life could have turned out, if only he'd trimmed those eyebrows. So simple! He could have had a wife by now. Behind him was Ethan, Joe's youngest brother, and then at the back, his other brothers, Rory and Simon, and then Joe. Joe's dad was at the front of it, all in his black funeral regalia. So he'd made it. But then, as if the Reverend Clifford Sawyer was going to let any other rev guide his beloved Marion on her final journey to the gates of Paradise.

I gave the coffin a wide berth and joined everyone else in the churchyard. Half of Kilterdale was there. Side on, you could see how all four Sawyer brothers had the same profile: long face, these big, deep-set doe eyes and a slightly beaky nose; all put together it was somehow very handsome. Ethan has Down's syndrome, so his features are obviously a little different, but they all have the same hair: light brown, with a hint of red, and so fine and straight you never have to brush it.

People's conversations tapered to a murmur and then that awful, sombre silence as they parted to make way for Marion's last journey.

The plan was, I'd slip in at the back, say a quick 'Hi' to Joe at the end of the service, then slip out again, unnoticed. I found a place on the back pew and kept a low profile, leafing through the Order of Service. The first, magical, angelic notes of 'In Paradisum' from Fauré's *Requiem* struck up just as they brought her in. Then, it was unbelievable: the whole place was illuminated by a freak beam of sunlight coming smack-bang from between Jesus's thighs, on the far right window. It really was like heaven in there – and I wished, not for the first time, that I was a believer. But then perhaps when you work with people who try to recruit disciples in Morrison's, you start to equate religion with madness.

A cough echoed around the cool caverns of the church. Some kid goes, 'Daddy, you're funny,' just as Marion was lowered onto the trestle. Joe's dad stood at the feet end, palms pressed together. 'Well,' he said, gesturing to the beam of sunlight, 'she's here, ladies and gentlemen.' And everyone laughed and shed a tear at the same time, including me.

The service was lovely. I know people always say that, but I feel I can comment with sincerity, since I've been to a few not-so-lovely ones in my time, including my own mother's. Joe's dad told funny stories: how Marion was working behind her parents' shrimp bar on Morecambe front when they met, but that even the ever-present whiff of cockles couldn't keep him away, such was her luminescent beauty.

Occasionally, during the hymns, I looked over at Joe's pew. Rory and Simon were grim but dry-eyed, Ethan looked confused as to where we were on the Order of Service, but I decided Ethan was probably fine, in Ethan's own world. Joe was on the end, crying his eyes out, wiping the snot and the tears on the back of his hand because Joe wouldn't think to bring such a banal item as a packet of tissues. And although I knew the pain he was feeling, I also thought: *Good for you, Joe.* Him being such an open book was always the thing I loved about him. In fact, when I look back to that time, I can probably remember Joe crying more than me.

It was such a warm day that they'd left the door open, and so if I looked to the left, down the hill on top of which the church teetered, and past the crumbly tombstones, I could see the sea, springing up the glossy, black rocks; the same sea Joe and I had played in as loved-up teenagers, and it comforted me for some reason. Here we were, in this church, half on land, half looking like it might slip away into the sea at any time. This was all so momentary; we were all just passing through, liable to drop off the end of the world at any given time.

Of course, I didn't philosophize like this at my mum's funeral. I was far too busy concentrating on the church door and whether my bloody sister was going to walk through it in time. If I'd known that when she did, the real trouble was going to start, I might have concentrated more on thinking about Mum. I guess I'm still a bit angry about that.

A funeral congregation always says so much about the person in the box, I've always thought, and there was every walk of life in that church: old and young; your floral-society twin-sets; as well as single mums and ASBOs and hoodies from the work she used to do with the Probation Service.

And me . . . I wished *I'd* had a chance to thank Marion. For feeding me, and often Niamh, in that year Dad was mainly AWOL; for being my mum, basically, when I didn't have mine. And when I thought about it like that, I felt really glad I'd come.

Ethan stood up and read a 'poem' he'd written, which was all of two lines and said: 'Mum, I miss you and I love you. I hope you can hear me, from Ethan.' That was it. Niagara Falls. Just as I was recovering, Joe stepped up to the lectern. He hugged Ethan, then unfolded a piece of A4 paper, his hands trembling. It was all I could do not to go up there and give him a hug.

'Words can't really express how much I'm going to miss my mum, or how much I loved her. She was so many things to so many people, but to me, to us, she was just our mum.'

Our eyes met briefly and I smiled at him, encouragingly.

'I wrote long lists of what she meant to me. I even tried writing a poem, then remembered why I'd put all those terrible love poems in the bin when I was a teen-ager.' There was the odd murmur of amusement from the congregation, including me. I still had some of those terrible poems sitting in a box, along with the doodles and sometimes multiple-choice quizzes (he was always very creative with his love letters). 'And then I found this,' continued Joe. 'I think if you replace "love" with "Mum", it describes her perfectly.'

He read 1 Corinthians 13:4–8.

'"Love is patient and kind; love is not jealous or boastful; it is not arrogant or rude. Love does not insist on its own way; it is not irritable or resentful; it does not rejoice at wrong but rejoices in the right. Love bears all things, believes all things, hopes all things, endures all things."'

He was doing so well until the last line, when he broke down. '"Love never ends . . ."'

And I cried again then, too: for Joe, Marion, my own mum, absent parties, it didn't matter. Crying was just a nice release.

I waited for the congregation, plus any undesirables from schooldays who might be lurking, to leave. Then I went to find Joe. He was standing near the gate, talking to an old woman in a floppy velvet hat.

'Then it was 1980 and I think your mum only had Rory . . . no, wait . . . maybe she had Simon, too.'

Joe spotted me and stretched his hand over the lady's shoulder so that our fingers touched. 'Sorry, excuse me, Betty. Here she is!' I couldn't help but notice how his face lit up.'

'Hi, look, I'm not stopping,' I said. 'I don't want to interrupt. I just wanted to say, beautiful service for a beautiful lady – and your reading, Joe, it made me cry.'

'Oh, I think Ethan stole the show.'

'They were both gorgeous,' I said. 'Your mum would have been really proud.'

The old lady started off on one again . . . 'No, I've just remembered, Simon was about five months old . . .' and I took the opportunity to study Joe's face. I'd last seen him three years ago, in the pub on one of the rare Christmases I'd spent in Kilterdale, and been surprised to feel a stab of jealously at the fact he was with Kate, his girlfriend at the time. That he'd even moved in with her. He'd aged since then (but then, grief does that to you). The dark circles he was always prone to around his eyes were more pronounced, and when he smiled, which was often, there were quite deep lines running from his eyes to his hairline, which when I studied him closer, was peppered with a few grey hairs. But older suited him; as though he'd always been older, his face just waiting to catch up. Every time our eyes met, I saw that behind his eyes was the same person I'd known.

The woman took a breath. I really had to go.

'Joe, I'll call you, okay?' I said, squeezing his hand. 'I don't want to interrupt,' but he squeezed mine tighter.

'But you're not interrupting.' His eyes were pleading with me. 'Come on, don't go yet. Please? This is Betty.'

Betty looked pretty cheesed off I'd waded in and ruined her flow.

'Betty used to be a lollipop lady, and knew us all from the very first week Mum and Dad moved to Kilterdale. She used to cross us over to primary school, didn't you, Bet? Hand me bootleg sweeties from her pocket.'

'He was a bloody nuisance,' she said, and Joe and I laughed. 'A few penny sweets and he was high as a kite.'

Joe had been diagnosed as hyperactive when he was little, and was never allowed sweets or stuff like Kia-Ora. By the time I met him, at sixteen, he was still bouncing off the walls most of the time, but I'd always loved that about him – his energy.

I said, 'He didn't improve with age.'

'How do you know?' said Joe. 'You haven't spent any time with me for sixteen years.' He was looking at me, quite intently. I couldn't help think that comment was loaded. 'Anyway, this is Robyn.' He said, eventually.

'Robyn, eh?' said Betty. 'That's a funny name for such a bonny girl. Is she the lucky lady?'

'No, no . . .' Joe said. 'There is no lucky lady at the moment, Bet.'

So he was no longer with Kate?

'Robyn's a friend. A very old, good friend.' His gaze was intense enough for it to make me look away.

'She's a l'il corker, too. Look at all that lovely thick hair,' Betty said.

'Now you're making me blush, Betty,' I replied.

'Oh, I still blush,' said Bet, 'and I'm eighty-six!'

Betty eventually gave Joe her condolences and shuffled off. I really did have to be getting back to Dad and Denise's, even though an evening with them – Dad watching *Gardener's World*, Denise bringing him endless, elaborate snacks, didn't exactly fill me with glee. I opened my mouth to say as much when, from out of the corner of my eye, I saw a thickset bald bloke making his way over. He had one child by the hand and was pushing a twin buggy – with twins in it – with the other. Stopping, he slapped an arm around Joe. 'Hey, Sawyer!' It was only when he was right up close that I realized it was Voz. 'You did really well, mate. I wouldn't have been able to stand up there and do that.'

'Cheers, Voz,' said Joe, giving Voz a manly back-slapping hug in return. 'That means a lot.'

'All right, Vozzy?' I said. I was adopting my old matey, blasé school tones, when really I was shocked. I hadn't seen Voz for years – since that day Joe nearly drowned at the Black Horse Quarry. Who was this beefcake before me? What had happened to runty Voz?

'All right, Kingy. How are you?' For some reason, I was touched that he'd used my nickname. 'You haven't changed a bit.'

'You have!' I said. Joe sniggered. 'I mean . . . you look like you've been busy.'

He giggled. When Voz used to giggle, he used to look like a cute rat; now he looked like a cute fat rat, all his pointy, ratty features concentrated in the middle of a big round face.

'Yep, this is Paige.' The chubby blonde child holding his hand stared back gormlessly at us. 'Paige is eight.' (*Eight?* What had I produced in the last eight years?) 'And these little monsters are Tate and Logan.'

Tate and Logan? Bloody hell.

'That's my missus, Lindsay, over there.' He pointed to a pretty, dark-haired girl chatting to Joe's brother. 'We've got another on the way in January.'

'Wow, Anthony, are you going for world domination?' asked Joe. 'An assembly line of Vozzies keeping the whole of the northwest in wallpaper?' (Voz's dad owned the Wojkovich Wallcoverings empire.)

'You've got to get cracking while you can.' Voz laughed. 'Any of you got kids yet?'

'No, no . . .' said Joe.

'Not that you know of, eh, Sawyer?'

'And what about you, Kingy?' said Voz, when nobody said anything. 'I hear you work up on the funny farm?'

'Yep. If you can't beat 'em, join 'em, eh?' I smiled.

'So are you like a shrink? A psychiatrist?' Voz asked.

'Well, no, I can't prescribe the drugs, but I can administer them.'

'What, someone leaves you in charge with a *needle?*' Voz seemed genuinely alarmed by this.

'Yes, and in people's own homes. I visit people at home who have mental-health problems.'

'Can you do something about my missus? She's got a few mental-health problems.'

'I tell you what – because it's you, Voz – I'll do a two-for-one.'

Voz turned round at the sound of two girls talking loudly. 'That's Saul Butler's wife, isn't it?' he said, gesturing to the one with red, bob-length hair. 'Is Butler not here, Joe?'

I looked quickly to Joe.

'No, I invited him – his kids all went to one of the playgroups Mum ran.'

So Saul Butler had kids?

'But he never got back to me, so – you know – his loss.'

Voz grinned at me and for a second he was just little ratty, giggly Voz again, who used to cry actual tears when he laughed. 'I reckon Butler always fancied you, Robyn. I bet he was well jealous of you, Joe.'

Joe smiled at me. 'Well, yes, I was a very lucky boy.'

'I always remember that time up at Black Horse Quarry, when you jumped in. D'you remember?' Voz said, adding, 'When you nearly died?'

'How could I forget?' said Joe.

'That was a competition for Butler, that was.' Voz said, pointing decisively. 'I'll never forget his face, standing at the top of that hundred-footer. Absolutely gutted that you had the balls to jump and he didn't.'

'Yeah, well, turned out he was the sensible one, didn't it?' said Joe. 'I might well have died if Robbie hadn't saved me that day.'

'Och,' I said, modestly. 'No . . .'

One of the twins in the buggy started to cry then,

60

thank God. 'Right, well, I'd better get these rug rats home,' said Voz. 'You take care.'

The moment Voz trundled off with his army of children, Joe's face collapsed. I remember that effort too.

'Tired?' I said.

'Yeah.' He took my hand. 'Look, don't go, Robbie. Come back for the wake.'

Robbie. Nobody but Joe ever called me Robbie.

'I can't, Joe. I have to get back to London.'

'So do I,' he said.

'You're in *London* now?'

'Well, Manchester, but you *see*,' he said, pointing, 'that stopped you. You didn't know that, did you? You didn't know I lived in Manchester. We've got so much to catch up on.'

'*Joe*,' I sighed. Didn't he get that I wasn't just some unfeeling cow but that I was trying to make a polite exit here without having to go into one?

'Come on, I haven't seen you for three years. I don't want to go back on my own and face all those people.'

Then it clicked.

It was a funeral, his mother's funeral. What was I *doing*?

Chapter Six

'Only plus of being a vicar's son,' Joe used to say, 'is that you get a big house'; and it *was* big compared to the houses most kids who went to our school lived in, but not, I noticed, anywhere near as big as I remembered it from the last time I was in it, years ago. Still, I'd always loved Joe's house, maybe because it was what ours might have been if Mum and Dad had spent less on socializing and throwing parties, and more on doing the house up (but then, 'You can't take it with you when you go,' Mum used to say. Obviously, she didn't expect to go quite so soon).

Our house was big too: 'The big pink house in Kilterdale.' But it was a wreck. Mum and Dad had bought it when I was six, for a pittance, with some big plans (Dad in particular was good at those) to do it up and turn it into a 'palace fit for a King!' It was always the party house – there was nothing to spoil, after all, since nothing had been done – and every summer, we'd hold the King Family Extravaganza, where Mum and Dad would dress up as some famous couple – Sonny and Cher, Marge and Homer, Torvill and Dean – and Dad would serve hot dogs and beer from his old ice-cream van. The big renovation plans began, finally, when I was eleven, but then Dad's work dried up and they'd always spent so much on socializing, on living for the now instead of thinking about the future (good job, as it turns out) that they couldn't finish. One year, we had to move into a caravan in the driveway, because we couldn't afford to finish off the plumbing. Leah (who was fourteen at the time and very unamused by the whole situation) would shout at the top of her voice things like: 'If I have to shove anyone else's shit down this septic tank, I am going to *throw it at them*!' I dread to think what people on that street thought of us.

It was a shock to the system then, dragged up amidst such chaos (and a lot of fun), to meet Joe, whose house was a vision of sombre, deep contemplation – at least, that was what I imagined. The first time I went there, his dad was wearing his dog collar. We all had tea and biscuits in the living room, making polite smalltalk to the background sound of the grandfather clock ticking away. I bit into a ginger nut and Joe looked at me like I'd just flashed my bra:

'Oh, *no*' he said.

'What?' I said.

'You didn't say Grace, and we always says Grace before we eat anything.'

I felt sick. They let me suffer for a good ten seconds before they *all* started killing themselves laughing. So that was the kind of 'good' church family *they* were. That was the kind of home the Sawyers had.

The vicarage was an Edwardian villa-type affair, with huge front windows and a big conservatory off the back. The front doors were open when I got there after the funeral, so you could see right through the sun-flooded hall of the house to the lawn, where people were milling in the sun, drinking cups of tea. The scene was very tame – mind you, I'm not sure what I expected: a free bar, like at Mum's (recipe for disaster in retrospect)? Most people were over fifty and very sedate. I was a bit disappointed the probation lot hadn't turned up; they'd have livened things up a bit.

I did a quick scan for alcohol and could see none, which panicked me. Then I spotted Mrs Murphy, our old deputy head, and panicked even more – this was exactly why I'd worried about coming: blasts-from-the-past absolutely everywhere. I looked around for Joe, but couldn't see him, and so I took myself off to the buffet table, before finding a quiet corner, where I was immediately joined by a woman who'd just got back from a Christian Aid mission in Somalia. I'd just put an entire mini pork pie into my mouth when she started telling me about all the horrors there, so all I could do was nod. She left soon after and so I went for a wander, to find Joe, and hopefully some alcohol. I ventured into the cool, dark hall, where one woman – angular and the colour of digestive biscuits – was talking at the top of her voice to an audience, who looked as if they'd not so much gathered, as been passing through and seized against their will.

'I'll never forget when Marion came to my Zumba class,' she was saying. 'It was last summer. Or was it the summer before? Or was it the one before then?'

Why was it always the one who knew the deceased the least, who talked the loudest at funerals?

I went on to the kitchen, where people were poring over clip-frame pictures of Marion, which I couldn't quite bring myself to look at. Old Potty was there with his Mexican-wave eyebrows. I was contemplating slipping out, texting Joe later, then I saw Mrs Murphy looking dangerously like she was making a beeline for me, and decided on a tactical toilet break. I sloped upstairs.

The house had hardly changed in eighteen years. It had the same smell: furniture, polish and books. The wide, dark staircase seemed modest enough now, whereas it used to seem so grand to me, so full of mystique, probably because it led to Joe's bedroom, which was the only place we could be alone, doing whatever we did in there – learning Zeppelin lyrics off by heart, discussing Potty's eyebrows . . . Joe's mum occasionally walking past with the Hoover.

'Joseph, leave your door open, please, otherwise Robyn will have to go home!'

Behind that door, we'd be sitting, holding our breath, often in various stages of undress. It seemed like an age ago, another life ago. Like it didn't even happen.

There was the same mahogany side table at the top of the stairs, with the photos on top. I paused to look at the one of all four boys, an eight-year-old Joe on the end, pulling a stupid face, desperate to dash off as soon as the picture was taken.

I gave myself a quick once-over in the long mirror just before you get to Joe's room.

I was wearing a black Monsoon shift dress. Last time I looked in this mirror, the girl staring back at me was terrified, with peroxide hair: white face, white hair. I just remember that.

The door to Joe's bedroom was half open, just a slice of the view of the rolling sheep-dotted fields, then the flat grey line of the sea. I couldn't resist it. I went inside. It smelt different, of a guest room, but it was still completely Joe's room. There was still the poster of Led Zeppelin's album *Physical Graffiti* (Joe and I were alone and, it has to be said, slightly ridiculed in our appreciation of Led Zeppelin, which as teenagers was enough to make us believe we were destined for one another) and, above his bed, Béatrice Dalle in *Betty Blue* pouted back at me. Clearly, Joe's older brothers had introduced him to *Betty Blue* and the wondrous sexiness that was Béatrice Dalle, since we were only little when the film came out, but I'd often looked at her in that poster; the tough, gap-toothed poutiness and the cleavage, and I'd wanted to *be* Béatrice Dalle at sixteen. I wanted to be French and insouciant and wild and sexy. I was kind of annoyed with this gawky, traumatised teenager, who just desperately missed her mum. I wandered around for a bit, examining Joe's odd collection of boy trinkets: rocks and fossils, and then – I couldn't believe he'd kept it this long! – the 'ironic' pen in the shape of a lady; when you tipped her up, her knickers came off. I'd brought it back from Palma Menorca for a laugh, in 1997. That year – the summer we got together – Joe went to Amsterdam and bought me a wooden clog specially engraved with my name. The fact he'd queued up to get that done (because '*Robyn*' was never on any merchandise in the land) thrilled me. 'He must *really* like me,' I'd thought, 'If he's willing to queue in front of his mum and dad, to get a wooden *clog* signed.'

'He's got tenacity, that one,' I remember Dad saying. A few months later, Joe wasn't allowed to set foot in our house. But I still have that clog, and sometimes, when I'm feeling down, I just like to turn it over in my hand; feel its wooden, smooth simplicity.

I stood in front of his bed – it was the same metal, tubular bed in 1980s grey that he'd had back then – and remembered how I'd had some of my most uncomfortable nights in it. It was like sleeping on a climbing frame, and yet, in the times we'd snatched together, it was also where I was happiest; where, for a while, I could forget about Mum, curling around Joe's warm, strong body. We'd lie there in the dark, thrilled just to be naked together.

Joe was obviously sleeping in this room because there was a wash bag on the bed. I stood looking at it, feeling a wave of sadness. Imagine coming home, to sleep in your childhood bed, knowing your mother is to be buried the next day. Just then, the door flew open, making me jump. It was Joe. He slammed it shut, his back towards me, swearing, leaning his forehead against it for a moment, before fiddling in his inside jacket pocket and producing a bottle of Jack Daniel's. He unscrewed the top, muttered something about *Sorry Mum* and *have to do this*, and then tipped his head back and took a swig. Then he saw me.

'Bloody hell, you nearly gave me a heart attack!' he said.

Then, when he'd realized what he'd said, 'That's going to keep on happening, isn't it?'

I smiled. 'Probably.'

'Do you want some?' he said, holding the bottle out. 'Can I just say, it was a huge oversight by me not to have organised booze at this wake.'

'Yup,' I said, taking a gulp. 'Still, I don't need booze to relax.'

'Really?' he said. ''Coz I do.'

I handed him the bottle back. 'Jack Daniel's? Going for the hard liquor, then?'

'I can't take any risks,' he said. 'It needs to reach my bloodstream instantly. I just can't *talk* to people any longer.'

There was a long silence, during which we just sort of looked at each other.

'So, er . . . the bathroom's two doors down,' he said, thumbing in that general direction when I just stood there, still clutching Miss Knickerless. 'Same place it's always been.'

I felt my cheeks grow hot.

'God, sorry. I couldn't resist, I just had this mad desire to—'

'Snoop around my bedroom?'

'Oh, shit, I'm sorry.'

'I'm joking, Robyn.' His eyebrows gave a little flicker of amusement. 'It's actually really sweet.'

He looked pale as anything, washed out. I'd forgotten about that bit, the *tiredness*, and he pushed the stuff to the side, collapsing on the bed.

'I should go,' I said. He'd come up here to be alone, lose himself, and here I was, making that impossible, but he said, 'Don't *go*. Why do you keep on wanting to go?'

He looked genuinely annoyed – Joe and his transparency.

'I don't know, because you want to be on your own?'

He tutted, dramatically. 'I don't want to be on my own. I just can't take much more of people, of Betty. We're only on 1978. There's thirty-odd years to get through yet.'

I laughed, despite myself.

'I needed someone to save me. Where were you, Robbie?' he said, turning on his side.

'Snooping round your bedroom?'

I sat down on the bed next to him. Up close, it was like he'd changed even less, and I had this urge to give him a hug, but wondered whether that was appropriate, him lying on a bed and all, so I said, 'It'll be over soon. They'll all bugger off home and then you can go to sleep or watch a film. That's what I did.'

'Really, what did you watch?'

'*The Evil Dead*.'

'You *are* joking?'

'I'm not, as it happens. It's my job, you see. You start off quite PC and normal and, before you know it, you can't operate in normal society.'

Joe thought this was really funny. 'So, basically, you've become like, the world's most un-PC mental-health nurse? Telling schizophrenics to get real?'

'Something like that, yes.'

We were both giggling now – funeral hysteria.

'So, anyway, let's get back to this *Evil Dead* thing,' he said. 'Talk me through that.'

'Well, I found that the key is distraction, not stimulation,' I tried to explain. 'No tear-jerkers, which rules out a lot more than you may think, for obvious reasons. No documentaries or kids films 'cause they just remind you of too much. So, yeah, slasher-horror really is your best bet. *The Evil Dead* is the ultimate wake-movie.'

Joe tried to be serious for a second, then smiled. 'You always did have all the best advice,' he said.

He turned on his back, closed his eyes and let out this huge sigh. I was looking at the shape of his lips, the Cupid's bow, the wideness of them, the way they always looked like he was about to say something amusing, trying to remember what it felt like to kiss him. Then remembering that I shouldn't even be here.

'*You* bought me that pen,' he said suddenly. I'd forgotten I was still holding it.

'Funny, wasn't I?' I said. 'Such a sophisticated, witty sixteen-year-old.'

'You were,' he said, taking it and tipping it upside down.

'No, I wasn't.'

'I thought you were – cute, complicated . . .'

I rolled my eyes. 'Oh, weren't we all?'

'I'm not surprised that you work for the Mental Health Service – the sidelined in our society . . . You always liked the underdog.'

'Me and you, too, then, hey?'

When I'd last seen Joe, three years ago, he'd been living with his girlfriend in Preston but seemed a bit lost, career-wise, working in a sports shop. In our brief email exchange during the last few days, he'd told me he was now teaching English to NEETs (Not in Education, Employment or Training) – kids who'd spent most of their lives skiving off school or inside, basically, and wanted to turn their lives around. He absolutely loved it, he said. The perfect job, if you took away the mounds of paperwork, which was exactly how I felt about my work.

'I can't say I'm surprised, either, Joe. All that energy had to go somewhere.'

'We were a pair of little revolutionaries.' He grinned.

'Were we? I can't remember. I just remember you used to say to me –' I assumed the younger voice of Joe's radical years – 'it's evolution, Robbie, not revolution.'

'Did I? God, what a dick. I was so *intense*!'

'Oh, Joe, you're still intense.'

'How would you know?' He said, tapping my thigh, as if chastising me for not getting in touch. I ignored it.

'Actually, you saying that really helped when things were grim,' I said, seriously. 'I sometimes say it to my clients.'

'Really?'

'Yeah, just to remind them that recovery . . . it takes time. Step by step. Rome wasn't built in a day and all that.'

He smiled. He knew what I was getting at.

The room was growing dim, it was getting late, and I was here, having a heart-to-heart, the very thing I'd promised myself not to do. I stood up.

'Look, I really should be going now,' I said. 'I'll just go downstairs and say, "Hi" to your dad, okay?'

But Joe suddenly got up from the bed and went rooting in a drawer for something.

'What are you doing?' I asked.

'Trying to make you stay.'

'Joseph Sawyer,' I said. 'I wasn't supposed to come in the first place!'

He turned around. He looked hurt.

72

'But why?'

Why did he not get it?

'Because,' I sighed, exasperated. 'Because . . . oh, God, it doesn't matter.' I'm really glad I did come.

He had something in his hand. He put it behind him and, walking backwards, picked up the bottle of JD off the table with his free hand and handed it to me. He always did have this way of making you do things. 'Come on, drink up,' he said. 'This is going to take you right back.'

That's what I'm worried about.

But then, there was a sound like someone loading a gun, a click, the whirr of a tape being rewound and then, the bluesy, achey riffs of Led Zeppelin's 'Since I've Been Loving You' – we used to listen to this track, this album, all the time – and when I saw Joe's face, the look in his eyes (well on his way to drunk, mainly), I understood that – even if I didn't want to – Joe needed to. He needed to be anywhere but here.

We swayed – it's one of those songs that make it impossible not to – but rather awkwardly, like the first self-conscious dancers on the floor at a wedding reception, and I suddenly felt old. It didn't feel like it used to feel, and when we smiled at one another, it was because we both knew this. I took off my shoes and we danced, passing the bottle between us. It felt like undressing, like a layer of tension was being peeled back. Joe held both arms out, his eyes shimmering with tears.

'Come here,' he said. 'Please? I need a hug.'

I wrapped both arms around his neck then; his suit jacket felt stiff and restrictive and so I took it off for him. We leaned our heads on each other's shoulders and,

73

as we danced, I could feel his whole body shudder. And I just held him like that, and let him cry as I stroked his hair. The song finished, I was still holding him. He looked up at me.

'Do you want to go for a walk?' He said. 'I can't stay here.'

We didn't talk about where to go, we just went; it was like our feet remembered the old route and took us there: down the long, sloping lawn, through the front gate and out onto the path. I didn't know what time it was, but everything was awash with a lilac hue and the tide was out, leaving sweeping, silver channels like liquid mercury. The air smelt like the inside of mussel shells. Were we drunk? I should hope so, the amount of Jack Daniel's we'd put away. We were holding hands – it just felt like the right thing to do. We turned left at the gate and out of the cul-de-sac that wraps itself around the bottom of the vicarage. The houses get lower, the closer you get to the sea around here, so you have the big old houses like Joe's and our old pink one, up on the hills, with a bottom tier of white bungalows petering out to the sea. And this is where we were now, walking – not entirely in a straight line – hand in hand, among the white underskirt of Kilterdale, with the lilac sky and the black shadows and the low houses with their big, glowing fly's-eye windows; and I didn't know whether it was because the houses were so low that the sky seemed so big, but it did; so big and empty, like everyone had deserted.

We passed Joe's hip flask between us. We'd filled it with the remainder of the Jack Daniel's and then sneaked into the kitchen and put some Coke in there, too, because we didn't want complete amnesia, just a blurring of the edges, and I could tell the edges were already blurred because we were getting onto fundamentals.

'So . . . relationships,' said Joe. 'You got some nice guy to look after you?'

'We just ended, actually.'

'Oh, shit. Sorry. Why?' There was a pause, where I knew what Joe was going to say next. Such a mix of self-absorption and selflessness, I haven't seen in anyone since. 'Was he just not as good as me?'

'No, he was just still married to another woman . . .'

'Robyn King,' he said, 'a marriage-wrecker?'

'Oh, no, he was separated. He had been for a long time. He was just eking out the longest, most painful divorce in the history of divorces, and I was his therapist. It was never going to work.'

'There you go, you see – I said you always liked the underdog.'

'I forgot how the only time you're sarcastic is when you're drunk.'

'It *is* my mother's funeral.'

'Like that's an excuse.'

We got to the stile that takes you over the fields to the other end of the village.

'So, what about you?' I asked. We were trapped in the stile, so were facing each other, our faces inches apart. 'You were with a girl called Kate, last time I saw you. What happened? Not as good as me?' I said grinning.

He'd been drinking from the flask again and he laughed, coughed.

Stop flirting, shut up.

'Nice girl,' he said, 'but she had thick ankles and I just couldn't get over it.

'See, I told you she wasn't as good as me,' I said, flashing my dainty ankles (my body improves as it peters to the ends) and resolving, really, to stop the flirting. I was getting carried away.

We stayed sitting on the stile for a bit, passing the flask to and fro. Beyond the fields, were the cliffs, and beyond the cliffs, you could hear the sea.

'You could be seventeen in this light,' said Joe. He had his hand over mine, and all I could feel was that hand, as though that warm area of skin was all that existed.

'Don't say that,' I said.

'Kiss me,' he said suddenly, and I laughed.

'Joe, I can't *kiss* you!'

'Who cares? Why not?'

'That's why.' *Because you don't care*, I thought, *because why would you? On a day like today? Whereas for me*, I was thinking to myself as I looked at the lovely shape of his mouth, *it's not that simple, Robyn, and you know it.*

He groaned. 'Come on,' he said, and we carried on walking over the fields. A pale disc moon was now intensifying in the sky. The poor old trees, after centuries of being blown mercilessly by North Sea gales, now leaned permanently over.

I leaned over, too.

'What are you doing?' said Joe.

'Checking they're really like that, or if I'm actually that drunk.'

'You're actually that drunk. Now give me some of that,' and he took the flask from me. It was much colder

76

now and we held onto one another, for warmth as much as anything else, dodging the turf-covered rocks and the sheep shit. Now and again, one of us would trip spectacularly, the other hoisting them up, and then we'd carry on, oblivious, conversation rolling like the fields themselves.

'You heard me talking to my mum,' said Joe. 'That's a bit embarrassing.'

'Joe, I used to go into my mum's wardrobe, put on her clothes, then prance around the house, pretending to *be* her. How's that for embarrassing?'

'And did it help?'

I loved that Joe didn't bat an eyelid. Andy would have given me that look, the one that said, 'Robyn, I really like you, but sometimes you scare me.'

'At the time, yes, and if chucking things at the wall helps you, or getting paralytic, or dressing up in your mum's clothes, then you should do that, too.'

'Excellent. I'll think of you when I'm wearing one of my mum's skirts and maybe a nice blouse.' He was holding out his hand for me to take it. 'Shall we go through the farm, like old times?'

The cold air and the walk had made the booze go more to my head now, and I didn't really care where we went or what we did. I just knew I didn't want to go home yet.

We trudged up the lane. The farmhouse had most of its lights on and there were sheets hanging on the washing line, billowing against the sky, like a child's idea of a ghost. Chickens were roaming around outside, doing their odd little jerking movements, like clockwork toys, and to our left, behind the milking shed, was the barn, the one that all the kids used to play in, much to the annoyance of Mr Fry, who'd come and shine his great big torch in your eyes and swear his head off.

'Come on,' said Joe, pulling me towards it. 'It's bloody freezing, let's go inside.'

'We'll get done,' I said.

Joe grabbed hold of my face; he was laughing. He put his forehead so it was touching mine.

'*Done?* You're so sweet,' he said. Then he kissed me once, hard on the lips, and I startled – Joe's face, that mouth, suddenly right there, like the last sixteen years hadn't happened at all. I lifted my face instinctively for more, but he was pulling me by the hand. 'We're not sixteen any more, you know,' he said. 'And, anyway, what happened to the naughty Robyn King I know and love?'

'She grew up,' I said, not knowing if he heard me. He took me inside anyway. The bales were piled right up to the ceiling, then graduated like steps to a cluster on the floor. There was an old wardrobe, timber stacked up on one side of it; to the right, there was a tractor – or the skeleton of a tractor – about to be mended or tended to, with all its doors and metalwork removed. It was huge and looming and really quite sinister. It reminded me of a prehistoric creature, about to stir and let out a deafening roar.

We leaned back on the bottom rung of hay, and finished what was in the flask. I wasn't wearing tights, and my legs were goose-pimpled. Joe took off his suit jacket and lay it over them. We lay back like that for a while, next to one another, just looking up at the stars that throbbed in the gaps of the corrugated-iron roof.

Then Joe said, 'I found her, you know.'

I turned my head to him. 'Your mum?'

'Yes. She'd stayed up after Dad went to bed. I got up to go to the toilet in the middle of the night and the light was still on in the front room. She was sitting in the chair, but sort of half sitting on it, half slumped over, and I thought, that's a funny position for anyone to go to sleep in – with her body all twisted, half her bum on the seat. And then I moved her hair from her face. God, it was horrible, Robbie. Her skin was grey, it looked like putty, and it had, like, slid off her face. And she was just absent, gone. All that was left was this shell . . .'

I took Joe's hand and stroked it with my thumb.

'I'm so scared I'll never be able to get that picture out of my mind,' he said.

I leaned over and I hugged him then. 'You will,' I said. 'It takes time, but you will.'

'Promise?'

'It's evolution, not revolution, remember?'

He nudged me and gave a little laugh.

'It *is*,' I said.

We stayed like that, lying down, our arms wrapped around each other, my cheek against his. I inhaled his smell. I already knew.

What did it matter? Who did care, anyway? Wasn't this what it was about, life? Seizing the day, just being; not thinking so much all the time? It was funny, I thought, how sometimes there was nothing like death to make you feel so alive.

He pulled away from me and we hesitated, then I lifted my hands to his face. He lifted his eyes to mine. I couldn't stop staring at that face, seeing how his eyes, or rather the person inside those eyes – his gaze – was the same. Did he see the same thing in me? Does that ever change?

'You're strong,' I said. 'Stronger than you know.'

'Not stronger than you, everything you've been through, all of that.'

'*We've* been through,' I said. 'You *are* strong.'

Silence, except for somewhere in the distance I could hear a chicken squawking. It was incongruous, a rude interruption.

'What did we do to each other?' he said, the words toppling out, 'that means nothing, nobody . . .' I kissed him then and the curve of his lips, the way it moved with mine, the little dance we did, it was so familiar, it shocked me; and when I looked at his face, his lovely face, I recognized it so much, it was like looking at myself. We lay back on the straw: it scratched and prickled the backs of my thighs and my arms like anything, but I couldn't have cared less, I didn't care about anything, I wasn't thinking anything – that was the beauty of it. And I looked into Joe's eyes and told myself that he didn't want to think either – not today. We kissed, but in a frenzy, as if we had no control over our movements because we were in shock, in shock that this was happening at all; at least, that's what it felt like. Involuntary. A brilliant, beautiful shock. I turned on my back, Joe was next to me and I wriggled my bum, so I could lift my skirt up, and started to take off my knickers.

'What are you doing?' whispered Joe.

'What?' I said, pausing.

He ran a finger down my arm.

'I want to savour you more than that yet,' he said.

'I've got lots more kissing to get through yet. Lift up your bum, come on.'

I shifted so I could do as I was told, and he gently pulled down my dress, then arranged it on my legs and lay down next to me. I looked at him, a bit unsure then, but he moved the hair from my face, gently slipping one hand under my head, so I didn't have to crane my neck to reach him, and kissed me – sweet, sweet kisses, on my forehead, my eyelids, my mouth. My throat had gone dry and I was trembling. He reached down and, very softly, ran the tip of his finger up my leg, just getting to my knickers, before he sent it in little circle movements across and between my thighs and, then, just as I felt I might explode, back down again. I buried my face in his chest and dug my heels into the straw, so I could bear it, this feeling that was so familiar and yet so wonderful that I doubted I could ever have had it before – like déjà vu.

He looked beautiful in the half-light – his eyes shone. The tractor skeleton loomed over us, the height of two men. But I wasn't scared one bit; I was safe. I leaned down to undo his flies, but he put his hand over mine, stopping me; he took my hand and kissed it, then lay it across my chest. I gave a low growl of frustration and he smiled. Then he continued stroking the other leg up to my knickers again, this time stroking underneath me, a feathery, gentle touch, barely detectable through the fabric, which was wet. He pushed the material to the side, slid one finger inside me, then another, and I gasped – I couldn't help it – and when I looked at him, my eyes wide, disbelieving, Joe looked so happy as my whole body bucked, then shuddered. I could bear it no longer.

I pulled at his trousers but my hands were shaking so much that I couldn't do it, so he kicked off his shoes, sat up and wriggled out of them.

'I haven't got one,' he said.

'It's okay,' I said, pulling his shoulders back. 'It's okay. It's fine, honestly.' I sat up and kissed him on the neck. 'Just come here, *please* . . . For God's sake.'

'Robyn . . .'

'Come *on*!'

I took my knickers off and flung them to the side; we were both giggling now and shivering, half with cold, half with desire.

I lay back down and then Joe was inside me, the length of his whole, warm, strong body against mine. I wanted to cry, I was so happy, and I cried out again. When I flung my head to the side, I saw that a chicken had wandered into the barn. I could make out its fat, black body silhouetted; its shadow was long on the straw floor, and in the moonlight its lidless eye was blinking at me.

Chapter Seven

'Right, how do you like your eggs, Robyn?'

The atmosphere at the breakfast table at Dad's the next day was frosty, to say the least. Denise was the martyred waitress, wafting dramatically in and out of the beaded curtain separating the dining room from the kitchen (I swear she only had it fitted so Dad could actually *hear* her go in and out of there). Dad was doing what he always did when there was an atmosphere: hiding behind his newspaper.

I watched him, reading the sports pages, picking his nose, unable to even believe myself, that I could possibly feel this bad. I'm not a big drinker, normally. I don't like the feeling of being out of control. This wasn't always the case. At university, I was *that* girl with traffic cones in my room, that girl to get in any old minicab. I once held up the traffic on Blackfriars Bridge when drunk (and spent a night in a police cell for the privilege). But there's only so long you can carry on like that before you realize it's not fair to have everyone worry constantly about you, even if you're not worrying about yourself. Now, I never drink so much I'm out of control. Last night, I did. Maybe I felt safe? Still, I wasn't going to let Denise have the satisfaction of knowing that.

I sat motionless at the dining table, my throbbing head slowly catching up with the pleasant dull ache between my thighs. If I sort of pursed my lips and closed my eyes, I could still smell Joe on my top lip: his muskiness, Jack Daniel's. When Denise came marching back from the kitchen, I felt like she'd caught me in the act.

She plonked a cup of tea down in front of me.

'You look like you need that,' she said. The slogan on it said: DO YOU TAKE ME FOR A MUG? I chose not to take this personally. Then she rattled through the beaded curtain, to make my poached eggs. I might have helped, but feared that, if I moved, I'd most definitely be sick.

From behind his newspaper, Dad tutted. 'How come madam here gets to choose what type of eggs she gets? It's not a bloody hotel, you know . . .'

'Really?' said Denise from the kitchen. 'You could have fooled me.'

I apologized for waking people up; it's much easier that way. Apparently, I'd come in at after 3 a.m., then set the smoke alarm off by making a bacon sandwich. Denise said my dress was left in a heap by the toilet, still in the shape that I'd stepped out of it (and I could go and pick it up when I was ready, too).

'Did you get back to sleep, Denny, love?' Dad said.

'No, but it's fine,' she said. (Fine, fine, *fine*.) 'I'll have a nap later, if I get the chance.'

Denise was huffing and puffing and clattering in the kitchen. I was taking slow, tentative slurps of tea, looking through the French doors at the dull grey sky and the grey concrete. When Mum was alive, that garden was a mass of wild flowers and colour; six months after Denise moved in (which was only two after Mum died, Christmas '96, just to add insult to injury), she had it paved over – apparently because she had a 'bad back and found it hard to garden'. Maybe it was this which angered me – this feeling I can't seem to shake, that Dad has let Denise pave over him, us. Maybe it was the thought that if Mum could see those grey slabs, she'd be so disappointed, or that last night had ignited something in me, set some kind of change in motion. Whatever it was, I felt daring. I was not leaving this house without the ashes.

'Right, so,' I announced suddenly, pressing my palms on the table for extra emphasis. From behind his newspaper, I saw Dad's eyelids flicker with alarm. 'Where are Mum's ashes? 'Cause I'm not going home without them.'

Dad coughed and put his paper down. Denise came out, carrying my eggs, a miasma of Elnett and frying fat, the tops of her jeans swish-swishing. She stopped when she got to the table, holding the plate in her hands.

'Well, Bruce, have you told her?' She'd overdrawn one of her brows with eye pencil, so it went too far towards her temple. It made her look even more mad than usual.

'Told me what?'

'He can't find them, Robyn,' she said, putting my plate down.

I felt my throat constrict with panic.

'What do you mean, you can't find them?' I said, my voice wobbling. 'Dad, are you saying that you have actually *lost* Mum?'

'Don't be bloody ridiculous,' he said.

85

'Well, where are they, then? Denise, any ideas?'

I didn't hate Denise but I didn't trust her either. Mum was a hard act to follow and she knew it. I always got the sense with her that she'd never got over one vital fact: Dad had never wanted to end it with Mum; it ended because she died. It would have been easier for Denise if it had been divorce.

'Because I don't mean to be rude, and please don't take this the wrong way, but I know you've sometimes found it difficult, looking at . . .' Dad was boring holes into me with his eyes. I stopped just in time. 'Just, maybe you moved them, that's all?'

The realization that, yes, I *was* accusing her of hiding my mother's ashes, made Denise's throat flush red – was that anger, or guilt? 'Don't look at me,' she said. 'I have polished that urn every single day. I do it at the same time as I do my cats and trophies.'

That was nice, I thought, ranking all that remained of my mother with her badminton trophies and ceramic cats. And, anyway, I didn't believe her.

'Also, if you three girls can't look after your mother's ashes yourselves, well . . .' She flounced off in the direction of the kitchen again. 'I've done my bit.'

'Denise, excuse me!'

Dad slammed his newspaper shut. It made me jump. 'That is enough, Robyn, thank you. Stop talking about the ashes in front of Denise. It's bad manners.'

Bad manners? My mum's memory was now a bad manner?

'And in front of your dad,' added Denise. 'It only upsets him.'

This was unbelievable.

'Look, I'm not saying anyone's put them anywhere,' I said, finally, even though this was exactly what I was saying. 'I just . . . I need them.' And, as soon as I started talking, I became more resolute that this was absolutely what had to happen. 'By August, by the time you move out.' Dad was still glaring at me, petrified about what I might say next. 'Mum wouldn't want to be in any other house but this one; so, if she can't be here, I want her with me.'

Chapter Eight

Dear Lily

I've so many emotions flying around, I don't know what to do with myself. I'm telling myself, I'm always like this when I've been back to Kilterdale, and this time was so much more poignant – for obvious reasons – but I'm sitting here, writing this on the train, crying my eyes out. God knows what the other passengers think of me.

It was so good to see your dad! It was wonderful. I felt like how I used to feel, before I lost Mum, and we lost you and I somehow lost *myself*. I felt like I was THAT girl I used to be, who I never thought I'd find again, and this horrible emptiness, which I realized is always with me, wasn't there any more.

And yet, I was so reckless, Lily. I can't believe how reckless I was. What was I thinking of?! What if I am pregnant? My God. I would never ever forgive myself.

*

As soon as I reached civilization at Euston Station the next day, I went to Boots and got the morning-after pill. I couldn't believe what I'd done. It was like I'd been under a spell, lawless for a moment. I decided to put down what happened to anxiety at being back in Kilterdale and total excitement at seeing Joe again, and resolved to get on with normal life as best I could.

I was still anxious about the ashes, however. Despite Dad searching high and low, he hadn't been able to find them, and I could tell he'd begun to panic himself. Denise was making a good show of acting concerned but I wasn't buying it. She was acting shifty, if you ask me, staring out of the kitchen window as Dad and I ransacked the place, as if she knew something we didn't.

It made me feel a bittersweet camaraderie with Leah, who would definitely hold Denise up as prime suspect. Sweet because I treasured any chance to feel bonded with my eldest sister these days, I suppose, and bitter because it took losing our mother's ashes and suspecting our stepmother had taken them, to do it.

Growing up, Leah and I had the classic big sister/little sister relationship: we hated and loved one another with equal fury. We knew one another better than anyone else. Then Mum got diagnosed with cancer in January 1995 and died in October 1996 and it felt like I lost not just Mum, but my big sister too. Not only did Leah behave outrageously at the funeral (turning up, just as they'd closed the curtain on the coffin, with her boyfriend at the time, who'd never even met our mother, and was wearing a back-to-front baseball cap – small detail, but I've never forgotten it), but she then proceeded to get off her head at the wake, shout at Denise and then leave to go back to university two days later, leaving me and Niamh to pick up the pieces. Our relationship has never really recovered from that. Sometimes, I wonder if I'd even see her much at all if it wasn't for her kids, who I adore. I feel like sometimes she uses them as a barricade; an excuse for not being able to do anything. She seems so angry all the time and, yet, I don't know what about. But I keep making the effort because, essentially, I miss her.

I call her as I'm walking home from the Tube. I'm thinking, perhaps the whereabouts of the ashes is something we can bond over, at least.

She picks up after two rings,

'So, can you believe it, Lee, they've lost our mother's ashes?' I said. 'They're still not on the mantelpiece. I reckon Denise is behind it.'

'Oh, really?' She was driving, and on the hands-free, but still, she sounded distracted, unfussed. 'Could we chat about this later? I'm trying to get home at the mo, kids going mad in the back . . .'

I couldn't hear any kids, which was odd. Also, it wasn't like Leah not to be outraged with Denise, which is her default setting at the best of times. 'I'm seeing you soon, aren't I? We can talk about it then.' Then she said she had to go.

Nobody talks about how Leah had a massive go at Denise in front of everyone at the funeral. It made no sense at all. Denise and mum were friends from the badminton club, so she had every right to be there. Nothing was going on between her and Dad at that point, and yet Leah just laid into her, shouting, *'Jump in your own grave so fast, would you?'* God, it was like a scene from

Eastenders and Leah and Dad have never really talked since, and us three girls don't talk about Mum much either, because of what happened, which I find really sad.

I arrived home, having made Leah, before she hung up, promise on her life that we'd discuss the ashes when I next went round. Then I made myself some soup and settled down to watch re-runs of some seventies sitcom . . . I felt calmer now the hangover had subsided and I was back in my own space. I felt like what had happened in Kilterdale was a dream; that it had happened to somebody else, in another life.

Then, the next day, Joe sent me an email: distinctly flirtatious and with a photo of me that made me actually gasp. I knew I couldn't do this with Joe. I had to nip it in the bud.

4 April 2013
From: robyn.king@nhs.uk.kingsbridge
To: JosephSawyer@man.edu.co.uk
Dear Joe, thanks for your email. I particularly enjoyed the picture of me wielding the bottle of JD and Miss No Knickers – just how one should behave at a funeral.

I've been thinking of you often. I found those days following my mum's funeral really tough, so I hope you're taking it easy and being extra nice to yourself. Did you manage to watch a good horror? I recommend it. I found it to be a bit of escapism, if any escapism is possible at the moment.

Joe, I want to apologize. As wonderful as it was to see you, I shouldn't have got so carried away and *drunk*. (*It was your mother's funeral, for God's*

sake!) You've no doubt got all sorts of emotions
going on at the moment and me just unleashing
myself on you like that can't have helped. So, I'm
sorry. I hope you can forgive me. We can never
talk of this again, and be friends. It's so great to
be back in touch. Call me any time. R xxx

'Right, Kingy, do you want to come in?'

Just as I often thank the lord for London and its ability
to swallow me up and allow me to disappear, so I am
thankful for my job. After my eventful weekend, I didn't
have a chance to stew in a pit of self-loathing, because
immediately I got to work, Jeremy called me into his
office.

He wanted to talk to me about Grace Bird, a forty-
one-year-old woman about to be discharged from
hospital, who had specifically requested me as her CPN.
I felt rather special, especially since, apparently, she'd
based her decision on watching me with other patients
at Kingfisher House Psychiatric Unit, where she'd spent
the last two months. I also knew this irked Jeremy,
because Jeremy is the sort of man who can even make
providing mental-health services a competition.

He gestured to the only spare seat in his office, one
of those low chairs, the colour of Dijon mustard, with
wooden arm rests mental-health services are full of them
– and shut the door. 'So, shall we talk Grace Bird?' he
said. The office smelt of a mixture of the egg sandwich
he was eating and TCP. He gargled with it every morning,
with his door wide open. 'How are we feeling about
meeting her?'

I felt like Clarice Starling in *The Silence of the Lambs*,

being prepped before meeting Hannibal Lecter, the way he was going on. This wasn't the first time he'd had a word with me about the infamous Grace.

'Um, fine, I think,' I said. Grace had schizophrenia, and a history of hearing persecutory voices. 'I've read Grace's case notes and chatted to people. I'm looking forward to meeting her. I think we'll get on.'

Jeremy nodded and excavated a bit of egg sandwich from his back molar.

'You know, she has got a challenging background, although nothing out of the ordinary: years of sexual abuse by her stepfather sent her over the edge – nasty piece of work by all accounts, he was. She was brought up in a hotel, and the stepfather was the manager, apparently. Used to abuse her in the guest bedrooms.' He made a face, as if he was describing a disgusting meal he'd had.

'Horrible,' I said. Jeremy was harmless and also quite passionate about his job in his own (his *very own*) way. But there was sometimes a salacious tone in his voice, when he talked about patients, that didn't sit well with me, like he enjoyed the drama.

'You do know she's had three CPNs beforehand who she's not got on with?' he said (you had to love his management style – so encouraging).

'Yes. I think I did know that.'

'Although, she's particularly requested a woman this time, so, you know, you might be okay.'

He told me how he'd been Grace's CPN for years; that they went back to the year 2003, when she had her breakdown and came into the system.

'Oh, so you know her well, then?' I said.

'Yes. And I can tell you, she has a very definite cycle.'

I laughed. 'A cycle? That makes her sound like a washing machine.'

He frowned, a bit affronted.

'What I *meant* was, if you would just let me finish, is that she runs like clockwork. She has . . .' He paused, belching quietly into his hand. 'And no, I won't make any apologies for this, 'cause it's true. She has a very definite "cycle" of behaviour.'

'Okay,' I said. 'So what does this cycle consist of?'

'Well, she has an episode every May, without fail, like we've just seen now, when she's generally found wandering the streets at night, starts hearing voices, saying people have broken into her flat at night. Then June, we're not usually too bad, but come August and we're downhill again. Always mid-August. Always the same time.'

'Is she not on a CTO this time?' I asked. It would make sense after so many admissions. A Community Treatment Order meant she'd have to sign a form to say she'd come into hospital for an injection, because she couldn't be relied upon to take her medication herself.

'I don't know,' Jeremy said, a bit defensively, like I was trying to get one up on him, which I wasn't. 'But this will be something you can discuss up at the hospital.'

He bit into his sandwich and chewed, breathing noisily through his nose. 'Sorry, you don't mind if I eat this now, do you? Molls is potty training – we had several accidents this morning, including a number two, and I didn't get time for breakfast.'

'No, not at all,' I said, although 'breakfast' and 'number two' in the same sentence made me gag.

'So, has anyone got to the bottom of Grace's . . . "cycle"? Why episodes happen at certain times?' I asked.

Jeremy carried on chewing. 'Well, it's obvious, isn't it? I mean, the summer – like Christmas – can be a very alienating time for people like Grace. Everyone's having barbecues, going on holidays . . .'

This seemed tangential but I nodded anyway.

'And also she's got this thing with taking people's photos – I'm sure they'll fill you in when you get there. Needless to say, it gets her into trouble on the ward. She's got no idea of personal boundaries.'

Having finished his sandwich, he started applying some cream to a flaky red patch on his elbow.

'Sorry,' he said. He made a wincing noise as the cream touched his skin. 'Psoriasis. It's really flared recently.'

I couldn't wait to meet Grace now. I'd read her case notes and there were things that chimed with me, things people had said to me about her, that reminded me of things people said about me, when I was younger, before Mum happened and that summer happened, and I probably grew up ten years in one: 'She's a handful, that Robyn King'; 'She's not at *all* as sensible as her big sister.' It made me want to rise to the challenge of her. To show Grace what I was made of.

When a patient was about to be discharged to the homecare team, us CPNs often went along to the hospital for ward round and what was called a 'discharge planning meeting', so we could meet the patient beforehand. As discharge planning meetings went, Grace's was pretty painless. Dr Manoor was Grace's consultant, which made things easy, because we've got quite a rapport going now, Dr Manoor and I. Whenever he calls me up to come in and assess, we always have a joke: 'Who've you got for me this time, Ramesh?'; 'Are we going to need a stiff drink after this?'

As well as Dr Manoor, there was Michelle, the OT – occupational therapist – who never seems as frazzled as the rest of us. I like Michelle. It was the senior nurse I didn't take to – someone called Brian Hillgarth, who I'd never dealt with before. He had dandruff and this off-putting habit of never meeting your gaze when he was talking to you. I didn't like the way he spoke about Grace either. He kept saying things like, 'Like all chronic schizophrenics, she has fixations about things . . .' What did he mean, 'Like *all* schizophrenics?' (*Like all people called Brian, you never meet people's eyes when you're talking to them.*) I felt like he spoke about her as if she was beyond help, beyond hope.

There was also this matter of her taking photographs.

'The problem is, she was putting that camera in patients' faces,' Hillgarth was saying. (I couldn't help thinking there were worse places she could have been putting her camera.) 'Taking pictures of them brushing their teeth, or in the art room. I mean, these patients are paranoid enough.' There was a pause during which everybody looked at one another as if to say, *We know, Brian, it's a mental hospital.*

'So, can I ask, what's with the photography in the first place?' I said. I was curious. 'Is Grace generally interested in photography? Is it something she does as a hobby?'

This seemed to completely confuse Brian, who said, 'I think my point is, she's abusive with it.'

'Abusive? What, with a camera? How do you mean?' Everyone sort of looked at the floor. As CPNs went, I was probably quite outspoken.

97

'She gets a bit upset, I think,' said Michelle, 'when people don't want their photo taken, you know.' Michelle was such a softy; if Grace had been beating people over the head with a mallet, she'd have put it down to her just being 'a bit upset'.

'No, I'd definitely say, she's abusive,' Brian said. 'Personal and insulting when people don't want their picture taken. She told one rather large patient that they were supposed to "eat what's in the fridge, not the fridge itself".' I had to bite my lip so I didn't laugh. I've always liked the naughty ones.

The meeting went on for forty-five minutes. It seemed Jeremy was right about one thing at least: there was a pattern to Grace's admissions (May and August figuring strongly), but nobody had got to the bottom of why.

'So she's not on a CTO?' I asked.

'She was trialled,' said Dr Manoor. 'But there were side effects with the injections: tremors, weight gain . . .' Often the side effects were worse than the mental illness itself but, without the CTO ensuring Grace would agree to come into hospital to have her injections, I'd have to work hard to keep her compliant.

Eventually, they called Grace in. She was *tiny* and ever so sweet-looking, with this delicate, fawn-like face and these big brown eyes shining out from beneath the Yankees baseball cap she was wearing. The skin on her face had been ravaged by fags and booze and emotional pain, but there was still a girlishness to her; then, she spoke.

'Wotcha?' she stuck a tiny hand out and I shook it. 'I'm Grace, and you are . . .?'

'Robyn.'

'Robyn,' she said, screwing her tiny nose up. 'Isn't that a boy's name?'

'And a girl's,' I said. 'Although, my theory is, my parents wanted a boy and so didn't really have any proper girls' names on their list.'

She laughed, but like it was an afterthought, then carried on staring at me, quite intently.

'You're pretty, ain't ya?' she said, eventually. 'She is, she's pretty, i'n't she?' she said to the rest of the room. I could feel myself glowing beetroot. 'It's the eyes – you've got lovely brown eyes. And great bone structure. Have you got Slavic in your blood?'

'I've got Cumbrian, does that count?' I said, and everyone including Grace laughed – although Grace a little later than everyone else. She swung a leg over the chair and almost bounced into the seat. She was wearing a grey poncho with reindeers on it, rust-coloured trousers, white trainers and the cap.

'I'm glad I demanded a girl,' she said. 'They normally give me smelly old men to look after me. One before last, looked like a massive strawberry,' and I smirked, because I knew exactly who she meant (Jezza – Jeremy), and he did, he looked *exactly* like a massive strawberry. 'He had this big fat red face with pits all over it, and this hair, sitting like a toupee on top . . .'

'*Grace* . . .' Michelle was laughing too but had her hand over her eyes, shaking her head. 'We've talked about being personal, haven't we? Sometimes you've got to *think before you speak*.'

'Oh, I know, I know,' Grace said, 'That's my problem, innit?' I never think before I open my big mouth.'

We had to get some of the big questions out of the

way: likelihood of her topping herself after discharge from hospital, for example (low, she assured us, the council were coming to do up her flat if she could stay out of hospital – and alive – long enough), and whether she promised to stick to taking her medication.: 'Well if it's that or a needle in my bum, then I'd better be a good girl, hadn't I?'

'And would you like to see one of the crisis team, Grace?' Dr Manoor asked. 'For a while, after you're discharged?'

'No,' she said, smiling at me. 'I just want to see Robyn.'

I felt this little bubble of pride.

Then, the most bizarre thing happened. Brian reached behind him, brought out something and held it out to Grace. 'My camera!' she gasped, turning it around in her hand, as though it was her engagement ring that had been found. 'I thought it was gone forever!'

'We had to pretend it was lost,' Brian said to me, like it was a dummy and she was two years old. 'She was just driving everyone mad.'

'Got time for a chat, Grace?' I said, as we were all getting up to leave. 'Just the two of us?'

She looked at me, a little suspiciously, before breaking into a gap-toothed smile. 'All right,' she shrugged. I followed her out of the door.

We went to Grace's room to collect her cigarettes.

'We'll have to freeze our bums off outside,' she said, rummaging around in her coat pocket. 'No more smoke rooms. As if they could make these places any more bloody depressing.'

We had to walk around a zigzag of corridors, before

we got to the lift that took us to the main entrance outside. The walls were filled with pictures of dodgy, replicated beach landscapes, in an attempt to brighten the place up. Grace gave me the lowdown as we were walking.

'Room Five. That's Harry. Hasn't said a word in two months. Spends all day watching DVDs about polar bears . . . All right, Harry?' She popped her head around the door. I could just see a large, white-haired man, sitting in a chair, staring straight ahead. 'Those polar bears behavin' themselves?'

I waved at Harry but he didn't wave back.

'Room Seven, Winnie – conked up to the eyeballs, bless her. Tried to hang herself on a curtain last week.'

'I know,' I said, 'I heard in the office.'

'And that's Rebecca's room,' she said as we passed room 10. 'Now *she's* a sandwich short of a picnic. *She thinks she's a millionairess*,' she whispered as we turned down another corridor.

'Maybe she is,' I said. 'You want to get in with her.'

'You're joking, aren't ya? She lives up at the Elephant in a council one-bed, like me. Day she came in, she'd blown three grand in Harvey Nicks; hired a security team and everything, just in case she was kidnapped, she was so convinced she was loaded.'

'So what happened?' I said. 'In the end?' This story hadn't yet made it back to the office, but I knew it would.

'Driver clocked, didn't he? Whilst she was having a champers lunch at The Ritz, no less. Story goes, he managed to get hold of her phone, called up her sister, who confirmed she was mad as a box of snakes, and she came to collect her. That was three weeks ago,' she said, holding the door open so we could go outside.

And that's the thing about this job, I thought. Just when you think nothing can surprise you, something does. Manic shopping sprees we'd had, but hiring security? This was a league above.

The smoking area's not such a good place for a 'private' chat in a mental hospital, since for 99 per cent of the patients it's their favourite place on the premises, possibly the world.

We sat together under the plastic shelter. The red-brick chimneys of south London were arranged, against a slate-grey sky, in perfect sloping lines, up in front of us.

I watched as Grace lit a cigarette.

'That's a long one,' I said.

'Vogues,' she said. 'More fag for your money. I may be in the loony bin, Robyn, but you've got to retain some of your glamour.' She inhaled and gave a throaty laugh. I smiled. Grace amused me.

We sat in silence for a while as she smoked. The city looked quite beautiful from up here. I wondered what thoughts had gone through the muddled heads of people sitting in this shelter: what fears, what hopes? How had the world looked to Grace during her months in hospital over the years?

She stuck out the packet of Vogues in my direction.

'No thanks, Grace. D'you know, it's one vice that's never, ever done it for me,' I said.

'You've more sense than me,' she sighed, lighting another one. 'Worst decision I ever made – and I've made a few. I bloody well need it here, though.' I noticed how her fingers were shaking now, with the meds, or anxiety, or the cold – probably a combination of all three. 'These people don't help.'

On the lawns opposite, two old women were shuffling along, hunched over. A guy who looked like he hadn't put his teeth in was staring at us from across the way.

'You must be looking forward to getting out,' I said, and she laughed. 'Wouldn't you, after being in the nuthouse all summer?'

'What you looking forward to most?' I said, and this smile spread, slow and wide, across her face.

'Talking to my daughter,' she said.

'You've a daughter?' I said, even though I knew she did from reading her notes, but I wanted her to tell me the story herself.

She reached inside her pocket and drew out a plastic cardholder with Hello Kitty on the front, opened it up and pulled a photo out.

'Isn't she beautiful?' she said, showing me a picture of a dark, petite teenager.

'She is,' I said. 'She looks like you.'

'D'you think so?'

'Definitely, same little face, big eyes. What's her name?'

'Cec – Cecily,' she said. 'I named her after my dad – Cecil. He died falling down an escalator.' I watched as she sucked on her cigarette. Was that story even true?

'Has she been to visit you here?' I said.

'Nah, she's really busy with her boyfriend, you know – typical fourteen-year-old. And who'd want to come and visit someone here?'

She paused for a moment and slipped the photo back in its card.

'Also, she's very talented, she wants to be an illustrator.'

'Wow, you must be very proud of her.'

103

'Oh, yeah, very. Shame, really, she can't say the same about me. Have you got kids?' she said, eventually, turning to face me.

'No,' I said. It had started to spot with rain. 'No, I haven't. Not yet.'

Joe didn't reply to my email, apologizing for my wanton behaviour at the funeral, for two days. I was beginning to think he never would, and also that that would be a shame; it was lovely to be back in touch with him. Perhaps we could be friends now? Perhaps, after sixteen years, we were ready for that?

Then he did reply. Only it wasn't the reply I was expecting.

6 April 2013
From: JosephSawyer@man.edu.co.uk
To: robyn.king@nhs.uk.kingsbridge
Do you want to know what the best escapism is? you+kissing+barn+JackDaniel's+nakedflesh. That really helped.
The Evil Dead – though good – doesn't cut it, I've found.

Clearly my strategy to nip any flirting in the bud had washed right over him, but what was surprising was how I reacted.

Oh. I *see*. Well, I'm glad. Even if that escapism took the form of helping you drink a bottle of Jack Daniel's, then taking all my clothes off in a barn, like some wanton milkmaid.

104

I thought I'd be scared off but I found myself flirting back!

It didn't take long for Joe to respond in similar fashion.

From: JosephSawyer@man.edu.co.uk
To: robyn.king@nhs.uk.kingsbridge
I know. I was being naughty (although the image of you as a wanton milkmaid is a *great* one) . . .

From: robyn.king@nhs.uk.kingsbridge
To: JosephSawyer@man.edu.co.uk
Why have you sent me a picture of a shark?

From: JosephSawyer@man.edu.co.uk
To: robyn.king@nhs.uk.kingsbridge
Oh. That's a nurse shark. I meant to attach a pic of a nurse. I'm on Ethan's desktop. He's still obsessed with animals, in particular sharks. I'm obsessed with nurses . . .

And there followed three wonderful weeks of emails between us – deep and meaningful emails, shamelessly flirtatious emails, silly emails – and it was wonderful. All the clichés were there. I was *that* girl in the heady first weeks of a new relationship (albeit a long-distance, electronic one that I constantly told myself I wasn't getting into at all. This wasn't a relationship, Joe was just my friend); giggling at my desk at his messages, staring into space in meetings. 'She's got her Joe face on,' Leon would say. 'I know, you can practically see the dirty workings of her mind,' Kaye would tease, narrowing her eyes. She was one to talk: Kaye has the dirtiest mind in the world – a penchant for the puerile. She knew that Joe was my first love. She just didn't know the rest of it.

A month after his mum's funeral, on 3 May, Joe emailed me to say he was coming to London to stay with his school friend, Bomber:

I'm staying at Bomber's on the weekend of 24 May – we could meet? In actual real life?

My heart was in my mouth but I wrote back immediately:

Great. Be lovely to see you and I promise to behave this time. Luckily, there aren't many barns in this part of the world . . .

*

To my Robyn, my Bobby, my middle one.
What is it they say about the middle child? That 'difficult' middle child? Well, for starters, you know, I've always hated labels. Also, we've had our moments, darling, I know we have, but you've never been anything but my amazing middle child to me. My firecracker. My super-duper girl.
  I remember the day you were born (how could I forget?!). Slipping out like a lamb in the back of Dad's Land Rover. How many times have I told you that story? You loved me to tell you it, again and again. You always loved my stories and now they are yours to keep.
  You made your entrance in a memorable way; and you've been that way ever since. People

106

remember you, Robyn. Remember that. You will always be one of life's special ones.

I can't believe this is goodbye, my love. I'm so sorry I didn't get to know you longer. But I have always said to you girls (admittedly, more lately), 'It's not the days of your life that matter, but the amount of life you pack into those days.'

And we've packed it in, haven't we? We've some good stories to tell, you and I. Stories that will last forever.

Do you remember when I brought Niamh home from hospital? How you were so smitten, you didn't want to go to school for days? Later, she would sit in her high chair and do that hilarious cackle as you did impressions of all the family – little dances and made-up songs (usually rude, but still!). I am so proud of what a brilliant big sister you have been, and I know you will continue to be. Niamh loves you to bits, you know, even if she is bonkers most of the time. Although, I think you have probably taught her all she knows.

Also, Leah loves you – I know it may not feel like it sometimes, but she does. I know this for a fact. In fact, I shall let you into a secret: You know when you didn't get into the Lancashire Swimming Squad? She burst into tears over her tea. You were over at Beth's and she was inconsolable. So, you see, you may not know this yet (although knowing you, you probably do), but you don't actually have a choice in how you love your siblings. You feel what they feel. That's just the way it is.

Be patient with Leah for me. She finds life harder

than you. Please try not to take her personally, because I guarantee you, behind all that angry stuff at the moment is just a scared, sensitive girl who loves you. Who needs you. And you could teach her a thing or two about how to live with her cup half full instead of half empty. About how to enjoy life, Robyn. You've always been so great at that.

You are going to make someone the best mother one day, darling. You were born to be a mum. You are also going to make someone a wonderful partner or wife; and you do not need me to tell you this, but only ever marry for LOVE. Love is all that matters at the end of the day. Your dad and I have despaired of one another at times, but it's always come back to love. So never settle for second best. Certainly never go for a Man City supporter or a southerner (I'd never forgive you! I'm joking of course). Basically, find someone who loves you at your best and your worst and never let them go.

Life is going to be good to you, Robyn, darling. Fortune favours the brave. Of the three of you, I am least worried about you because I know you are going to be fine. I know you are strong. Of course, I'd be lying if I said that this will not affect you in some way for the rest of your life, but it won't hurt forever like it does now, and it doesn't mean you can't be as happy. In fact, if I were to say one thing to you, do not use this as an excuse to be unhappy. I'd be so disappointed.

Look after your dad – he loves you so much too, remember, even if he's terrible at showing it sometimes. Don't let him swear too much in front of Niamh (it's too late for you and Leah, I'm afraid). He may go to pieces but, one day, he will be happy again, and whatever it takes (I think you will know what I mean here), I want him to be happy.

Also know this: Even though I have to go now, if I could have a life again, a much longer one but without knowing you, I'd still choose this one in the blink of an eye.

Be happy for me, darling. Be strong.

I love you, always.

Mum x

*

5 May 2013
From: robyn.king@nhs.uk.kingsbridge
To: JosephSawyer@man.edu.co.uk

I'm really sorry, Joe, I can't meet you on the 24th now. Something's come up.

R x

PART TWO

Chapter Nine

Mid-May

Can I take your name?

The girl on the other end of the phone was called Faith and sounded young, younger than me.

'*Robyn King.*'

'And your date of birth?'

'*11th January 1981.*'

'And you're calling to enquire about terminating your pregnancy?'

Two women walked past my kitchen window pushing prams. I swear, it was like a film. I half imagined a director to shout, 'Cut! The prams are too obvious.'

'*Yes, that's right.*'

'Can you remember, approximately, the first day of your last period?'

I could do better than that. I'd spent the last two weeks since I found out, counting on my fingers – on cars going by as I sat on the bus, people's feet on the Tube, the little staples that run around the office carpet.

'*Ninth of March? I'm seventeen days late.*'

'So you're about eight to nine weeks into your pregnancy.' She said it so breezily. 'Have you been to your GP?'

'No, *but I've done three pregnancy tests and they were all positive.*'

I could hear Faith typing, putting all my details into her computer. 'Three. Positive. Tests. Okay, Robyn . . . well, I think we can safely say you're pregnant . . .'

I felt like I might throw up.

'*Well, no, not really,*' I said. '*I don't think we can safely say anything, can we? You don't understand, I can't have a baby. I took the morning-after pill because I was taking absolutely no chances.*'

She didn't say anything. I knew what she was thinking: 'But you already took a chance, didn't you, love?'

I can't say I blamed her, I was thinking the same thing.

She was much less breezy now. She lowered her voice as if this were a secret we were sharing.

'The morning-after pill is only around ninety-per-cent effective, Robyn, okay?' *No. It's not okay. None of this is okay!* 'So, it's rare, but sometimes it doesn't work. The other thing is that it becomes less effective the longer you leave to take it.'

I thought, I didn't know this. I'm thirty-two and I *didn't know this*.

I started crying now.

'How long after having unprotected sex did you take the morning-after pill?'

'*Not the day after, but the one after that. It was hard*

114

for me to get hold of it immediately, you see, because I was up in Cumbria, in a village . . .'

I remembered how I'd sat there at Dad and Denise's dining table, stuffing lasagne down my gullet, the night after the funeral, when I could have got on a bus, I could have gone into town, to A&E, an emergency pharmacy . . .

Her silence told me there really wasn't any point going on.

'Do you feel you've considered all your other options? Adoption, fostering, continuing with this pregnancy . . .?'

This pregnancy. It was really happening then. I had this strange, out-of-body experience then, like I was looking at myself from the outside in; like I was one of the women outside, watching me, as I stood crying in my kitchen, planning to get rid of my baby.

'*Yes, although I wouldn't exactly say they were options.'*

A tear fell then, right onto my top.

'We offer counselling before and after. Do you think you might benefit from that?'

I thought about this.

'*I don't want it before, thanks,'* I said. '*As for after, I don't really know how I'm going to feel then, do I?'*

I don't know why I was taking it out on her. It wasn't her fault.

Silence on the other end as I cried. She must get this all the time, I thought, Faith. Grown women snivelling down the phone at her, like they'd never heard of the facts of life.

She was quiet for a while as I sobbed.

115

'Have you talked through your feelings with somebody, Robyn, or do you have someone you could talk to now? A partner, a best friend, your mum . . .?'

I just wanted to get off the phone now.

'Yes. I've got people I could talk to.'

I was on the phone for another ten minutes, while she went through the 'options' I had available to me. There was the 'surgical abortion'; I could choose to be put to sleep, or be aware but sedated for that one. Then there was the 'medical abortion' option, but I'd have to make my mind up very quickly for that as it was only 'available' up to eight weeks and six days; like the turkey option at the office Christmas do. I'd take two pills, several hours apart. This would bring on a miscarriage: heavy bleeding and cramps and possibly sickness and diarrhoea too, whilst the pills were doing their thing. Apparently, it might not even work, but at least it was 'non-invasive', she said.

I stood in my kitchen after I put the phone down, unable to get the image out of my mind of an eight-week-old foetus being sucked out of me. Most of all I was so angry. *So angry* I had let this happen – How could I have taken a risk like that? When I finally moved, I realized I had bitten my fingernail down so much that the raw skin was exposed underneath and little spots of blood were starting to show. I went to find a plaster in the bathroom. Then, I got in the shower. I didn't know what else to do.

It was just after six. Usually, at this time on a Friday, I'd be going for Friday beers with Kaye and everyone from work. I imagined Kaye with her Guinness moustache, standing outside the Hermit's Cave in the evening sunshine, and I *longed* to be there with her, having a laugh, Kaye doing her impressions of Levi Holden's mum. 'He lazy, dat boy.' (Genevieve would say this whilst he was sitting, catatonic with depression.) 'He bin lazy since the good Lord sent him to me.'

I washed my hair, trying not to look at my sore, veiny boobs that didn't look like my breasts any more. They looked like they'd been pumped up and hardened. They looked like steroid boobs.

I got out of the shower and wrapped a towel around myself. Then, I sat on my bed and called Kaye.

She was already in the pub.

'Hey, Kingy! It's Kingy, everyone!'

There was a lot of cheering and whooping – they were well oiled already.

'How you doing, darlin'? Still chucking up and shitting through the eye of a needle?' (I'd spun them some yarn about having the Norovirus.) 'Poor you. Stomach bugs are the pits . . .'

'She means the shits,' someone shouted – Leon or Rik. I couldn't have cared less if they knew I had the shits.

'Tell her to get her runny arse down here now, these people are boring me to death,' someone else shouted, voice like a foghorn: Parvinder.

'Parv says come down, we're boring her to death,' said Kaye.

'I know.' I laughed. 'I heard her.'

'Oooh, I hate to think of the Kingster led-up-poo-erly.' You can always tell when Kaye's had a few because she starts taking the mick out of my northern accent, even though she can't do it for toffee. Kaye's born-and-bred East End.

'Are you seriously not feeling any better?'

117

'Yeah, course, loads better. I'll definitely be back on Monday. Look, Kaye . . .' I needed to tell her. I just needed to tell someone. To get it out.

But the line went all muffled, like when someone calls you by accident and you can just hear the inside of their pocket. There was laughing and squealing and obviously people trying to grab the phone because Kaye was going, 'In a minute, in a *minute*!'

Then Parv came on. She was talking really loudly and I had to hold the phone away from my ear because it hurt.

'Now, listen here, darling Robyn.' The line crackled, probably as she swayed about. Bloody hell, they were all *legless*. It was the first properly warm day of the year and they'd all been in the drinking mood. 'It's Parvinder here. You need to get dressed and get yourself down here – I'll pay for the cab – and stop pretending you're ill, 'coz we all know you've taken a skivey Friday and have probably got Joe there, bonking as we speak.'

Joe. Just the mention of his name made my stomach lurch.

'And I am struggling here,' she went on. 'These people are dangerous to anyone's mental health. I've got Leon banging on about his root-canal surgery, Kaye who can only be funny when she's got you around . . .' (I heard Kaye snort with laughter in the background) '. . . and Leon who's about to abandon us, to go and have hot gay sex with someone called Yves – as in Yves Saint Laurent . . .' They all laughed. 'I *need* you!'

A strange noise was coming out of me. I looked at myself in the mirror on the wardrobe door. I'd gone grey and goose-pimpled with cold. My mouth was pulled into a grin. The sound was laughter, but it didn't sound like my laughter. I looked like a mannequin.

I said, 'Honestly, I leave you alone for five minutes and you're a mess, you lot. A mess, I tell you!' I was jabbing a finger at the laughing person in the mirror. I looked so unfamiliar, I was freaking myself out.

Silence on the other end. Parv had obviously wandered off.

'Sorry, I can't come down,' I said to nobody.

Then another voice: male. Leon.

'Kingy, Robyn, are you still there?'

'Yes, I'm still here.'

'Another reason you have to be here on Monday is because Levi is having none of it. When I went down there today and it wasn't you, he wouldn't answer the door. He just kept shouting, "F-off," through the letterbox, "I want Robyn, my Robyn." Then when I asked him how he was, he opened the letterbox, chucked a bit of cat litter through it, and said, "How do you think I fucking feel? Like this. Like cat shit!"'

I felt a wave of affection for Levi, which was good; it made me feel better. I couldn't fall apart, because Levi, the people I looked after, they needed me. 'Oh, God,' I said. 'Levi really does tell it like it is, doesn't he?'

Then the phone went dead.

My hair was dripping down my shoulders. I sat on the edge of the bed, holding the phone in my hand, until I was so cold, I was shaking. Then I picked up the photo on the side of my bed. I often like to look at it when I'm feeling down or anxious. It's of all five of us on Blackpool Beach – I'm about ten, Leah's thirteen and Niamh is a chubby one-year-old. You can only see Mum's and Dad's

119

heads because we buried them in the sand. They're both killing themselves laughing. That evening, we'd all gone to see the Blackpool Illuminations and Leah and I sang Take That songs really loudly, out of the car windows. For once, she didn't seem to mind hanging out with me. In fact, she seemed to enjoy it. It was one of the best days we spent together as a family, perhaps of my entire childhood.

I turned the picture over in my hand, then I put some clothes on and left. If I hurried, Kaye would still be at the Hermit's Cave in Camberwell. I would go and find her. I would tell her everything. If I didn't tell someone, I might combust. There were workmen relaying tarmac on my road when I got outside – the most banal, everyday thing . . . And, yet, perhaps it was the smell of fresh tarmac, or the vibrations that the digger sent reverberating around my body, but immediately a memory struck me: October 1997, nearly six months after Joe and I started going out, practically a year to the day since Mum died, and I have locked myself in our big but shabby bathroom, with its avocado suite, to do a pregnancy test. Leah is banging on the door, shouting (I kid you not), 'Bloody hell, Robyn, what are you doing in there, having a baby?' And outside, they are digging our road up, and there is the same thick smell of tarmac wafting through the bathroom window and the same vibrations beneath my feet. At least, I think it's the digger doing that now.

It was still rush hour when I got to Archway Tube. The escalator was spewing out suits who were straight on their iPhones, as if something major might have happened whilst they were underground. I went to the bit where you top up your Oyster card. 'I'm going to

Zumba,' I heard one girl say on the phone. She was wearing a pinstriped skirt suit and court shoes. 'But there's that Sainsbury's fish pie in the freezer.'

I'd never really yearned after a pinstriped-skirt-suit and fish-pie-in-the-freezer type of existence, but now it was all I wanted. In fact, I yearned for it, ached for it, like you yearn for something you once had, but had lost.

It was busy on the Tube and I started to feel my heart go. Since I found out I was pregnant two weeks ago, literally the day after Joe had told me he was coming to London, I've had a couple of funny turns: one catastrophic one on the Tube that resulted in St John Ambulance being called out (how stupid did I feel?) and one at work. At first, I was petrified. It honestly felt like I was going to die. Now, at least I had some warning that one was coming on, because my heart beat faster, my limbs grew hot; but also there was this sensation, like when you're underwater or walking alone in the dark and you become aware that you can't hear anything but your own breath; like you're all alone in the world. Like if anything went wrong, nobody would be able to help you.

I didn't want to become one of those people who can't even get on the Tube, though, so now I was concentrating hard and I was talking to myself, soothing myself: *It's okay, it's okay* . . . and I was counting to seven, seven times on my fingers and people's feet, which I know sounds mad, but for some reason it helps – most of the time. This time it didn't, and all I could think of was that last time I was on the Tube, and the man in the boiler suit who smelt of turps. By some miracle, I managed to make it off the Tube before I was rendered immobile by sheer terror, and was now standing outside Camden Station, shivering. I thought about going to find Kaye, getting back on the Tube, and I knew I couldn't do it. I decided I'd go and sit in the pub across the road.

'Could I have a ginger beer please?' My voice seemed extra loud in the pub. I knew my mouth was moving but it felt like the words coming out of it were somebody else's. There was a copy of *Reveal* magazine on one of the tables. I intended to sit there, reading nothing more taxing than an article about Kerry Katona's bikini diet, until my heart had slowed down, but I'd been reading perhaps fifteen minutes when someone said, 'Hello, Robyn.'

I looked up at the person like you look at anyone you can't place because they're in the wrong context: personal trainer in the pub, your local vicar in the crisis unit, for example. Then, it twigged.

'Oh, hello, Tim.' Tim lived in the flat below me. 'How are you?' I said, remembering too late that Tim is the sort of person who thinks that 'How are you?' is a real question.

'No Fujiko?' I said, when we'd gone through the leak in his bathroom and his nephew's birthday party. Fujiko is Tim's Japanese wife. They're attached at the hip.

'She's gone to the specialist Asian hairdresser just round the corner. Apparently, they're the only ones who can do her hair properly. Don't ask . . .' He chuckled. I smiled politely. 'But I'm off back home now, coming back to pick up Fuji in an hour. Would you like a lift?'

It looked a bit grey out now; a lift would be good. Otherwise, I'd have to walk home or get on the Tube again, and I certainly didn't fancy that.

'Yes, if you're sure. Yes, that would be great.'

'I'll sit in the back,' I said.

'Are you sure? You can sit in the front. You may have to put up with my conversation but, I promise, I don't bite.' I smiled. I knew he was harmless. 'No, really, I get sick in the front,' I said. 'I know it's usually the other way round, but there we go, I'm a bit strange.'

Tim chuckled again. 'No bother, you pop yourself in the back.'

Elton John was playing.

'Fuji and I love Elton,' Tim said. 'Have I told you the story about our first dance at our wedding?'

He hadn't, so, as we drove along, Tim told me the story about their first dance to Elton's 'Rocket Man' and how they'd choreographed a whole routine themselves. The sun was at that level in the sky where, no matter how far you pull the visor down, it's in your eyes. Its white-heat spokes were casting starbursts off buildings and Tim was having to lean right back, his arms straightened, so he could see. I couldn't take my eyes off his arms: they were stocky and covered in freckles and dense, curly, amber hairs. When I looked at his face, I noticed his stubble glowed orange in the sun.

Elton John was whacking out 'Rocket Man' and Tim banged a chunky, freckled hand on the steering wheel in time with the music, singing along. He banged the steering wheel again and I flinched. 'Sorry, did I make you jump?'

'No, no, I'm okay.' I said, but my heart was going again like someone hammering on a door. The sun was showing up every particle of dust and dandruff on the dashboard. I still couldn't take my eyes off Tim's arms, swapping over each other as he turned the wheel, those amber hairs glistening in the light. I closed my eyes and

123

tried to think about Joe; about his kind, sloping eyes, the colour of moss, his tender touch when he held me in the barn; but all I could see, playing on the mottled red of my eyelids, was that chicken with its beady eye, standing in the glow of the barn. The fan-shaped shadow it cast on the floor.

Tim said something, laughing, and I looked up to acknowledge him, but then my neck ran icy cold because it wasn't Tim's face I saw staring out at me from the rear-view mirror, it was Saul Butler's.

My heart thumped horribly. 'You can just drop me here.' I said.

'No, you're all right, we're only five minutes away.' There was the tick-tick of his indicator as we turned right.

'It's okay, I can walk,' I said again, more desperate this time.

'All right, if you're sure.' Tim did a double take in the mirror. 'But it's really no . . .'

That face was still there: pale piggy eyes in a huge moon face; amber stubble twinkling in the evening light. I squeezed my eyes shut.

'*Tim* . . .' I pulled quickly at the handle.

'Hey!' he said, pulling into the kerb sharply, alarmed. 'Okay, okay . . . I'll let you out.'

He clicked the central locking off. He said something, but I wasn't listening. I managed, 'Thank you,' before I slammed the door shut and walked quickly away, or tried to because, as I did so, my legs almost gave way, like they'd gone dead; like they weren't my legs at all.

Chapter Ten

Joe hadn't responded to my email cancelling our meeting on the 24th like I'd hoped. He hadn't seemed to notice I was cancelling at all, in fact, and had emailed back the next day, saying simply . . .

> Something came up? This is all very enigmatic. Don't worry, I'm going to be at Bomber's for a few days, so maybe we could meet on the Sunday instead? The 26th?

I didn't reply to that email for three days and when I did, it was about inconsequential things. I didn't mention meeting up. For the two weeks that followed, there were a couple more emails from him but I didn't reply. I felt terrible about it. He'd lost his mum just weeks ago. He was still so raw. In between the flirty banter and the jokes about nurses in those first emails, before I'd found out I was pregnant, there'd been calls where he'd just cried down the phone; one particular one where he'd been in Curry's in Lancaster, of all places. Michael Ball's *Showtime Greats* had come on (Michael Ball being his mum's favourite) and he'd had to flee the store in floods. 'The worst thing was, Robbie,' he said (he rang me whilst still standing in the car park, having inadvertently shoplifted a Dusterbuster), 'people must have thought I was moved to tears by Michael Ball singing Barnham.'

He still made me smile, even with these phone calls. I was only too happy to take them, because it only seemed like yesterday when I was calling him, distraught, from some car park or shop or pub where I'd been suddenly struck down with grief.

Finding out I was pregnant, however, had changed everything because, suddenly, I was reminded of everything. It felt like my life was on repeat and so I'd cut him off and I felt terrible about it but I just didn't know what else to do. I couldn't believe this was happening. Some things are not supposed to happen once, let alone twice. Perhaps, if I ignored it, it would all go away.

Fat chance with the number of pregnant women everywhere. London seemed suddenly teeming with them. Every other woman on the high street, the bus, in Tesco Metro, was Mr Greedy-shaped: fat and happy. I, more than anyone, knew that how people's lives appeared on the outside was rarely what was really going on inside but, even so, I couldn't help but feel cheated, that what was supposed to be a joyful event – finding out you're pregnant – was for me the worst thing imaginable. Perhaps even worse because it wasn't that I didn't want a baby – I wanted nothing more than to be someone's mum one day, but because I couldn't have a baby like this. I couldn't have a baby with Joe. Of all the people in the world, it couldn't be Joe.

It had been precisely seventeen days since I'd found out I was pregnant and, in that time, the panic attacks had got steadily worse, to the point where they were happening almost daily. I've never been in any doubt that's what they are, of course, these funny turns I've been having. I've seen enough people in my line of work hyperventilate and shake like a pile of crockery in an earthquake to work that out. What I didn't know was that you don't need to be in a panic-inducing situation to have one. I've had them at home, in the supermarket. I had one watching telly the other evening, so, like I say, not exactly threatening (although some people may say that watching Gordon Ramsay's *Kitchen Nightmares* counts as very threatening). The other thing I didn't know was that, like the pain of childbirth, until you've experienced a panic attack yourself, you'll never be able to convey how real the belief is that you are certainly going to die.

On the upside, I felt I now had more insight into my clients' conditions. One of the symptoms of schizophrenia, for example, being the 'rigid upholding of false beliefs', because when I had the first few ones, the belief I was going to die felt as real as the change from day to night. Now I knew what they were, I was less scared, but the frequency of them was becoming alarming. My biggest worry was that they were starting to happen when I was with clients. I was able to hide them now, but how long could I keep that up?

It was 21 May, only the start of summer, and yet we'd already had one heat wave in London and were now on the cusp of another. No doubt June and July would be a washout. Everything felt bleached in this bright, white light: workers lunched on homemade salad boxes in any patch of green they could find, straps down, trousers rolled up, going back to the office smelling of Ambre Solaire. I had a chocker morning that day: an eventful trip to Peckham to buy one of my patients, Yolanda, some shoes (Yolanda thinks she's Beyoncé at the moment, so getting her to consider anything but Perspex hooker platforms was a challenge). Then I visited Levi. We went for a walk in Ruskin Park. It was so peaceful up there and we sat on a bench and talked for ages.

The sky was blue but smudged with clouds, which, for some reason, brought to mind my childhood bedroom – the one I'd shared with Leah, when we were little, before Leah left home for uni and Mum was diagnosed. There'd been a fashion around about that time for 'sponge effect' walls, and we'd had our room done like that – pale blue walls with pale pink splodges. Mum had spent two days doing it, black leggings and a chambray shirt on; Paul Weller turned up. 'It's like the sunset over the Bay, girls!' she'd said when she'd finished her handiwork. (Possibly, if you really, really squinted!) 'Or a dawn sky, with those pink clouds.'

Leah and I had fought like cat and dog in the daytime – two totally different personalities, two different sets of friends. And, yet, there'd been this sisterly bond that came

128

out in the privacy of our own room, almost as if, away from the public gaze, we'd allowed ourselves to love one another.

Mum never knew it, but sometimes we'd set our alarms so we could watch that dawn sky, the real one, not the one on the walls; watch the sun rise, huge and red, over Kilterdale Bay from the Velux window in our bedroom. It would be then – the back garden in a shroud of sea mist, us still in our nighties – that we'd have our best times, Leah and I; our special times, when we'd talk about how we imagined our lives to turn out: I wanted to be a midwife like Mum. I loved babies and was still dining out on the story of my birth, in the back of a Land Rover. Leah wanted to be an 'entrepreneur' – 'like Melanie Griffith in *Working Girl*', she'd once told me, in all seriousness. (Leah said a lot of things that made us laugh that weren't meant to.) 'And I'm never having kids,' she'd said. 'Gross! They ruin your figure and your career.'

I was the maternal one in the family, everyone said, the one who would provide our parents with oodles of grandchildren.

The memory retreated and I was back with Levi, sitting on the bench in Ruskin Park. He had his long, fit legs stretched out in front of him, his hands clasped on his lap, looking up at the sky.

'So, how you doing?' I said. I'd thought it was best to get to the nitty-gritty whilst he looked so relaxed. 'What's going on in that head that I should know about, Levi? Are you having suicidal thoughts at the moment?' Mine must be one of the few jobs where that is a perfectly normal, necessary question.

129

He swallowed. I watched the muscles in his throat move.

'I think about dyin', man,' he said. 'I think about it all the time.'

The sun was casting a beam across his flawless mocha skin. He looked so alive for someone who thought about death so much.

'And have you got plans?' I said, and he laughed; this long, deep, oddly joyful laugh.

'I always got plans, innit?' he said, turning to look at me. 'I always got plans, Miss Robyn, you know dat.'

I looked at the sky, too. 'Yeah, I know,' I said.

Neither of us said anything for a while, then, as if he'd read my mind, Levi said, 'I ain't gonna do it, though. I know deep down, if I hold on, it will get better and I've decided, anyway, I c'dn't do it to my mum.'

'Yep, she'd be devastated, Levi,' I said, trying to hide the excitement in my voice. This was progress; he'd never spoken like this before. 'And we're going to help you. I'm going to try my best to help you. You won't feel so bad forever.'

He smiled. 'Yeah, also, I'm her boy, innit?' he said. 'Her son. The only person she got.'

I walked back to the office, thinking that the way Levi felt about doing himself in was, in many ways, the way I felt about having a termination: 'Suicidal ideation', that's the psychiatric term for it. He'd never do it, but he thought about it a lot, fantasized about the escape route . . '*I don't wanna die, I just want out*,' he'd say to me. And, right now, I could relate to that.

I went in to see Jezza on my return to the office,

which proved to be a mistake. The egg-sandwich/TCP fusion proved too much for my delicate, hormonal stomach (the sickness had started with a vengeance, almost immediately), and I'd only just made it to the Ladies' in time and was leaning on the basins outside, sipping somewhat pathetically on a bottle of water, when Kaye burst through the door, so desperate for the loo that she was already undoing her flies.

There was a torrent, as she told me from the toilet cubicle how Patrick the locum wasn't pulling his weight. 'I swear to God, he's so lazy, he'd have a catheter fitted to spare him the trouble of going to loo, if he could,' she said. It was only as she was washing her hands that she clocked my face in the mirror.

'My God, you look like shit. Are you all right?'

I just came straight out with it: 'Oh, God, Kaye, I'm pregnant.' What was the point of doing anything else? It felt like a valve had been unscrewed in my chest. I immediately felt so much better just for telling someone. 'It's Joe's,' I added. Just in case there was any confusion on that front.

She didn't move or say anything for what felt like forever. Then, she slapped both hands to her cheeks and made a squealing sound of delight that was just so girly and un-Kaye, it was even more touching. And it struck me: Oh, my God. This is how I'm supposed to react. This is how it's meant to feel. It must have been written all over my face because, immediately, hers dropped. 'Oh,' she said. 'Oh, you're not pleased, are you?'

She tried for a while, bless her. 'Look, I know it's a shock, a huge, *huge* head-fuck, Robyn, but you're gonna be a mum!' And it was the next bit that really made me cry because it reminded me exactly of my own mother's words to me, the words she'd written to me in the letter a week before she died, a letter I'd read over and over again since I'd found out I was pregnant. It comforted me to read her words: 'You were born to be a mum. You're already one to all of us here. You're gonna be just the best mummy.'

The tears started spilling then, which was annoying because I didn't want Kaye to worry about me (which being Kaye, she would; I purposefully hadn't mentioned the panic attacks and did not intend to).

'I-I don't know . . .' I started. 'I don't know yet if . . .'

I could see what she was thinking: 'You're thirty-two, you're clearly into Joe. It's not like he's some stranger. Worse things happen to people.'

'I rang Marie Stopes,' I said eventually.

Kaye was searching my eyes, frowning at me.

'Really? That bad?' she said, and I nodded.

'Oh, Kingy,' she said, bringing me into a Kaye-style embrace, almost crushing me with her kick-boxing-toned arms. 'Surely not. I'm sure once you've spoken to Joe, it will seem so much better. So much easier?'

I looked up at her. 'It's not that simple, Kaye. I wish it was, but it's not.'

And when I said that to Kaye, I felt like I was saying that to my mum, too, kind of letting her down, too. All this life she'd not been part of, it was becoming bigger than the part she'd been in.

Chapter Eleven

It is summer; I know that, because in front of us is a huge shimmering sun, like a gong, and riding into the centre of it is my mother, in her terry-towelling playsuit. The playsuit is dusky pink and strapless – the next best thing to naked – and Lil's been sporting it since the first rays of April, lost in the gardening, nattering over the fence, so all her freckles have joined up and she's as brown as a berry.

We are cycling down a sea front, I know that much. There are blue railings that curve, like Morecambe prom, and a steep grass verge to our right, like the prom at Grange. But this is not Morecambe or Grange prom, it is a promenade only we know about; one we've just discovered, untouched but for our bicycle tyres. We sneaked between two tall buildings, down a cool, dark alleyway, and there it was, in all its blue, quivering glory.

We stood back and marvelled, Mum and I, at the pulsating sun, the shimmering sea, and the smooth, red tarmac of our promenade, which curves and hugs the bay and leads . . . we don't know where, 'But that's the fun of it, Robyn!' says my mother.

And I can see her now in front of me, those fierce little legs pedalling like nobody's business, her big straw sunhat like a smaller sun, against the real one. I am wearing a green-and-white sundress, nipped in at the waist and tied at the shoulders. I'm sure Mum made it for me when I was little – seven, maybe eight – but the legs that pedal beneath it are fully grown and athletic, tanned; and I am very pleased about this. I can't take my eyes off my amazing legs!

We've got quite a speed up now. I tip my head back and fill my lungs with the warm, salty air. I'm admiring my mum's posture from behind: such a straight, toned back, she has – I can make out individual muscles. Then the square shoulders, and her thick auburn hair, which flows from her hat like flames. Every now and again, she turns and looks to check I'm still with her. She's wearing huge, white-framed sunglasses and lipstick. She looks like a film star.

We ride on; the grass to our right is getting hillier and craggier now. If I follow the line of the land, up the hill, I see there's a column-shaped monument at the top, glinting in the sun, and I know, instinctively, that this is where we're heading. We're going to climb that hill, to our monument, and admire our newly discovered land from up high, where it will be laid out like a patchwork quilt. Mum veers off the promenade onto the craggy foot of the hill, and we have to stand up from our seats to heave our bikes up. When we get to the top, our thigh muscles burning, we see how the road dips and rises; a

*valley, a hill, a valley, and then on top of the final hill,
our monument, winking at us. Mum turns and smiles at
me. 'I'll race you,' she says. And then we're off, feet off
the pedals, over the crags and the grassy knolls, squealing,
our hearts in our mouths.*

'Hi, it's me, Joe.'

I woke up, violently and gasping, as if from the dead,
just as the shrill beeps stopped and the answerphone
kicked in.

'I'm just checking you're not dead in a ditch, because
I've left a few messages on your mobile and I haven't
heard anything . . .'

I sat up. It took me a bit for the dream to subside and
reality to kick in, to realize who it was, and everything
else. Every day for the past three weeks or so, it's been
like this when I've woken up. Like finding out all over
again.

'. . . Anyway, I'm just checking on arrangements for
today . . .'

Today? What day was it? I had to glance at my radio
alarm to check: Sunday, 26. Shit! I'd never said anything
concrete but he assumed it was on.

'Are we still meeting? Are you taking me somewhere
posh? Are we doing booze or cultural, because this will
inform my outfit choice. Also, actually, I have a request
– somewhere I'd really like to go.'

I smiled. I'd forgotten how much Joe could *talk*.

There was a pause. I clutched the duvet to me, holding
my breath, watching the blossom outside my bedroom
window flutter to the ground like confetti.

'But you're not there, so . . . maybe you're busy in

135

the kitchen, rustling up one of your Kingy Breakfast Specials.'

I smiled. The Kingy Breakfast Special. I'd forgotten about those: a tower of fruit in a sundae glass, with an irresistible layer of yoghurt-soaked Frosties, and topped with crumbled digestive biscuit. Streets ahead of a Müller Corner. At least it was in '97. I used to make stuff whilst Joe did a ridiculous running commentary, as if we were on a cookery programme. We called it Twits TV – God knows why . . .

'On the other hand, perhaps you were fast asleep and are now cursing me. Go on, you are, aren't you? You're lying there in your scratcher, going, for God's sake, Sawyer, will you just piss off? I've been trying to get rid of you for years . . .'

In spite of myself, I was laughing . . . a scratcher? What the hell was a scratcher? Only Joe would come out with a word like scratcher.

'On the off chance you are awake, call me back, will you?'

I couldn't bear it any longer. I lurched forward and picked up the phone.

'Joe, I'm here.'

'Hello . . .' He actually sounded breathless with relief. I could hear his smile. 'I thought something had happened to you.'

I almost choked on the next line. 'No, Joe, nothing's happened to me.'

'Oh . . .' Long pause. 'So why the long silence? Have you been ignoring me?'

'No, don't be daft, I haven't been ignoring you.' Oh, God, to think his mum had just died and he thought I'd

136

been ignoring him. 'I'm sorry I didn't get back in touch about today. Things have been a bit . . . tricky,' I said eventually. That was the understatement of the year.

'What like, "tricky"?' asked Joe.

'Oh, work stuff.'

'Right.' I could see him nodding to himself. 'Work stuff. I see.' There was an air of suspicion – or was it confusion? – in his voice. Joe always hated to be confused, to feel you were keeping something from him; not in a possessive way, just because he likes people, *life*, to be transparent; he doesn't know any other way to be. 'You've always told me about work stuff before,' he added.

I had, it was true. In the emails we'd exchanged after the funeral, I'd told him loads about life as a CPN. 'What's going on at work?' he said.

'Oh, nothing specific, just my caseload is getting bigger and then there's Levi . . . Have I told you about Levi?'

'Chronic depressive? Mum called Genevieve?' He paused for effect. '*Beautiful*?'

I sniggered. Was I always going on about how beautiful Levi was? How unprofessional!

'Yes, well, he keeps taking overdoses. He's okay at the moment, but I'm worried, one day soon, he's going to succeed,' I said, grasping at straws.

'*Okay*.' Joe was genuinely thinking about this when I'd only said it as an excuse for not getting back to him. Levi was on the straight and narrow, for now, anyway. 'Well, I guess you can't save everyone,' he said. 'People are going to do what they want to do in the end. You can't control other people's behaviour, only your own. It's a very good piece of advice I was once told. I always tell my students.'

'It's true,' I said, even though I desperately wanted to save Levi, Grace, all my clients, and wished I could. 'That's a very good piece of advice.'

'So, what else?' he asked. 'What's your other excuse?'

I didn't have any more excuses.

'Because I'm free all day and I'd love to see you. If I stay one more hour in godforsaken Parson's Green, I might descend into a pit of mourning and loneliness so bad that I might end up in one of your units, and you'd have to talk sense to me as I rocked silently in a corner.'

I was giggling at the same time as wanting just to hug him through the phone; I was thinking, 'God, I wish this hadn't happened.' I wish so much I hadn't let this happen, then maybe I could have left the past where it belonged and started afresh, made a go of it with Joe, at least had some fun, seen where it went. Also, I just wanted to be there for him, when he needed me – like he had been there for me – not consumed by all this other stuff going on. 'How are you?' I asked. 'How have you been?'

'Oh, up and down, you know.'

'Yeah, I know.'

'One minute I'm fine, the next I'm in the foetal position, bawling my eyes out.'

'It's really healthy to have a cry,' I offered. 'It's normal and it does get easier, I promise you. Someone once told me that grief starts out feeling like a big house you're carrying on your shoulders, and eventually ends up as something you can put in your back pocket. I found that really comforting.'

Joe sniffed. 'I really like that, thanks,' he said. Although I knew it was no real compensation for not being on the end of the phone these last few weeks. I wanted to make it up to him.

'Okay,' I said, simply. 'Okay, no more crap excuses. I'm available today. Now, where do you fancy meeting?'

'Fossils,' he said. He wanted to go and see the fossils at the Natural History Museum.

'I'm massively into fossils, don't you remember?' he said. I joked I couldn't imagine choosing, of my own free will, as my first boyfriend, someone who ever claimed to be 'massively into fossils', but then he jogged my memory about the caravan weekend we'd taken with Dad, Denise and Niamh to Lyme Regis, during that summer we got together. It was only nine months after Mum had died and I think Dad realized within the first hour that it was too soon to take us anywhere with Denise, who had been so overexcited, she'd spent two hours packing the car with the entire Lakeland Plastics catalogue: gadgets such as egg separators and orange peelers that we were never going to need over the course of forty-eight hours in a caravan in Lyme Regis.

Desperate to get away, Joe had spent an hour in The Fossil Shop one day, buying shark teeth and ammonites. I'd got bored and got chatting to a homeless tramp outside. I always sniffed them out, even then.

'We can go and see fossils, if that's what you want to do,' I said. I thought the Natural History Museum might be good, actually; doing something other than sitting opposite one another at a table – I knew there was no way I'd be able to keep my mouth shut in that situation. Or worse, going to the pub and all the lying that would entail. I had to tell him about the baby soon, but not today. I didn't have to tell him today, did I?

Of course, though, once we got to the Natural History Museum, all I could think about was the baby. Mainly because everything seemed to be about babies; the circle of life. We went to see the sea creatures – everything looked like an embryo; we saw an exhibition about the evolution of mankind, and all I could think about was the evolution going on inside me. There was even a photography exhibition called 'Genesis': THE BEGINNING OF CREATION, it said in huge blue neon letters. (I still hadn't decided if this felt like the beginning or the end.) And then, just when I didn't think I could take much more, Joe suggested we go into the Human Biology gallery, only to be met by a video playing about the baby in the womb, and a model, five times the size of a real one, of a baby *in utero*.

I steered us to the fossils.

'My issue with fossils,' I said, as we stood, noses up, to two separate glass cabinets, displaying in one ancient fossils and in another not-so-ancient fossils (which is about all I understood of the names with a gazillion letters in them, describing the different 'eras'), 'is that they're not actually a thing, are they? They're the imprint, traces of a thing. That to me just isn't that exciting.'

Joe turned and looked at me, mock-horrified. He was wearing his glasses for the trip. They were a bit too big for his face and made him look very sweet. 'You are kidding?' he said. 'Fossils are fucking fascinating.'

'I'm going to quote you on that,' I said. 'Joseph Sawyer of Didsbury, Manchester, says, "Fossils are fucking fascinating."'

'You're evil,' he said, pretending to look studiously over his glasses at me before going back to the cabinet. 'Anyway, they're not always imprints or traces – sometimes they're the actual thing. Come here.'

I did as I was told and joined him at the cabinet displaying the fossils of the 'Palaeozoic Era' that he was lusting over. 'Fossils are *remains*,' he read, emphasizing the words from the information panel entitled: *What is a fossil?* 'Or traces of animals and plants preserved in rocks . . . See that . . .?' he pointed to something that reminded me of those marshmallow sweets you used to get called Flumps, but in rock version. 'That is the actual shell of a creature that went extinct maybe five hundred million years ago. *That's* how old it is!' he said, excitedly jabbing his finger against the glass for extra emphasis. Joe was still, was *always*, when we were going out, so excited by life. Don't get me wrong, it was annoying at times (making me walk in the pissing-down rain and the cold up Catbells fell in the Lake District, for example, 'because the view at the top would be out of this world' (you could barely see your own hand, it was so foggy, and he'd had to pretty much sit on me so I didn't blow away). But I always loved that about him, and was thinking how great it was that he was still like that, especially after everything; how he could still make me feel surrounded by a kind of Ready Brek glow. Then, I'd remember the news I had to tell him, and that warmth would evaporate, leaving me with this emptiness inside. It could never work. I could never do it.

'I guess that is pretty amazing,' I said, pushing that feeling aside. 'To think that we are looking at the same thing that perhaps Neanderthals or dinosaur eyes have seen.'

'Oh, it's way before there were dinosaurs, and definitely Neanderthals,' said Joe. I loved his flat, northern vowels; leaving the North so early on, I'd lost much of my accent. 'This is so old, fish were only just beginning to evolve.'

'Wow.'

'I know. We're standing here in 2013, looking at something that existed millions and millions of years before man.'

I watched him from the side. The expression on his face reminded me of the expression my nephew wears when you take him to the ice-cream parlour bit of Pizza Hut and ask him to choose his toppings. It was an expression very much reserved for boys, I thought: to be so completely absorbed by something that you were incapable of thinking about anything else. How I wished for that gift right now.

'What I love, too,' Joe carried on, running a hand through that fine hair that never did anything, just flopped back down again, 'is that these little fossil things can tell you so much about the past.' We read from another information panel, which described how the earth below was effectively layers and layers of small rock fragments squeezed together, and that within these layers were remains of plants or animals, creating a fossil record of Britain's past life.

'*That's an entire history of Britain, on the ground we're standing on!*' he read. Which did kind of blow my mind.

Joe cocked his head to the side.

'That's kind of like us, too, don't you think?' he said, after a moment's reflection.

142

'What do you mean?'

'Well, we're like a big rock, with remnants, fragments from the past squeezed between the layers, aren't we? You only need to study all those fossils to get an entire history of us, too.'

We got a sandwich from a little kiosk and went to sit on the daisy-strewn grass outside the museum. Joe had picked up a leaflet about palaeontology and was lying down, reading it, absorbed. My mind was going over and over what he'd said.

After a while he put down his leaflet and turned on his side. 'What are you thinking about?' he said.

'What you said in there, just now,' I replied. The sky was cloudless and powder blue. The sun throbbed. I imagined it was Mum urging me, pushing me to go on. 'About us being like rocks, layers and layers of fossilized past *stuff*.'

'Yeah, I quite like that analogy.' He yawned, content. I pulled at tufts of grass, feeling something inside me tighten like a rope.

'It scares me,' I said.

'What do you mean?'

I turned on my side, too, now, so I was facing him. 'Just this idea that the past is always there; it doesn't fade away, it leaves an indelible imprint. I mean, people go on about the Internet and how whatever you write on there, is out there forever, but it's the same in life, too, isn't it? You can't actually erase your past.'

The hormones were making me philosophical, high-minded. I'd started reading Ted Hughes in bed, for God's sake. Poetry seemed to be the only thing I was in the mood for.

The sun was shining directly onto Joe's head, making the reddish tints in his hair stand out. He was looking downwards, picking at a daisy. I was admiring the handsome androgyny of his features; the angles of his cheekbones, the sweeping thickness of his lashes. His deep-set, generous lids.

'I think it just becomes part of us,' he said. 'All that pain, those experiences, they makes us who we are.'

So what of my clients who had no end of pain? I bet they didn't like how it made them who they are.

It was like Joe read my mind, because he lifted his head and, closing one eye against the sun, said, 'That's not to say I'm not totally fucked off at the universe for making certain things happen. My mum, your mum . . . everything.' We both knew what he was talking about. 'But the way I see it, everyone gets bad luck.'

I smiled, thinly. 'Yeah, I know.'

'You can't give up on life,' he said. 'Otherwise, it just gives up on you.'

He looked at me, for a long time, and took a breath, as if he was about to say something then stopped himself. I was aware of him shifting his body towards me, the rustle the grass made, but it was only when he was milli-metres from my lips that I realized he was actually going to kiss me. I wanted to kiss him back so badly and yet I knew, with some instinctive, self-preserving part of me, that that kiss was a line, between the past and the present, and that if I crossed it now I could be sucked back into a dark place that I'd find it very hard to draw back from, that I'd have to tell him the whole story of what happened that summer – and what would that do to him? Most of all, I didn't want to drag him there with me.

I pulled away, suddenly.

'God, sorry,' Joe sprang back from me, his hand over his mouth, mortified.

'No, *I'm* sorry.'

'It's just . . .'

'Honestly, it's okay,' I said, sitting up.

'You looked so lovely there, in the sun, and I thought . . . Shit, what a dick.' He sat up too then, his head in his hands. 'I'm sorry.'

'It's *okay*,' I said, embarrassed

Could I not just pretend the baby, the pregnancy, hadn't happened for a while? I wanted so badly to kiss him! Could we not just snog, and it all be fine, it all not be so dangerous and intense for a while?

'Robyn?' he reached out and stroked my arm then. I knew I just couldn't keep it in any longer. 'Joe,' I said. 'I'm pregnant.'

Somewhere, far on the other side of the lawn, a crowd burst into 'Happy Birthday'. A text arrived in someone's inbox with a sound like a bird whistling, a paper cup still with liquid inside made a thud into a bin. Everything was magnified, stilled. In that clichéd way people talk of, the world really did come to a standstill, and then I was underwater again and all I could feel was the beating of my heart, the blood in my ears, like I was outside of my body, watching us.

Joe sat, blinking, trying to compute this information.

'*Pregnant?*' he said at last.

'I nodded.'

'Have you done a test?'

'Three. All positive.'

'Are you . . .? *Fuck.*' He put his head in his hands,

145

and it was only when he turned to me that I saw he was actually smiling. 'But I thought you said it was fine, that . . .?'

'It wasn't fine. It *wasn't*, Joe,' I said, panicking. 'I took a risk, an unbelievably stupid risk. I was very drunk, and it was just so –' I stopped myself, tempered it, because what I wanted to say, what I would have said if none of this had happened, was that it was the most wondrous, amazing night, the best night of the last sixteen years '– *lovely* to see you again, after so long. I got carried away. I've no idea what I was thinking! I took the morning-after pill as soon as I got back. I thought I could no way be pregnant. But it turns out the longer you leave before you take it, the less effective it is, and it's not even a hundred-per-cent effective, anyway. I didn't know that . . .' I was crying now and I wiped the tears away with the cuff of my top and, as I did, I caught Joe's face again and stopped. There was no doubt about it, he looked actually *pleased*. 'You'd have thought of all people, I would, wouldn't you? But I didn't and I'm so sorry.'

Joe reached for my hand. 'But why are you sorry?'

He *was* pleased! 'Well, because this is a nightmare, Joe. After everything. I can't go through that again.'

'Darling, it's not going to happen again.' He said. (How could he sound so sure?) 'You'd have to be seriously unlucky for that to happen again.' He was frowning and smiling at me all at the same time, peering at me as if he thought I'd gone mad. He actually thought I was mad for considering not having it. Like this was absolute lunacy. Why hadn't I predicted this response? Of course he'd be happy and optimistic. Joe was always optimistic.

146

'Anyway, I called up Marie Stopes,' I said, rambling. 'Because I didn't know what the hell to do and I thought that might be the answer but, in the end, I couldn't go through with it. There was just no way I could have ever gone through with it.'

'Wait a minute,' said Joe. The expression on his face had darkened. 'You spoke to Marie Stopes?'

'Yes.'

'Isn't that where you call if you want an abortion?'

I'd never seen this expression on his face before: all his features had hardened, even his eyes. It was horrible.

'Joe, I never would have actually—'

'You were going to have an abortion and not even tell me?'

'*No*,' I said, knowing that at the height of my panic and desperation, I had considered it.

'After everything we've been through, you would have even considered that?'

But I thought you might have wanted that, too, I thought, that you'd have thought it was best for everyone. That you would have thanked me in the long run.

Looking at his face now, he was right, I *must* have been actually mad. What was I thinking of?

'Joe,' I said, making him look at me. 'I never would have gone through with it. But this is a nightmare. I mean, you know *why*?' I was searching his face – didn't he?

'*Jesus*, Robyn.' The expression on his face was disdain and sadness rolled into one. 'My *mother* just died.' He said it so quietly.

I felt so ashamed then. How could I get rid of a life when he'd just lost one that was so close to him? But also just those words, those simple words: a pregnancy, the loss of a mother. This was déjà vu on a whole new, awful level. I stumbled to my feet.

My heart was already firing like bullets as I left Joe. I don't remember making a decision about getting on the Tube, I simply went down to South Kensington on auto-pilot, my only thought that I needed to get away from Joe, from talking about the baby, from myself, and that disappearing underground seemed like the obvious way to do it. I have never wanted the dark, grimy underbelly of London to suck me in and swallow me up and make me disappear as much as I did then, but realized as soon as I was standing on the District and Circle eastbound platform that it couldn't, because I couldn't take the Tube any more.

Just the warm air, gusting through the tunnel, signalling an approaching train, was bringing on a panic attack.

The problem was, I couldn't move. No matter how much my heart was pummelling the inside of my chest, or my teeth were chattering, I was paralysed. It was like one of those awful nightmares, where your conscious mind knows you're having a nightmare but your body can't wake itself up.

I looked down the black mouth of the tunnel, trying to focus my eyes on something, focus my breathing, but the two dim lights of the train hurtling towards us were wobbling through my tears. The train eventually slowed and hissed into the station, and I staggered back. 'Breathe,' I was telling myself, 'just *breathe*.' Then, it stopped. The doors opened, people piled out, then on. Someone tutted loudly then knocked my shoulder to get past me. '*Are you getting on, or what?*' Whoever it was did me a favour, however, because it brought me momentarily to my senses, out of my bad dream and into the world. I peeled my feet right off that platform, turned and walked away, up the stairs, to the sun.

I felt instantly better once I was in the fresh air; and walked, in a daze for a while, just regulating my breathing, feeling the warm breeze on my skin, noticing the blue sky, the trees thick with creamy blossom, but aware of this twisting feeling in my gut: I'd made the mistake of telling Joe that I'd considered an abortion. I don't know why I had done that. In that minute, when I'd got up off the grass and walked away, I'd wanted to be as far from Joe as possible, as far away from everything he reminded me of; so why, suddenly, did I now desperately want to be back with him? It didn't make any sense.

My phone beeped. Someone had left a voicemail whilst I'd been underground and I knew instinctively who it was. I always used to think, when people's phones beeped as soon as they came up from the Tube, what important things could have possibly happened to so many people, for there to be so many messages left during a short journey? Now, I thought, how possible it was for life-changing things to happen to so many people, all the time. How life-changing events just flew out of nowhere, like a train from a dark tunnel.

'Robbie, listen, this is totally fucking ridiculous. You don't have to do this on your own . . . Call me back, will you?'

The message had been left two minutes after I'd left him and I thought, how typical this was of Joe. He could never let the dust settle after an argument. He always had to sort it out immediately. Whereas I needed time to process and form my opinions, he always knew how he felt, about everything, and he'd been like that right from the beginning. It's part of the reason I loved him so much.

I put my phone in my pocket and made my way down the street, thinking about those first few weeks of our relationship, back in that hot May of 1997, when life had felt so intense. I'd lost Mum just seven months previously, in the October, and now I was falling in love for the first time.

Even in the shadow of my mum's death, however, that falling in love felt as liberating and exhilarating as freewheeling, and I thought about how sure Joe had been then, even when, unbeknownst to him, his would-be girlfriend was still drowning in grief, and therefore prone to leaving cinemas in the middle of films and bursting into tears in the middle of supermarket car parks. And yet, perversely, post losing Mum, there's never been a happier time for me than that summer I got together with Joe.

After the near-drowning incident at the Black Horse Quarry, we'd all gone to the pub for the night, hyper with the drama of the day. I'd got drunk, quickly, and spent the whole evening sitting on Joe's knee, flapping my hand away at people who said I was a hero – *'No, really, anyone else would have done the same,'* knowing inside that nobody actually did.

'Robyn King saved my life,' Joe had kept whispering in my ear, even though I already had a feeling he was going to be the one to save mine; to be a light in these

dark times. Little did I know what darkness there was still to come. I can still feel the thrill now, of sitting on his knee, with the giddy anticipation of what the summer might hold. My sunburn had been heating up his thighs. 'You're like a little radiator,' he'd said. The intimacy of the comment had thrilled me. 'Your sunburn is actually burning through my jeans . . . feel *that*.' When he'd laid his hand on my bare, hot thigh, I swear, it was the most exciting thing that had ever happened to me. This tsunami of desire rose up in me. I remember feeling like, *This has got to go somewhere or I'll explode*. As it was, there was somewhere, because that night in the car park of the pub, the Lakeland fells black and sleeping in the distance, we kissed for the first time. Bomber honked his horn all the way through because he was supposed to be giving Joe a lift, but all the while we kissed, Joe held one finger up to Bomber over my shoulder. That kiss was the first proper kiss I'd ever had and also the best. It still is. I can still remember the sound of our eager breath, the feel of his lips, gossamer-soft, the glorious bloom in my belly – like a craving you could never fill; like no other feeling I'd ever known. I remember the taste of him, the slightly sunken shadow of his cheek under the lamplight as a train roared past and laughter broke out inside the pub, and the big sky enveloped us in its thick, blue, starry velvet.

'So, like, will you be my girlfriend?' he'd said.

'I'll think about it,' I'd teased, kissing him again.

'Can I see you tomorrow then?' he'd said, and I couldn't believe it because who says that?! Even if you want to? (Which I did, desperately.) Wasn't he supposed to play it cool? But I said, yes, he could.

151

'Can I see you every night this week?' he'd added, kissing me again, at which point I'd done this big, snorty snigger (wholly attractive) into his mouth.

'Are you joking?' I'd said.

'No.' He'd looked almost offended I could ever think he was.

The irony was, I thought, as I wandered towards Knightsbridge, along the Brompton Road, the warm air like a soft sheet around me, I'd been in love with Joe from afar for months before that night; since he'd played Christy Brown in the Year 11 Christmas production of *My Left Foot*. After all, who'd dare play a wheelchair-bound man with cerebral palsy in a school like ours and expect life to ever be the same again? But Joe stormed it. He wheeled on, his hands contorted, talking through the side of his mouth, and he didn't care what anyone thought. I don't think he was even aware of the audience. We went to the pub after that. I remember I minced over with my Bacardi and Coke, and I said:

'Joe, we don't really know each other, but I just wanted to say, I thought you were unbelievable tonight. I mean, do you actually have cerebral palsy, or . . .?'

He burst out laughing. 'No. But my little brother is disabled.'

I was the one to laugh then, because I thought he was joking.

'No, he is,' Joe had said. I've never been so mortified in my life.

He'd been getting some stick from so-called mates. One said, 'All right, Sawyer, you spaz,' or something like that. Joe replied, 'I was acting, mate, what's your excuse?' I spat

152

my Bacardi out, I was laughing so much. I thought, I'm going to marry Joseph Sawyer.

I eventually caught a bus heading to Highgate and sat at the top, where the blossom-laden trees lolled and brushed against the windows; candy-floss-pink against the cloudless sky. Now I'd calmed down, I could start to unpick why I'd had such a strong reaction; why I'd had to make off like that, some textbook example of the 'flight or fight' response, mine clearly being flight. The truth was, I knew Joe wouldn't have been able to hear my news and walk away from it, any more than I could have walked into a Marie Stopes clinic and had an abortion. It was just wishful thinking. Because I couldn't handle the potential fallout of this, the risk of him hurting more than he already did; because I couldn't handle his emotions as well as mine, I was hoping he wouldn't have any. And, yes, I do know how mental that sounds.

Even when the bus finally got to Archway, I didn't want to go home. Normally, I didn't have a problem with living alone but, today, I could not bear to turn the key in the lock, knowing that only silence lay on the other side. Then I'd end up calling Joe back, and I didn't want to call Joe back yet. I hadn't worked out what to say to Joe, or what I was going to do. I sauntered in the general direction of home, thinking of the look on Joe's face as I'd left: disbelief, confusion but, most of all, in his big, hazel, sloping eyes, was the sort of pain that a man of thirty-two shouldn't know and, if he'd never met me, wouldn't. And now I felt like I'd come back into his life, carrying the risk of it happening again, like the carrier of a dangerous disease. If I could have turned back time,

I'd have never even have gone to the funeral and none of this would have happened. The worst thing was, I couldn't even tell him the whole story, I couldn't explain why I'd had to run away like that. Still, I couldn't just leave him with absolutely nothing from me. I texted him:

Joe, I'm so sorry I said. And I WILL call you. I just need some time.

Chapter Twelve

Joe and I are in my childhood bedroom in Kilterdale, the one with the sponge-effect walls that I share with my sister. It is September 1997 and we are lying on my bed. I have found out I am pregnant a week previously. I am still mute with shock. Joe is trying to be positive.

'I think if you can give a baby everything it needs – clothes and milk and love – then it doesn't matter how old you are,' he's saying, so innocently and naively. I can only nod, unable to meet his eyes.

'If it's a boy, I want to be the kind of dad my son feels he can cry in front of, but also go down the pub to watch the footie with. If it's a girl . . . honestly, Robbie –' he sighs and shakes his head so seriously – 'if any man dares hurt her . . .'

I am gripped by this memory as I lie in bed now, in my double bed in Archway, London, not my single one that squeaks and that Leah crawls into most nights – it is almost 3D, it feels so real, like I could reach inside it and touch the squishiness of the duvet, pass a hand over my already-swelling belly. I can remember the conversation word for word:

'*God, I wish I had a dad like you,*' I'd said, *gutted that I had this amazing boyfriend, whom I was so in love with; that, actually, new life should be such a precious thing after losing Mum and yet, here I am, sixteen and scared out of my wits, unable to be excited like Joe.*

'Grace?' The only way I have ever known how to cope is to throw myself into the job I love and this time was no exception. 'Grace, are you there?'

Two and a half weeks after that horrific conversation with Faith from Marie Stopes and three days after meeting Joe at the museum, I stood knocking on Grace Bird's front door. 'It's just Robyn, here, Robyn King, your CPN?'

I was really looking forward to seeing Grace again. In fact, in these past three weeks of total insanity, it had ironically been the thing that had kept me sane. The eight-week, six-day deadline Faith had informed me about had been and gone, as I knew it would, with me coiled tightly inside in some kind of madness of my own. Nine weeks passed. Ten . . . I never made an appointment or even called her back.

It was fair to say that in this dark and brooding mood in which I found myself, the Mr Greedy-alikes with their BABY ON BOARD badges and their 'we are just absolutely ecstatic' faces, were not just doing me no good but were alien to me. Which is why I was looking forward to being with Grace: it's pretty hard to think about your own problems while you're helping someone else with theirs, for a start, but also, I felt an affinity with Grace. There was something in her eyes that I recognized; I knew all that stuff would be alien to her, too.

I rapped again on her door. It looked industrially heavy and was painted burgundy, with a glass panel on the top, from which hung a curious home-made wreath: a ring of plastic, green foliage, within which nestled various woodland creatures and flowers made out of papier-mâché and lolly sticks and fur – *Possibly something she'd made at a mental-health craft group*? I thought. But no, there was something incongruous about it here. It looked too jolly and playful, like it belonged in the sunny Cath Kidston kitchen of one of those huge Edwardian houses in Dulwich village.

As is often the case for people with mental illness, a bright young woman who would have been destined for great things – had her mind not collapsed under the deluge of shit life had thrown at her – had wound up living on the umpteenth floor of an inner-city, concrete monstrosity. Just on the walk from the lift, along the gangway to Grace's front door, I'd counted a latex glove, a condom and a syringe. A miasma of urine, beer and fried food hung thickly in the air. It was sickly metallic; like how your hands might smell if you'd been gripping the bars of a rusty climbing frame. Just being here made me feel better about everything, if I'm honest. Things were tricky, to say the least, but my job can be a great leveller.

I knocked again, much harder this time, because the TV was blaring from behind, so I guessed she wouldn't be able to hear me. Eventually, however, there was the sliding of a lock, like the barrel of a gun, the jangling of a chain. One lash-fringed, fawn-like eye peered back at me through the gap.

'Who is it?' came Grace's high-pitched estuary twang. The obligatory Vogue dangled from her lip and I watched the blazing redness of the ash intensify as she sucked hard. Smoke snaked upwards through the two-inch gap in the door and across my face.

I coughed. 'Hello, it's Robyn,' I said, cheerfully. 'Robyn from the mental-health team.' She didn't look too happy, but then I wonder how most of us would feel if someone from the local mental-health team was the only person who ever came to your door.

I lifted up the NHS card and smiled, so she could see.

There were a few seconds before recognition lit up her face – 'Oh! Robyn, it's *you*!' – and she undid the chain and opened the door. The plastic wreath plunged immediately to the floor. Grace looked forlornly at the little mound of fur and pipe cleaners on the dirty concrete. 'It keeps bloody doing that.' She sighed, before pinning it back up above the door.

She walked inside and gestured me to follow. 'Sorry darlin', I thought you might be some weirdo, some odd-bod. I forgot you had a boy's name.'

She was wearing a satin dress-could-be-nightie, a crocheted black cardigan over the top and the bright blue Yankees cap again. Her skinny girl's calves were clad in black tights. And, on her feet, bright white Reebok high-tops, which looked like they'd been nicked off the back of a lorry.

She stopped and surveyed me for a few seconds, the telltale clozapine blankness descending – a little absence – and then she was back again, engaged.

'D'you like my dress?' she said. 'I got it down the Red Cross. It's a wedding dress, you know.'

'It's lovely, Grace.'

'So, shall I take your jacket, darling?' she said, in a mock-posh voice like she'd heard people say things on the telly.

'Thank you,' I said, handing it to her. She exhaled smoke all over it, then lay it – as carefully as if it were a baby – but on the floor (along with ash stains and about a gazillion pizza-delivery leaflets). I thought about my baby as I followed her through to the lounge, about the dangers of passive smoking (unavoidable in my job), and felt encouraged: I'd had a maternal thought; a protective, normal thought. This was a start.

The flat was much bigger inside than it looked on the outside and I stood in the spacious, yet cluttered, lounge as Grace picked up various piles of stuff and moved them from one place to another, trying to make space for me to sit down. Eventually, she pushed a tide of papers off a grubby, floral two-seater, which was so small that, when she sat down, her face was just centimetres from mine. This seemed to alarm her and she sprang up. Clearly, she didn't often have other people sitting on her sofa. And to my dismay, just this thought brought a lump to my throat.

Hormones? Already?

'Shall I make a drink first?' she asked.

'Yes, that would be lovely, Grace. Why don't you do that, then we can have a chat?'

I leaned down to get my notes out of my bag, but sensed she was still standing there, fiddling with the gold chains around her neck.

'What shall I make?'

'I don't mind. Tea? Coffee? What are you having?'

'Dr Pepper, darlin' . . .' The ash from her Vogue finally surrendered and fell to the floor, making a fizzing sound, which both of us ignored. 'Or coffee. I haven't decided yet.'

'Coffee's great for me,' I said. 'Just milk, no sugar.'

I could feel her eyes on me for a few seconds longer.

'All right,' she said when I looked up again. 'Coming up!' And she glided into the kitchen, from where she sounded as if she was building an extension, not making a coffee, but I decided to leave her to it.

The lounge was big but grimy: blue carpet dotted with fag burns, like bullet holes; mismatched furniture; an old, unplugged microwave in the corner, looking as if it might actually start talking, it was covered in so much crusted food.

There was so much *stuff*. Little deposits of it everywhere, like molehills, as if she'd decided to do something vaguely productive – some knitting (there were needles and balls of brown wool strewn across the carpet as though the moles had escaped from those molehills); paperwork (an avalanche of it on top of the coffee table) – or make herself some food (a pan with a boiled egg sat on top of the telly), before she got distracted by something terrible and had had to leave it all there, like someone who'd had to run naked and screaming from a house fire.

The walls were nicotine-stained and the wallpaper

peeling, but there were also attempts at domesticity and home-making – ornaments and trinkets and pretty cushions that broke my heart, because it was obvious Grace knew what a home should look like, but her disordered thoughts meant she hadn't quite managed it. Her illness had robbed her of what was probably, once, a natural sense of style.

There was a bit of a commotion in the kitchen.

'You all right in there, Grace? Shall I come and help?'

Another bang.

'What did you want again?' she shouted.

'Coffee.'

'I can't find the coffee – what about Dr Pepper?'

'Yes, Dr Pepper. Dr Pepper is great.' I hadn't had Dr Pepper since the days of sitting outside Mr Fry's in Kilterdale with Mum and everyone; it would be nice.

I wandered towards the window. It was one of those huge 1960s ones that take up the whole of the wall – not stylish, but it let in a lot of light at least. It looked over the grimy congestion of the Walworth Road: more concrete rabbit hutches; an Esso petrol station; the dark red Victorian arches of the entrance to Elephant and Castle station.

If you looked down below, there was a rather threadbare football pitch, more scrubland than pitch, and the mellow afternoon light was playing on it in such a way that a memory suddenly assailed me, so vivid I could almost taste it on my tongue. I was seventeen and watching an eight-year-old Niamh play for Kilterdale Primary football team. It was autumn and sunny, that glassy autumn light. It reminded me of the same time the previous year when we'd lost Mum – she'd spent her last days on a Marie

161

Curie bed in the lounge, looking out on a garden bathed in light just like that.

Niamh's pale, stocky legs were flushed with cold in this memory. She was sturdy, still with a rounded little girl's tummy but, God, she flew like a hummingbird around that pitch.

Her side won, and all the kids ran cheering, arms pumping the air, to the sidelines to meet their mums. I remember the look on her face at the moment she embraced me, the moment she clocked that she was the only one without her mum there. I remember, as we walked home together across the golden fields, her saying, quite casually, 'Do you think Mum saw that today? My goal? Do you think she was watching when I scored?' I'd had to bite down hard so I didn't cry.

'Won't be a sec now, darlin',' Grace called from the kitchen. Then I heard the pop-fizz of the Dr Pepper can being opened. Something caught my eye as she brought it in: a collection of photos, like a shrine on a table beneath the window. They all pictured the same girl, with dark eyes like Grace's and black hair in plaits, that Grace had shown me in the Hello Kitty wallet: Cecily.

'Here we are.' Grace handed me the can, rather proudly, and I took a sip. Immediately, I was transported to outside Mr Fry's with Mum and everyone, the can cold in my hand, the fiery heat in my throat. So happy.

Grace sat down, but on the armchair opposite this time. She took another cigarette out of the packet and lit it. It took several goes, her hands were shaking so much.

I picked up my notebook and pen. 'So,' I said, 'I know we've met but it's great to see you back home, in your own surroundings. Today is really about getting to know one another and seeing how you're doing, but also to get an idea of how you'd like to use our time together, what makes you happy, how we can get you out and feeling part of things again.'

Grace and I chatted easily for half an hour. As I suspected, having a diagnosis of schizophrenia was about the least interesting thing about her. She used to be a professional photographer for one (why Jeremy had never told me this, and why they'd taken the one thing she loved away from her in hospital, I'd never know). She used to have a studio where she did portraits – babies and families and so on – but would also travel and do her own projects. It was on one of these photographic trips, Grace told me, that she'd met Cecily's father.

'He was a Cambodian tribesman,' she said, as matter-of-factly as if she'd said, 'He was called Chris and he worked in IT.' Like the escalator story, I even wondered if it were true. But then she picked up one of the photos: it was of Grace with her dad and, lo and behold, he was standing outside some sort of hut in the Cambodian jungle, dressed in Western clothes and very handsome, but in the Cambodian jungle, after all.

'She gorgeous, i'nt she?' she said. 'My Cec.'

'She really is,' I said. 'She's a beauty.'

There were so many photos: Cecily as a baby in black and white in a studio; Cecily wearing an I AM 5 badge, standing outside a green front door. Then, the most heart-breaking one of all: Cecily with a woman dressed in shorts and strappy top, arms wrapped around one another in some exotic garden (you could tell by the palm trees that it was somewhere abroad), and it took me a few seconds to realize that the woman was Grace, because it wasn't the ravaged face I saw staring back at me, but a normal, shiny-eyed mother, just enjoying time with her child.

'That were in Mallorca,' Grace said, the photo shaking like a leaf in her hand. 'The three of us and my mum and dad. Thomson package, all in. Grace would have been six – no, just turned seven.' Her face had lit up, like that of the woman in the palm-tree picture. 'She was incredible; she'd go out in the waves with her dad. Six foot, they were, and she wasn't scared one bit. Such a little dare-devil, she was,' she said, laughing again. Then her eyes narrowed, the smile dropped. She took another deep tug on that Vogue. 'She's ever so arty, too. You see that wreath on the door?' She made it. She was only six when she made that.'

'Your whole face lights up when you talk about her, you know,' I said.

'That's 'cause she's the light of my life,' Grace said, like this was a universal truth. 'She loves her mum, too. Such a mummy's girl, she is.'

I nodded, smiling.

'Attached at the hip when she was growing up. We still are now, although she's much busier these days – you know, boyfriend, her studies, hobbies . . .' She didn't say which hobbies, which studies, I noticed.

'She's the only thing –' Grace paused, almost to gather herself – 'I look forward to, darlin'.'

I reached out and put my hand on hers. 'And you have her,' I said. We were supposed to be doing her care plan, but we were having such a nice chat, I'd abandoned the form-filling. 'Nobody can take that away from you, Grace.'

She smiled and drifted off into the distance for a minute or two, then she turned to me. It was like she knew.

'You're so lucky,' she said. 'You've got it all to come. The babies, the life. How old are you? Twenty-five, twenty-six?'

I laughed. 'Well, I'm extremely flattered, but I'm thirty-two!'

'And you've no babies?' My cheeks grew hot. Could she tell?

'No.'

'And you don't want 'em?'

'Oh, yes, yes,' I said. 'Very much. One day.'

'Good.' Grace reached over then, and patted my thigh, like she was satisfied. 'Because I've seen you with those patients and you're born to be a mum. Not like me. I messed it all up and it was hard, darlin', so hard for my Cec. But, you know, despite everything, I don't regret it. 'Not for one second of my sorry little life have I ever regretted my Cec.'

I left Grace's flat a good hour after I'd intended. Grace wanted to accompany me downstairs and outside. I wondered if she wanted me to go at all. The wreath fell off her door again as we closed it. She sighed again and pinned it back up. I wondered how many times she'd done that.

We went down in the lift. Outside, just a small patch of grass separated us from the heaving, wheezing jam of the Walworth Road. 'Oooh, it's nice to have some fresh air,' she said, taking out a Vogue from her cardigan pocket and lighting it, with not even a flicker of recognition at the irony. I wondered if she meant to be funny?

The air was warm and I felt this calm descend. A plane

soared noisily overhead on its way to Gatwick. A stream of white froth in its wake.

'Bloody noisy, them planes,' said Grace.

'They are,' I agreed. 'Hurts your ears.'

'Always talking to me. Bla bla bla, all bloody day.'

'What do they say to you, Grace?'

'Oh, just messages,' she said, inhaling. 'Some nice, some not so nice. I never quite know what I'm going to get.'

I looked at Grace as she stubbed that fag out, in her Yankees cap and her satin wedding dress-slash-nightie, and I thought, even though you think planes are talking to you, and you have a plastic wreath of small animals on your door, you've made me feel saner than anyone else has in weeks. Grace Bird might not have the best grip on reality, but she had held her child in her arms and was clear on one universal truth: nobody, no matter how hard it is, no matter how unplanned, regrets a baby.

By the time I left Grace, thick grey cloud had rolled in over the blue sky, like a canopy over a swimming pool, and the world looked saturated in colour, the sky almost navy, the clouds pencil-grey, and the trees so green they looked fake. It looked lit, like a stage set.

I couldn't stop thinking about how Grace had looked the same when she talked about Cecily. 'My Cec,' she'd kept saying. 'My girl.' Grace spent her days in the murky, grey world of her mind – like living in the smoker's room – and her daughter was this spotlight, there. She lit her up.

I'm not saying that I, or even the baby and I together, were all Joe had, because Joe had a rich, full life before I turned up and wreaked havoc. But, whereas I'd only seen this baby as something that could potentially cause

166

more heartache for Joe, now I considered the possibility that it could be *his* spotlight, in what must seem a fairly dark world for him at the moment – a glimmer of hope. I thought about that look on his face, when we'd been lying on the grass outside the museum, just seconds before his face contorted with hurt – and that was what it was, it was hope. And by me just making off like that, I'd taken that hope away from him. Oh, God, what had I done?

I had to call him, tell him it was going to be okay. That I was going to have this baby. I walked faster, fumbling in my bag for my phone, but it was out of battery, which was just so completely typical. I could go to the office, I thought, but Kaye and Leon were on late shift; it wouldn't be in any way private. If I waited until I got home to charge my phone, it could be an hour, and suddenly I couldn't bear one more minute of Joe worrying. I spotted a phone box, just as the big grey belly of sky collapsed and it started hurling it down; so I ran, with my bag over my head, the few metres to it. The door wouldn't shut properly, so I wedged the bag in the doorway. The inside smelt faintly of wee and it occurred to me how many hours I used to spend doing this during that time Joe and I were together, standing in a pissy phone box, whenever I wasn't at home, pushing coin after coin into the slot, frantically searching for more coins in my pocket so I didn't have to hang up.

He answered in the same way he had since I'd known him – 'Hello, Joseph' – the intonation going up at the end.

'Joe, it's me. It's Robyn.'

There was silence. I prepared myself for a torrent of

anger but he simply said, 'Robyn?' and it came out as an exhalation, as relief. 'Are you okay?'

'Yeah, I'm fine.'

'Why are you out of breath?'

''Cause my mobile died and I just ran to call you on a payphone and also . . .' I felt like once it was out there, it was out there, in the universe – it was fact. 'I *am* three months pregnant.'

I leaned against the glass, tracing the rain, which fell in rivulets, listening to Joe make this little noise, somewhere between a sob and a laugh. Had he thought I might still go through with an abortion? Surely, he knew I'd never do that? But then, judging by my behaviour at his mum's funeral, how did he know what I was capable of any more?

'Joe, you do know I would never ever have gone through with a termination, don't you? I should never have even told you I called them up – it was totally stupid and insensitive of me.'

He was very quiet. I silently kicked the side of the phone box. 'How have you been?'

'All right . . .'

'Tell me the truth.'

'It's been one of the worst weeks of my life. You didn't call me back, Robyn. I didn't know what you were thinking. I wondered if . . .'

'Oh, God, Joe, I'm sorry, but it's all right,' I said. 'I'm having the baby. *We're* having the baby. I've got used to the idea now. I feel okay about it.'

'Okay?'

'Even happy, sometimes. It's just, it's really hard.'

He sighed. 'Yeah, I know, darling.'

'And a massive shock.'

'Maybe it's just meant to be?'

There was a long silence when it was clear both of us were thinking, *So what now?* I felt a heaviness in my chest. Why couldn't things be simpler?

'Look, Joe, I'm sorry, but I still feel like I can't see you,' I said. 'Not just yet . . .' The rain was hammering the roof, exploding like little water bombs on the pavement.

'But why?'

'I don't know,' I said, lamely. How could I tell him? How could I ever explain, that him just being near me made me anxious because he was part of the whole story, not just of losing Lily. That if I were to be with him, I would have to tell him everything, and I couldn't do that. 'I just can't handle it at the moment. It's too much, emotionally,' I said. 'It's not forever. I'm sure we'll be able to meet up soon, to be friends . . .'

'It's okay, you don't have to marry me,' he said, laughing, and I felt a bit embarrassed.

Was I totally overthinking this? Was he not expecting anything anyway?

'I just want to be involved, to help you.'

'Okay.' It seemed so mean to shut out Joe like this, but I needed to compartmentalize, to do what I had to do, on my own, at least for a little while. 'Listen, I've got my first scan next week,' I said. 'I'll give you a call after and let you know how it's gone, I promise.'

'When's the scan?' he said.

'Next Thursday afternoon. At the Whittington, it's really near me.'

'Right, okay,' he said. Then, taking a breath, as if he'd found new determination not to let me get away with this, he said, 'At least let me come to the scan, then? I promise I'll be good. I won't ask too many questions. I'll behave myself.'

I briefly thought of Joe, with his orang-utan arms and legs filling that nice, quiet space.

'Oh, Joe, I know you will,' I said. 'I'm really sorry. Please, just understand I need do this on my own. I can't bear the thought of you being in the room and anything—'

'I'm thirty-two, Robbie, I'm a big boy.'

'Joe, you're lovely. And I'll call you. Immediately after, I promise.'

Chapter Thirteen

I'd arranged to see Niamh for dinner that evening at Wagamama's in Soho. (Niamh is new to London, and noodles are the current gastro-novelty of choice.)

I was excited. I was looking forward to seeing my little sister in the same way I'd been looking forward to seeing Grace, maybe because there were similarities between Niamh and Grace. Niamh might not have mental-health issues, but she'd never conformed in life either; never adhered to the marriage, house, baby mantra, and not just because she was gay. As she joked she'd say to Dad and Denise when eventually she came clean: '*If it wasn't lesbianism, then it would have been something else. Something much worse.*'

Leah, our elder sister, has always had a 'normal' life – as in the trampoline-in-the-back-garden-and-the-Ford-Focus-in-the-driveway kind of normal (although, if you'd have done a straw poll when we were young, she would definitely have been 'least likely'), but it wasn't for me or Niamh. Maybe that's why we bonded more than either of us bonded with Leah these days, despite the fact we loved her all the same.

I was thinking about Niamh all the way to meet her, about that chubby eight-year-old on the football pitch, the straggly blonde hair (now glossy and a drama-student henna-red) that was always tangled across her face, as if she'd just emerged from the Great Deep. Did fate know it then? That 'normal' was not what was in store for Niamh, like it wasn't in store for me? Did losing Mum have anything to do with her being gay? The fact that Leah left Kilterdale two weeks after Mum died and I left as soon as I could, too? Maybe she felt she needed to replace that sisterly intimacy with someone.

Sometimes, I still think about that moment, when Dad's pick-up truck with Niamh in the front seat drew away from Kilterdale Station after dropping me off for my train to start a new life in London. It was May 1999. Literally days after I'd finished my A levels. A year and four months since Joe and I had finished. I have never willed a year over like that one.

Both Niamh and I were sobbing our hearts out. It tore me apart to leave her. The worse thing was, I could never explain to her or Dad exactly why I felt the need *to* leave like that. They must have thought I was mad, swapping a nice, cosy house (with Denise in it, but at least all my meals would have been provided) for a life crashing on the floor of a friend's sister's flat in Seven Sisters. I must have been desperate! I was. To stay in Kilterdale any longer meant constantly being surrounded by memories, risking bumping into people I didn't want to see.

Of course, she'd laugh wryly if I said this to her. Niamh is very much of the belief that you're born gay or straight, like you're born male or female – she always knew deep down. I didn't doubt that at all, but it's not the being gay thing that worries me, it's the being happy thing. And I wonder sometimes how happy she is, and if being gay and in the closet with her close family adds a dimension of difficulty to her life that I wish wasn't there.

I had decided to tell her I was pregnant tonight. I'd decided her reaction would do me good. She'd be shocked; but mainly she'd just be excited and 'Yay!' and uncomplicated about it. She wouldn't think of the practicalities or even the complicated emotions, and that was fine by me. No, she'd think of a cute, new baby, a new niece or nephew. The baby clothes she could buy.

As soon as I saw her, however, rabidly searching for my face among the diners of Wagamama, Soho, eyebrows knotted, every inch the struggling actress, I knew this wasn't going to happen. She was crying – which is by no means unusual or alarming for Niamh, but I felt my stomach tense with maternal instinct. It also put a spanner in the works for my own plans to offload.

'Oh, my *God*.' She put her various bags down on top of the bench, swung her legs over and slumped forward on the bench. 'I've got to come out to Dad, I've *got* to, it's driving me mad.'

My sister rarely arrived anywhere and just said, 'Hello.' When she was little, we used to take bets on what bombshell she'd drop literally as she walked through the door.

'Ellie's mum's had a hysterectomy.'

'Miss Buck's off school with a mental breakdown.'

Or what strange, tangential question:

173

'How long do you think a monitor lizard can hold its breath?'

She always did have a feel for drama, even then. Still, I felt my sisterly instincts sharpen.

'What's happened?' I asked. 'Has Denise said something? Has Dad said something?'

After a crap start (most memories of her mother being of her in the oncology ward of Westmoreland Hospital, rigged up to a chemo drip), I dared to think life was finally going well for Niamh. She'd fallen in love, recently got her first acting job and had come out to her friends and me. Being in the closet as far as Denise, Dad and Leah were concerned seemed to be the only thing that was spoiling it.

'No. But that's the point,' she said. 'You know the other weekend when you went to Joe's mum's funeral, which we'll get on to in a minute, I promise you . . .' I smiled, I loved how Niamh always had such good intentions of asking me about me, but that it usually happened as we were kissing goodbye. 'Well, I went home with Mary, because we were doing the Three Peaks challenge, and it was just *so* obvious. I mean, could they not hear her creeping into my bed in the middle of the night? Did they not see me lusting at her over the breakfast table, ogling at her rack?'

Niamh has an unusually loud voice, and the two girls on our bench all shot her a look, but Niamh carried on, oblivious: 'It's just painful, Robyn, honestly. We were all having a barbie on Sunday and Dad was going, "You two will never get yourselves a husband if you don't stop spending all your time together; people will think you like women."'

I cringed. 'Oh, Jesus. What did Denise say?'

'Nothing, it wasn't Denise,' said Niamh, and I felt the familiar pang of guilt that I was bitchy-fishing about the woman who had basically been Niamh's mum since she was seven. 'She isn't homophobic. I don't think Dad is either, deep down, but that's different to *me* being gay, isn't it? What if they, you know . . . reject me?'

Just the thought made me feel murderous. 'Well, if they dare,' I said, 'I'll reject them.'

Our noodles came.

'How was Joe, anyway?' said Niamh, slurping her chicken ramen. She'd brightened after our little pep talk. 'Lovely Joe Sawyer. He's such a good 'un that boy.'

I nearly choked on mine.

'Hey, do you think now you've finished with Andy, you could get back together with Joe?'

That noodle seemed to be winding its way around my windpipe.

'Then Ethan would be my brother-in-law, which would be so unbelievably epic!'

Niamh loves Ethan. She and he spent a lot of time together that year after Mum died and I was with Joe. They're similar ages – Niamh would have been seven and Ethan eight – and Niamh, with no concept of him being different, used to lead him everywhere by the hand like her pet; Ethan gladly following, exploring bits of the vicarage garden, making up games – '*Right, you be the burglar and I'll be the policeman.*' I can see her now, with that mermaid hair and her bossy little face.

I steered the subject away from Joe, swiftly. I couldn't trust myself not to just spill. 'It was really good to see Ethan, actually. He's got a little job up at the garden

175

centre where Joe used to work, remember? It's such a shame this has happened with his mum because he seemed really happy.'

'That's fantastic. I'm so glad he's happy,' said Niamh, geniuinely.

Did that mean *she* wasn't?

After the meal, we wandered around Soho for a bit, Niamh telling me about her new contract (going around schools with the police service, doing role play about crime and punishment – it wasn't Hollywood, but it was a start) and the million different reasons why she was in love with Mary – or 'Mary Crane' as she calls her, because she always gives her girlfriend her full title, in the way that lovers do. She pointed out all the gay bars they'd been to together – a kind of impromptu and personal tour charting their love affair. How sad that out of our entire family, she only had me she could talk to about this stuff, I thought. The important stuff, that really matters.

Around 10 p.m., I walked her to the Tube. My little sister going back to *her* house, that she shared with *her* girlfriend. It all seemed so terribly grown up. When did that happen?

'You're not getting on the Tube?' she said.

'Um, no, I think I'll take the bus.'

'Okay, weirdo,' she said, nudging me jokingly. Niamh lived in Nottingham, where she went to university, until five months ago. The Tube – like noodles in Soho – is also a novelty.

I took a moment to look at her, illuminated by the city lights, outside Leicester Square Tube, and felt a lump in my throat (the hormones were making me hyper-emotional;

176

must get a grip). Her face had changed, become edgier somehow; but no less beautiful: she had a new, blunt fringe and together with the steel-grey eyes, the ivory skin, the slightly prominent jawline, there was an air of toughness to her that belied the childlikeness behind the eyes. Or maybe it was just that, to me, she'll always be seven years old.

'I'm glad I got to see you,' I said, hugging her. I hadn't told her my secret and in the same way a mother might worry about telling her first-born there was a baby on the way, I felt this was a betrayal.

'You, too, Rob. You sorted my head out as usual.' She pulled back and wrapped her arms around her leather jacket. 'Although I don't feel like I asked you how you are.'

I could have laughed. 'Oh, I'm fine,' I said. Now was neither the time nor the place. 'But I do have one question: You don't happen to know anything about Mum's ashes, do you?'

'What about Mum's ashes? That's a strange question.'

'Well, don't panic, but we can't find them. They haven't been where they usually are on the mantelpiece up at Dad's any more. I've asked Leah, but she didn't know, and, also, she was all funny about it, and I thought you might know where they are, or why she was being odd?'

'No, no idea, I'm afraid. Who knows the inner workings of that woman's mind.'

'Well, yeah, quite.'

'Anyway, bye,' she said, pecking me on the cheek. Mary's watching *Strictly* re-runs and wants us to watch it together.'

'Look at you two with your rock-and-roll life. Bye then, darling,' I said. 'Behave yourself.'

She pulled a silly face at me as she went down the steps to the Tube. Funny: should she perhaps have been more worried about the fact that we can't find our mother's ashes? But then as I walked to the bus stop, I considered that perhaps our mother is a collection of retold memories to Niamh. She was only seven when she died. She doesn't have many of her own memories. And it's good she's not too upset. It means she got off lightly.

I can't help but think, though, that Mum would have been cool, more than cool, she'd have been pleased, knowing that one of her girls was gay. She always did like to stick two fingers up to convention. This is the woman who held funerals for goldfish, after all.

Chapter Fourteen

Mid-June

I spoke to Joe another couple of times in the week before the scan appointment. He wanted to talk about the big picture: What the hell we were going to do? How was this co-parenting thing going to pan out? (I hadn't thought that far; it was all I could do to deal with the present.) But mainly about me and how I was feeling. He was tremendously keen that I look after myself and take it easy, that I sit on my expanding backside as much as possible and eat cake. I told him that shouldn't be a problem. Only at the end of the second conversation did he bring up the scan: 'But it's all right, I *know* you don't want me to come. I know when I'm not wanted.'

'Joe, it's not like that.'

'I know, I'm teasing.'

'I want you to be involved, I'd love for you to come to the scan with me, I just . . . at the moment. What if

179

there's something wrong? I'm worried if . . . It's not long since you lost your Mum.'

'Hey, hey, it's all right,' he said. 'Shuddup going on.'

We both laughed. I felt better.

On the morning of the scan, I was so nervous I thought I was going to throw up. I bumped into Eva on the way out – literally. She had her vast bottom in the air, rummaging in one of the five hundred bin bags she has piled up on the corridor outside our flats, wearing one of her psychedelic tent dresses. I wondered if she wore this stuff so she could be located in an emergency among her hoards of stuff.

She blocked my way with fake concern when she saw me.

'Mrs King. Where *you* goin' so early?'

'I've got a hospital appointment' I said. I really wasn't in a position to come up with anything cleverer on the spot.

You should have seen her eyes – wide as saucers.

'Nothin serious, I 'ope?'

Eva doesn't just hoard stuff, but information. She probably has files on everyone in this block, stacked high with the Polish newspapers going back several decades.

'No, no,' I said. 'Just a checkup. Anyway, Eva, about these bags. I need you to tell me at least when they might be moved . . . Is that reasonable . . .?' Was it? I'd lost track.

Eva put her hands on my shoulders then and looked at me through those eyes that widened and narrowed, like she was trying to hypnotise you.

'I bin sick,' she said, shaking her head gravely . . 'These

last few weeks. I bin teerrrible, terrrible, sickness, Mrs King. I bin to the doctor and is not good news . . .'

'I'm sorry to hear that,' I said with a sigh. The woman was a pathological liar, what can you do? I was going to have to chuck the bin bags out myself. 'Maybe we'll have a chat about this later,' I said, as I made my way down the stairwell.

'I like that,' she shouted after me. 'I make you cabbage Polish-style and tea!'

I made the short walk to the hospital, trying not to think too much about where I was going. Since I'd got the appointment in a long brown envelope marked NHS, this is how I'd dealt with it. One day at a time, trying not to think about it too much. I couldn't believe I'd made it to thirteen weeks without anyone at work guessing (except Kaye, of course).

I've lost count of the number of times I've made excuses at work these past five weeks. It's hard to keep your breakfast down at the best of times, many of the clients not exactly being big on hygiene. But John Urwin's flat was really getting to me: my morning gag reflex wasn't holding up to the skiddy pants left all over the flat, or the mugs of fag ends or (his new trick) the little piles of thick yellow nail clippings, sitting like mounds of tiny bones on the coffee table. In the end, I had to get Parv to go and do my visits to John for a few weeks, citing a sudden dust-mite allergy (like dust even figures on John's radar . . .). Then there's the recurrent stomach upset. I've had to avoid Friday beers.

'Are you getting sickly on us, Kingy?' Parv said the other day. 'I thought you were from the North?'

181

Thankfully, everyone's been mad busy recently. Jeremy's on the warpath about assessment forms, professionalism, 'boundaries' – honestly, you'd think patients were a different species, the way he carries on. Work has been a great distraction, but also it's been scary, sometimes, how adept I've been at pushing all this to the back of my mind. How I've been able, sometimes, to convince myself it's not happening at all.

I spotted him as soon as I turned the corner into Magdala Avenue. He was sitting on the steps of the hospital, feet wide, head in a newspaper, innocent as anything! And I thought, 'You bugger, Joe. You total bugger for turning up when I specifically told you not to.' And yet, I was smiling. Joe has one of those annoying faces you can't help smiling at: it's in his mobile eyebrows, the way his mouth twitches when he's lying or the way his nostrils flare slightly when he's excited, or concentrating, like he was now. I hung back and watched him. He was reading his paper, but every time someone walked up the steps, he said hello. It astounded me still, how friendly Joe was – far more friendly than me, who posed as an extrovert, but led a secret life, avoiding the phone and cursing uninvited guests. Joe would never *not* answer a phone-call, ever. He'd not just open the door gladly to any uninvited guest, but invite them in for a cup of tea and a chat. He stopped, looked around, and when he couldn't see me, put his newspaper down and lay back, arms behind his head.

I strode right over and stood, straddling him, blocking the light. 'Joseph,' I said.

He bolted upright. '*Shit!* What are you doing?' I was

laughing, served him right. 'You scared the living daylights out of me!'

'I feel maybe I should be saying that to you. What the hell are you *doing* here? I told you not to come.'

He grimaced, sheepishly. It was no use – I couldn't be cross with him.

'Well, I weighed it up, and I decided, whatever happens, I'd have to know some time.'

I sat down next to him. 'Know what?' I said, even though I knew what.

He put his arm around me. 'That you're gonna be fine, silly,' he said, pulling me into him in a way you might do to encourage a flagging kid on the football pitch. 'You and that baby are going to be absolutely fine.'

We sat there for a minute or two, in the sun, just watching people come and go – the odd hardcore smoker, in their pyjamas, the colour of tobacco themselves; relatives holding flowers and overnight bags; a heavily pregnant woman.

It was lovely to be sitting there with Joe's arm around me, the familiarity of it. Then I'd remember what we were there for. 'What if there's nothing there, Joe?' I said, resting my head on his shoulder. I felt his chest do a little puff. He thought I was being ridiculous. This was good.

'Then how's about we just make one anyway?' he said.

Dear Lily
I write to you from a purple chair, fixed to the floor of the dating-scans waiting room of the maternity department of the Whittington Hospital. I'm not good at hospitals at the best of times, but maybe that's because I have only ever been in them at the

183

worst of times. (I'm determined to work on this.) As soon as that gravy-mixed-with-chemicals smell hits me, I'm back in the chemo ward at Cumberland Hospital, with my bald, yellow Mum, doing puzzles with her, crossword after crossword.

I dreamt about her the other night – your grandma, that is. It was the most gorgeous dream – one of those you wake up from and want desperately to go back into, but never can. They always make me cry, those ones. In this dream, Mum and I were cycling along a promenade (Dreams never quite translate when you tell them in real time, do they?). But it was glorious, this prom, and the sea was sparkling, like it had silver sequins scattered all over it. Mum was wearing the terry-towelling short-suit she used to wear from May to October. She looked strong and beautiful and we were pedalling into this huge red sun. It was SO good to see her! I was pedalling really hard, trying to catch up, to touch her; but it didn't matter how fast I pedalled, I never could. Then, of course, I woke up.

Why am I telling you this? I think I'm more telling myself this, in the hope that by recounting that feeling the dream stirred in me last night, some of that Lillian King optimism might rub off on me, because I could really do with it today.

I'm scared, Lily. REALLY scared. Your father is sitting in the hospital canteen downstairs – because obviously he was going to turn up – and I didn't tell him this, but I've never been so glad to see someone in my life. The worst thing is, I used to be the

184

'sunny' child. I was the one your grandmother trusted to have her cup half full. Now, I don't know if it's even true of me. Sometimes I feel like I've let my mum down. Like that person she thought I was . . . Am I actually that person still? Or did what happen change me forever? I really hope not . . .

I put the notebook and pen in my bag. The waiting room was packed now: fifteen, twenty women, most with their partners (but, like me – Joe had agreed to wait in the hospital canteen – not all), sitting clutching notes, clutching hands, anxiously jiggling knees. The walls were filled with posters of doom – it was farcical – the dangers of catching whooping cough in pregnancy, of MRSA. There was one opposite me with the headline: HAVE YOU FELT YOUR BABY MOVE TODAY? If they were trying to scare the living daylights out of us, they were doing well.

Everyone looked so 'professionally' pregnant, too, so natural with it. I felt like a fraud, an impostor.

'So is this your twelve-week scan?' someone said.

I glanced briefly at her, the woman opposite, with a blonde bob and the creamy skin, but then I let my eyes drift to the poster about hand-washing above her head – I didn't think she could be talking to me.

'Sorry, I'm *so* nosy.' Then, I realized, she *was* talking to me.

'No, not at all . . .' I said. (Even though I thought she was a bit nosy, to tell you the truth.) 'Yes, it is . . .' but I could feel myself go red, like I'd been caught out, like that feeling you have when you're supposed to be introducing someone and suddenly find you've forgotten their name.

185

She looked at my midriff. 'Ooh, you're showing, for twelve weeks,' she said.

My hand flew to my stomach. 'Am I?'

'You've quite a little bump there, already, haven't you? Is it your first?'

'*Lorna*,' a man – her husband? – said. He had reddish, cropped hair and a friendly face. He rolled his eyes, affectionately.

'But that's *good*,' she said, nodding towards my stomach. A few other people had begun to look too; I was starting to feel self-conscious. 'It's good if you're big for your dates, means baby's healthy.'

'Or you've been eating for two since day one,' I said, and they both laughed.

'Sorry about my wife,' said the husband. 'She's obsessed. She's been talking to strangers like this ever since we found out.'

'It's true.' She giggled. She had one of those faces that looks like it's permanently on the cusp of a giggle. 'I've got this game: I eye up pregnant ladies then guess how pregnant they are. I'm usually right.'

'And she asks them,' he said.

'Um, yeah, *and* I ask them,' she admitted, giggling again.

'Maybe wise to keep that game to ladies in antenatal waiting rooms,' I said. 'Just in case they're not pregnant, they've just eaten all the pies.'

And we all laughed. There was a brief silence.

'So how many weeks *are* you?' she said, eventually.

'*Lorna!*'

'It's fine,' I said. 'About twelve, I think, maybe . . .' I didn't really feel like giving this stranger the exact details of my pregnancy.

'Maybe?' he said. 'About? *Gawd*, this one knows how many hours pregnant she is. Never off that Baby Central website thing.'

'It's Baby *Centre*, Ian, and you'd be complaining if I wasn't interested.'

'First, it's the size of an avocado.' He made the shape with his hands. I could tell he was the showman in this relationship, this one. That he married her because she was still wetting herself at his jokes, several years on. 'Then it's half a banana. Apparently, this week it can blink . . .'

'Aw,' said the woman, 'how sweet is that?'

'And if it's a boy, the balls will have descended.'

'Really?' I said. I was interested now. I generally approve of anyone who says words like 'balls' and 'descended' in public places. 'So I'm guessing this is your twenty-week scan then?' I said. If she was going to be nosy, so was I.

'Yes.' She beamed, rubbing her bump.

'And what are you hoping for – a boy?' I asked. She looked like a boy sort of mum. The homely outdoorsy type you could imagine standing around the rugby pitch in a few years' time.

'No, a girl.'

'Yes, a boy,' said the husband, and she gave him a withering look, 'with ginger hair.'

'I do *not* want ginger hair,' she said, slapping his leg. I could see the woman next to her – *bright* red hair – smirk and look at the ceiling.

Ian tugged at the hair he had left. 'We need to keep this Viking living on!'

'I'd love a little girl,' she said, 'with blonde hair and brown eyes. I've always loved that combination.'

'Mrs Lawley?' Just then, a nurse popped her head around the door. 'You can come through now, if you're ready.'

'Good luck,' I said, as they were ushered excitedly into a room.

I watched as he gently closed the door behind them. I thought, *I don't care if it's a boy or a girl. I just want everything to be okay.*

The scanning room was perfectly white and quiet, with a small square window from which you could see a courtyard of the hospital. The sonographer had a soft, kind voice, which set me off as soon as she started talking, and she was so covered in freckles that they joined up – like Mum. This was going to be interesting.

'So, Mrs King . . .' she said, looking at her clipboard.

'Actually, it's Miss,' I said.

'Oh. I'm so sorry,' she said. 'Honestly, these GPs. Sometimes I wonder if they actually listen; do you know what I mean?'

I did. The GP I'd seen had looked about twenty-one, still with the remnants of teenage acne and, frankly, looked terrified by what I'd told him.

She smiled as she amended my notes. '*Miss* King; there we are, let's get it right from the start, shall we?' I watched her as she wrote on my pink notes. I wondered what was on those notes.

'Now, if you'd just like to pop yourself on the bed, and roll your jeans and knickers down to your hip bones.'

I got up on the bed, the paper lining dry and rustling beneath me, and began to undo the belt of my jeans, but my fingers were trembling so much it was difficult. She smiled, encouragingly. 'Everything okay?'

'Yes, sorry.'

Do not have a panic attack in here. Hold it together. Breathe.

'They're fiddly those things, aren't they?' she said. 'You take your time, there's no rush . . .'

She must know, I thought. She must. Or maybe she was being extra nice to me because I was here on my own. I thought of Joe sitting in the hospital canteen and really wished I wasn't. I'd realized far too late that he was the only person in the world who knew how I was feeling.

'Okay, lovely, so just lie back and relax,' she said, when I'd finally got it together enough to undo my belt. I stared at the blinking monitor in front of me. I felt suddenly powerless before this thing, at its mercy. My hands were shaking so much, I thought she might think I was mad, or a raging alcoholic with DTs, and couldn't decide which was worse.

She turned around away from me. I could hear the 'slick, slick' as the latex gloves went on.

'Ah, you're a leg wiggler,' she said, turning back. 'We get so many leg-wigglers, I can't tell you, and the problem is, it makes baby wiggle too.' I tried to smile at her, but my lips had gone so dry they stuck to my teeth. 'No need to worry, we're not at the dentist now.'

I managed a pathetic laugh. 'Okay, now this might be a bit cold . . .'

I felt the jelly go on, then the scanner glide over my belly, like a detector searching for precious metal. 'Right, baby,' she said. 'This is your moment.'

Suddenly, everything seemed to hang on that moment. Everything. The rest of my life like I was balancing on a tightrope and one way was happiness and one wasn't and it really could go either way.

Above all, I suddenly wanted this baby more than I'd ever wanted anything in my whole life but, to my horror, there was nothing, just quiet. As she slid the scanner over my skin, soundlessly, I could hear a heartbeat, but it was my own. There were black and white shapes on the screen, but they were fuzzy; shifting and morphing, like a storm tracker, and I couldn't make anything out. What were probably six or seven seconds went by but it felt like an age and, without warning, my chest heaved and I let out this almighty sob; so big and uncontrollable that a bubble of snot escaped from my nose. It was violent crying, like I hadn't known since I was a child.

'Oh, gosh.' The nurse looked very alarmed and I felt guilty, like she'd just been witness to a trauma, inches from her, and that that trauma was me. 'Oh, dear, sweetheart, you are nervous, aren't you? . . . Should I . . .? Do you want me to . . .?' I had my hand over my face, I was hiccupping, mortified.

Then, a soft knock at the door. 'Can I come in?' someone said.

And then there was Joe, poking his head around the door, holding a cup of coffee, his eyes full of concern, and I've never been so glad to see someone in my life.

'*Yes*,' I said. The relief must have been so obvious in my voice, because the nurse kind of laughed. 'Yes, please,' I said. 'Can he? This is Joe, he's the father.'

'Oh, well,' she said. 'Oh, good. Well come in, Joe, take a pew.' Joe drew up a chair, and took my hand. It was warm from the coffee. 'She's a little bit upset,' said the nurse, unnecessarily. Joe didn't say a thing; he just pulled some tissue from a dispenser on the wall and wiped my face.

'Baby's heartbeat's just being a bit shy at the moment. But I am sure, any minute now . . .'

The nurse cleared her throat. I squeezed Joe's hand. I swear, it was like ten minutes had gone past, then, like one of those visual tricks that you have to stare at for several seconds before something emerges, it was there: a head, the very clear outline of eye sockets, a nose, a little stomach, limbs. Tears were sliding down my temples into my ears. I was willing it with every cell in my body.

'The heartbeat?' I said. 'I can't hear . . .'

And then came this noise; the most glorious noise, like a horse galloping across a beach.

'*There* we are!' The relief in the sonographer's voice was tangible – you could have held it in your hands. '*Lovely* strong heartbeat. And look! Baby's waving at you . . .'

I looked at Joe. He was grinning, his eyes full of tears too.

'Oh, bless,' said the nurse. 'It's so nice when you get the emotional ones – it's always so emotional when it's your first.'

I looked at the ceiling. I felt like laughing, I don't know why.

'It's not my first,' I said.

Chapter Fifteen

'Did you hear that heartbeat?' I said to Joe, on the way down in the lift, like our baby's heartbeat was special, more miraculous than anyone else's baby's heartbeat. 'It was going like the clappers!'

We had to get off at Level 3, to change lifts to get down to the main entrance, and I could hear a woman screaming in the labour ward, and then the cry of a baby – we looked at one another, eyebrows raised. To think, in six months, this could actually happen! I did not dare.

Outside, the sun had come out. Joe looked at me. 'I wish they gave you an audio of the heartbeat, as well as a visual scan – I'd play it in the bath,' he said, as we walked down the steps of the hospital and out into the still warmth of the day. 'On surround sound.'

'Exactly,' I said. 'Don't they do apps for that, anyway? Where you can listen to your baby's heart? You're going to become like one of those super-parents, who puts their scan pic on Facebook, has their baby's footprint framed, plays the heartbeat soundtrack at dinner parties . . .'

'Yeah, and . . .?' said Joe, shrugging. 'What's wrong with that?'

I squeezed his hand. He probably would too. He was so fabulously unashamed.

We decided to go to Waterlow Park. I couldn't remember feeling so happy in a long time. We turned up Dartmouth Park Hill and it was only as we were scaling it – or at least it felt like that for me – that we realized we were still holding hands, that we'd been holding them since we'd been in the lift. We looked at one another and laughed shyly, then dropped them, even though I could have quite happily held Joe's hand all day. It felt lovely – soft and big and familiar in mine. I was thinking about that place where our fingers inter-linked, about the warmth radiating from his body and flowing into mine. After the intimacy of what had just happened, I felt almost postcoital, bathed in loveliness and feel-good hormones. I felt close to Joe in a way I'd never felt about Andy, and yet I knew that holding hands was as far as I could go now with Joe; that trying to have a proper (i.e. physical and romantic) relation-ship with him now I was pregnant again would bring back memories of that terrible time in my life that I'd kept in a locked box until this happened. All those painful memories.

But it couldn't have been a more beautiful day to catch the first glimpse of your baby. The air smelt of honeysuckle and promise. I closed my eyes and inhaled as I slowly made my way up the hill, Joe at my side, trying to be in this moment, to push away the other thing trying to seep its way into my consciousness – a memory: Joe and I, a wet autumn day; me in a red coat and bad roots – the

194

green-tinged blonde growing out. I won't be able to dye it for a while.

We are sitting on the swings in Kilterdale Park, there are damp leaves at our feet – and this strange fungus. I don't know why I remember the fungus – it somehow adds to the awfulness of that time in my head – but it is yellow and looks like soggy little pancakes stacked on top of one another.

I have the positive-pregnancy test in my hand. Joe has his arm around me, rubbing my back; trying to be a man when he is still a boy. And it feels like the world as I know it, has ended. Like the earth has literally fallen through my feet. I am sixteen. My mother is dead and I am about to be a mother myself, to a baby I don't want and don't think I can love, and I am petrified.

Joe suddenly spoke, bringing me back to the present. 'God, I feel so happy,' he said.

It made me physically jolt. Joe wore not just his heart on his sleeve, but his soul. What must that be like? To have no secrets? No demons? To have nothing come to haunt you in the small hours?

He said, 'I told you it would be fine, didn't I?'

'You did,' I said, laying my head on his shoulder. 'You did.'

'I was so nervous, though.'

'I knew it!' I said. 'I knew you were deep down. I was picturing you pacing around the canteen.'

Things of course could still go wrong, I knew that, although it didn't feel like the time to talk about this. No, this was a good moment. The air out here was fresh and scented with blossom. Everything was so verdant. It was the start of summer and, if I could just let it, it could be the start of something else, too.

We passed Highgate Mental Hospital.

'You see,' said Joe, 'you go mad with this pregnancy and it's just a hop, skip and a jump to the local mental facility.'

'Ha-ha, very funny,' I said, while at the same time thinking, 'Don't joke, Joe.' I hadn't mentioned to him about the panic attacks, or the episode in Tim's car, or the fact that since I'd found out I was pregnant again, scenes from the past – unwanted, intrusive scenes – kept coming at me like meteorites to earth. I didn't want to. Joe had already been through enough recently without having to deal with my internal drama. No, this was now, and now was good, and that was all that mattered.

I had one eye on where we were going and one on the scan picture. I couldn't take my eyes off it. Joe craned his neck to look at it, too.

'It's pretty amazing, isn't it?' he said. I watched him looking at the picture: holding it up this way and that, the way his eyes crinkled at the side, the half-smile of delight that played on his lips, and this little firework of hope exploded inside of me. I stopped.

'It feels like a second chance, Joe,' I said, and in that moment I believed it. I really did. 'It feels like someone, somewhere, thought, "Actually, those two would make quite cool parents. Shall we give them another chance?"'

Joe lifted up his arms, as if to the heavens: 'At last!' he cried, dramatically, sillily. 'At last the woman sees sense!'

'Honestly. So rude,' I said. He put his arm around me and we walked together in the sunshine.

Waterlow Park was blissfully peaceful: squares of mani-cured gardens, undulating pathways, and weeping willows falling into sun-dappled ponds. The sun shone through the lace pattern that the leaves of the trees made and, whenever you came to a clearing, it was so bright and still you could have traced the jagged skyline of London: the Barbican, the Gherkin, glowing orange like a rocket, and the sprawl beyond them. St Paul's floated out on a limb, looking like it was from another world.

'What time's your train?' I asked Joe.

'Oh, I've got time.'

I don't think either of us wanted the day to end.

We ended up going back to my flat, since it was only a short walk away. Joe said he'd have a cup of tea and then get off. I took us a different way, so we didn't pass the Tube.

The streets were warm and the houses looked bleached, in that way they do after a long, hot day. We had our arms around each other and were dragging our feet, not really out of necessity, but because we wanted the journey to last longer, even though I was genuinely tired from all the walking. It didn't take much these days to tire me out.

I looked over at Joe.

'So, don't you think this is kind of . . . odd?' I said, at last. He frowned. He looked a bit hurt. 'I don't mean in a bad way.'

'Explain yourself, King.'

'Well, just, we're having a *baby*! We've just been to the first scan of *our baby* and, yet, we haven't seen one another properly for sixteen years, and the first time we do, I'm up the duff, and now here you are, and you're still Joe, and yet a different Joe, and yet the same Joe . . . and . . .' He was smirking at my ramblings. The unsaid, the main point, the events of the past, hung above us like a huge cloud, threatening rain. 'Well, doesn't it freak you out a bit?'

He had his sunglasses on so I couldn't read his eyes.

'Maybe.' He shrugged. 'But then it's nice, isn't it? This has been a great day. You're my friend.'

'And you're my friend, too,' I said, somewhat overzealously. (I didn't have to worry. He wasn't expecting anything more.)

'I really like you. I happen to think you're rather clever and funny and interesting.'

'Oh, Joe,' I said.

'I can think of worse people to have a baby with.'

'Me too.'

'It's so nice, after everything, to have a new life to think about.'

'It is,' I thought, 'it really is.'

It was like Eva was waiting for us. As soon as we approached her flat and were about to navigate the bin bags, she flung open the door.

'*Oh*,' she said, looking Joe up and down. Her greasy hair was clumped at the back, like she'd just got up. 'Zis your man-friend, Mrs King?'

'Actually, I'm her husband,' said Joe, straight-faced. I'd told him about Eva, 'touched' on the bin-bag situation. Eva's mouth made an 'O' and her eyebrows looked like they might sail right over her head, they went so high.

'Don't believe him, Eva,' I said, shooting Joe a look, and taking his hand to guide him around the bin bags. Eva certainly didn't need anyone to fuel her imaginings. God knows what story she'd concoct – whatever it was, it couldn't be as good as the real one. I leaned against the bin bags, scrabbling in my bag for my keys, trying to get inside the flat as quickly as possible.

'You moving?' said Joe.

'Nooo,' said Eva, 'not moving.'

'She's moving her bags soon, though, aren't you, Eva?' I said, opening the door.

'She harass me all the time,' she said, wagging her finger at me. 'She lovely girl, but she so impatient.'

I took Joe's coat, to hang it up in the hallway.

'Has she always had those bags there?' he asked.

'Yep, and they just keep growing,' I said, taking his bag from him, too. He'd brought a little rucksack with supplies, which was just so Joe.

'Have you ever asked her to move them?'

'Er, yes! Don't get me started.'

'Do you know how mad that is? To step over those every day. You're as crazy as her.'

'Joe, you have a lot to learn about me and my life, and my job, if you think that's even close to crazy,' I joked, gesturing for him to follow me into the kitchen.

I made tea, while Joe walked from room to room with slow, even footsteps. It was so quiet, I could hear his breathing. I strained the tea bag against the side of the mug for far too long, my stomach tense. It felt like I was selling and he was a prospective buyer.

Eventually, he appeared at the kitchen door. After the intensity of the day, I was extra aware of his gaze, his presence. Joe Sawyer was in my flat. He was in my home. I was carrying his baby . . . I don't know whether it was the sheer absurdity of this, or the atmosphere – which had stretched so taut I thought something might snap – but

I started laughing, and Joe joined in. Maybe he was thinking the same thing.

'So this is chez Robbie?' he said, when we'd stopped.

'Yep, my humble abode.' I was pleased someone had said something, anything.

'It's cute,' he said, 'but what's that noise?'

I handed him his tea. 'What noise?' I said.

'That one like we're in an aeroplane and we're about to take off.'

I listened, then felt my cheeks grow hot. It had gone on so long I barely noticed it any more.

'Oh, now, that'll be the dehumidifiers.'

'The dehumidifiers?'

'Yes.'

'How many have you got?'

'Um, four.'

'*Four?*' he said, loudly.

'It is quite damp,' I said, 'riddled with it, unfortunately, but I am getting it sorted.' I cringed. Suddenly, the dehumidifiers seemed to roar, drowning out our voices. 'I promise you, I am!'

Joe sighed and cocked his head mock-sternly. 'Now, Robyn King, you are carrying my child,' he joked, even though I could see he wasn't joking, not really, 'and as of now, no child of mine, or any mother carrying my child, is going to live in a flat that smells of the inside of a tent and sounds like a wind tunnel.'

I made pasta and we played music – Led Zeppelin (naturally), but also Red Hot Chili Peppers, Stereophonics, stuff we'd listened to that year in our bedrooms and on crackly tapes in Joe's rubbish Metro – the soundtrack of summer

200

1997. Joe had got excited telling me about such-and-such a band he'd heard or seen play in Manchester. I hadn't heard of any of them.

'What have you been doing for the last sixteen years?'

Thing is, I didn't know. It felt like I'd been sleep-walking through a sixteen-year fog and, now Joe was here, I was remembering a little of what life used to feel like, during those golden three months, May to August 1997. Before Butler, the pregnancy and, losing Lily.

'Well, I have spent probably more time than the average person in mental asylums,' I said.

It wasn't long before Joe gravitated, as people do, to the many photographs I had around the flat. I stood watching him, self-consciously, taking in the map of his profile – the same face as the one of sixteen years ago, but sharper, somehow; more defined. More Joe. I liked it more. I wondered what he was thinking, what he expected of all this, of us. I knew two things: I was loving him being here; but also, when I thought about being with him, as a couple again, my stomach tied in knots with the fear that the past would repeat itself, that I wouldn't be able to finish what I'd started and that I'd hurt him all over again.

He shuffled his way around the flat, nose close to the photographs, making little noises of amusement at such-and-such a hair disaster, fashion disaster. I was thinking about that first time I ended it with Joe – his face then, how hurt he'd been . . .

'I feel like we're back in the museum,' I said, Joe still looking at my photos. 'All my Palaeozoic eras laid out for you to see. See what joys and pleasures you missed out on?' I added, as he worked his way through the

201

poodle perm and my vampy university days with the dark lips and the pale face – waaaay too much make-up. Around the millennium, there was a scary foray into a business image, as I tried to tell myself I'd be a lot happier, if I just got myself a job in recruitment, a boyfriend who worked in sales and was normal. Joe peered at the result, shaking his head: me in a pale grey suit, my curly hair straightened and highlighted blonde, and pulling a face. 'I call those my "Karren Brady" years,' I said. 'Before I realized my true spiritual home was working with the clinically insane.'

He gave me a once-over. 'I like you much more like this,' he said. 'Much, much more.'

He moved into the hallway, while I hid in the kitchen, but then I heard him say, 'Oh, *God*,' and rushed out to see what the fuss was about. 'Was this the day . . .?'

I peered over his shoulder at the photo. Me, Beth and some other girls from school at Tania Richardson's wedding. I was looking middle-aged in a beige linen trouser suit and straw hat, holding the hand of my beloved at the time: Brendan Lloyd Yeomans (he was known to introduce himself using his full title). After several years of feeling lost and off the rails, I had finally found 'security' in B.L.Y. when I worked in the university holidays at Clinton Cards and he was area manager.

Joe peered even more closely at the photo. 'Is that . . .?' he said again.

'Yep.'

'Is that that wedding where . . .?'

'You told my boyfriend he was a prick with a ridiculous name then proceeded to throw up all over his shoes?'

Joe put a hand on my shoulder and gave it an

apologetic pat. 'I was just crushed with jealousy,' he said, 'and also, I've never forgiven myself.'

Then we said in unison, 'Yeah, but he so was.'

The flat glowed buttery yellow, orange and pink with the setting sun, and nobody said anything about a train home to Manchester. I was glad. For the first time in weeks, I felt completely calm, like everything was going to be okay – that, whatever happened, today would be a good memory, and I definitely needed more of those.

We somehow ended up in my bedroom, looking at more old pictures of us: in fancy dress at a friend's seventies party; lying on the school field, outside the caravan in Lyme Regis; that weird first holiday with Denise and her plethora of Lakeland Plastics gadgets, Joe gaunt, pasty and centre-parted, floppy-haired. 'God, and I thought you were literally beautiful,' I said. I did, too, but the truth was he was more beautiful now, more fully formed – dare I say it, a man! I'd said this to him that fated night in the barn, while hammered on Jack Daniel's, and he'd laughed his head off at me, but it was true.

Afterwards, we lay on my bed. I felt like I could fall asleep. After a few seconds, Joe sighed, dramatically. 'God, this is awful,' he said. 'Am I allowed to touch you?'

I sighed and wriggled closer to him. I guessed the 'What about us?' conversation had to come soon, I just wasn't expecting it to be *so* soon and for Joe to be *so* blatant.

The room was almost dark, just his white-towelling socks glowing. He always did wear terrible white socks. I felt my chest tighten.

'Joe?' I said.

'Mmm?'

'You do know I can't do it, don't you?'

203

I had my head right next to his chest and swore I felt his heart thud. 'Do what?' he said.

'Oh, not the baby,' I said, realizing he might think I meant that. Even though I worried every day I couldn't do the baby, or rather the baby wouldn't do me. 'I mean, a relationship, a proper one. The physical side of things?'

He was quiet. What had I said?

'I know I pounced on you at your mum's funeral, and I know I must have given that impression, but now this has happened . . .'

'You realize now the shit has hit the fan that you don't feel that way about me?'

He didn't say it in a wounded way, just as a statement of fact, but he sounded disappointed.

'No. Yes,' I said, then, 'I just can't Joe, I'm sorry.'

He gave a long sigh. I felt suddenly so empty, hollow. Why did life have to be so complicated? Then he said, 'It's okay. I had the brush-off outside the museum. I get the picture.'

'Oh, Joe,' I said, 'I'm sorry.'

'It's all right, you'll come round,' he said. He made it sound like a joke but I knew it wasn't.

'There's just too much that's gone on with us,' I continued. 'Losing Lily . . .'

It was the first time I had said her name out loud and he went very quiet, just shifted his head on the pillow, but it was enough to tell me that those feelings were still close to the surface. 'We've been through too much . . .'

He raised his eyebrows at me. 'Um excuse me. Don't tell me what I can't handle,' he said.

'Okay, I feel *I've* been through too much – to handle it,'

I corrected myself. 'Too much water under the bridge. It's my fault. I'm so sorry.'

He sighed, ruefully, and looked at me for rather a long time. Then he took my hand and kissed it. 'It's okay,' he said, quietly, as if he'd needed that time to square everything in his head. 'It's okay, I understand.'

We lay there for a while, then Joe spoke suddenly into the half-light: 'I don't want to be a weekend dad, that's all I'll say,' he said, as if he was telepathic, as if he could read my thoughts exactly: *So what the hell do we do now?* 'I don't want to be the kind of dad who just takes him or her swimming and to Pizza Hut. I want to be there for the hard bits, too; the interesting, tricky bits. I want to deal with the potty training and when they're naughty and the homework and the teaching him or her about life, you know?'

'Worry not,' I said, 'I'm sure that can be arranged. You're going to be great at that, Joe,' I added, feeling a new surge of optimism. 'Really great.'

'I want to be useful.'

'Joe,' I said, 'you already are.'

I turned on my side, so I was facing him. I was inches from his mouth and I wondered if I should just kiss him, because part of me wanted nothing more; and the other part of me was telling myself, *No*: it'd been a wonderful but emotional day but I shouldn't try to run before I walked. If I was patient, maybe I'd be able to just go with it. Maybe we'd have a chance?

'Do you know what I'm dreading?' I asked. 'Bloody antenatal classes. I saw one advertised today in the hospital – it was called Bump Club.'

'*Bum* Club? Sounds a bit suspect.'

I laughed. That was just *so* Joe. 'No, you idiot. *Bump* Club.'

'Oh,' said Joe, 'still sounds suspect.' I loved how I didn't have to explain why I didn't want to go to any antenatal class. Then he said, 'Well, I've got an idea. How about, if you don't want to go to antenatal classes and have me massage your coccyx or whatever it is they get you to do, and I want to be useful . . . how about we create a kind of *Alternative* Antenatal Class? A list of stuff you can do to prepare for the baby and keep your mind occupied that's not preparing your nipples, or doing pelvic workouts . . .'

I was laughing into the pillow, with despair more than anything else, and because I knew he wasn't even trying to make me laugh; he probably did think they did these sorts of things at antenatal class. Joe could easily get the wrong end of the stick like that – run with an idea and that would be it.

'What like, a programme of tasks?' I said.

'Yes, exactly,' said Joe. 'Just so you have something to focus on, to fill that head of yours –' he tapped my forehead – 'with actual useful, practical things, rather than incessant worrying about stuff you can't control.'

He still knows me, I thought. *He still knows me really well.*

'Because you can't control it, Robbie, you know?' he said seriously. 'And I can't, nobody can make you a hundred-per-cent promise that it won't happen again. But I want you to know that I'm here, whatever, and that I *believe* it, won't happen again. And I want you to believe it, too – that's all I ask.'

I smiled, thinly. 'I'll do my best,' I said.

'Good. So since it's my Alternative Antenatal Class—' he continued.

'Oh, it's yours now, is it?'

'We can just call it AA. Keep it simple. The Twelve Step AA. Nobody need know what it stands for.'

'Right, so they'll just think I'm like a pregnant alcoholic? Which is nice, which is classy.'

'You know what I mean,' said Joe, sitting up. 'You in?' I rattled around in my bedside table for some paper and a pen.

'Yeah, I'm in.' I smiled. Joe still had the ability to make me feel better.

And so we sat up in bed, like an old married couple, trying to come up with twelve points – just so it fitted in with the Twelve Step AA theme, really, not because there really were twelve to speak of. Some of them were there just to amuse us, like 'massage nipples daily' and 'knit range of unisex matinee coats', but most were practical, or just stuff that was worrying me, taking up emotional energy where I needed it all for the job in hand, stuff I'd been putting off for ages:

- Sort out damp.
- Find Mum's ASHES!!
- Get Eva to move her bags.
- Help Niamh to come out to the rest of the family. (We decided, if all else failed, I'd just tell everyone. It had been so long, I doubted Niamh was ever going to do it, and she'd just moan to me and pretend to be someone she wasn't with them forever. It wouldn't do . . .)
- Make more effort with Leah. I suspected some of

207

the reason we weren't as close as we were before was because I was also guilty of communicating through the kids (they were much easier, after all, but that was no excuse).

- Exercise (Joe had always done loads of exercise, like cycling, karate; whereas, over the years, work had encroached on everything). Start making time for swimming again.
- Help Grace: help her reconnect with the things that matter to her: photography, her daughter.
- BUT stop thinking you can *save* everyone, however – you can only do your best. Emotional vampires are out; thinking about Number One and Baby is in.
- Decorate the flat – de-clutter AND decorate spare room for baby.
- BELIEVE – Joe wrote this one on the end and underlined it twice.

We lay back again afterwards, the day's setting sun throwing a warm and very pleasant blanket around our legs. I was so tired, so relaxed, so content (I couldn't actually recall the last time I had felt content), I could easily have fallen asleep there, if I hadn't been next to Joe: he's one of those people who's very difficult to share a tent or a bed with because, when everyone else understands that point where you stop talking and go to sleep, he keeps talking.

I shut my eyes, just as he took a breath.

'So, Robbie . . .'

'Mmm.'

'I was thinking . . .' He turned his head. 'Are you asleep?'

208

'This is very pleasant, actually, Joe. I was thinking of having a little nap.' I patted his thigh, sleepily. 'Maybe you should have one, too.'

'Okay,' he said. He cleared his throat and wriggled for a bit longer, put one arm behind his head and an arm by his side. I could feel the edge of his little finger touching my thigh, the warmth emanating from it, like, if I were to look down there, there would be a spotlight. We lay there, still, listening to the soothing coo of a wood pigeon outside, the sigh of far-off traffic. I was thinking how lovely it would be just for him to fall asleep here for the night. Nothing else. Just for there to be Joe when I woke up, so we could hang out and I could make him one of my Kingy Breakfast Specials, make some Twits TV.

'Robyn?' he said again.

I sighed. 'What? You always used to do that, you *still* do that, just go on and on. Never let me just go to sleep, have any peace. *Jesus . . .*' I pretended to punch my pillow and weep for comic effect. 'I just want to go to sleep!'

He thumped my leg. 'Stop saying I always did this and I always did that,' he said, laughing and yet irritated, I could tell. 'I have grown up a little bit in sixteen years, you know. I'm a *man* now,' he added in a stupid low voice, then, in this voice filled with wonder, said, 'I'm going to be a *dad.*'

'Well shut up then.' I teased.

'Okay,' he said. 'I'm shutting up *now.*'

We must have fallen asleep, because I woke up to find it was dark and Joe was in silhouette, sitting up on the bed, his back to me.

'What are you doing?' I said.

209

'Going,' he whispered.

He stood up, straightened his T-shirt and rubbed his face. When he glanced down at me, his eyes were still unfocused, his face crumpled with sleep. It took all my resolve in that moment not to pull him back onto the bed.

'You don't have to,' I said.

He was patting his pocket for his wallet and keys but stopped. 'I do,' he said.

I got up to say goodbye to him at the door. It was 9.25 p.m. and the stairwell outside my flat was dark, save for two sidelights that automatically come on when they sense someone.

'So you are disappearing into the London night?' I said.

'Yes, that's what I do, you see,' he whispered, leaning in. 'I lure exes to funerals, sow my seed, turn up unannounced at their scans, just to check the seed is sown and my work here is done, then I disappear into the London night, leaving them wanting more. It's my MO.'

He drew back, clicking his tongue, smoothly. He could still act.

'It's flawless,' I said.

'Isn't it just?'

'And your hair is sticking up,' I whispered. It was casting a great big horn-shaped shadow on the wall behind him. 'It looks like you've got a huge rhino horn on your head.'

He inhaled through his nose, as if to say something important and intelligent but actually said, 'I'm going to resist the urge to make jokes about horniness. And I'm going to go . . .'

'You really can stay on the sofa,' I said. 'I'm worried, it's late. I'm worried you're not going to be back in

Manchester till like one a.m. What if you fall asleep and end up in Carlisle?' It was cold now and I was shivering.

'Check *you* out,' he said. 'You get a bun in the oven and you can't resist me, hormones all over the place.'

'*Joe.*' I tutted, but he had a point. I was confusing him, giving out mixed messages. No, it wasn't fair. 'Yes, you're right, you have to go.'

'I am going,' he said, but he was manhandling me by the shoulders and pushing me back inside. 'And I'm joking about the not being able to resist me bit. Well, sort of.'

'Go. It's freezing,' I said.

'Okay. Bye . . .' he said.

'Bye,' I said.

Then he kissed me on the cheek, once, and he left. I could hear him whistling, going two at a time down the steps. I stood, the door open for a few minutes, then I went back inside, and I pulled out the box of letters and I went down to the bottom of the pile, to find the first one I ever wrote.

Kilterdale
12 October 1997

Dear Lily
Hello. You don't know me yet but I am your mum. You are sixteen weeks old, but I have only known about you for three. Right now, I am sitting on my bed, writing this, listening to 'Bron-Yr-Aur' by Led Zeppelin. It is so beautiful. One day, I want to walk down the aisle with your father to this song.

Since telling Dad and Dad's girlfriend, Denise,

about you, three days ago, this is where I have mainly been. I'm banned from seeing Joe at the moment, which is ridiculous; because your dad (who is seventeen, lest we not forget) is dealing with this situation far better than my own father at the moment, who CANNOT COPE!! I'm angry with him, but I feel guilty, too. He loses his wife, and now, his middle daughter – the one supposed to be the 'strong' one – gets pregnant at sixteen. I hate the fact this has happened, but I realize that this, and how you came to be, has nothing to do with YOU, this little life growing inside of me. And that's why it helps me to write to you, because you're separate to everything, so I can tell you everything. I'm going to imagine that you live in a place where nothing bad happens and life is wonderful. And I'm going to do my best to write only lovely stuff: to tell you about what your grandma was like, how great she was, how great your dad is.

I've seen you on a scan, and since that scan, a week ago, I've kept the little picture in my wallet. I often get it out to remind myself that you are real, and that you are mine and that, whatever happens, you are half me. Your father has been amazing. I don't care what they say about teenage dads, he's been absolutely amazing – especially at school, because some people have been pretty nasty. Still, at least I've stopped being sick now. They say that if you're sick a lot, you're probably having a girl, and I really hope you're a girl, because I want to call you Lily after my mum. She is part of you, after all.

Chapter Sixteen

There's a promenade again; the sea, but this time it's dark and it's late and there are lights; illuminations. Blackpool Illuminations, perhaps? But they're grander, much brighter than I remember them; strings and strings of them, hung up like necklaces made of the brightest jewels and all in different shapes: flowers and stars and dancers and sea creatures. Mum is here, of course – she's next to me, but this time we are travelling fast, rolling along this prom in some sort of contraption. It's red and yellow metal with a canopy over our heads, and it's being driven by a girl with a swishy, golden ponytail.

We're moving quite fast now, through this lit-up night-world, Mum and I, the breeze pushing the hair from our faces, our thighs jostling when we go over bumps. The air smells of candy-floss and home, salty, briny and slightly fetid – that North Sea pungent smell – and, if we look to our right, the lights from the illuminations are playing on the water: smudged, muted discs of colour, like Smarties with the coating sucked off, changing formation like far-off dancers. I am mesmerized by these lights. I let them burn the backs of my retinas with their warmth. I turn back to Mum, to say something, to tell her how beautiful they are, how I'm having the night of my life! But when I turn back, she's fading from view and I'm saying, 'Mum, Mum, don't go!' But she's gone. Vanished. And then I am travelling all alone and the air has grown cold.

I am woken up by the sound of my breath being expelled from me, as if coming back from the dead – it's always the same with these dreams; then there's the ringing in my ears like I've just stepped from a nightclub or circus, from the kaleidoscope brightness of the world with my mother in, to the dark, cool quiet of my room.

I put a hand to my belly and could be sixteen again, doing the same thing, lying bewildered in my childhood bed and wanting my mum. I miss her all over again and ten-fold. Damn these dreams, they always make me cry.

A sound starts up next door. Eva, ferreting around like a cat, or a trapped pigeon, rearranging boxes, no doubt, so she can sleep lying down. I remember the AA list of last night, Joe's face as he wrote it, the way he sent a hand across the stubble on his cheekbones, so thought-fully, conscientiously. I really must get tough about those bags.

I look at the clock. It's 3.26 a.m. At 3.30 a.m., the record player goes on: 'Bridge Over Troubled Water', which is seven minutes, thirty-four seconds long; I know, because I've timed it. Usually, I am cursing her. This time, however, I am glad of the company because my mind is racing. The dream has disturbed things, brought up more scenes from the past that play, as clearly as film clips, in my mind. Hormones probably heightening things, making them sharper.

Right now, it's 22 August, the day my life changed forever. It's odd, but when I think back to what happened that late summer's evening down Friars Lanes, it's like I've got peripheral vision: I remember in vivid detail what happened before and immediately after, but when it comes to the central event itself, it's a blurred black spot, a sensory wasteland.

I'd been to Bubbles Waterpark with Beth that afternoon. She'd been getting it on all summer with a twenty-year-old lifeguard called Sean, and he'd let us in for free – Beth had been so proud. My penance was, she then talked to him all day or pranced about in the wave machine, losing her bikini top on purpose. I didn't mind. I was too busy sunbathing, keeping one eye on the entrance, hoping Joe's lovely face might appear at the door. We'd only been seeing one another for three months – since that day at the Blackhorse Quarry – and were still in that stage of wanting to spend every minute of every day with one another. I miss those times of longing and missing and hoping; those times before mobile phones.

We'd gone to the slot machines after Bubbles and won some money. The plan was, we'd buy a bottle of Taboo for the party that night. The party was at one of the Farmer's houses – a boy called Tony Middleton – and everyone was going to be there, all my friends, the Farmers, the Townies and, of course, Joe. Tony's parents were away somewhere exotic; it was to be the party of the summer. I couldn't wait.

The plan was, Joe would pick me up and we'd walk

together to the party about a mile away. But when I got home from being out with Beth, he rang to say he'd been out on a boat with his mates all day near the party, so would it be okay if he met me there? I said that was fine – Dad could give me a lift.

But Dad wouldn't give me a lift.

'You're not going to a bloody party in the middle of nowhere and that is final.'

Everything was 'final' in those days with Dad, mainly because he just didn't have the energy or motivation to argue or negotiate about anything.

I left it till late – 8.30 p.m.-ish – then spun him some tale that Beth wasn't allowed to go either and that I was going over to hers for a sleepover instead. He was several pints of Boddingtons down then, so he didn't argue.

I put on my new flippy frock with the pink roses all over it, nicked some booze from the drinks cabinet and set off. And that's where I was, now, in the movie of my mind, sauntering down Friars Lanes in the balmy dusk, the sun diminishing like melting butter behind the hedges, the sandpipers and the flycatchers, in their V formation overhead, heading for warmer climes, and, at my side, the odd roaming chicken from the nearby farm.

I'd maybe walked for fifteen minutes, sipping on the vile concoction I'd put in a Tupperware beaker, when Butler pulled up. He had his window wound down, one chunky, freckled arm sticking out. I bent down to talk to him, saw his small, pale eyes flit to my cleavage and up again.

I made a joke about his choice of music: 'Is that INXS you're playing, Saul? Shame on you,' or something like that. It was only a joke but he turned it off.

216

'I presume you're off to this party then?' I said.

'Yeah, are you?' he mumbled. 'Do you wanna lift?'

I was desperate to see Joe. It had been a full twenty-four hours, after all, so I said, 'Yes, please. If you don't mind?'

'I wouldn't have offered if I minded, would I?' he said.

I got in the front. The car stank – not unpleasant, just strong. A bit like paint and petrol put together. It got you right between the eyes.

'Sorry about the smell,' said Saul. 'It's the rags in the back, they're covered in turps.'

He told me he'd been doing some decorating job up at the new estate in Kilterdale. The new houses 'for people with more money than sense', he said. 'Swimming pools and fucking kitchen gadgets nobody's going to use in a million years.'

He sounded a bit cross. Saul's family lived on the council estate in town. I wondered if he was actually jealous of those people in their plush new houses. They weren't a far cry from the sort of house my sister Leah would eventually live in, years later, in Berkhamsted, where, as far as I can tell, she now spends most of her time going to barbeques, book clubs and dinner parties. The sort of place parents come 'for the schools' and with what must be one of the highest concentrations of pregnant women and trampolines-in-back-gardens in Britain, if not the world. Her house has pillars, like the ones on the estate Saul was working on at that time. He'd probably hate my sister if he knew her now.

I turned to Saul, then, in the car. 'Who knows, eh? One day, you might live in one,' I said. 'Saul Butler in his executive five-bed!'

He just looked at me. He didn't seem interested in banter.

We were driving quite slowly, for some reason, something to do with the tyres, he said, which didn't exactly inspire confidence but, like I say, I'd had more than a few sips of my lethal cocktail and was well on my way to being drunk.

'So where's Joe then? How come he's not going with you? I wouldn't be letting any girlfriend of mine walk down a lane like this on her own.'

'Oh, it's complicated, he was already near Tony's house, so there was no point him coming all the way back to pick me up. I said my dad would give me a lift, then my dad wouldn't give me a lift.'

Saul Butler gave a disapproving grunt.

'Some dad,' he said. 'Some boyfriend.'

I shrugged. It felt like he was trying to make a competition out of something but I didn't really know why.

'Well, you look very nice, anyway,' he said. 'Nice dress. I haven't seen you in a dress before.'

'No. They're not usually my thing.'

'Well, you should wear them more often.' He smiled. 'It looks really nice on you.'

'Thanks,' I said, feeling flattered.

He changed gear, his hand on the gear-stick thick and freckled and looking like it would be really dry to the touch. In the distance, you could hear the trains racing through the fields, with their ghostly cries, like the last, long exhalation before someone dies. Like their last breath.

I must have lain awake for an hour or more, enough to hear the music and Eva's clattering reach a crescendo, as it often does, and to see the slither of sky, through the gap in the curtains, turn from impenetrable velvet black to the denim blue of dawn.

The scenes from the past kept coming: sometimes they were just fragments, sometimes the whole thing. I felt that now, at thirty-two, I should feel so different to how frightened I was back then, and yet, too much about how it had all happened so far – the recklessness in getting pregnant in the first place, the death of our mothers, the basic fact that this baby was Joe's – was so similar; it was like 1997 all over again. Losing Lily, losing Mum . . . and the other thing. My secret. My huge, terrible secret. The real reason I couldn't be with Joe because I knew, if I were, I'd have to tell him.

I told myself everything always seemed so much worse at this hour of the night, turned on my side, forced my brain to shut down and myself to go back to sleep.

For the next two or three weeks, Joe and I spoke to one another almost every day. I tried at first to keep some distance – to speak, say, every few days – but it was clear Joe wasn't interested whatsoever in approaching his new role as Joe, Antenatal Guru, in a part-time fashion. The excuses he came up with to call or email me became hilarious in themselves.

'What do you think of the name Oswald?' he asked one day. 'Oswald Sawyer-King. One of life's winners, right there . . .'

'Joe,' I said, walking into another room, politely away from the patient who was standing, pants down, ready for me to inject him. 'I'm about to administer anti-psychotics into someone's bottom; can we talk about this later?'

They got less baby-focused, more just random, such as: 'How do you cook artichoke?' Or: 'I'm in Blockbuster's, what do you recommend?'

I was wary at first. I don't want to sound presumptuous – after all, I am pretty easy to resist at the moment, with hormonal spots and not so much a bump as a thickening waist – but I didn't want Joe to get too close. It's perhaps excusable to be reckless once, and for the fallout to be so monumental, but *twice*? I could just about cope with me getting hurt, but not Joe. I couldn't do that to him again. I felt sometimes like I wasn't carrying a baby but a bomb. So I tried not calling or answering his calls every time, but it'd get to 10 p.m. and I could almost feel him, up there, pacing his little bachelor pad in Manchester, trying to resist. He always cracked. I remembered this about Joe: if he wanted to ring you, he rang, no game-playing; and I always took his calls in the end, because they were becoming the best part of my day.

In some ways, it felt like we'd never been apart, and yet, in others, it was like I was getting to know someone new. But then, it had been sixteen years since we were last together. We'd seen each other on various occasions over the years – a few times in the pub in Kilterdale over Christmas; Tania Richardson's wedding; the fated night of the puke-on-my-boyfriend's-shoes; and an unannounced visit while I was in my third year at university (less said about that the better) – but there had been no sustained time spent together over those sixteen years so, yes, I was getting to know someone new, and yet, parts of Joe had not changed one bit, either.

He was so light, so confident about everything. It was

good for me. And those phone calls were a good opportunity to piece together the last sixteen years. He kept tabs on my progress with the AA list and it focused my mind, took me away from the dark thoughts that would come at me without warning; the panic attacks that were happening far more regularly than I cared to admit, especially when I was with Grace. Not that I would ever have told her that, because, after all, I was the one supposed to be helping her. And I really wanted to help her. I wanted to help all my patients, but Grace, I felt I had a connection with, I don't know why. Maybe because we'd been through similar things or that when I looked at her, I got a flash of, 'There but for the grace of God . . .'

I suppose we'd become quite friendly in the last few weeks, too. Tuesdays were our day for seeing one another, but sometimes I'd pop round, if I was in her neck of the woods, with a photography magazine I thought she'd like, or just for a cup of tea.

I'd told work and Grace (only because she said I looked like I'd put on a few pounds!) about the baby a week after the scan. There were a few embarrassing 'Who's the father?' questions to contend with at work, and Jeremy was as tactful as ever but, to be honest, none of it had touched the sides due to the emotional rollercoaster going on. This had been the second time I'd told the world I was pregnant and people were more shocked than congratulatory, so I was kind of used to it. Of all the people I'd told, aside from Kaye, Grace was probably the sweetest about it. She wanted a day-by-day commentary of how I was feeling, what side the baby was lying, when my due date was. She'd then forget everything and ask me all over again the next time I saw her, but I didn't care. It was just nice to have someone being so positive and asking questions – wasn't that supposed to be what happened?

Grace had a soft spot for Selim, the owner of the Turkish café on East Street Market, and so sometimes we'd go there on a Tuesday, and Grace would flirt with Selim, who would slip us a couple of free *bourekas* and we'd chat about all sorts: her old life; her twenties when she was in love with Cecily's father; the years she spent as a working photographer.

She'd also chat to me often about the photographs in her flat: the technique she'd used, the composition. I loved how animated she became when she talked about her photography and her daughter and her twenties – they seemed like the happiest days of her life. The more she trusted me, the more she would tell me about this life – the one before her breakdown, aged thirty-one, triggered by the death of her stepfather and the realization she could never bring him to justice – but also, about her other life – the horrendous details of her childhood. She'd throw them into conversation and they'd pierce me, like tiny shards of glass, when I wasn't expecting it. Like last week, when she took off her Yankees baseball cap for the first time and showed me the scar across her forehead, where her stepfather had struck her with a broken Heineken bottle, and the time we were in the launderette, and she'd casually dropped into the conversation how her stepfather would rape her in one of the guest bedrooms of the hotel they lived in, then make her take the sheets for a service wash.

It was difficult, when she got onto this line of thought, to bring her back from the darkness of the past to her present. It was like she wanted to wallow there, berating herself about how she'd been a bad mother – there was a lot of that. 'I'm a mad, bad mother, darlin',' she'd say. 'I've let my Cec down.'

It didn't matter how much I told her that it wasn't her fault or that there was no point going over things that couldn't be changed, she'd get stuck, like a broken record. In order to help Grace achieve some sort of recovery, I needed to help her find a way to her future. And maybe it was that I, too, had lost a daughter, but I decided that Cecily was the key.

Chapter Seventeen

Kilterdale
13 May 1998

Dear Lily

Oh, God, I don't think I'll ever stop crying and I've
hurt Joe so much. This morning, he asked me to
marry him!! We were planting your tree in the
woods – because today is the day you were due.
And now, not only do I not have you, but I don't
have Joe, either.

The tree is a lovely oak tree that we can both
visit whenever we want to remember you. We
planted it, then Joe said he had something to ask
me. He got down on one knee and he said that in
spite of, and because of, what we'd been through,
he still loved me. In fact, he loved me even more
because he could see how strong I was and, even
though we were still a bit young to get married, he
wanted to get engaged and make a commitment. He

said, we could have more babies, we could have a family together, later on.

I love him so much. The most awful thing is that if none of this had happened, I would have said yes in a heartbeat. I can't imagine wanting children with anyone but Joe, but how could I marry him, knowing what I know? If I married him, I'd have to tell him everything, and how can I tell him that all the pain he has been through during the last few months might have been for nothing, because you might not even have been his? How can I tell him that I am not the strong person he thinks I am, that for the first few months, I desperately wished I wasn't pregnant?!

Is that why you died? Why the universe decided I didn't deserve you? Because I might not have wanted you for the first few weeks but when I felt you move and saw your face on the scan, you were MY baby then, and I wanted you so much. You were the light keeping me going.

One Monday evening, Joe called earlier than usual, around 6 p.m. I was in the car, just coming back from assessing a patient up at the hospital. He told me to call him when I got home. He hated me talking while I was driving. He never actually said that, but I knew.

I called him back. He was checking in on the AA list, in particular about progress with the ashes. I was grateful for the kick up the bum, to be honest. I'd made such a fuss about the ashes when I was in Kilterdale, but so much had happened since then, I couldn't face bringing it up again with Dad and Denise. Denise would feel attacked and victimized. I'd feel guilty and resentful (and also a little bit attacked and victimized). Also, if I called them about the ashes, I'd have to tell them about the baby, and I wasn't ready for that yet. Turned out I didn't have to anyway, because Joe being Joe had gone over to Dad's that morning, around 11 a.m., and asked about the ashes anyway. What he told me next, floored me.

'I'm afraid they definitely don't have them.'

'What? What do you mean, they don't have them?'

Worst-case scenario was now playing in my head: we'd never find them, we'd have lost all that's left of Mum; mine and Denise's relationship would be over forever, which means mine and Dad's relationship would be over forever. It's fragile, anyway. I couldn't bear that.

'Your dad looked really worried,' said Joe. 'I think he genuinely doesn't know.'

How could he *not KNOW*?

'But that's my mother we're talking about. Dad's wife, the woman he loved and adored, once.' I leaned against the sink and actually started to cry a bit then. 'I *bet* Denise has moved them. Or, Jesus, what if they've been nicked?'

'Robyn, listen to me, calm down . . .' Joe had started to do this every time I got stressy. He didn't want my pulse to go above resting, in case it was bad for the baby (he'd never admit this but I knew that was what he was thinking). 'We'll find them. If I have to go over there and gag and bind Denise till she surrenders, we'll get them.' He paused, cleared his throat. 'Also, I told them you were pregnant.'

'*What?*'

'I can explain.'

'*Joe!*'

I wasn't ready for them to know yet. It was different now I was solvent and out of my teens, but it would still come as shock, and it would be telling them all over again, like last time, and I wasn't ready to remember all that, too; all the tears and the heartache and Dad being so disappointed.

'What about your education?' was all he'd kept saying. 'Such a waste, Robyn. Your mother would have been so disappointed.'

That had cut like a knife.

'She'd have handled it better than you! You would have thought life would be precious to you after losing Mum!' I'd yelled, but really I was yelling at myself, trying to convince myself that life was precious, however it had come about. Now I just feel sorry I had to put him through that; he'd just lost his wife and then his teenage daughter was knocked up. It's a miracle he didn't drop down dead, too, of a heart attack.

On the other end of the line, Joe started rambling, nervously.

'Rob, I'm sorry, but I wanted them to know how important it was that we got the ashes, that it was making you anxious. Also, it was on the list and I thought it might help with you focusing, you know, small achievements and all that, things going right for a change . . .' His voice trailed off as he realized he might have overstepped the mark. Impulsiveness may be Joe's worst trait. 'Are you angry with me?' he said, finally.

'*No,*' I said. Was I? I wasn't sure. Mainly, I was incredulous my life had become this ridiculous in a matter of weeks, but I wasn't angry, I was relieved. 'How was it?

I mean, what did they say?' Yes, that was it. I was actually relieved.

Joe gave a little laugh, relaxed now I'd softened. 'Well, it was hilarious, because Bruce answered the door and just said "Jo-seph," like that, in a very stern voice, without looking at me, and then just stood aside to let me know it was okay to cross the threshold. Clearly, he still hadn't forgiven me.'

I pictured the scene: Dad with chest puffed out like a partridge. Joe towering over him. Dad doing something ridiculous because he was nervous, like . . .

'He lit up a cigar and offered me one. Then he offered me a whisky.'

'Oh, God,' I said. 'Who does that at 11 a.m.?'

'S'alright, I had one.'

'What? You did not.'

'I'm not passing up a cigar and a drink – plus, it served as a good ice-breaker because then I said, "Hey, Bruce, you know how I got your daughter pregnant at sixteen and you were *delighted*? Well, it's happened again! Turns out, we only have to look at one another."'

'Oh, my God, tell me you didn't.'

'No, I didn't! Wow, you really don't know me any more, do you? Of course I bloody didn't. I was very much the gent – I said it was unexpected but that, whatever happened . . .'

I wondered what this meant. 'Whatever happened?'

'Well, whether we were together or we weren't,' he said, 'I'd step up, I'd be there. "I won't shirk my responsibilities, Bruce," I said.' I stood in my kitchen and smiled down the phone then, because I was imagining us together. I was thinking, *Maybe?* I was trying to believe.

229

I was relieved the actual 'telling my dad' bit had been taken out of my hands, but there was still the very pressing issue of the ashes – all that remained of our mother, lost! I had to confront Denise. I had to ring her. She had to know what had happened to them. I was suddenly terrified by the possibility that she hadn't just hidden them, but lost them, or accidentally knocked them over while on one of her dusting odysseys and then hoovered them up in a panic. I'd never forgive her. I'd hate her. And I didn't want to hate her, I didn't have the energy.

Literally, just as I was about to pick up the phone, however, it rang.

'Hello, Robyn, it's Denise here. I'm calling about the ashes.'

It was so odd, it was like Mum made it happen.

'Oh, right. Okay.' The rant I'd planned went straight out of the window with the fear that she really was calling to confess, that this was the moment I learned our mother's remains were in the Henry Hoover.

'I think Leah has them,' she said.

'*Leah?* Why on earth would Leah have them?' And then the penny dropped. Leah had gone up to Kilterdale before me – something that hardly ever happened, due to the longstanding tensions between her and Dad and Denise. She knew they were moving; she'd been strange on the phone when I'd asked her about them. She'd been avoiding my calls ever since. Of course Leah had them!

Denise gave a little cough. 'You know I'm not Leah's favourite person at the best of times, and we'd had a row that afternoon. Or rather, Leah had been quite rude to me.'

I didn't say anything, I wanted Denise to talk. Trying

to get anything out of Dad or Leah was impossible, and any insight was good.

'The usual sniping about how I'd railroaded your father into this . . .'

'This?'

'Oh, us being together.'

'Oh, God.' Was she really still going on about that, sixteen years later? Denise wasn't exactly my favourite person either, but surely there came a time when you had to let it lie?

Denise said, 'I think, I *know*, she took them because she didn't want us to take them to our new house, she wanted her mum with her.' I pictured Denise: all big hair and tight jeans and spidery lashes, speaking through pursed lips 'And I understand that, Robyn.'

'Ok*aay*,' I said, tentatively.

'Despite general opinion to the contrary, I'm not actually some kind of witch, you know?'

I was frozen in the middle of my kitchen. I had never in my life had this sort of conversation with my stepmother.

'I know,' I said. I didn't have the foggiest what else to say. 'Thank you for telling me about the ashes, Denise, it was thoughtful of you.'

'That's okay,' she said. 'Just, will you do me a favour? Don't tell your dad I told you. Things are tense enough as it is between your sister, your dad and me, and I don't want to look like I'm dobbing anyone in, or stirring things up. I told you because I knew not knowing where they were would be stressing you out, and I didn't want you to be stressed in your condition.' She paused. 'When you're pregnant.'

It was the first time she'd said the word and I started.

'Thank you,' I said.

'Your father's going to call you. He was upset you didn't feel you could tell him yourself.'

I winced. Bloody Joe. I would have got round to it.

'He's very happy for you – concerned, but happy.'

There was a pause, while I tried to take all this in. 'Really?'

'Yes. He's no ogre, either, you know?' She laughed. 'I don't know sometimes, what you have him down as.'

Nor did I any more. Sometimes I felt like he'd sailed away from me the moment I got pregnant the first time around, because he just couldn't handle it, like a boat floating away from the quayside.

Something went *ding* in the background.

'Right, that'll be my dishcloths boiled, I'd better go.'

The woman was certifiable but perhaps, no, not a witch.

'Bye Denise,' I managed.

I was about to hang up when she took a little breath, as if to say something. 'Perhaps,' she said, 'if you could send us a picture of your scan?'

'Definitely.'

'Also, Robyn . . .?' She hesitated.

'It is going to be okay, you know. This time. It's going to be fine.'

232

Chapter Eighteen

Kilterdale
May 1999

Dear Lily

I thought today might be hard, but I don't think I had any idea how hard. It started out well – Beth totally lived up to her best friend status and had a whole day of distraction laid on for me. She never said – I think she's worried about upsetting me – but she definitely knows what day it is today.

She booked for us to have our nails done this morning, then she treated me to lunch. We had to go into the pharmacy for something afterwards. I haven't seen the woman who works in the pharmacy since I was pregnant, and she asked how old you were now and how you were doing. I wasn't prepared at all, and just said, 'She died,' because I knew if I carried on talking, I'd start crying. But now I'm thinking it might have been better if I had, because the silence was awful and she was so mortified that I was the one who ended up feeling bad.

After that, we went back to the pub, for that fatal 'one pint'. Perhaps if I'd gone home then, to sober up, I'd have been okay (I'm so mad at myself for not doing that, for not coming home and spending some time thinking about you rather than writing this letter now, which probably makes no sense because I'm pissed). Anyway, we stayed in the pub till 6 p.m., which meant that by the time we went to the rugby club for my cousin Nathan's 21st, I was drunk AND emotional. The last time I saw Nathan was at Mum's funeral, when I was also emotional. He must think I spend my life crying. All my family were there – Dad propping up the bar, in his new sheepskin, buying Denise an endless stream of Campari. I kept out of their way, until Dad came over and saw that I looked upset. It was then that I had to remind Dad what day it was. We had a chat and we cuddled. He was pissed but it was lovely, it was better than nothing. I'd forgotten that Nathan was friends with some of the Townies so Saul Butler was there. It's the first time I've seen him since that night last year and not ideal, to say the least – but I was handling it. I was no way going to leave for him. But then Joe turned up, with a girl, and I haven't been able to stop crying since.

I didn't dare look at the girl and was just going to leave, but then Joe cornered me as I was queuing for the loo. He looked so handsome – which only made things worse – and then he was telling me he still loved me and that he missed me and he was trying to cuddle me, and wanting to talk, because of what day it was and everything. So then he was crying and I was crying and I could see this girl he'd come with out of the corner of my eye – she MUST have been able to see us. I just left.

When I got home, just now, there was a letter for me, which must have come in the post after I left this morning. It was a photograph of your tree and a note from Joe that said: Thinking of you both, especially today. Maybe one day, when you're ready, we could meet here . . .

Denise reassuring me it was all going to be fine was probably the nicest thing she'd ever said to me in her life, and I wished I believed her but I didn't. I was split in two: the sane me, who was excited about this new life growing inside me, who remembered what Mum had said in her letter, 'You know how to enjoy life, Robyn, how to live with your cup half full . . .'; and the other, secret me, the evil twin, who believed that I didn't deserve to be a mum, that it was my fault Lily had died, that the baby or I were fundamentally unviable. That it was going to happen again. The panic attacks were getting worse and I missed Mum like nothing else: I missed not being able to talk to her about the baby; I missed the future grandmother she'd never get to be. If I couldn't give her that, then I needed to give her something, and it dawned on me that scattering her ashes was it. I needed to set her free.

And so, two days after the phone call from Denise, I found myself on the M1, on the way to Leah's, all fired up. I'd told her I was just coming for a visit but I promised myself I was not leaving that house until I'd seen the urn with my very own eyes.

The Grand Union Canal winds through Berkhamsted and it was gorgeous at this time of the year, with a confetti of blossom scattered on the surface, brightly painted barges moored up to its banks (and the maddest, most vicious geese you've ever seen in your life). It was a lovely place to live, I could see that, but there was something about its tightly packed streets and neat gardens, its tight-knit-ness, that made me want to hotfoot it back to Archway, with its ever-present whiff of petrol fumes and Chicken Cottage and be absorbed by it. Perhaps, I just wasn't quite 'there' yet. Leah always said I was a 'young thirty-two' (short translation: childless). Perhaps, once I'd popped one out, I'd spend my weekends going to barbecues and dinner parties and retire to the shires, too. She was in for a shocker.

Leah's house was a four-bed, 'executive pillared' number on a cul-de-sac, with a gleaming BMW four-wheel-drive in the driveway (although I doubted she'd ever been further than Waitrose in it), next to several other 'executive pillared' houses with big cars and manicured hedges. My brother-in-law, Russell, answered the door looking exhausted and wearing a green, Superdry sweatshirt and jeans (this, I'd deduced, was the weekend uniform of the Berkhamsted commuting dad. Russell worked in the city as a management consultant) and a grim expression on his face, like he was a carer for the long-term infirm: *No change today, I'm afraid . . .*

We did the strange hug that is reserved for me and my brother-in-law. He lunges as if to hug me, but then just ends up patting me on the back. I always feel like he is *this* far away from hissing in my ear: 'Anything, I'll pay you anything for respite care; you work with the mentally ill, don't you?'

'Surviving, Russ?' I said.

There was a lot of thumping coming from upstairs. '*Russ!!!*' I heard Leah yell. Through the gap in the lounge door, I could see that Niamh was here already, jousting with Jack, clad only in his pants. '*CAN YOU GET UP HERE, PLEASE. YOUR DAUGHTER IS CUTTING HER OWN HAIR!*'

'Surviving? This is living . . .' Russ deadpanned, before trudging up the stairs.

I escaped to the lounge, to join Jack and Niamh. I'd called my little sister immediately after Denise had called me and offered to pick her up and bring her here for the official 'ashes showdown', but the police job had taken her to a school nearby today and so she had just come straight from work.

'Aunty Robyn, I'm gonna get you.' Jack was now operating his light-sabre attack from on top of the settee. We'd just got into a three-way battle, when Leah opened the door: 'JACK MITCHELL. IT IS QUARTER PAST SEVEN. IF YOU DO NOT GET DOWN FROM THERE AND UPSTAIRS TO THAT BATH NOW . . .!' She disappeared again, leaving Niamh and I wondering what terrible fate awaited Jack if he didn't do as he was told. Jack didn't look too concerned, however.

He surrendered his *Star Wars* light sabre to Niamh and dutifully made his way towards the door. 'Honestly,' he sighed. 'She's driving me up the wall.'

I love my sister. She is loyal, she is fearless, she is brilliant at her three-day-a-week job as PA to a family lawyer, more

237

organized and decisive than I ever hope to be in my life. She loves her kids and I'm sure, deep down, she loves her husband, too, but, my God, is she mad? Niamh and I sat in the immaculate lounge – every single toy put away – barely daring to speak, cowering under the elephantine-stomping and shouting from upstairs, pretending not to have noticed the screaming irony of the four solid-silver letters spelling out the word LOVE on the mantelpiece; the wedding pictures in their gleaming silver frames; the canvas over the fireplace. It was of all four of them – Leah, Russ, Jack and our three-year-old niece, Eden, taken in a studio. Russ and Leah were lying on their stomachs, grinning, as the kids larked about on their backs.

Niamh was gazing at it, mesmerized.

'Do you think they ever do that at home?' she asked, so genuinely, it made me laugh.

Russell came in, looking like he'd just been twenty-four hours in a labour ward (him being the one to be in labour).

'Just thought I'd check, are any of you staying?' he said.

Niamh raised her hand tentatively. 'I was going to.'

'Because we're . . . um . . .' He scratched his head. I remarked to myself how there was definitely less hair than there was even six months ago. 'We're using the spare bedroom at the moment, so it's fine, but I'll have to make up the sofa.'

I was feeling any anger and resolve I'd arrived with (plus any lingering desires for normality – if normality meant marriage and two kids and love being something you had to display on the mantelpiece) dissipate, the more I saw the reality of my sister's life, which was kind of annoying. Must stick to the plan.

There was more shouting and then, suddenly, deadly

calm upstairs, possibly as the drugs went in. Then, the landline phone rang. Leah came running down the stairs and picked up.

'Hello?'

Long pause.

'Oh, hello, Joanna.' Her phone voice. The three of us sat in the lounge pretending to look at the walls. 'Yes, of course.'

Longer pause; some light, tinkling laughter. Niamh jabbed me in the side of the thigh. I jabbed her back, feeling the dreaded bubble of laughter in my throat.

'No, that's absolutely fine! You know we're more than happy to have Amelie any time . . . *Aw.*' Long pause. Then a bigger 'AW! They're so sweet together! Peas in a pod. Well, listen, don't rush back, six-thirty is fine.' I coughed to mask the little snort that escaped. 'I'm basically a single mother in the week, anyway, so makes no difference to me . . .' More tinkling laughter. 'I know! Bye, Joanna, bye . . .'

She hung up. 'JACK MITCHELL, DON'T THINK I CAN'T HEAR YOU STLL UP AND ABOUT UP THERE!' she shouted. Two minutes later, she opened the door, carrying a bottle of wine and three glasses, her black hair held on top of her head with a bulldog clip, eyes slightly manic, looking unhealthily thin. She only had to look at Russ for him to sidle out of the room, like a dog that has to go to his basket at mealtimes. 'Right,' she said, unscrewing the bottle, 'to what honour do I owe this? A visit from *both* my little sisters on a school night?'

I took a deep breath and looked at Niamh. It was best just to get this over and done with. 'Leah,' I said, 'we've come about Mum's ashes. You have them, don't you?'

*

She confessed immediately (after practically inhaling what was basically a third of a bottle of wine; perhaps there was something in those hideous headlines in the *Daily Mail* about middle-class, suburban alcoholic mothers, after all).

'I just didn't want Dad and Denise taking *our* mother's ashes to their new, horrid little house.'

It surprised me quite how full of venom she still was for Dad and Denise. It looked exhausting.

'But, Leah,' I said, 'nor did I!'

'And I knew Dad wouldn't give them to me, so I just took them.'

We all knew the reason Dad wouldn't give them to her. But, like I've said, nobody ever mentions the funeral. Sometimes I wonder what would have happened if *I'd* have done that, but try not to, because it makes me so cross.

All three of us sat there, Leah and I arguing over Niamh who was sitting in the middle, quietly sipping her wine; probably thinking how awfully bourgeois and uncool this all was – drinking Chardonnay on a vast, cream sofa in suburbia, her two middle-aged sisters arguing over their mother's ashes – but I couldn't help myself. I got why Leah didn't want the ashes to be moved to Dad and Denise's house, but why did she sneak off with them? And why not just tell me the truth when I asked her straight?

Leah poured herself another glass of wine. Neither sister had noticed so far that I'd barely touched mine.

'I just wanted them for a bit,' she said, childishly.

'You could have told me. I was worried Denise had hoovered them up.'

'Oh, Robyn, don't be so dramatic.'

I thought this was rich coming from the woman who once took her daughter to A&E for a headache because she worried she might have a brain tumour.

'I'm not! They're not bits of Lego, Leah, they're all we have left of our mum – they *are* quite important.'

'I know! That's why I took them!'

'*Guys*,' Niamh sighed. 'Listen to yourselves, seriously.'

'Oh, for crying out loud,' said Leah, suddenly getting up off the sofa and walking out of the room.

I heard the front door being opened.

'*Where are you going now?*' I shouted.

'*To the car!* They're in the glove compartment.'

Niamh and I looked at one another in disbelief.

The *glove compartment*? I could have killed her.

But I was so utterly relieved to see the urn, safe and sound, that I didn't go into this. Now was not the time.

Leah set Mum on the coffee table. 'Happy now?' she said.

'Yes, I am, actually,' I replied.

'I just don't know why we're in such a rush to scatter them,' she added.

'I just think it's the right time.'

'Why though? Why suddenly now?'

I'd pictured this lovely, sisterly scene. Me announcing my shocking yet exciting news as we drank tea and ate cake and reminisced about Mum, but this would have to do:

'Uh, well, it turns out I'm pregnant.'

Leah leaped off the sofa like she'd been stung by a wasp.

'Oh my God,' was all she could say, for what seemed forever. 'Oh. My. God.'

Never having followed my big sister down any path in life so far, she clearly could not conceive of her little sister (who worked with loonies and was a spinster at thirty-two) doing anything in life that she had.

Niamh was hugging me. 'I'm going to be an auntie again! This is so cool!' Which is exactly how I'd predicted she'd respond.

'Whose?' said Leah, eventually.

'Joe's,' I said.

'*Joe's?*' Niamh said. 'That is so romantic!' (Again, exactly how I'd predicted.)

Leah, however, grew very quiet and pale.

'Joe *Sawyer's?*' she said, eventually. It was barely a whisper. 'Joe from Kilterdale?'

'Yes,' I said, cowering into the sofa.

Then, she burst into tears.

She claimed it was just shock, but I knew she was crying because of what happened with Lily, because last time I was pregnant it didn't end well. I also suspected it was because she knew the whole story of what happened that summer. This, I couldn't be one-hundred-per-cent sure of, but there had been a weekend in February 1999, exactly a year after I'd lost Lily, and eighteen months since what happened down Friars Lanes, where I'd gone to visit Leah at university and ended up, in some nightclub, drunk on beers with Sambuca chasers, attempting to confide in her, but I'm not sure how much she remembers. Either way, I now felt a bond I don't often feel with my eldest sister these days. I was touched she'd got so emotional.

We didn't get too far with the ashes after that. I'd hoped we might discuss possible places where we could scatter them, but Niamh was just drunk and excitable and Leah was drunk and wanted only to discuss the baby. She got completely carried away, rooting out all her old baby equipment.

Despite my protestations, she insisted on going up in the loft.

'Breast pump?' she was shouting down, as Niamh and I waited at the bottom of the stairs, shaking our heads in despair. 'Moses basket? Sterilizer? I've got a whole bag of nipple creams and maternity bras here, if you like . . .'

'You're all right, Lee,' I said. 'Bit prem, perhaps.'

Niamh was killing herself laughing.

Every time I tried to bring the conversation back to the ashes (we'd got as far as Leah making a spreadsheet, with 'no'/'yes' possible locations), Leah would change the subject to the baby. It was bizarre and also quite lovely; it was like she'd been waiting for this moment all her life.

We went to sit in the kitchen and Leah made me a cup of tea (decaf – defies the entire point of tea, surely, I said, but she insisted on grounds of responsible older sister) and poured her and Niamh yet more wine.

'Okay, so, also, Robyn, you have to do Gina Ford,' she slurred. 'Made everything so much more bearable.'

'What the hell is "doing Gina Ford"?' I said. 'Is it like doing the tango or the quickstep, a special dance routine you practise while pregnant so the baby slips out like a dream?'

Niamh sniggered. Leah waved her hand at me, mouth full of wine, too hell-bent on imparting her baby-whispering wisdom to laugh at any jokes. 'The woman is a genius,' she gushed, refilling her wine glass. 'Her whole mantra is about controlled crying and not letting the baby think they're in control and absolutely, *never* cuddling your baby – gives completely the wrong message.'

'What the hell?' Niamh and I said in unison. 'Never cuddling your baby? Can't you get done for neglect for that sort of behaviour?'

Leah wafted us away with her hand. 'During sleep time, I mean! Obviously.'

Obviously.

We did eventually get round to discussing the ashes again, and various suggestions were bandied about: Kilterdale beach (mine), in the garden along with all our pets (Niamh's), not scattering them at all and just having Mum on rotation (Leah's), so one daughter has her for a few weeks, then another, but I said that made her sound like the guinea pig we used to take it in turns to bring home from school. Also, I had to move the ashes in the end, because Leah kept gesticulating drunkenly as she talked and more than once nearly swiped Mum right off the table.

It seemed that we were completely unable to make a decision because things I remembered about Mum and our childhood, Leah remembered differently, and Niamh didn't remember much at all. Then there was the sore subject of the funeral (still skirted around), and how Leah had disappeared off to university in Brighton – about as far away as it was possible to get – and I'd hardly seen her for months. I missed her desperately then; it was almost visceral. I missed her like you might ache for a lover, which I found embarrassing at the time, and kind of still do. I missed the smell of her perfume

244

(Poison by Dior; the entire house stank of it for four years), the soles of her feet on my thighs, on the settee, watching Saturday-morning TV, even stepping over her legs in the hall, where she'd sit for hours on the phone, having monosyllabic 'conversations' with whichever bloke she was with at the time, our cat-fights where we'd throttle one another, then feel terrible and declare our undying love. Plus, I felt like I knew things about Leah that nobody else in the world did: she might have acted like I was the shit on her shoes in front of her friends, but I knew that sometimes, in the middle of the night, she'd crawl into my bed because she'd had a nightmare.

But I had nightmares too after Mum died, and she wasn't there. As we tried and failed for two hours to agree on where to scatter Mum's remains, it occurred to me that maybe I still hadn't forgiven Leah for this. It also occurred to me that this apocalyptic thing had blown apart all our childhoods and yet we'd never really talked about it.

At 9.30 p.m., I announced I was leaving. I was good for nothing after about 10.30 p.m. these days anyway and, as much as I love and adore them, my sisters are exhausting for entirely different reasons. I had Niamh in tow – she'd decided to pass on the offer of the sofa on the frontline of domestic war and get a lift with me to the station and get the train home. (I had offered her a bed at mine but she'd declined on the basis that the damp wasn't good for her voice and she needed her voice for her job. Unbelievable!)

She went to the loo before we left (no doubt just an excuse to creep into Jack and Eden's rooms and give

245

them a kiss), while I stood chatting to Leah in the front porch. The air was thick with the smell of sweet peas in Hawthorn Gardens, the cul-de-sac Leah had made a life in. Who'd have thought that the angry, Morrissey-loving, grief-stricken nineteen-year-old with whom I'd last lived in 1997 would ever live in a cul-de-sac that smelled of sweet peas?

I looked at her now, still in her suit skirt and blouse from work, and felt a strong pull of nostalgia for this time, but mostly for a time before all that, even before Niamh came along, when we were just two kids with a really happy life. It made me sad that I'd never live again with my sister. That that bit was so short.

Leah leaned against the pillar, tipsily. She was cute when she was drunk, I decided: softer, easier to love; like a child when they're ill.

'My little sis, pregnant, eh?' she said. 'I can't believe it . . .'

'You can't believe it? Think how I feel.'

'So what's this about Joe, then?'

I leaned against the other pillar, facing her. I wasn't sure I wanted to go into this when she was drunk, but it's not every day you get to have a proper intimate conversation with my sister. 'I don't know, we just met up again at his mum's funeral and we just clicked, you know? It was weird, it was like we'd never had time apart.'

Leah frowned, working it all out. 'So, the baby . . . his mum's funeral. So like . . .?'

'Yes,' I said, quickly. 'Please don't lecture me, Leah, not now.'

But she didn't lecture me, she just sniggered affectionately, stepped forward and hugged me.

246

'Oh, Robyn Elizabeth,' she said, 'I do love you. You're priceless.'

'Thanks.'

'Also, do you know what I think?' she said, drawing back and tenderly moving the hair from my face.

'What's that?'

'I think Joe is special. I think people like him are rare. He was only seventeen when Mum died and look how well he looked after you. Look how grown up he was when everything happened . . . unlike me.'

I shook my head. There wasn't any point going over that now.

'I think you were mad to let him go.'

'It was hard, Leah. I didn't want to . . .'

'Yeah, I know. Just, if I can be the bossy big sister for a second, people like Joe don't come along very often.'

'I know,' I said. And I did. 'And, what about you, Lee? Are you okay? You and Russell?'

She rolled her eyes. 'Oh, yeah, he's just *pissing me off*.' She was whispering – not very successfully – in case he could hear her from the spare room above. 'Sometimes I feel like I could just do everything better on my own, you know?' *Poor Russ*, I thought. He was fighting a losing battle because nobody comes up to Leah's standards.

'You do still love him, though, don't you?' I asked. I wanted to ascertain how much the booze was talking.

'Oh, yeah, I *love* him,' she said, although more like he was her annoying brother than her husband. 'I just don't know what extra he adds to my life, or if I want to be actually married to anyone any more, you know?'

I tried to say something about how maybe he didn't

247

have to add anything 'extra' (this seemed like an awful pressure, like he was her acupuncturist or healer or something), rather that he should complement her. Or something. Jeez, what the hell did I know about marriage?

'Anyway, I'm sure you don't want to hear me witter on about my boring marriage woes,' she said, even though I was quite happy to. 'I just want you to know, that you can talk to me any time, okay?' And I smiled because I knew she meant it, but also that 'any time' was any time other than mealtime, bedtime, story-time or bath-time, which didn't leave much time, let's face it, but I was grateful she'd said it, nonetheless. This was the most intimate conversation I'd had with my sister for years, and I made a promise to myself, then and there, that we should have more of them.

She hugged me again and speaking over my shoulder, said, 'I do understand, you know, much more than you know. I've always regretted the fact I never protected you – I was your big sister, I should have protected you.' The hairs on my arms stood on end then – so she did remember the drunken conversation we'd had in the back of some dodgy nightclub in Brighton, in the February of 1999. But how much? And how much detail had I gone into? I didn't dare ask.

She must have sensed that she'd crossed a line, and that perhaps I didn't want to go there, because she said, more lightly, 'Anyway, are *you* okay, honey? I mean, in general? This baby must be a massive shock.'

'I'm okay,' I said. 'I just still don't understand why you took the ashes and, in particular, why you didn't tell me.'

She bristled, stood back a little. 'I just wanted Mum to myself for a bit,' she said.

248

'Okay,' I said, still not really understanding.

She sighed, 'Okay, I felt guilty. I've *always* felt guilty – about how I behaved at the funeral. I wanted to talk to her, make it up to her, -s, before we scatter her and she's gone forever. Does that make sense?'

'Yeah.' I shrugged, but there was still that vital question that nobody has ever dared asked. I had to take my chance.

'But why *did* you behave like that at the funeral?'

'Why . . .?' she said, wide-eyed – but I knew she was just trying to stall the answer – '. . . Because I was angry.'

'What? About the fact Mum died?'

'Yes,' she sighed. 'No. Something else, too. Something I've never told you.'

'Oh? Well I don't think after my big news tonight there should really be any more secrets, do you?'

Leah looked a little sad and shook her head.

'Okay. Well, you know how you've always thought that Dad and Denise got together after Mum died?'

'Yes.' I could guess already where this was going.

'Well, they didn't. They were together before she died.'

I paused, trying to rewind to that time.

'What? How do you know?'

'Because I saw them kissing, Robyn,' she whispered, missing her footing again. 'In Denise's car, outside, when Mum was basically on her deathbed.'

'Oh . . . Oh God . . .'

'Sorry, I'm coming!!!' Then Niamh shouted at the top of her lungs from the top of the stairs, like she used to do when she was little, and Leah *must* have been drunk, because she didn't bat an eyelid over the children being woken up.

249

Instead, she hugged me again. 'I'm sorry if it was the wrong thing to do to tell you that,' she said. I was shaking my head. I didn't really know what I felt yet, I hadn't processed it. 'But I have to say, it's made me feel better.' She touched my belly. 'And I'm so excited about this, the baby,' she added.

'Are you? Good. Because I'm mainly shitting myself . . .' I said, truthfully.

'Do you know what I'm most looking forward to?'

'No, what?'

'Being there this time.'

'She's an alien,' said Niamh, darkly, flatly. We sat in my car outside Berkhamsted Station, just recovering for a bit before Niamh was due to catch the train. 'Are you sure she isn't adopted?'

I laughed but I was miles away. So Leah had protected me, after all. All these years that I thought she'd not cared, she'd been keeping this secret about Denise and Dad from me because she thought it would hurt me. And she was right, it probably would have back then, but now, weirdly, it seemed irrelevant. Now I understood that Dad lost Mum months before she actually died, that he was her carer not her husband for the last few months of her life. Also, I couldn't stop thinking about what Mum had said in her letter to me about wanting Dad to be happy. 'You'll know what I mean,' she'd said. Who knows? Maybe she even knew what was going on. But anyway. Now I did, and Dad was happy. It was time for Leah and all of us to accept that. Even if Denise boiled her dishcloths and insisted on a car valet every week.

I felt bad, after Leah had been so sweet about the baby, sitting with Niamh and taking the mick out of her phone voice, her OCD, her *Stepford Wives*-ness but, then, it was also irresistible.

'I think she's got first-born neurosis,' I said. 'You know, high expectations of everything, perfectionism . . .'

'*Mentalism*,' said Niamh, putting her feet up on the dashboard, and I smirked, while feeling hypocritical, considering my mental state lately. I got this a lot with Niamh, this feeling I had to be sane, I had to be solid, because our mum was dead, our dad had been usurped by a control freak, and Leah was – well, Leah was Leah. I suppose it was a pressure of sorts.

'Anyway, I'm so pleased for you,' Niamh said, turning to me. She had the loveliest smile, my sister. Her mother's wide smile. 'I know it's probably not how you planned it, but . . .'

'What, I'm getting on a bit?'

'Well, yeah . . . I didn't want to say that but, yeah, you are like, ancient.'

'Nice,' I said. I bet thirty-two did seem ancient to Niamh, too, whereas to me, on a good day, this felt like a second shot at life.

She gave a big sigh, with her shoulders, as if she was about to cry. 'God, I feel like, now you're going to become an actual mother, you won't have time to be my mum, too, and I might have to actually grow up. Can you believe it?' she said, and when I looked at her, I realized her eyes were glittering with tears. 'I might have to be a really big girl, and tell everyone who I *really* am.'

'Aw, Niamh. Or I could just do it for you?' I said, hugging her, thinking of the AA list, how this could be the one thing I could do for my sister, how I didn't want any more secrets in the family ruining things.

She frowned at me from under her electric-blue lashes. That beautiful, chiselled face she has. The tough chin.

'That would be a massive cop-out.'

'No, it wouldn't. I let Joe tell Dad I was pregnant.'

'Oh, did you?'

'Well, he sort of did it without consulting me, but that's academic. What I'm trying to say is that sometimes it's okay to go with the easy option. Save your energy. Choose your battles.'

She thought about this. 'Would you?' she said, eventually.

'Course,' I said. 'Consider it my last big favour as your *mother*,' I joked.

She took my hand and squeezed it, sweetly. 'You have been like a mum to me,' she said. 'An amazing mum. I'm lucky.'

Chapter Nineteen

Westminster University Halls, London
September 2000

Dear Lily,
So today is the first day of the rest of my life. How
long have I waited to write that? Have I waited to
be FREE from Kilterdale and the past? And now it's
finally here: my first day at university.

So, how do I feel on this momentous day? Dizzy
with possibility, yes. After all, I could completely
reinvent myself if I wanted. I could erase my entire
past or say I was a countess from Dumfries and
nobody would ask any questions. I am freer than I
have ever been in my life. So why do I feel sad?
Bittersweet sad, but sad all the same. I've come to
the conclusion it's because, while I feel like I am
welcoming a whole new era, I am saying goodbye to
an old one. And even though so much happened in
that era that I want to forget, there was some

wonderful stuff too; wonderful people that I never want to forget: Joe, for instance, and my mum, and I feel like they won't be a part of this new life.

Very soon after the twelve-week scan, I'd received a brown letter in the post marked with the NHS logo. My anxiety levels must have been such, that even the sight of that envelope with the clear window and those letters 'N-H-S' made my stomach turn over; I physically recoiled from it, like it might actually contain a death sentence:

Dear Miss King, Unfortunately, the sonographer got it wrong, didn't look at the scan properly and your baby has no heartbeat/there was nothing there.

Of course, it didn't say this, but I believed it was perfectly possible it would, which, even by my standards, was a crazy way to carry on. What the letter actually said, when I opened it, was that I had an appointment with a consultant, 'just to reassure me and to answer some of my questions', since I'd lost a baby before, even though I knew the only thing that would reassure me now would be to fast-forward to thirty-something weeks, and have my baby delivered pink and crying.

I toyed with the idea of not telling Joe about the appointment – there were things I wanted to ask Consultant Gynaecologist and Obstetrician, Mr Gordon Love (that was his real name), without Joe being there. Then I thought back to how that went at the twelve-week scan – the trying-to-be-brave thing – and decided otherwise. I'd still not recovered from blowing a snot bubble, I was crying so hard.

I told Joe he didn't have to come, but he took the afternoon off work and came anyway. I was beginning to worry his students were one of the main casualties of the past few months' events. I couldn't see how Joe could have been fully present at work with all this going on, even though he insisted he was. (As well as joking some of them wouldn't notice anyway as they came to class stoned.)

I was glad he came in the end, anyway, because it turned out that even just walking past the room labelled TRIAGE set me off. All I could think about was how much blood there'd been that awful day in February 1999. Fresh, scarlet blood. And of Lily's beautiful face: utterly beautiful but lifeless. 'She looks like she's sleeping,' the midwife had said, and I'd wanted to slap her, because she didn't look like she was sleeping at all, she looked like she was dead. That was what I found the hardest, looking back, the fact that I'd carried my daughter for twenty-seven weeks and she'd gone before I'd even got to clap eyes on her. That's partly why I wrote to her, I suppose, to validate her existence; to say, YOU LIVED ONCE – only inside me, but you did.

So, having Joe at my side, trying to make conversation with every nurse, every midwife – in fact, everyone that we passed as we walked down seemingly endless peach-painted corridors – was a godsend.

I could tell he was trying to distract me in the waiting room, too, trying to keep things light. We tried to think of other people we'd heard of, also with names perfect (or just ridiculous) for their profession. As well as Dr Love, Joe told me that, when he used to live in Preston with the girlfriend (I tried always to keep a neutral expression when he talked about the two years he'd lived with Kate), there had been a policeman called PC Robin Banks. I then remembered a dermatologist Niamh had once seen called Dr Creamer, and Joe told me how he once temped for a company that exported handbags from the Far East, and had to deal with a Mr Baggoyshyt, which made me snort out loud in the waiting room.

'It's called nominative determinism,' said Joe.

'What is?'

'When your name determines your job.'

'Sawyer, you are an endless stream of useless trivia.'

'Robyn King?'

Then, Dr Love opened the door, and I felt guilty for laughing and being happy. Of course, we were plunged immediately into discussions I didn't want to have. I wanted to be back in the waiting room, talking about silly names.

'Well, the good news . . .' Dr Love began. He had a preposterously jolly face and I wondered what he looked like when it was bad news – did he still smile like that? '. . . is that baby is doing very nicely indeed. The scans look great, the measurements are fine, and how is Mum?'

For a second, I wondered who he meant, then clocked.

'Oh, fine,' I said. I was turning that word around in my head – '*Mum*' – trying it out for size. 'Great. Just . . . what's the bad news?'

Joe was looking at me, shaking his head.

'There is no bad news,' said Dr Love, smiling, looking at me, then Joe, for some sort of clue of what I was talking about. 'Why should there be bad news?'

'Um, you said there was good news?'

He laughed. 'I did, so I did.'

'She likes to look on the bright side,' said Joe, sarcastically.

'Well,' said Dr Love, with a little chuckle, 'there really

is nothing you should be worrying about. Everything is utterly as it should be so far.'

I swallowed.

So far.

'Now, Robyn, I have your notes here,' Dr Love continued, turning back the front page, and I caught a glimpse of the Sands teardrop sticker. It shows a womb, in the shape of an eye, with a baby inside, and a teardrop coming out of it. I'd found out about it when I'd been having one of my sessions torturing myself with research on the Internet – not that I would *ever* tell Joe about those – and knew that it was often added to notes of women who had previously lost a baby, to prevent any hiccups such as the one we'd had with the sonographer. Clearly, it had since been added to mine. 'So,' said Dr Love, 'perhaps you could tell me what happened with your first pregnancy, in your own words, and we can go from there?'

'Okay,' I said. 'You should know that Joe here was also the father of that baby, our daughter, Lily.'

Dr Love raised his eyebrows, just a fraction. It was the first time I'd seen him look anything but cool and composed.

I relayed the whole story. It was the first time I had done so in front of Joe, and it wasn't as awful as I'd worried it would be. In fact, it was cathartic, comforting in some odd way, to reduce it all to medical facts. I told Dr Love how everything had been as normal – for as much as it's normal to be sixteen and pregnant – until I'd got to twenty-seven weeks, when I'd had terrible stomach pains and started bleeding heavily. It had been in the middle of General Studies, and there'd been a huge drama involving an ambulance and pupils crying. I'd been too traumatized to shed even a tear; too convinced this was somehow my fault, that I'd caused this to happen, that I was tainted – clearly. I didn't tell Dr Love that bit, though, I just told him how we'd been told it was unlucky, one of those things, and that the placenta had basically come away.

I managed not to cry, the whole way through. Joe was staring at me when I'd finished, his eyes glistening, like *he* might cry.

'Often with stillbirths . . .' said Dr Love, gently, when I'd finished. *Often? Did they happen often?* '. . . there is no known cause, and that is one of the hardest things for the parents but, yes, what you had is what's known as a placenta abruption, which as I'm sure you're aware means there was a bleed behind the placenta, which meant the placenta came away. More common than you'd think, but still rare, relatively and, yes, hugely unlucky.'

'How rare?' I said.

I wanted statistics, even though I already had statistics, because I'd looked them up on Google, but I wanted them from the horse's mouth, from Dr Love.

'It's *very* unlikely.'

Joe took my hand. 'I think, if possible, Robyn needs to know facts, statistics,' he said. 'Even though I don't particularly think that is helpful myself.'

Dr Love nodded. 'Mmm, probably best not to scare yourselves unnecessarily.' (I wondered what scaring yourself necessarily consisted of.) 'But, stats-wise, about one in a thousand women will have a stillbirth.'

I was picturing a thousand women in my head – what would a thousand people look like? It still seemed quite common. It was quite common. 'But a lot fewer than that will have it happen twice,' he added. 'In fact, in my twenty-seven years of practice, I've never met a woman who it has happened to twice.'

'Hear that?' said Joe, squeezing my hand. I was picking at my bottom lip.

'That's not to say it wouldn't,' said Dr Love.

'He has to say that to cover his back, don't you, Doctor?' said Joe.

Dr Love crossed his legs, folded his arms and smiled in a noncommittal fashion.

'The most important thing *I* think,' he said, 'is not speculating on what might happen, but looking at the situation now, which is that you are in very good health, the baby is in very good health and we've no need to worry.'

With all due respect, and as nice as he was, I could tell that Dr Love had never held his dead baby in his arms.

'One stat perhaps it *is* important to remember,' he added, 'is that a third of women will experience some bleeding during pregnancy and, if you do, you should come straight to the Day Assessment Unit, just to alleviate any worry.'

Even though I was worrying, all the time.

Joe was all for just getting it out as soon as possible and I can't say I disagreed with him. 'And what if you delivered the baby early?' he said. 'What chance of survival would the baby have if we just took it out sooner?' For some reason, I found Joe's complete lack of medical terminology very endearing.

'A baby born at twenty-six weeks has around an

eighty-per-cent chance of survival,' he said. 'At twenty-eight weeks, it goes up to ninety to ninety-five, and at thirty weeks plus, we expect pretty much the same survival rate as full-term.'

Joe grinned at me. I had to admit, this was far better than I had thought.

'See, you're seventeen weeks or thereabouts now, so you only need to go another twelve weeks,' he said, 'to be basically out of the woods.' *You're so optimistic*, I was thinking. *How can you be so optimistic?* 'That's a week per step of the AA plan.'

Dr Love looked at me, then Joe. Joe and I looked at one another.

'Sorry, that's our, er, personal joke. I didn't mean AA as in Alcoholics Anonymous . . .' said Joe. 'It's basically . . . AA stands for 'Alternative Antenatal'. It's this list Robyn and I drew up, stuff for us to concentrate on other than, you know, what could happen.'

Dr Love was nodding. You could tell he was confused but didn't take it any further.

I changed the subject. 'What I want to know is, how much can stress be a contributing factor?' I'd thought about sending Joe out of the room and having a private conversation with Dr Love about this, but then, I figured, Joe would worry more if I did that, he'd think there was something I wasn't telling him. Better to double-bluff him, as it were.

'There are no statistics to say that stress has any bearing on stillbirth,' said Dr Love, 'but I do think it's down to attitude. While many women see having a child as a very natural part of life, some see it as an inherent danger. And there is research to say that you and the baby have an easier time in labour and childbirth if you *don't* see it as an inherent danger . . . If you let nature take its course. If you relax.'

He clocked the look on my face. 'Although, obviously, in your situation, that is easier said than done.'

I thought for one mad second about confessing to not being able to get on the Tube and to the panic attacks. (That week, I'd had one in Tesco's, where I'd gone to get some milk, but had made the mistake of going down the nappy aisle. It had triggered a memory of the nappies we had piled high in my bedroom for weeks when I was pregnant with Lily. When we'd come home with no baby, I'd made Joe give them to charity immediately, because I couldn't bear to look at them.) But, thankfully, just as I opened my mouth to speak, Dr Love said, 'Most importantly, try and relax and enjoy this pregnancy. You deserve to. You've been through enough.'

We went to Waterlow Park again after the meeting. It felt even more exciting than the last time we were here because, back then, after the first scan, the baby had felt more like a dream, an idea. Now, I was seventeen weeks and showing (only a little, but there was definitely a comforting protrusion when I stood to the side). This was really happening.

We stood on the bridge of the lake and watched the ducks.

'I'm so proud of you,' said Joe.

'And I'm proud of you,' I said. 'Of how positive you're being, especially considering what else you're going through at the moment.' Joe was leaning on the bridge, waving at the ducks as they drifted beneath us. He was actually trying to strike up a friendship with a duck. 'How are *you*, Joe?' I said.

'Me?'

'Yes, you,' I repeated. 'I feel like, in all the drama of the baby, the fact you've just lost your mum has got lost. I'm sorry.'

'Yeah, taking all the limelight. Can't bear not to be the centre of attention for two minutes, so has to go and have a baby,' he said, then adding quickly, 'Sorry,' when he saw I wasn't laughing, that I was actually trying to have a serious conversation. 'But I don't need to tell you how I am, do I? Because you know. You understand what it feels like.'

'Yeah,' I said. 'Yeah, I guess I do, but then everyone's different.'

There was a pause.

'It still feels unreal, I suppose,' he said, eventually. 'These things happen to other people, don't they? But it's happened to my mum. Our mum.'

'How *are* your brothers?'

'That's the thing, I don't really know. We're usually close – I thought we were close – and yet we've hardly talked about it. I think it's too painful, like we can barely cope with our own grief, let alone one another's. So now, when we talk on the phone, we chat about the frigging football scores. I've never talked about football with my brothers, ever, in my life! And the other day, when we all called round one another because it was Mum's birthday, I ended up having a ten-minute conversation with Rory about verrucas – about whether I'd ever had a verruca frozen off and did it hurt? I mean, nuts!'

I was laughing. 'I think it's normal,' I said. 'Just because this massive thing has happened, doesn't mean life is any less banal, which I found comforting in an odd way. I remember when Mum's ashes were delivered to our door by the guy from the crematorium and Leah's exercise bike from Argos Online turned up at the same time. There was this kerfuffle at the door. For a second, I don't think Dad knew who to talk to first.'

'I miss her like hell, though,' Joe said, when we'd stopped laughing. 'It's like a physical pain, grief, isn't it? Right there.' He put a hand to his heart. 'I know what people mean now when they say, "I felt like I'd been stabbed in the chest."'

'Well, just remember, the reason you hurt so much is because you loved her so much.'

He nodded. 'That's a lovely thing to say,' he said. 'Yes. Such a comforting thing to remember.'

'Yeah, she's your mum and you love her. Nobody can take that away from you.' I said. I was thinking about Grace, too, and Cec. I was thinking of those bonds that can never be broken, not ever.

Joe sighed and lifted his face to the sun. Then he put his hand on mine. 'See,' he said. 'We can still talk.'

Chapter Twenty

London, 2001

Dear Lily

I'm thinking about you so much today. I miss your dad. I even miss Kilterdale. I miss what we never got to have.

I'm having fun at uni and I've got some great friends but, some days, I can't help thinking about how life might have been: about being your mum, and us being a family.

Today, you'd be three. (That's if you'd been born on your due date, of course, which is unlikely, but I find it helps to have a date I can remember you by. A positive date.) Maybe we'd be going to feed the ducks, or having a little party. Sometimes, when I can't sleep, I like to imagine what you'd be like and where we'd live and what our family would be like: I imagine we'd live in Lancaster, in a Georgian townhouse, and we'd run a café, or your dad would be a teacher and I'd run a bookshop and look after you. You'd have my thick hair and your dad's beautiful hazel eyes. I know I'm lucky to be at university with all the opportunities it offers, but sometimes I wonder if I'd have preferred that life. Sometimes all the opportunities confuse me. Take boys: I've met some lovely guys here, but none that come close to Joe, which, to be honest, has been a shock. Everyone said: 'You wait till you get to university, you'll have so much choice!' But what if you choose right first time? What if you found The One but just too early?

Most of the time I don't think about what happened too much, because it's too painful but, today, the worst thing is not having anyone to talk about you with – because it's like you never existed. But I want to talk about you sometimes because you are still my baby. That's why I write to you and I always will.

It was Tuesday, my 'official' day to see Grace. On this particular Tuesday, I arrived a little earlier than usual. Her door was ajar when I got there. I knocked, softly, before popping my head inside.

'Hi, Grace, it's just Robyn . . .'

She didn't reply but I could hear her chatting to someone on the phone. She sounded upset. 'I'm sorry, darlin' . . .' she was saying. 'I'm sorry, Cec, I'd hate me, too, but please don't go.' I hovered in the entrance, feeling bad for listening. 'I've been an awful mother. I've let you down.'

Oh, Grace, I thought, *don't get back on that again.*

I could see through to the kitchen. Sunlight flooded in through the big window and Grace was standing with her back to me, on the phone, her tiny frame silhouetted. She was wearing a blue Chinese silk dressing gown and had her hair up. A plume of bluish smoke rose up from her right hand. She could have been a rather decadent, elegant star, if you ignored the mould growing on the corners of her kitchen walls, the yellow film of tobacco that covered everything, and the fact that the hand holding a lit cigarette up in the air was trembling violently.

'Will you ever forgive me?' I heard her say. I stood there, not knowing whether I should make my presence known or not. Then, a crack in her voice: 'Oh, darlin', don't say that.'

I went into the lounge, to make myself busy, but could still hear her through the flimsy walls: 'Did I ruin you, sweetheart? Are you happy? It's my fault. Do you hate me, darlin'?'

I was looking at the Cecily shrine – all those pictures she'd arranged with a precision you didn't see anywhere else in the flat – and cringed at how exposed she was making herself. How vulnerable she sounded. If I were a teenage Cecily and all my mother did was to tell me how awful she was, would I want to speak to her or visit her? I think not. There was one picture I'd not noticed before. I picked it up. It was Grace – can't have been more than twenty – sitting at a pub table with a pint and some friends, wearing a maroon leather jacket with her dark hair in a topknot. She looked so level, so normal, it was heartbreaking. She was looking straight into the camera with those eyes with the fiery amber centre. That fire was still there, it just needed reigniting.

'I was a looker, weren't I?' Grace was standing at the living-room door. 'I used to win beauty pageants when I was a girl. My Cec still could.'

'It's a lovely pic,' I said. 'Were you a student there?'

'Yeah, Brighton Art College, darlin'. Best years of my life.'

She hovered in the open doorway. I put the photo, in its heart-shaped frame, down again.

'Nice to talk to Cecily?' I said. I wanted to give her a way in.

She paused, as if deciding which way she was going to play this. Then she said, 'I'm going to make myself a coffee,' and wandered into the kitchen. 'Fancy one?'

'That'd be lovely, Grace.'

I followed her into the tiny, cluttered kitchen. Two ashtrays, overflowing with fag ends, sat on the table, with a half-full bottle of Dr Pepper and the remains of a fish pie.

Grace took the kettle off the stand and filled it up at the tap.

'That was my Cec on the phone,' she said. 'My Cecily, my beautiful girl.' Her voice had changed. It was high and tense. 'She was telling me all about this boyfriend she's got – 'cause she's very grown up now, fifteen last week! She was just talking and talking, I couldn't get her off there. She's so like me, you know. We're peas in a pod, me and Cec. She says we could meet next week, maybe go shoppin', up at the Elephant, maybe even Oxford Street, Selfridges – you know, a nice girly shopping trip . . .' She stopped talking. The tap was still on and the kettle was overflowing. Her hand was shaking so much I could hear the silver bangles she wore, jangling like prison chains. She eventually turned the tap off, but her head was still bowed.

'Grace,' I said, softly. 'I heard you – on the phone. Do you want to . . .?'

'I lied,' she said, turning to me, nervously biting her fingers, like a child who thinks they're about to be told off. 'About Cecily. I lied, darlin'. I haven't seen her for years. She don't even wanna talk to me.'

I took a step towards her, and put my hand on her shoulder.

'I know,' I said, gently, and I can't imagine how hard that must be. But I'm going to try and help you.'

I'd known before I'd even met Grace, that's the truth. Jezza had told me and, anyway, it was written in her notes. I suppose I could have come clean straightaway, not humoured her stories about the visits, her phone conversations with Cec, but when I saw how her face lit up when she talked about her, I couldn't bring myself to. Also, I understood her need to talk about her as if everything she were saying were real. Her need to talk to Cec in her head. To somehow be close to her. That's what I'd always done with Lily, after all. It had just been in letter form.

I also knew it was important for Grace to tell me in her own words what really happened and, working her way through several Vogues, she did.

After she'd had her breakdown, she'd been so ill, spent so much time in hospital, that Cecily had had to go and live with her grandma, Grace's mum. There'd then been a court order taken out, meaning she could only see Cecily, supervised, for an hour a week but, over the years, she didn't even get that, because Cecily didn't want to

269

see her, and when Grace rang her, she rarely wanted to speak to her.

'I wasn't fit to be a mum. I was living in a fantasy world. I was taking her to see priests, because I thought I'd contaminated her,' Grace told me.

'With what?'

'With that nasty business he did to me,' she said. 'My stepfather. I thought that badness must have got through to her, because she was mine, you know . . .?'

Poor Grace. Here she was, only forty-one, with yellow teeth and yellow fingers, with the only person in the world she loves rejecting her. Life could have been so different, if perhaps she'd had more support. If the abuse she'd suffered had been a one off, not sustained over so many years. I was beginning to realise, I was one of the lucky ones, that so many people go through trauma in their lives, and it's down to luck, really, and the people around you, as to how you come out the other side.

I shuffled right up to her, because she was crying. A solitary tear was rolling down her face.

'You know none of this is your fault, Grace?' I said. 'I know we've been through this but it's important you understand.'

'Oh, it was, I was a terrible mother.'

'No,' I said, emphatically. 'You weren't. You got pushed to the limits, you had a breakdown. You were very poorly.'

She took my hand. 'Lovely girl,' she said, and squeezed it, then very gently brought it to my belly – eighteen weeks and swollen now – and put hers over it. 'You look after that baby of yours. You need to be as healthy as you can be.' I wondered whether passive smoking was really the way to go. 'Not lose your marbles like me.

270

End up in the nuthouse with mental-mind disease. Rattling when you walk, you're on so many pills.'

'Oh, Grace,' I said. 'Now come on, there's lots more to you than your illness and I'm going to try and help you get back in touch with Cecily. It's going to take some time, but we're going to build up that relationship, that trust again and, do you know what the first step is towards that?'

'Electric-shock therapy,' she said.

'No, *not* electric-shock therapy, Grace Bird. Happiness,' I said. 'We need to find what makes you happy, what you enjoy doing, because then you can talk to Cecily about new things you've done and not go over the past all the time.'

She gave me this very unconvinced look that made me laugh.

'So, apart from Cecily, what *do* you enjoy?'

'Photography,' she said, quickly. 'Taking photos, my camera. But I haven't done it properly for so long.'

'Then we shall take you out with your camera,' I said.

'Oh, I dunno.'

'It'll cheer you up,' I said. 'Relax you. Things will improve Grace, okay? Perhaps not get better completely, but things will improve.'

'Thanks but . . . I don't think I'll ever get over it,' she said, eventually. 'Some people just don't, darlin'.'

Chapter Twenty-One

A few days after the meeting with Dr Love, Joe called me to ask if I would accompany him and Ethan to London Zoo the following week. Ethan still loved animals and Joe wanted to do something to cheer him up after losing his mum. I was more than happy to do anything that would help cheer up Ethan but, as the day approached, I became *more* excited about seeing Joe, at the same time as worrying what seeing him again might do to me, of what my heart might feel, no matter what my head was telling me.

And what was my head telling me? That it would be madness to try to make it work with Joe (properly, as a couple). That all that had to be kept in the past, where I had kept it the last sixteen years. (And I had survived perfectly well, hadn't I? Even if my emotional wellbeing was measured against the clinically insane and I hadn't had a successful relationship with a man since.) It was telling me that to revive that side of things would also revive so many painful memories. Just having him back in my life seemed to have brought on panic attacks. I couldn't go out with him, even if I wanted to. It would tip me over the edge. And yet, I was becoming aware that Joe was the last person I thought of before I went to sleep and the first person I thought of when I woke up and that that feeling had only ever happened with one person in my life before, and what this meant.

I felt I was at the precipice of a slippery slope that once, the first time around, I had freewheeled down and now I was too scared to even stand close to the edge.

The other thing that had struck me, during the hours and hours I had spent pondering *Joe, Me and the Future* during the past weeks, was that even if we were to make a go of it, it would be nothing like getting together the first time around, would it (before the pregnancy and Lily, of course), when life was so carefree and fluid? Back then, Joe and I were professional romantics. Our favourite thing to do, especially on a grey, drizzly day, was to go to Brucciano's ice-cream parlour on Morecambe prom, slip into one of the red leather booths, feed one another Knickerbocker Glories and snog. How shameless we were with our public displays of affection! How louche! Joe would regularly slip a hand up my back, or kiss me full on the lips in front of my dad, even his dad (who occasionally would still give Joe his 'friendly' sermon on temptation), his mates, the poor waitresses at Brucciano's. He really couldn't have cared less. I loved that about him. He was so unashamed, so proud of me, of us.

I imagined how it would be this time: we'd be a family (all being well) and part of me yearned for that – we could be so happy! – while the other part felt it was a risk I couldn't take – for me, but most of all for Joe – because, what if I got so far and then had to pull back?

What if it was already too late?

In the days leading up to seeing him again, I'd got myself into quite a state and so, on the morning of the zoo visit, I literally sat myself in front of the mirror and gave myself a talking-to. *He's asked you to the zoo, with his brother, not to marry him or to move in with him: nobody needs panic.*

Once I'd done that, I felt a bit better. This was a chance to see Joe, my old friend, father of my child (minor detail), on neutral ground. And I knew he'd hinted that it wasn't just Ethan who needed cheering up. Even if I couldn't 'be' with Joe, I wanted to 'be there' for him. Whether we liked it or not, this baby would mean that we would be forever linked, so it made sense for us to spend time together.

'Robbieeeee!' I could hear someone calling my name as soon as I walked into the café at London Zoo where we'd arranged to meet, because Ethan needs to eat regularly and wanted breakfast there before we started. The café was called The Oasis – a joke if ever I'd heard one, since it more resembled the orang-utan enclosure than any kind of refuge (talk about feeding time at the zoo), with a gazillion under-fives running around, steam rising from their damp coats, chucking food, screaming from their highchairs.

'Blake!' one woman was shouting at a child – aged three? four? I've no idea – but he was standing on a chair, doing an impression of a gorilla. 'I'm giving you five seconds to get down from that chair.' *Blake, quit while you're ahead,* I thought. *My sister only gives her kids three.*

'Robbieeee . . .!' I looked around again, trying to identify where the voice was coming from and then spotted Ethan: he was standing at the back of the café, looking at everyone through a pair of binoculars. 'I'm over here!' he shouted.

I gave him a very small wave, not that there was really

any point in trying to be inconspicuous now, and weaved my way towards him through the crowds.

'Hi, Eth. What's going on?'

'I'm bird-watching,' he said.

I laughed. 'Awesome. Well don't get us arrested, will you?' I said, putting my bag down on the table next to him. 'Perhaps save the binoculars till we see some actual birds. I think the flamingos are around here somewhere. Where's your brother?'

'Gone to the toilet.'

About three seconds later, I felt a hand on my back. I turned around to find Joe grinning, inanely. I felt sure my face was doing similar things.

He threw an arm around my shoulder. 'Hello. How are you doing since I last saw you?' he said.

'Good,' I said, aware of his hand, golden-brown and slender fingered with just the right amount of dark hair at the wrist, hovering, just above my left breast. 'Looking forward to this.'

Joe stood there, apparently unaware of his fingers near my breast. While I could be gauche in the wrong environment, Joe was so natural, so at ease with anyone and in any situation. You could sit Joe next to Bob Geldof or the Queen at a dinner party and he wouldn't necessarily know the right thing to say, he'd just say what he wanted and they'd love him anyway. My grandma used to adore him. 'No Joseph?' she'd say, whenever I went to visit her (no effort made at all to hide the crushing disappointment in her voice).

She'd take all her friends to the garden-centre café where he worked, just so she could show him off, and he would give them extra cake.

'Grandma, Joe is *my* boyfriend, you know,' I'd tease 'He's not actually yours.'

'I've seen a really big hippo!' said Ethan, suddenly, very loudly.

There was a very large woman sitting not far from us. This was probably merely a coincidence but Joe was taking no chances.

'Ethan, put those *down*,' he hissed, bolting towards him and snatching the binoculars. 'You can't shout things like that in public places!'

Ethan giggled mischievously as he let Joe put the binoculars back in their box and his drink back in his backpack for him.

'Don't worry, we'll take some pictures for Penny,' Joe was saying. Penny was Ethan's new girlfriend. She also had Down's syndrome. She was meant to be coming today but her rabbit had died and she was too upset. Joe had texted me beforehand to say not to mention it because Ethan was extra-sensitive at the moment with losing his mum.

'I really love Penny, Joe,' Ethan was saying, while Joe wrapped up what remained of Ethan's sausage breakfast bun in a napkin, to take with us.

'I know but, Eth, it's only been a week, best wait to say those three little words; otherwise, she might run a mile. Women get very easily scared off, you know.'

I watched them have this man-to-man chat; how tender Joe was with his brother. Yes, I had feelings there for Joe, still. Big feelings, that scared me. And I knew it was mutual. That was the scariest thing of all.

Joe turned, breaking my thoughts. 'Right, are we just going to stay here discussing Ethan's love life, which is

277

better, frankly, than yours and mine put together, or are we actually going to see some animals?' he asked.

I've always thought there was something romantic, melancholic about zoos – especially London Zoo. Maybe because it always seems to rain when I go, like it was today. Not a full-on downpour, just a damp, warm, summer drizzle that doesn't really get going but never stops either. The animals looked even more lost and sad in the rain. It was almost as if the giraffes, with their huge black lashes and their slow-motion munching, were silently pleading with you to take them back to the Serengeti; as if the lion, sitting regally in his enclosure, was secretly sending you telepathic messages with each slow, elegant blink, willing you to set him free, take him back to home to Africa.

I said this to Joe. He knew what I meant.

'I think that's *exactly* why the zoo feels melancholic,' he said, as we drifted around, arm in arm in the drizzle. Typically, neither of us had brought an umbrella. 'Because really, we shouldn't be here, the animals shouldn't be here. They should be running free in their natural habitat . . . They're all just making the best of a bad lot, at the mercy of us humans to save them.'

'That's sometimes how I feel when I go to see patients on the wards,' I said. 'Or when I take Grace down to Millbank Day Centre, and she looks at me with that face.'

'What face is that?' said Joe.

'The one that says: Get me out of this hellhole now! Some of the day centres are fantastic but we don't go to that one any more. Last time, Grace said to me afterwards, "Listen darlin', just because I've got mental-mind disorder" – that's her own description of schizophrenia, by the way;

she never uses the S word – "doesn't mean I like doing jigsaws or playing fucking Connect 4, any more than the next person." I thought that was fair dos, really.'

Joe agreed. 'How is Grace anyway?' he asked. We were sitting in the hippo enclosure, watching them waddle to the edge of their pool, then sink into the festering, brown, poo-strewn water. It stank in there but nobody seemed to mind.

'She's a bit all over the place, to be honest. I'm worried about her at the moment.'

What I didn't tell him was that I was worried about me, too. That I'd had several panic attacks at Grace's in recent weeks. Although I'd managed to hide them so far, I suspected it was only a matter of time before I could no longer do so. That they were affecting my life more and more. I knew how to manage them but that didn't take away how they made me feel, and it wasn't that much fun feeling like I might die several times a day.

'Well, remember what we said on the AA list?' he said. 'That you can't save everyone? You can help, but you can't save?'

Ethan had discovered that the hippo house was echoey and was enjoying hippo-type snorting noises. It was keeping him amused.

'Yeah, I know.' I shrugged. 'I'm just hoping I can help her.'

I gave Joe a brief breakdown of the situation, how Grace had lost custody of Cec, but how much she missed her. How she made things up about their relationship.

'God, that's so sad,' said Joe.

'I know. I'm trying to get her to see that there's no way she's going to have a relationship with her daughter if she keeps harking back to the past and telling herself what an awful person she is.'

'Well, I've no doubt you'll get through to her,' said Joe. 'Also, human beings are resilient: they can go through the most horrendous stuff and still come out the other side.'

I liked to watch his face when he talked. He had such an open face, eyes that held no secrets. 'I really believe that,' he said, turning to me. 'That there's always hope.'

We left the hippo house for the elephants. Ethan ran ahead, excitedly.

So what do you say to her?' Joe asked as we walked. 'How do you deal with it in your job when people are so damaged?'

'You can't "deal with it" as such,' I said. 'It's happened. You can't change the past. I just tell her that it's not her fault, that she's ill and that I'll do my best to help her have some sort of relationship with her daughter again, because ultimately I think that's the key to her recovery, anyone's recovery. I mean, she'll never be fully recovered, but she could be better.'

'What's the key?'

'Human relationships. Love. That's what experience at work has taught me anyway . . . What?' I said self-conciously. I realized Joe was looking at me as we walked and talked.

'Nothing, just, I really admire your passion, I suppose, your belief that you can help them. Sometimes I just want to scream at my students.'

'Oh, believe me, I sometimes want to do that too. So what's the deal with your students?' I asked. 'I'm guessing most of them have not had the easiest start in life either?'

Joe blew air through his lips. 'Yeah, I dunno, you've made me think, I suppose. I spend most of my time telling them not to let their past define them. That blaming your

280

past is not a good enough excuse – but maybe it is? Maybe I'm too harsh on them? Expect too much.'

I shrugged. 'No, I think that's a healthy message. Also, it's different. They're not ill as such, are they?'

'Not as *such*,' Joe said. 'Some of them are just bone idle. They're so young and yet so lazy, Robbie, and *hopeless* – in the true sense of the word, it's really sad – in that they think, because they had this shitty past, and Mum was an alky and Dad was a gambler, whatever, that nothing can change, so they may as well give up. It annoys the hell out of me.'

I smirked, I couldn't help it.

'I know, great teacher I'm turning out to be, eh? Listen, you lazy bastards, you've only yourselves to blame!'

'Actually, I think they're lucky to have you,' I said. 'At least you care enough about them to *get* angry.'

'Oh, yeah, I do care. I love my job. No matter how frustrating it can be.'

'Me too,' I said. 'But also, I get it. I get angry about some of my suicidal patients, I can't help it – especially the young ones, especially ones like Levi with his beautiful, healthy body. I mean, what a *waste*. I think about my mum – how much she wanted to live – and now your mum, and then I think about them fantasizing constantly about throwing themselves off the nearest bridge or whatever, and I think, *Fine love, you do yourself in; move over for someone who does want to live.*' Joe was nodding, as we meandered, arm in arm, listening to me. 'Actually, I've never admitted that to anyone,' I said.

Obviously, in my CPN head, I knew some of my patients' depression was so devastating, if you'd given them the choice between life and terminal cancer, they'd have chosen, *begged*, for cancer to take them quickly (that's the thing with suicide, once they get to that point, they want it so badly) but, intellectually, I found it hard to grasp. Literally having no hope. No hope of hope. So that was something, wasn't it? That was hopeful. 'So, you see,' I added. '*Great* psychiatric nurse I'm turning out to be.'

'Yeah, we should develop a new care programme,' said Joe. 'You've only yourself to blame, mate, Limited.'

'Very limited,' I said.

Joe laughed.

We went to see the elephants, then had our packed lunch, sitting on a bench, under a shelter, watching the sun fight with the drizzle. A rainbow arced across the fields. 'Are you two going to get married?' Ethan said out of the blue. We both stopped mid-sandwich.

'No,' Joe coughed. 'Not as far as I know. Not unless Robyn has any plans up her sleeve.'

I shot Joe a look. 'Why do you say that, Ethan?' I said.

''Cause you're having a baby. And you have to get married if you are having a baby. I'm going to marry Penny before we have a baby.'

'God, when are you living, Eth?' said Joe. 'The 1950s? Things have moved on, mate. You don't have to get married to have a baby. You don't even have to be in a couple.'

I was the one to cough this time.

'I love her, Robbie,' Ethan said . . 'I love Penny. She's beautiful.'

'She sounds beautiful. Have you got a picture of her?' I said.

Ethan jigged up and down excited: 'Joe. The picture! The picture on your phone! Show Robbie!'

Joe put down his sandwich, rummaged in his pocket for

282

the phone and, once he'd found the picture, passed it to me. It showed Ethan hand in hand with a dark-haired Penny. She had her hair up and was wearing a white cotton summer dress. They were standing in front of an enclosure with pigs in it. They looked so happy.

'We were at the farm,' Ethan said. 'Penny loves animals as much as me.'

'Match made in heaven,' I said. 'And she is beautiful, you're right.'

I passed the phone back to Joe. 'Yeah, just . . .' he said, his mouth full of sandwich as he talked, which made Ethan giggle. 'Don't get carried away with that lady of yours, Ethan Sawyer. Don't go getting married, either. Bloody women.' He winked at me. 'They're more trouble than they're worth.'

We finished our lunch, then Joe said, 'Right, who's for turtles?'

'Yeah!' said Ethan. 'They were Mum's favourite. I miss my mum,' he said, looking very deflated all of a sudden.

'Yeah, I miss her, too, mate,' said Joe, putting an arm around his brother. I put an arm around Joe. 'I miss her, too. Come on, let's go and see the turtles, for Mum.'

I sat there for a minute or two, watching them run across the field, their coats flapping behind them, thinking again how I wished the pregnancy thing hadn't happened, that Joe and I had got back in touch but that the baby hadn't happened.

The reptile house was tropically warm and lovely and I was aware of how much I was enjoying myself, at the same time as being aware of the nagging worry at the back of my mind that I was getting into something I couldn't handle, and that I was pulling Joe with me. But what was the alternative? To shut him out completely? I didn't want to do that either.

I didn't notice the two teenage boys at first, I was too busy admiring Dolly and Dolores, the two giant Galapagos turtles; and was only aware, somewhere in my peripheral consciousness, of two male voices, laughing, that honking, hoarse kind of noise that boys on the cusp of their voice breaking make. I was standing next to Ethan, who was peering at Dolores through his binoculars, giving a running commentary, David Attenborough-style. Joe and I were providing supplementary material à la 'Twits TV' and the Kingy Breakfast Specials. It was one of those rare moments – I'd had a few of them recently – where it felt like we were sixteen again, but even before Lily, before the bad stuff.

The next thing I knew, Joe was saying, 'What did you say?' to someone in a tone of voice that didn't sound right, that didn't sound like Joe. I turned around, to hear him say, again, 'I asked you a question, mate: "What did you say?"' in a more aggressive tone, and realized he was talking to the two boys who had made the honking noise, that he was practically spitting, he was so livid.

The boys looked about fourteen and had teeth too big for their mouths and skin that looked like they didn't know what a vegetable was. 'Noffin',' one said, 'I didn't say noffin'. What you on about?' The other was looking a cross between gormless and shit-scared.

'You said, move up, you spaz,' said Joe, moving away from Ethan so he couldn't hear. 'You called that guy there, who happens to be my brother, a spaz. I heard you, with my own ears.'

'Joe,' I said, gently touching him on the arm. I looked back to check on Ethan. Thankfully, he was still having a tête à tête with Dolores and completely oblivious to what was going on.

'No, it's all right, Robbie,' Joe said. 'I'm dealing with this. I just want them to admit what they said.'

There was a bit of an audience gathered now. A group of girls watching as the two boys tried to slope away and Joe followed, shouting, 'Oi! I'm not going to hit you or anything. I just want you to be man enough to admit what you've said and to apologize, since, in actual fact, my brother has Down's syndrome.' But the boys carried on walking. 'And you look old enough to know better!' Joe shouted after them.

One of them turned around. 'Not as old as you, you dickhead!' he shouted.

'Yeah, and your brother's a mong,' the other joined in and, with that, they both ran off, doing their seal-like honking laughter.

'Little fuckers,' I heard Joe say under his breath. He looked furious but still, I thought he might leave it there. But no, he did not leave it there. He turned to me, sighed regretfully, as if to say, *I really don't want to do this but I have to*, and then he ran after them, dodging dawdling families, parting groups of kids, past a load of buggies and a tantrum-ing toddler.

'Joe!' I shouted after him. I knew what Joe could get like when it came to Ethan, but that was back when he was sixteen, seventeen. Now he was thirty-two, but I worried he'd forgotten that, that he still thought he could run and fight like a sixteen-year-old. 'Joe, come back, they're not worth it!'

Ethan turned around now. 'Where's Joe?' he said

'Oh . . . just going for a wee,' I said, cursing him.

'But why is he running so fast? Is he desperate?'

'Yes, yes, it was a close call. Look,' I put my hand on Ethan's shoulder, 'can you just stay here for a second? I'll be right back, okay?'

'Okay.'

'Don't wander off so we can't find you, will you?'

'No, I'll stay with Dolores!'

The ground was wet with rain and I was worried about slipping as I ran after Joe – well, I say 'run', it was more of a light jog. As it was, I didn't have to go very far, however, because suddenly I heard this '*Ow, Jesus!*' followed by an almighty smack.

And then I saw Joe, about fifteen metres in front of me. He'd tried to hurdle over a bollard but had somehow got his foot stuck, meaning he'd landed pretty much face first. I ran over to him. He'd immediately got himself sitting up – I think he felt more stupid than anything else – and, in fact, on closer inspection, his injuries weren't as bad as the accident may have suggested (he was lucky he hadn't broken his neck, the force with which he'd buckarooed over that bollard).

He had a badly grazed chin with a Dracula-esque dribble of blood running from it. He'd also taken the top layer of skin off by his right temple.

I knelt down beside him. 'Oh, Joe,' I said.

'Where's Eth?' he said. 'Is he all right?'

'He's fine and, considering he didn't hear anything those boys said and thinks you just went for a wee, he's going to be pretty confused.'

'Ow, shit. Call yourself a nurse?'

'Behave,' I said, wiping gently at Joe's face with an

286

antiseptic wipe. We were back at mine, sitting on the bed while I cleaned him up. Ethan was in the lounge, watching *Pirates of the Caribbean* on DVD. 'I've known patients have electric-shock therapy and whinge less than you.'

He rolled his eyes.

'And keep your face still,' I said. 'I can't do this properly if you keep jigging about.'

His injuries didn't warrant this much cleaning, but I was just enjoying being this close to his face. I was so close, I could see how his eyelashes were dark and glossy but then went lighter at the roots; the crease in his deep, smooth eyelids (Joe's eyes are wasted on a bloke, he would look incredible in make-up), the tiny capillaries on the curved, narrow bridge of his nose. The way his two front teeth turn inwards on themselves. Things you'd only know about someone's face if you'd spent a long time studying it, which I had. All those years ago, and during the last few hours, too. I suspected that Joe also knew that his wounds were clean long ago.

'This is going to be a nice scab in a few days,' I said, rubbing Sudocrem onto the graze next to his temple. 'And you'll probably have a nice shiner, too.' To be fair, that bit was quite bad. The top layer of skin had come off and it was raw and glistening underneath.

'Do you think I'll look hard?' said Joe.

'Uh, nope,' I said. 'I think you'll look like you tried to hurdle over a bollard and fell flat on your face.'

Joe tutted. 'I'm really not hard, am I? I can't even run after a couple of teenagers without doing myself some damage.'

'You were quite angry,' I said.

'He's my brother,' Joe said. 'My little brother. I won't have anyone talk about him like that.'

287

I'd forgotten how protective Joe was. The scrapes he'd got into over Ethan, how he'd stuck up for me when girls had been bitchy at school – you know, just the stuff you'd imagine. Calling me a slut because I was knocked up at sixteen. I can't say I was ever that surprised. I had other things on my mind, anyway, like ever bumping into Saul Butler. Like Joe ever finding out the truth.

Joe winced again. I was convinced he was doing it for attention.

'You're a terrible patient,' I said, dabbing some more. It was becoming increasingly obvious that I wasn't so much tending to wounds now, just caressing his face with a tissue. I could feel myself softening, weakening. I knew the risks but I wasn't sure I could hold back anymore. I ditched the tissue and just stroked his face.

Joe shifted closer to me, so our noses were almost touching.

'I think that might be enough now, what do you think?' he said.

'Um, I think you might be right.'

'So how come you're still keeping me as some sort of Münchausen by proxy hostage, then? Is this giving you sexual kicks? Next, you'll be putting arsenic in my dinner then taking me to A&E.'

'Shut up,' I said. I was looking into his eyes. We both knew where this was going. We hadn't been kneeling on my bed facing one another for half an hour with one wet wipe for nothing. I hesitated for a long time and then, almost quickly, as if I didn't dare, kissed him on the lips and he kissed me back.

Joe reached out and stroked the side of my face, then

stuck his tongue in my mouth, dirtily, sillily, but it was lovely. I giggled.

'Now that's definitely not medical,' I whispered.

He went back to stroking my face, ever so slowly, with the back of his hand, and I closed my eyes, felt the undulation of every single knuckle, feeling at an impasse; like my life from now on would be split into before this kiss and after it. I imagined ten years from now, twenty years, thirty years, and I decided I wanted it so much, that it had to be worth the risk. Joe cupped his hand around the back of my neck and I leaned into him. In the other room, I was faintly aware of the babble of the television, but otherwise it was like we were in a bubble, a cocoon. When our mouths met, I felt like I'd let go of something and was in freefall and had no idea how I would land. 'Joe,' I said.

We were kneeling opposite one another and he shuffled even nearer on his knees so that our bodies touched, our necks interlocked and he was cradling the back of my head in his hands and planting kisses on my neck.

'I don't know,' I whispered. 'I don't know if . . . Oh God, I'm scared.'

'Of what, baby?'

Never, ever being able to tell you the whole story. Being with that, alone, for the rest of my life. Our baby dying again, because I don't deserve it, I don't deserve to be a mum, I thought. But then I thought about Grace: 'I'll never get over it, darlin',' she'd said. 'Some people just don't.' Well, I didn't want to be like Grace, I didn't want *Grace* to be like Grace: one of life's Great Irrecoverably Damaged. I did not want to wind up in Highgate Mental Hospital in too-short tracksuit bottoms and Crocs, mumbling about that gorgeous man called Joe I once knew, who came back into my life, giving me a new chance at happiness, and I screwed it up just because I was scared. I wanted to move forward, to be happy, to be a family with Joe.

'What of?' he said again, gently pulling me onto the bed. I let myself go.

'Nothing,' I said. 'Nothing.' I knew in that moment that this was the right thing to do. 'You got me,' I said. And he kissed me.

'After sixteen years. I got you back,' he said. 'Jesus Christ alive, you know how to make a man wait.'

We kissed then, for a very long time, and it was the sweetest, most wonderful kiss. Sweeter even, perhaps, than the kisses in the barn, because I had decided on this, rather than got carried away.

After a while, when our jaws were starting to ache, Joe said, 'So like, are you my girlfriend?'

I rolled my eyes. 'What are you, sixteen?'

'I feel like it.'

I smiled, hesitantly. 'I guess I am then,' I said.

'Can I see you tomorrow then?'

'*What?*'

'Can I see you tomorrow?' he said, and I started to laugh because I remembered when he'd last said that to me, standing outside the pub, the night after his Black Horse Quarry near-death experience.

'Can I see you every night this week?' he added. He was laughing, too, kissing me again and again.

'No, you can see me Thursday, *if* you play your cards right.'

Suddenly, from the kitchen, came an almighty din: the sound of cupboard doors being opened and closed, something dropping to the floor, the scraping of a stool against the tiles. I looked at Joe. 'What the . . .?'

'That'll be Eth,' he said, not taking his eyes from mine. 'Making a start on tea.'

'Right,' I said. 'Should I be worried?'

'No, but you should come here for another kiss.'

There was another bang.

'You okay there, Eth?' shouted Joe. 'We won't be long. We'll go and get pizza in a minute.' Joe turned back to me. 'He gets hungry a lot. It's part of the Down's.'

More clatter from the kitchen.

'Well we can't just leave him,' I said, slightly panicked now. 'He must be starving, poor thing. I'll have to go and help.'

'Oh-wer,' Joe groaned, dramatically, rolling onto his side as I got up. He tried to pull me back to bed but I resisted.

'Poor thing hasn't eaten for hours,' I said, pulling on the nearest thing: Joe's T-shirt, just long enough to cover my bum, and smelling of him.

'He ruins everything that boy,' Joe teased as I went into the kitchen.

The kitchen was a state. There were various tins and packets out on the side, including a box of Weetabix, the white packet with half of the biscuits gone and a sweep of Weetabix crumbs across the worktops. It looked like some sort of conceptual-art installation. Ethan was sitting at the breakfast bar, eating a dry Weetabix like it was a sandwich. I frowned at him.

'Ethan,' I said, 'what are you doing? You know you can have some milk with that.'

But he just carried on chomping, bits of Weetabix exploding out of the sides of his mouth.

I went over to the fridge. 'Were you starving?' I asked, looking for milk. 'I'm so sorry, I bet you thought we'd forgotten about you; we really will go and get pizzas now, don't worry.'

I closed the fridge door and was just standing there, holding the milk and some yoghurts, when Ethan stopped eating and pointed at me, grinning.

'What?' I said, glancing down at myself. For an awful second, I wondered if I'd walked out of the bedroom naked.

'Baby's coming!' he said, pointing at me, spraying Weetabix everywhere. 'Baby's coming soon.'

I looked down again, and realized the view was blocked from around the belly-button onwards. Sure enough, my eighteen-week-old bump was round and perfectly visible.

'Baby's coming,' he said again, a look of delight on his face. We both started laughing.

'It is, Eth,' I said. 'You're right.'

When Joe got dressed, we did eventually go to Domino's on the high street and pick up some pizzas. The sky was bruise-coloured, threatening more rain. And yet, as the three of us walked home, Joe, in the middle, balancing three pizza boxes and a garlic bread box like some sort of magician, reminiscing about all the amazing pizzas he'd had in his life (nothing beat the American Hot he'd had on holiday in Devon once; this we named the Holy Pepperoni, which Ethan thought was hilarious), I felt oddly happy. Hopeful. Maybe this was a new start; maybe I could learn something from Ethan's design for living, his version, of the world: a simple version, where people got married before they had babies, and whose memories didn't amount to anything more serious than the last great pizza they'd eaten.

Chapter Twenty-Two

September 2002
Kilburn, London

Dear Lily

So, last night, Joe turned up completely uninvited
and unannounced at our house (God knows how he
even knows where my student house is), having
driven all the way from Kilterdale to London in his
Metro with the wing mirror on the driver's side held
together with a rubber band and a dodgy exhaust
(it's a wonder he made it here alive). And do you
know what he said, when I asked him why he'd
come? He said, 'I just had an urge to see you.' Who
drives 250 miles just because they have an urge to
'see you'? And without telling you? I could have
been in bed with someone else.

I wouldn't mind (at least I'd understand) if he then
declared his undying love for me, said that he'd come
all that way because he couldn't live without me, but

he didn't say anything like that, he just sort of loafed around, got drunk at the pub with me, then slagged off my friends; then, when I suggested that he couldn't get over the fact that I'd moved on with my life, he said I was flattering myself. I mean, I can't win!

My head is all over the place now. I'm totally pissed off with him; I felt like I'd moved on; I've got new friends, I'm starting to meet guys, I'm starting, just, to put 1997 behind me, and then he turns up and it all comes flooding back again. I think I still have feelings for him, but I'm only twenty-one and he's only twenty-two. Even if he is The One, it's too soon for us to settle down with him. I think we both need to get out there.

Kaye guessed the second she saw me at work that something momentous had happened over the weekend. Jezza had called everyone into a meeting. He loves a meeting, does Jezza. He gets this look on his face when he announces we need to have one: sort of grim, but with barely concealed joy. In the same way some people live to be on stage, Jeremy lives to get into one of those rooms with a carpet that makes your hair go static, and lecture us about well, anything really; the subject matter is not important. He's been known to talk for half an hour, for example, about the hazards of bringing wet umbrellas into the office and not 'shaking them out'. I imagine he has a notebook somewhere, entitled 'Things I Could Have Useless Meetings About'.

Anyway, we all piled into this meeting. Jeremy was banging on about professional boundaries. Too many of us were treating our clients like 'friends', he said, we were seeing them outside designated times (so inconsiderate, these people who call us from the top of a cliff, armed with a bottle of vodka, with an urge to kill themselves when it's not our shift); we were buying them *coffees*; it had come to his attention that someone had bought a client a present. That someone was me – I knew by the way he was eyeballing me. I'd bought Grace a copy of *The Photographer* magazine because it had a feature about a photographer she liked in it. It was £3 from WH Smith, so hardly a present.

I was at the back of the meeting room. Kaye was standing with Parv and Leon near the window at the front.

'As I've said before,' Jeremy was saying, 'it is not advisable to cross professional boundaries because, to be completely and honestly frank' (he was a fan of tautology was Jezza; what you could say in ten words, he could string out to fifty) 'with some people, especially people not exactly hot on boundaries themselves, you give them an inch and they take a mile.'

There was a long pause, during which I considered just how much of a tossy comment that was. When I looked over at Kaye, to see if she was thinking the same thing, she was shaking her head at me, doing that thing with her fingers that says, *I'm watching you.*

'What?' I mouthed back to her.

'Right, Kingy?' But then I had to look at Jeremy because he was talking straight at me. 'You have to remember you can be friendly, but you are not their *friends*, okay?'

So who were their friends? I wondered. Because I knew for a fact that Grace, that John Urwin, that Levi and Sam – just to name a few off the top of my head – saw nobody else except me, sometimes for as long as a week. And what could be worse for their mental health? Us buying them the odd magazine, at risk of 'crossing boundaries', or loneliness and isolation (which so far seemed to me to be the biggest contributor to people losing the plot)?

Kaye demanded a kitchen debrief as soon as we left the meeting.

'So what's going on?' she said. 'Because you look totally and utterly pleased with yourself!'

When I'd caught sight of myself in the reflection of the bus window that morning, it was true, I was actually grinning. 'Well, me and Joe,' I said, 'we sort of got it together this weekend.'

'"Sort of" got it together?' asked Kaye, her ice-blue eyes narrowing. 'What does that mean?'

'Well, we decided to make a go of it. Me, him, the baby. To be a couple.'

Kaye gasped with delight. 'What, like a normal couple?'

'Yes, I guess so. So far as Joe and I are ever able to be a normal couple.'

She gave me one of her rib-cracking hugs.

'Well thank God for that,' she said. 'Thank God, you've stopped being so, well, *odd*. I mean, clearly, you adore him, the rate you go on about him, and you're having his baby – so, you have to agree it does sort of make sense for you to go out with him as opposed to someone else?'

'Well yes, yes, I suppose it does,' I said sheepishly.

She hugged me again. 'I'm so pleased for you.'

She did look inordinately pleased, it had to be said, and again it occurred to me: oh, this is how it's supposed to go. You meet someone, you fall in love with them, you have their baby. Everyone's happy. Sometimes I had to remind myself of that.

Kaye handed me a mug of tea and offered me the biscuit tin. I took a chocolate digestive. 'I'm taking three Oreos in celebration and commiseration,' she said.

'Why commiseration?' I said.

'Well, because I'm going to have to find a new partner to move into the hippy commune with now, aren't I? You're going to abandon me for a country pile and dinner parties in the Home Counties. Boden catalogue. Suburbia. Normality?'

I snorted then.

'Er, no, this is Joe we're talking about,' I said. 'Joe doesn't do country pile in the Home Counties. Or suburbia. Or normal. Joe is a lot of things, but I wouldn't say "normal" figures particularly highly. I'll introduce you soon. You'll see what I mean.'

Later that day, Jeremy sidled up to me in the corridor: 'Hi, Kingy,' he said, all friendly like he'd just thought of this as he was passing rather than the fact he'd been gagging to get me all day. 'Look, I, er . . . I know you're a fantastic nurse, Robyn, and I'd never question that, but I just think it would be an idea not to get overly emotionally involved with clients, especially Grace.'

'If you're talking about the photography magazine or our plans to go out and take some pictures,' (I'd mentioned this to Jezza briefly, before) 'I'm confident it'll help her. Photography is what Grace is passionate about. It makes her happy. I think it could be really good.'

Jeremy sucked air in between his teeth, as if to say, *Right love, whatever you say*, but actually said, 'It's just that camera of hers, I worry it's what gets her into trouble. I worry it makes her worse, because she gets overexcited, she starts annoying the staff and the patients.'

'Yes, when she's psychotic and ill and in hospital,' I said, trying not to get irate. 'But what if she wasn't admitted in the first place? What if she could get to some point of recovery, of being settled enough, where she wasn't admitted every few months?'

Jeremy looked at me. I could tell he was thinking: *Here she goes again, idealistic, naive, wants to save the world.* But truly, I didn't believe it was that hard to make a difference to someone's life. He could be so defeatist sometimes.

'Also, I'm hoping that encouraging her with the photography will go some way to helping her with her relationship with her daughter,' I said, 'Cecily.'

'Ah, yes, Cecily,' he said. 'That *is* very sad.'

I explained to him what Grace and I had discussed when we did our care plan: that one way for her to re-engage with Cecily was to chat to her about photography, something new that she was also interested in – hopefully working up to going to an exhibition together; something Mum and daughter could do together that would help their relationship to move forward. Jeremy touched me on the arm. I could tell I'd lost him.

'You're doing a fine job,' he said. 'Just . . . just be clear about your boundaries. And don't expect too much from Grace. Oh, and Robyn?' he added, as I was about to walk off. 'Is everything okay with the baby?'

'Yes, thanks.'

'And you?' he said. 'Is everything all right with you?'

'Couldn't be much better really,' I said; and it couldn't, not where Joe and I were concerned. All I had to do now was to stay perfectly sane. Keep my wits about me, not let my demons get the better of me. I needed to stay perfectly sane.

Chapter Twenty-Three

Three weeks later

It's Christmas Day and Kilterdale beach is empty, but for a man walking his dog, wearing a Russian hat. I am here with Mum. We are wearing swimming costumes – mine red, Mum's pink – and we are clambering over the rocks of the stone jetty, which curves sharp as a rhino horn towards the water. The sea is leaden grey; there is just a band of golden wintry sun, pushing itself out, like light under a door, turning the salt marsh at either side of us into a golden tapestry. It's December but I can't feel the cold; all I can feel is the smooth certainty of the stone beneath my bare feet and the secret thrill of doing this annual ritual with just Mum. The King Christmas Day Swim. Arms outstretched for balance, we quicken our pace now. There is the songful, soulful call of curlews and, every now and again, a little yelp from Mum in front as she negotiates the rocks with the litheness of a dancer. And now our bare feet are slapping the sand as we run towards the silver sea dancing with shards of light; Mum in front in her pink bathing suit, her hair fanning behind her. She turns around, her mouth open, smiling. She's wearing huge white sunglasses; she looks like a film star. I smile back and run to catch her up, but although I have my hands stretched out and my lungs are screaming with the effort, I still can't reach her. Suddenly, she enters the sea and then, she's gone, just disappears beneath the water like a mermaid, and I am standing in the middle of a vast, empty beach, as if there was never anyone else there in the first place.

When I wake up, I am crying. My pillow is wet with tears.

Joe was coming down pretty much every weekend. We had a routine: on the Friday, I'd meet him at King's Cross Station. We'd go to the gilded, high-ceilinged bar at St Pancras Renaissance Hotel. He'd have a cocktail and I'd have a virgin cocktail, and we'd make a plan about which of the AA list we were tackling that weekend. Of course, after about five minutes of that, we'd just end up talking about our lives: work, our families . . . and, sometimes, we'd talk about Lily, what happened.

It was a huge relief, like someone lifting a great slab of concrete that had been sitting on my chest for years. For sixteen years, I'd barely said a word about my baby, for fear of raking up the pain, or making people feel uncomfortable, and now I was able to and, better still, with the only other person in the world who had known her. One Friday, however, we were sitting on the high stools at the Renaissance bar, me saying how I felt when

300

we did this, like Juliette Binoche, in some French film about a torrid affair, when Joe stirred his Old Fashioned, took a sip and said to me: 'Why did you just run away all those years ago?'

I'd known it was coming but I still felt in no way prepared.

'Was it because I asked you to marry me? Was that it? Did I just scare you off?'

I felt sure I'd gone very pale.

'I'm not having a go or anything. I just want to know, because you never really told me.'

Disappointingly, and because I was caught completely off guard, I found myself on the defensive. 'Well, asking someone to get engaged at sixteen *is* quite scary,' I said, even though I knew fine well that in other circumstances I would have been ecstatic to get engaged to Joe. 'But especially because of everything that happened. Losing Mum, then losing Lily. I was sixteen, Joe, I couldn't cope . . .'

And what about me? Don't you think I lost all that too? I imagined he was thinking.

'We were so young,' I stuttered on. The echoey clattering of china and chatter seemed to be drowned out by the sudden silence between us.

'I would have stayed with you,' he said, looking up at me. He said it so quietly, I barely caught what he said. 'We could have worked things through together. The only person who understood how I felt was you, and you weren't there. Sometimes I feel like we wasted, we missed out on sixteen years, all those years, we could have been together.'

I tried to say something but the breath caught in my throat.

'You see, I've always known,' he said. I was looking into his eyes – those soulful, hazel eyes he has, thinking, *Me too. ME TOO! But things happened, awful things that I couldn't cope with, I couldn't tell you.* 'I've always known you were the girl for me. When I saw you at that stupid wedding with Brendan fucking Yeomans, whatever he's called, I literally couldn't stand it and that was *nine years ago* and, I realize, nothing's changed, Robbie. Nothing. I look back on all those years, all the girlfriends I've had, Kate, who I even lived with, they've never come even close, and I realize I . . .'

I put my drink on the bar and my hand on the side of his face. 'Sssh,' I said. My heart was beating wildly. 'Let's not go back over all that. We got each other back again, that's all that matters. We have to concentrate on the here and now.' And even as the words left my mouth, I felt like a fraud, because I knew how much I wasn't able to do that; how, essentially, I wasn't practising what I preached, because no matter how much I wanted this, this future with Joe, there was still our past, those fossils between the layers and layers of us. It would always be there, I just didn't know if I could ever get over it.

We had a kiss, a hug and nothing more was said. We went back to talking about the AA list – safe ground – but I was still reeling. What he'd said had thrown me off the balance I'd found during the past two and a half months. A feeling of promise – despite the turmoil going on in my head, despite my demons of the past coming back to haunt me – that I felt was worth fighting for. The list was helping me focus and Joe was so good for me. In the four years since noticing the damp in the hallway of my flat, I'd got as far as getting several workmen over, all of whom gave

302

me a different diagnosis, only succeeding in confusing me further. In six weeks, Joe had got his mate over (Joe being one of those people who has useful mates in all corners of the globe), who'd sussed it was a leak in the bathroom and fixed it. So now I was in the process of getting a new bathroom, courtesy of the insurance pay-out I'd been promised from the council, but had to wait for the walls to dry out, so the new, gleaming white toilet was sitting in my hallway and I was having to flush the loo with a bucket.

Joe wanted to put me in a hotel: 'No mother carrying a child of mine,' he said, 'will be flushing her poo down the bog with a bucket.'

'When you're used to clearing away people's skiddy pants all day,' I assured him, 'believe me, my flat is five-star luxury.' It seemed that the groundwork we'd put down all those years ago meant that we'd reached a kind of bodily function intimacy very quickly, Joe and I. And the toilet in the kitchen didn't bother me one bit. Even Eva's bags weren't bothering me as much as usual, because – try as I might to stop it happening – I was in love with Joe all over again. I wondered whether I'd ever *not* been in love with him, in fact, and it thrilled and terrified me in equal measure. My logical mind was telling me *don't do it*, because I knew if I were to lose him again – twice – I'd have lost him forever. I knew there was a good chance I would lose him, too, when he knew everything, because he would *have* to know everything. I'd have to tell him, I knew that now. I knew that the minute I kissed him on my bed when we'd got back from the zoo. I'd made that choice. But then I'd see him walking, so poised, with that half-smile, in the evening sunshine, down platform five; I'd watch his face as he talked; how animated he was, the way his chest kind of puffed out when he got excited – Joe actually needed to take in more oxygen, he was so excited by life – and I knew it was worth the risk.

We'd had the twenty-week scan at twenty-one weeks and we knew it was a girl. We both cried, although hopefully this time the sonographer didn't think we were quite so overemotional. Dr Love said everything was as it should be. 'Nine weeks,' we'd say to one another, then, 'Eight weeks,' 'Seven weeks,' . . . that's all we needed to get through. That's all we needed to get to twenty-eight weeks, when the chances of survival, Dr Love had said, were ninety per cent. Normal if we got past thirty. Thirty weeks pregnant! Imagine that. When Joe and I lay cocooned in bed together and I could see the silhouette of his face in the half-light, the rise and fall of his chest as he slept, I doubted I'd ever felt happier, or more certain about the fact that he was the right person. And yet, the panic attacks were getting worse. It felt like the truth, the past, was running towards me like lava and I couldn't run away fast enough. Everything was going to be subsumed.

Chapter Twenty-Four

June 2004

Dear Lily,

I've been going through some of my old letters to you recently and it's occurred to me, that while my intention was always to write only about lovely stuff, this has not always been possible – Maybe because I've needed to let off steam.

You see, I realize that you're the only person I can tell the truth to (bit tragic, when you come to think of it, since you don't actually exist), and the truth is not always that nice, I'm afraid. However, I've decided that this letter will be only lovely. It will be full of all the great things about my mum that I'm scared I'll forget over time. That I'm already forgetting. It will be a record between all three of us: me, you, Mum. I promised, before we lost you, that I'd tell you about Mum, so here we are.

Surprising things about Lillian King (your grandma, my mum):

- She couldn't cook for toffee, so she'd do party food for tea all the time: cheese and pineapple on sticks, mini-sausages, sausage rolls . . .
- She used to make up brilliant games for us to play, her favourite being a 'make the most realistic poo competition'. On a rainy afternoon when we were bored, she would challenge all three of us to make the most realistic poo: 20 mins on the clock, free rein of all ingredients in the cupboard (cocoa powder, bread etc.). At the end, she'd give us marks out of ten. That was, at one time, our all-time favourite family game. Not Scrabble, or Monopoly, no. 'Make the most realistic poo' competition.
- She was always fair. She never let any of us go to bed without giving each other a hug (even if, when Leah and I got to the bedroom, we almost killed one another).
- She played the ukulele (badly) and we all had to go and watch her.
- She was a Man Utd supporter through and through.
- She put up with my dad's potty mouth and his general cantankerousness. But he had to put up with her extreme untidiness (there is a reason he is now with a woman who boils her dishcloths).
- She had a phobia of baked beans. Not spiders, or bats, baked beans.

*

Joe put down his paintbrush and blew air through his lips. 'Do you think we could just give Carol Smillie a call? I'm done in,' he said.

On this particular weekend – the week after Joe had poured his heart out in the Renaissance Hotel bar – we'd decided to decorate the baby's room. I say 'we', because it was us who decided, and us who put it on the AA list. We'd talked about whether it was tempting fate, but decided that not to do it was also tempting fate, just in a far darker and more morbid way, and so decided just to get on and do it now, before I was too hefty and offended by the paint smell. The smell was all over the flat, anyway, which is why Joe suggested I leave the flat and I wasn't complaining. That afternoon, I'd spent the day mooching round Portobello with Kaye and Parv, buying sunglasses and ethnic jewellery and feeling young and cool again.

Now I was home and felt bad for being out all day having a lovely time while Joe slaved away, because he really did look done in. I dropped my bags and strode over to him. 'Thank you for doing this,' I said, kissing him on his cheek. It was damp with sweat. He had white paint all over his eyelashes and in his hair. I stepped back, crunching my eyes up. 'I can imagine what you might look like when you're seventy, if I do this,' I said.

'Really?' said Joe, amused. 'What do you care, anyway? I'll be married off and emigrated to Australia by then.'

I opened my mouth at him in mock shock.

'Or maybe just Spain. A nice villa in Andalucia . . .'

I rolled my eyes. 'In your dreams,' I said.

Joe started with the paint roller again, continuing with his second coat of white. I stood back in the centre of the room, so I could get the big picture, as it were. It was late afternoon – 4.30-ish by now – and the room was warm as toast and drenched in sun. It was so bright, you could see each roller stroke on the wall, each tiny drip, each movement Joe had made, and I felt this sudden little surge of excitement for the future, and what it might hold. I wanted to hold onto that feeling forever. Looking forward to things. For so many years, I'd forgotten what it was like. Now I was fighting for it.

'It's looking so nice in here, Joe,' I said. After things getting a little heated in Ikea (Joe had wanted to go out all bling and pink, I said we weren't doing anything so gender-specific, not until I was holding that baby girl, alive, in my arms), we'd eventually agreed on a unisex rabbits theme (sounds weird, looked cute). Joe had made a nappy-changing table to put on top of a set of drawers. He'd now got as far as painting the walls white, the skirting boards yellow and had grand plans to make a cot. Carpentry being one of the many things he did with his NEETs students, he was great with his hands. Cliché it may be, but in the past few weeks I'd discovered that there was nothing sexier in this world than watching Joe, pencil over his ear, decorating scruffs on, moving with the rhythm of the wood-sander. I'd told him so too, to which he'd (after he'd picked himself up off the floor, laughing) given me an Elvis lip and said, 'Hey, honey, if you want to take black-and-white pictures of me in my pants, over the Black and Decker, knock yourself out.'

While Joe had started work on the cot, I'd been tentatively knitting items, including a teddy and a little dove-grey cardigan, which sat around the flat, like little stepping-stones in my head: just get to twenty-seven weeks and a day. Then, twenty-eight weeks, twenty-nine. Thirty. If I could get to thirty, I'd feel much better. It wouldn't be perfect, but I'd relax. A little.

I went into the kitchen to make tea. That decorating smell hit me right between my eyes and I felt kind of headachey, like you sometimes do before a storm.

'Jeez, this place stinks. What paint are you using?' I shouted to Joe in the spare room.

'Sorry, that's the turps.' I was filling up the kettle and I stopped. Turps. Course it was. 'Are you sure you should be in a house that stinks of chemicals?'

I took him a mug of tea, setting it on the bottom rung of the stepladder he'd used for the ceiling. I'd get used to the smell.

'Are you operating a secret brothel?' I said. 'You keep on wanting to kick me out.'

'Sorry, darlin'. I just want to do everything right. You read this stuff on the Internet . . .'

'Oh, Joe, you've not been doing that, have you?' I said, knowing full well that things had taken a downturn on that front. One night last week, I'd got stuck on Google and I couldn't get off. Of course, I'd found torturous stories immediately:

The Ultimate Grief Twice. It's devastating enough to lose one baby, but to Emma Connor, it happened twice . . .

Google Search: How could anxiety attacks affect my baby?

Google Search: Risk of stillbirth happening twice.

I read blogs, studies and message forums, until my neck ached from sitting at my laptop and statistics seemed to glow from the screen, like cancerous tissue showing up on a PET scan. I still remembered the horror of those, from when Mum was ill. My brain was screaming at me to stop and yet, feverishly, my finger kept on clicking:

. . . women who have had a stillbirth are five times more likely to have a subsequent stillbirth.

But then another study concluded: *In mothers who have already given birth to a stillborn . . . there is NO increased risk of subsequent stillbirths.*

But that study was small and Australian, so did that even count? No increased risk was the overall consensus, but I couldn't stop myself thinking the unthinkable. It was perfectly feasible, after all: the universe had already dealt me quite a lot in one go, several years ago. The universe was clearly not interested in fairness. I became hyper-attuned to other people's stories of unmitigated misery and runs of bad luck; which is no mean feat in my job, given most of our clients have pulled the short straw in life (as if abuse and loss and trauma weren't enough, the universe then throws schizophrenia into the mix). Lightning-strikes-twice stories in the press leaped out at me: 'Woman loses son and husband to cancer in one day'; 'Man killed on way home from wife's funeral'. Like an addict, I'd promise myself I was never doing it again, until the next night. I knew Joe would kill me if he knew. But it was like a little voice inside me was dragging me to that laptop, urging me to gather more evidence to support the story my evil twin was telling me: that I didn't deserve this happiness, that when Joe knew the truth, he wouldn't want me any more, that this couldn't last.

I sat in a puddle of sunlight on the floor with my cup of tea and admired the muscles in Joe's arms as he painted, waited for the tantalizing glimpses of his smooth, golden back every time his T-shirt rode up. He stopped for a second and stepped back, surveying his work.

'Do you think they'd have looked like each other?' he said. It was completely out of the blue and my stomach flipped. 'Who?' I said, even though I knew who.

'Lily,' he said, turning to me. 'And the new baby. After all, they're full sisters, aren't they . . .?' I swallowed. Did he suspect something?

We'd talked once about this: how while this baby, or any baby, would never, ever replace Lily, she'd give us more to go on than just the imaginings we had. She'd be a window into what Lily might have been that we never had before. Despite this, we'd never talked about what she might look like before, more about personality traits, talents, that sort of thing. And we'd only talked about it once and then it was enough, we didn't need to keep bringing it up. I wondered why Joe had.

'Robyn?' Joe said, when I didn't say anything. 'You alright?'

My mouth was frozen. I couldn't speak. Did he know?

'I don't know,' I said eventually, pathetically. 'But it would be nice to think so, wouldn't it?'

Joe stuck his paintbrush in the can of turps and came over, putting his arms around me. That smell. It seemed to seep into every orifice, every pore of me, hardening something inside, making it hard for me to breathe, to think. 'Will we tell her about her?' he said.

'Course,' I said. 'Of course. As soon as she's old enough to understand, we'll tell her she had a sister called Lily Grace Sawyer.'

'Good name,' Joe said, resting his chin on my shoulder, wrapping his arms around my waist. I closed my eyes. Maybe I was just imagining it. Maybe he didn't suspect at all. Why would he? I'd never mentioned anything about Saul Butler, nothing at all.

'Yeah, top name.'

'It sounds like a writer or a musician, or a fashion designer . . .'

We both stood in that warm orb of sun, gently rocking, and I knew we were both thinking the same thing. That she never got to be any of those things.

I leaned my head on Joe's chest; and, as if she could hear us talking, the baby stirred inside me. I took Joe's paint-speckled hands and placed them on my belly. 'Feel that?' I said, and there was the fluttering – more than a fluttering now, more of a wriggling inside, like tiny people were moving tiny furniture. I smiled, excited. 'She's up and about.'

Joe looked skywards, concentrating; then, when she did it again, he smiled this slow, wide, smile. 'And to think people go out and get off their heads,' he said (like he'd never got off his head in his life), 'when there are natural highs to be had in life like that.'

Our noses were millimetres apart. 'Joseph,' I said, 'you're like a *poet* or something.'

He slapped my bum once, sharply, making me yelp. 'Sarcastic! Horrible girl,' he said. Then he put his hands in my hair, arranged his head and shifted his feet – Joe takes kissing very seriously – and put his mouth to mine.

The sun slowly made its way around the room as we kissed, the light it emanated kind of extraterrestrial. Joe's face and hair were damp from the exertion of painting. I drank in the scent of him, the pheromonal deliciousness. My hands made their way up his T-shirt, to the sun-warmed dune between his shoulder blades. Joe was caressing, marvelling at my bump, with both his hands in a circular, rhythmic motion, like he was fashioning a pot on a potter's wheel; at the same time as kissing me in that slow, very artful way in which only Joe can kiss.

He rested his forehead on mine. 'You're so sexy,' he said. 'I might have to take you to bed. Would that be okay with you?'

The dull nag of dread began in my stomach. I pushed it away.

'I think I could go with that,' I said. I let him take me by the hand.

My bedroom is at the back of the house, away from the afternoon sun, and was lovely and cool. We undressed and lay facing one another, Joe slipping one arm, gently under my head, me snaking a thigh around his smooth, warm body. I closed my eyes and concentrated on the taste of him; the sounds our mouths made, on our hands, feeling their way around our bodies, which were now familiar enough again for that feeling of togetherness, but still strange enough after all this time for it to be a total thrill. I'd rediscovered the simple pleasure, these last few weeks, of just Joe Sawyer's bare skin next to mine.

'You okay?' he whispered, as he lowered his pelvis onto mine, as our hip bones met and I nodded because, more than anything else in the world, I wanted to be. And for some time I was okay; more than okay, it was bliss. I was managing to think of absolutely nothing other than what was happening in that moment – meditating, basically; something I was doing in and out of bed, to try to help me with the panic attacks. But then, suddenly, I was far from okay. As much as I tried to fight it, my mind and body were betraying me and – just as had happened so many other times we'd tried to have sex these past few weeks since I'd caved, that afternoon after the zoo – Joe's face and his touch were being eclipsed by Butler's.

I knew what it was now. When it had happened in the back of my neighbour Tim's car the first time, when he was giving me a lift home, I hadn't realized. But now I knew I'd believed that it was really happening again, that I was sitting in a car with Saul Butler and he was driving me down Friars Lanes. It was in the way the sun had hit the windscreen, caught the light on the amber hairs on Tim's arms; it was in the way it had flashed behind buildings, like it had behind the high hedges that summer's evening, sixteen years ago, like a malevolent star, leading us somewhere dark and terrible.

There was a red, silk dressing gown hanging on the back of my door. Kaye had brought it back for me from her trip to Hong Kong in February. As Joe's breath quickened and he moved inside me, I fixed my eyes on it. It was something from the here and now. It couldn't be from my past because I didn't have it then. I was telling myself that this wasn't a real experience and I wouldn't let it be. This wasn't happening now and I wouldn't believe it was. This was a flashback, a defective memory; like toxic sediment being dragged up from my mind and, yet, every time I opened my eyes, for a second, before I was assailed by unwanted awful images and clamped them shut again, it wasn't Joe's hazel doe eyes looking back at me, it was his watery blue ones. It wasn't Joe's beautiful firm skin I could feel, but that fat, white belly slapping against mine like dough, and me, my head turned to the side, the beady eye of that chicken staring at me; the only witness.

314

I slowed and buried my face in Joe's chest, determined not to cry in front of him . . 'Robbie?' Joe said, gently.

'It's okay, carry on.' I stopped moving completely.

'Robyn, what's wrong?'

I kind of shifted my body, so annoyed at myself, and looked up into his face; as suddenly as that awful vision had started, it stopped. 'Nothing,' I said, kissing him, fully, as if for compensation, I suppose. But we both knew it was no use.

We lay there, cuddling for a bit, in a silence we both knew was loaded, but still neither of us said a word. I felt so guilty, like I'd let him down, that I'd failed. But most of all I was angry with myself and my body because I wanted nothing more than to just have sex with the man I was in love with, and it wasn't letting me. 'Are you all right?' Joe asked again. He'd turned on his back now, I had moved, so my body wasn't touching his and he was brushing the hair from my forehead, tenderly. 'You're not worrying about anything, are you?'

'Don't be silly,' I said.

'Good, because you know what Dr Love said about not thinking the worst, trying to relax. You would tell me if there was something?'

I felt a momentary flicker of annoyance. Wasn't losing a baby enough to put you off sex when you got pregnant again? Wasn't that the 'something'? But I didn't want to get into one. Best just to move on, and not make a big deal of it.

'No, I'm fine, honestly,' I said, as breezily as I could, kissing him on the forehead and getting up to go to the bathroom.

'Maybe you just don't fancy me any more, then?' said

315

Joe. 'Now I've got nostril hair and a pot belly . . .' (He didn't have either; not that it would matter if he did. I fancied him even more than I did at sixteen.)

'*Joe*,' I said. I knew he was teasing but my sense of humour had escaped me and, also, I couldn't bear for him to think that. 'Please, I'm so sorry.'

'I'm only kidding,' he said, puffing up his pillows and sitting up. 'I guess it must be weird, when you're pregnant, hey?'

'What?' I said, searching around for my knickers.

'Sex.'

'Yes, a bit,' I said. I was in the bathroom now, having a go at my eyebrows, which had gone so bushy with pregnancy, astonished, as I always was, by the sight of my changing body, my twenty-three-week bump. The S shape I made from the side. It always felt like it was someone else's body.

'Are you kind of worried it'll . . .?' He stopped. I walked to the door of the bedroom, still holding the tweezers.

He was lying, his arms behind his head. Two dark tufts of underarm hair.

'Worried it'll what?' I said.

'Sort of . . . poke the baby's head?'

I shook my head and sighed. 'Well, Joe, if I didn't have problems already, I do now!' I said, feeling the hot spring of tears threaten, the smile fade from my face. Joe's face fell too. We both knew this was getting to be a bit of a charade.

'Robyn, this has happened every time.'

'I know', I said. I couldn't even look at him.

'And, honestly, besides the fact that I would like to ravish you day and night. That I want to have you, constantly, because you're so frigging sexy with that

316

bump and those magnificent breasts and that face, I'm worried there's something deeper going on.'

I didn't say anything. I felt completely exposed, just standing there in my knickers. I unhooked the dressing gown off the back of the door and put it on, almost like a barrier, a defence.

'You don't get the Tube any more, do you?' said Joe.

'It's hot and cramped and I don't always get a seat'

'You've been scaring yourself with stuff on the Internet, too, haven't you?'

'How do *you* know? Have you been snooping?'

'I didn't have to, you'd printed loads of stuff out. It was just sitting there on the side when I was checking my emails.'

'*Shit*,' I said under my breath. I couldn't believe I'd left them out, that he'd had to read that stuff, besides anything else.

He didn't look cross with me, he just looked sad – that was the worst thing.

'Look, it was only one night,' I said, as lightly as I could, going back into the bathroom so he couldn't see my face. 'I won't make a habit of it, I promise, don't worry.'

'Good, 'cause you'll be in trouble with Dr Love and me if you do. You heard what he said about stress and the birth and labour.' I began washing my face, as if a quick splash of cold water might make me feel better.

'Also, anyway, I've got a bone to pick with you,' he said. I could hear him getting up and getting dressed in the other room.

'What, another one?' I teased, turning off the taps and reaching for the towel.

'Yeah, you know that conversation we were having

317

the other day, when we were talking about all the people back in Kilterdale that we'd ever had a thing with?'

'A thing with?'

'Yeah, a snog, or gone out with, or even just a crafty fumble down Hobbit's Cave.' 'Hobbit's Cave' being a cave on Kilterdale beach where many a crafty fumble had taken place in our youth.

'What, and you confessed to me about having it off with half of my year, feeling up Tania Richardson, you hussy,' I said, feeling better we were at least having a joke now that the atmosphere had lightened.

'I was fifteen!' Joe said. I could hear him giggling. 'And anyway, never mind about her, what about Saul Butler, eh?' I froze. Ice crept up my neck, my mouth filled immediately with water. 'Apparently, you had a thing with him, too?'

I immediately started to tremble; it was a reflex I couldn't control.

'Who told you that?' I said, desperately trying to make my voice sound normal. I tried to dry my face but my hands were shaking so much, I dropped the towel from the towel rail. I bent to pick it up.

'Bomber said Saul told him a couple of years ago,' said Joe. I could hear the jangle of his belt as he did up his jeans. 'When I was staying with him a few weeks ago, you crafty little minx.'

I was forming an answer in my mouth, when a shrill noise started up in the lounge: my phone ringing. When I walked to answer it, it took every cell of strength I possessed to remain upstanding, for my legs not to give way.

'Robyn?' It was Niamh. 'Have you got a few minutes to chat?'

Chapter Twenty-Five

Kilterdale
August 2006

Dear Lily
Sometimes I wonder if your father is still hyperactive or has some sort of problem that would explain his behaviour last night. Sadly, I just think he's turned into a common-or-garden moron! I've just been to Tania Richardson's wedding in Kilterdale. It was beautiful – the sun shone and Tania was so happy (even if she looked like she was having a Big Fat Gypsy Wedding; I would ONLY say that to you). I took Brendan with me, who I've now been seeing for two years, so it's not like he's 'a phase', but it's the first time I have dared take him up North to meet my dad and it went well – Dad loved him. He can see that Brendan is a proper grown-up, although offering him a whisky on arrival (Denise had put some in a decanter – who does that?!) was embarrassing to say the least.

I don't know what got into Joe. One minute he seemed to be having a perfectly friendly chat with Brendan, the next he was threatening to punch him. Then, ten minutes later, he was sick on Bren's shoes! What made it worse was that on the way to the wedding, I'd been telling Bren how much he'd love Joe – because 'everyone loves Joe'. I've never seen Joe behave like that – like he had not just a chip but a jacket potato on his shoulder. I'm torn now, because I'm worried about him at the same time as being annoyed he could show me up like that . . . At the same time (and I would only ever disclose this to you, too), I felt stuff when I saw him, Lily. I actually wonder if I don't still love him.

'I just don't feel like I know her, Robyn.'

Like I've said, it was not unusual for my little sister to begin whole conversations like this, at the eye of her personal storm. However, at first, what I actually heard was, 'I just don't feel like I know Robyn.' (An insight into just how self-absorbed this 'mental-mind disorder' was making me.) I stopped, stood there in the middle of my lounge in the red silk dressing gown, disoriented from what Joe had said; about to say, *You, too? So I'm not imagining then? I really have gone fucking AWOL?* In the nick of time, I realized she meant Mum.

'I feel like she never got a chance to know me.'

Since that evening at Leah's house, Niamh has called me and come over, wanting to talk about Mum. It was almost as if the possibility that we might have lost

Mum's ashes had panicked her, kick-started a desire to find out about Mum and to tell her things before she 'let her go' (in whichever way Niamh decided she would do this).

Since we couldn't make any joint decision on what to do with our mother's ashes, we'd decided to split them three ways so that people could do whatever they wanted to do with their share: scatter them, keep them in the airing cupboard – the glove compartment, if they so desired. That was what Mum always used to do with anything when we fought over stuff: split it up and let us work it out.

I got how Niamh felt. Whatever I decided to do with Mum's ashes, I needed to tell her my secrets first, too, but Niamh felt this more acutely. This was because Niamh's memory of Mum was patchy, at best. Sometimes completely imagined. It broke my heart, really, how she'd come up with this and that story and I'd have to nod my head and say I didn't remember. Sometimes I just pretended I did. I figured this was probably why Niamh was such a good actress, why she had such a wild and free imagination: she'd had to make up an entire parent in her head.

Selfishly at first, I was worried that exhuming memories of my mother with Niamh might make things worse for me. But, actually, it made me feel better.

I suppose I've always seen my life as pre-1997 and post-1997 and never given much thought to the first part, due to the energy it took to survive the latter. I was changed and that was good, because I had to be changed to survive it.

And yet on the few occasions lately when Niamh has

come over and we've looked at the few photos I have of Mum (just a small, raffia boxful, kept next to the box of my letters to the granddaughter she never knew), I'd suddenly unearth a lovely memory from that pre-1997 time, that sacred time, that had been buried for years beneath all the dark stuff, and it was like finding something precious beneath the devastation of a landslide, the retelling of the story, better than being there first time around.

Niamh loved the story of getting lost in Asda when she was five and how Mum had had a stand-up row with the manager about his total lack of procedure for this sort of thing (when really it was Mum's fault; she'd been gassing with someone and Niamh had wandered off); how, when Niamh's goldfish died and she was out at a sleepover, Mum put the goldfish in the freezer, so that they could give him a proper burial the next day (Mum insisted on proper funerals, complete with songs and readings, for all our pets). Her favourite story was how when Mum brought Niamh home from hospital and took her to show her off, round to every Tom, Dick and Harry's house in the village. (She was never one for false modesty, was Mum. If she had something to show off about, she showed off, and trusted that people would be generous enough to be happy for her, like she was for them.) I'd gone with Mum, and to every single person who said to the nine-year-old me, 'And you must be such a proud big sister?', I'd beamed, and said, 'She's *my* baby,' and they'd all laughed.

I told Niamh how I'd loved her so much from day one, and so had Mum, how she was a much-wanted third baby (not the late accident she suspected she might be), a final girl to complete the set of three Mum had always wanted. Had Dad? Sod Dad! She'd always said, 'God knows how he survived in that house full of hormones.' Because he loved Mum and us, I suppose; because he loved their life together.

After our little chats, Niamh would sigh like she'd been satiated and now could sleep easy, but now there was this other matter.

'It's not just that I feel like I don't know her enough. It's the other way round, too. I know it sounds silly, but I need Mum to know I'm gay,' she said.

'It doesn't sound silly at all.' I could hear Joe moving about, drawers going, doors going, and I hoped I didn't sound as distracted as I felt. The flashback had been horrific. I couldn't risk that happening again. And if I couldn't have sex with my boyfriend because I couldn't risk that happening again, where did that leave us?

There are things I want Mum to know, too, before I scatter her ashes. I almost said it aloud to myself, to Mum.

That's if I *was* to scatter them. It depended on how strong I was feeling. Right now, I just wanted her with me, close to me.

'I can't let Mum go until I've come out, Robyn,' she said. 'I've decided, I need her blessing. It's important to me.'

I came fully to now. 'Oh, Niamh, now listen. She wouldn't have cared if you were straight, gay, bi or anything else; all she ever wanted for any of us was for us to be happy, and be true to ourselves. She probably would have bloody loved it, anyway. She was always against convention. This is the woman who conducted actual funerals for goldfish . . . Who made us go swimming in the sea on Christmas Day.'

'Yeah, I see your point,' said Niamh. 'So, Robyn?' I was squinting at the piece of paper Joe was holding up in front of me which said: GOING OUT, BACK SOON. I gave him a look that said, *If you don't come back, I'd understand*.

'Yeah?' I said.

'When do you think you might tell Dad about me? You know, like you said you would?'

'Oh, God, Neevy, I'm sorry.' It was alarming how self-absorbed I was becoming with all this going on. I'd completely forgotten, I felt *terrible*. 'As soon as I find the right moment, I'll do it, okay? I have to do it before I have the baby anyway.'

'Why?' she said, and I hesitated. I hadn't told anyone about the AA plan and I didn't want to, really. It was Joe and mine's thing.

'Oh,' I said. 'Just because.'

I hung up just as I heard Joe leave, pulling the door shut behind him. As soon as I knew he was safely out of the house, I went into my bedroom and retrieved the spotty Ikea box from under my bed. There was a specific letter I wanted to read.

December 1997

Dear Lily

I knew this would happen sooner or later but I'm reeling. I can't get my breathing to go normal! I just bumped into Saul Butler. I was in the hardware shop, getting some fuses for Dad and he was in there, just lurking in one of the aisles, probably buying something for work.

'Hi,' he said. Hi? Hi?!! How can he just say hi to me like nothing happened? When I'm standing there with a bump? The worst thing was I was so shocked, I said 'Hi' back.

The one thing I regret most about the whole thing is that as I got out of the car, I told him not to tell anyone. What message would that have given him? That I thought I'd done something wrong. That what happened was like normal sex, like I'd just got off with him and betrayed Joe? Because that's not how it felt for me. But now it's occurred to me that maybe that's how he sees it? That it was all perfectly normal? And me just saying 'hi' like that can't have helped.

At precisely 9.05 a.m. on the Monday after Joe had been down for the weekend, I called Dr Love directly in his office – I was desperate.

'Beta-blockers during pregnancy? Mmm, I would say, probably not, no.'

'Oh,' I said. I was standing in the corridor at work, looking out of the window at London coming alive, failing to hide the disappointment in my voice.

'Can I ask why you think you need beta-blockers?' asked Dr Love. I briefly checked that nobody was coming down the corridor and pushed my forehead against the window, talking as quietly as possible.

'I've been having these . . . panic attacks, anxiety

attacks – you know, shaking, beating heart, overwhelming feelings of terror that I'm about to keel over and die.' I don't know why I was sounding so cheerful, laughing almost. Years of practice, I suppose.

'How often?' said Dr Love.

'It was just occasionally at first, but now it can be up to several times a day . . .' I paused. The next bit was hard to say out loud. 'It's starting to affect my work.'

'Mmm,' said Dr Love again. 'Well, Robyn, don't worry about work, you need to protect yourself and the baby. Although there's no research to suggest that panic attacks will harm your baby, so don't load yourself with that worry, too . . . Do there seem to be triggers?' he asked.

'Sex,' I said. It was a bit too late in the day to feel any sort of embarrassment about saying this. *Having sex with the one man in the world I trust, whom I love, who loves me!* I wanted to add. I was so angry with it all. 'I find it hard – no, impossible, to have sex.' *Also, the smell of turps, chickens and their beady eyes*, I wanted to add, *getting in the front passenger seat of any car, the Tube* – but felt sure he would think I was quite patently mad; I was pretty convinced I was going that way. And what if he deemed me too mad to look after my baby? It had happened to Grace . . .

Dr Love was quiet for a moment.

'There is an anti-depressant you could take,' he said, finally. 'It would help with the anxiety. It's an old type of medication and poses no known risk to your baby.'

No *known* risk.

'I would suggest that you go and see your GP and tell him or her what you just told me.'

'Okay,' I said, even though I knew, even now, that I

wouldn't be able to take anything with no 'known' risk, so I don't know how I thought Dr Love was supposed to help me, how anyone could help me now. I was a lost cause.

'The main thing, I'd say, however,' he added, 'is that after what happened to you, it's entirely normal – especially now you are pregnant again – to be having these feelings. It's just your mind's way of processing it.'

Yes, I thought, *but I haven't told you everything that happened to me.*

I couldn't concentrate all morning. At lunch, the strain of keeping everything to myself for so long was proving too much, so I decided I'd talk to Kaye in a casual way about it. Maybe it was just the nature of the job to be anxious and panic-ridden? Working with the mentally ill had to affect you eventually. If I was suffering in silence, then maybe other people were, too.

Kaye and I were sitting, sunning ourselves in the garden of Bella Café; I had my cheese toastie resting on my bump. 'Kaye, do you ever get affected by stuff at work?' I said, trying to keep my tone light.

Kaye put down the newspaper she'd been reading. 'How do you mean?' she asked.

'Well, like, emotionally,' I said. 'Do you find it a difficult job?'

'It depends how you mean . . . Do I find it emotionally difficult that we never get the chance to talk to anyone properly, because we're far too busy filling in forms? Then, yes. Do I find it emotionally difficult visiting people like Mrs Patel? Then, also yes.'

I laughed. Mrs Patel was one of those patients it was best to visit in twos. The week previously, Kaye and I had gone, and she'd locked the door behind us, then proceeded to force-feed us an entire Indian banquet for four hours. I rather enjoyed myself. Kaye, unbeknown to me, was secretly on hostage alert, back to the office on her phone, the whole time.

'Is that what you meant?' she asked.

'Not exactly,' I said. 'I suppose I meant more: Do you take clients' issues home with you? Does what they tell you ever affect you? You know, badly?'

She put down her paper. 'Not really,' she said. 'I think I'd crack up myself if I let that happen. I mean, I worry about them . . .'

'Oh, okay.' I bit into my toastie. 'I just wondered.'

I chewed, feeling Kaye's eyes boring into me. 'Are you okay, Kingy?' she said, eventually.

I looked up. 'Yeah, fine.'

'Is something bothering you at work?'

'No. No, not at all. I just wondered. You know sometimes you just wonder about this stuff but never really ask?'

Kaye looked at me, smiling, but you could tell her mind was whirring away.

'Okay,' she said, nodding. 'Yeah, I get that.' Then, staring at my midriff, she added, 'Your bump looks absolutely massive today, by the way.' Then, she went back to her paper.

Joe and I hadn't discussed, when he'd got back that afternoon, the fact we'd failed to have sex again. He'd just come home, armed with more paint from Homebase, a Thai takeaway and a DVD, and I'd hugged him, in that slightly platonic and apologetic way that says, *I'm really sorry but I don't want to talk about this now*, and that was it, we didn't. Instead, we lay on the sofa, sharing a bag of Revels, watching the film *Eternal Sunshine of the Spotless Mind* (about a couple who have each other erased from their memories – a controversial choice, all things considered), laughing in the right places, making all the right noises; but I knew he was worrying about me, worrying about the baby, about us. As I was too, of course. I was reeling from what Saul Butler had said to Bomber. I was going over and over events in my mind. Had I misconstrued things? Had I had a thing with Butler and forgotten it? I thought back to one night, must have been even before that summer of 1997, when I'd seen him in Boon's – Kilterdale's only club. He'd chatted me up: 'You look nice, Robyn, like the hair . . .'

And I'd smiled and replied, 'Thank you, Saul. It's not every man who notices things like that.'

Had I led him on? Had he kissed me then and I'd been so drunk I couldn't remember? I was doubting myself. It was like falling pregnant had unlocked a roomful of boxed-up memories from the last time I was pregnant, but they'd been boxed up for so long they'd faded, I couldn't trust which were real and which were imagined.

What has always disturbed me most about what happened down Friars Lanes at the end of that summer, is not what happened in the car (although, believe me, that still disturbs me), but what happened immediately afterwards. I knew I was changed, that life would never be quite the same again, but Butler carried on like nothing had happened, like he'd done nothing wrong. The sky was streaked with pink. The breeze was causing rippling waves across the citrus-yellow fields of

329

rapeseed. Pollen floated about us like minuscule airborne dancers on a lit stage. It was idyllic. How could something horrific have happened here? Maybe because it didn't? Because I somehow got the wrong end of the stick. I remember what happened next in minute detail, like I'm looking at it through a microscope. We drove to the party. Saul was chatting to me, looking at me through the rear-view mirror, normal as anything. The radio was on: Prefab Sprout – that song about hot dogs and jumping frogs.

We got to Tony Middleton's house and I opened the car door as the car was still pulling into the driveway. 'Easy Tiger,' Butler said. I was horrified to find when I stepped out that my legs wouldn't work – like they'd been drained of blood, like they are after you've been sitting on them a long time – but I pulled on every molecule of strength I had to stand up. That's when I told him not to tell anyone. Why had I said that? Because *I* felt like I'd betrayed Joe? I went straight inside the house and searched for Joe. I remembered how when I finally found him, upstairs, in Tony's room, earphones on, playing on Tony's decks, I flung myself into his arms. 'Baby, what's the matter?' he said, shocked, wrapping his arms around me. I'd just arrived at this party and now I was saying I wanted to leave. I spun some yarn about feeling ill on the way and would he take me home?

I don't know what time it was when I got in, but I could hear the bathroom tap running and Dad doing that slightly disgusting thing he still does when he's brushing his teeth, which is to honk up really loudly and spit into the sink. Fleetwood Mac were on the radio singing, 'Everywhere . . .', which was Mum's favourite song; and so I stood in the hallway and listened because I thought it might make me feel better, but I knew that song was ruined now. It had been Mum's favourite song and now it was my worst. And there wasn't even anything I could do about it.

Dad honked and spat again, then he shouted, '*Robyn*? Is that you? I thought you were going to Beth's?'

I froze to the spot because I didn't want to see Dad. I didn't want to see anyone. I just wanted to go upstairs, get in the shower and go to bed.

'Bobby?' he called again.

'Yeah, it's me,' I called back, but it didn't sound like me: my voice was small and weak and like Mum's when she was lying on the sofa – dying, if I'm honest. I sounded like *I* was dying. I *felt* like I was dying.

I closed the front door, as softly as I could, and put my bag down. The sun was pouring in right down the hallway, so I was kind of standing in this tunnel of light and, it sounds silly, but I imagined it was a sign from Mum. She was there; she was watching over me. She knew everything. I got in the shower. I made the water as hot as I could bear and scrubbed every molecule of Butler off me, but when I got out, I still felt soiled with him. I needed to cancel it out somehow. I went to bed, telling Dad I didn't feel well, and tried to sleep, but all I did was lie in the dark, images of Butler's face coming at me, that chicken standing in the middle of Friars Lanes, its horrible beedy eye jerking in its socket.

Dad popped in to check I was all right. He was unshaven and wearing only a pair of white Y-fronts. That was his look most of the time, after Mum died. Niamh and I used to call him, 'The ghost in white Y-fronts.'

'I'm fine,' I said, trying to disguise my voice, which was thick with snot and tears.

I'd told Joe I wanted to be on my own but now I was, all I wanted was him. He'd be up now with his parents, watching Saturday-night TV in the cosy vicarage lounge with its Tiffany lamps and its warm red rugs. Normality. Oh, God, how I longed for normal. It felt like nothing would be normal again.

I lay in the dark for hours, not being able to sleep, just crying. I wanted a hug so badly. A hug like only Joe could give me. I imagined his arms around me, my head lying on his chest, listening to his heart-beat, his smell. I imagined telling him everything, but then I had no idea what words I'd use. Above all, I wanted to cancel out what had happened with Butler. I lay there until it was light, and then I got up – it was Sunday morning – and I went straight round to Joe's. We went to his room and, immediately, I took off my clothes, pretty much threw myself at him. He wasn't complaining. Then we made love and, even though I was so sore and it hurt like hell, I didn't make a sound. I had to do it. I had to cancel it out.

Chapter Twenty-Six

I could have predicted almost to the second when Joe would call me at my desk on that Monday morning, after he'd gone back to Manchester: 11.05 a.m. (he had a teaching break starting at 11 a.m.).

'How're you feeling?' he said.

'Good. Great. Nothing to report,' I said, trying to sound as cheerful as possible.

'Did you go for your swim this morning?'

'Yes,' I lied. (I'd lain in bed, going over and over the scenes with Butler, wondering if there was anything I'd said, anything I did.)

He paused. I carried on typing.

'How's *your* day?' I said.

'Fine. Caught some kid dealing weed outside on the college grounds.'

I laughed. 'Shit.'

'Robyn?'

'Yeah.'

'You've not been scaring yourself on the Internet again, have you? You're being calm, trying to stay positive. Are you staying late at work again tonight?'

It was so sweet he cared but, also, I felt this bristle of annoyance: *Who was he? My dad?* My dad hassled me less than Joe. In fact, we'd had all of about three conversations on the phone since I'd told him the news I was pregnant again, and there'd been Denise in the background feeding him questions: 'Ask her if they're being understanding at work, Bruce. Ask her if she's told them what happened to her; she shouldn't be working, anyway, not at six months gone.'

It had endeared Denise to me. (Even if she had mad, 1980s ideas about maternity leave and confinement.) It was nice that she cared, I just wished Dad could have asked those questions himself.

Joe, however, was overdoing it.

'For God's sake, Joe.' I'd never snapped at him like this before and he was taken aback, silent. 'You're not my dad. You're my boyfriend.'

Joe wasn't the only person I was getting tetchy with. I felt irritated and angry. I felt my life was spinning out of control and the more I felt I was losing control, the more I was frantically trying to claw it back. Grace needed me, Levi and Yolanda; all my clients needed me. I couldn't go mad.

I was especially worried about Grace: her behaviour was becoming more erratic, her flat more untidy (if that were humanly possible). Sometimes she wouldn't turn up when we'd arranged to meet, which was most unlike her, and, if I wasn't there to watch her swallow her medication, I couldn't be sure she was taking it. I was beginning to see that Jeremy had a point about her having a very 'definite cycle' (not that I would ever give him the satisfaction of telling him that). And this cycle, I had identified, was down to anniversaries. Anniversaries were Grace's trigger: June – the last time she was hospitalized – being the month her abusive stepfather died, the event that triggered her original breakdown, and September – just weeks off – was the month that Cecily went to live with her grandma and Grace ceased to be a mother at all.

The problem was, it was a vicious circle – she loathed hospital: hospital made her worse, but the nearing of an anniversary made her worse, too; so life became chaotic, she stopped taking her medication, then became more unwell and likely to be sectioned. Things had reached a whole new level of chaos in her flat: mouldy food, smoking paraphernalia everywhere. I'd found a packet of ham dated May, lodged behind the radiator. And so I was checking on her more. I wanted to help Grace. Most of all, I wanted to keep her out of hospital. However, I was also becoming aware that helping her didn't seem to be helping me. Maybe we had more in common than I wanted to admit?

The most frustrating thing was that, actually, as far as making bridges with Cecily was concerned, we were making progress. Rather than constantly telling Cecily how awful she was, Grace had started to ask Cec questions about her life now, the things she was interested in. I'd been delighted when I'd gone to meet her at Peckham Library and she was on the phone. She'd put her hand up to me: 'Just give me a minute, darlin'. Cec and me are having a chat.' That moment was a proud moment. I was proud of her, proud of us for getting to that point. It may have sounded like a small thing, but to Grace, this was huge progress.

But still I could tell she was becoming ill. You had to listen carefully, because things were just muttered or insinuated; but there were constant clues left, like spots of blood leading to the scene of the crime, to the full darkness at work in Grace's mind. *Yeah well, is it any surprise, after what he did to me, that I ended up in the nuthouse?* She'd tag snippets from her past on the end of a conversation about something entirely different: a benefits form we were filling in, a risk assessment. Sometimes she was less obtuse, and the voices and her battles with them would be made perfectly public, say when we were sitting in a café, or on a bus, and she would just talk to them out loud: 'If you hadn't have dropped dead, I woulda murdered you myself, I would, with my bare hands!' People would turn around and stare. Grace was *that* mad woman on the bus that everyone avoids but I felt she was counting on me not to let her end up in hospital. 'They're not gonna put me in there, are they?' she'd say. 'You won't let them lock me up, will you darlin'?'

'Not if I can help it, Grace,' I'd say. And I meant it.

On the Tuesday of the week after Joe had dropped the bombshell about Butler, I went to see Grace for our normal weekly session. There was no answer, however, and so I called through the letterbox:

'Grace, it's just Robyn.' I always said 'just Robyn', I don't know why. To distinguish me from any other foreign body she feared it might be, I suppose.

There was no answer so I knocked again more loudly.

336

Silence, for a few moments. Then she shouted, 'I'm well!'

This wasn't a good sign. This meant she really wasn't well. I opened the letterbox and could just make out her shins, the hair on them visible in the shaft of sunlight. She was barefoot. I could hear rustling and she was padding about the kitchen, clearly no intention of answering the door. After a few minutes of talking to her through the letterbox, trying and failing to get her to open the door, I popped a note through, asking her to call me. She did, a day or so later, and we arranged to meet at the Subway sandwich shop in Peckham, so I relaxed a little. I assumed she was just embarrassed about the state of her flat.

She was agitated when we met, giving microscopic detail of her past life, in an almost manic way: as if literally turning over the earth with a hoe, wanting to examine everything it brought to the surface. We went halves on a 'New York Deli' sub. Grace also ordered a side-plate of jalapeño peppers, which she was munching through like they were peanuts.

'He said we would meet again in the afterlife,' she said, suddenly.

'Who?'

'Him – Larry.' I knew exactly who she meant, although it was the first time she'd used his name. 'He told me just before he died, that we would meet again in the afterlife, where he would have me again but this time for Eternity.'

I felt the prying eyes of the woman next to us – mental patients were well known around these parts and Grace was no exception – but didn't give her the satisfaction of turning to look.

337

'Grace, you know that's absolutely not true, don't you?' I said. 'Larry is dead and can't harm you any more.'

'Larry used to tell me he would snap my neck with one hand if I ever told anyone,' she said, ignoring me, tipping her head back and throwing another handful of jalapeños down her neck, like a fire-eater. 'But I will snap his.' Her eyes were beginning to stream with the heat, but she didn't so much as blink. 'Even if I have to do it in the afterlife, I will snap his.'

I knew she was getting worse and I was right to be worried. The following day, I found her standing in the centre of her lounge, among piles of old photographs – some in albums, most just loose, but all of them of her and Cecily, as if the only way to anchor herself was to literally place herself in the past, with her daughter, when she was well.

I stood on the threshold of the lounge and surveyed the scene. 'Oh, Grace,' I said. She looked bewildered, as small and vulnerable as a child herself, like she'd literally woken up and found that this had happened to her. She looked up at me. The next thing she said really broke my heart. 'I want her,' she said. 'I really, really want her.'

I went over then, stepped over the pictures – I didn't give a damn about boundaries – and I gave her a hug. 'And you will have her again,' I said. 'You will have her in your life again. But you must be patient, you are doing so well. Come on,' I said, 'let's get all this cleared up.'

In clinical, later that day (clinical meetings being where we talk about the patients we are most worried about), I brought up Grace and how I planned to take her out to do some photography. I thought it would calm her down to be absorbed in something she enjoyed, something that was hers. It would take her out of her own head, which was, of course, the last place she wanted to be.

Jeremy called me back afterwards. He was sitting on his desk, tapping a biro, this off-putting intense look in his eyes.

'Is everything all right, Kingy?' he asked. (Jeremy once said to me: 'I really should have been a psychologist, Robyn. I could analyse anyone.' I thought then, as I thought now, that these were dangerous times indeed.)

'Yes, why?'

'Just, you seem a little on edge lately. I'm worried about you.'

Oh, God, maybe I really was going mad. Even those that worked with the mad could see I was going mad . . .

'You seem to be very preoccupied with Grace,' he said.

I blinked. Perhaps I was, but I was still doing all my visits with my other clients. I wasn't neglecting anyone.

'I was just telling you what my worries are with Grace,' I said. 'So you know where I am with her.'

Jeremy nodded, slowly. 'Right,' he said. 'And where are you with *you*, Robyn?'

I froze. 'Fine.' What did he mean? There'd only ever been the patient and myself present whenever I'd had a panic attack and, so far, I felt sure I'd managed to keep them secret, hadn't I?

'Because we've been a bit worried about you in the office lately, to be honest. Is everything okay with you and the baby and with Jack . . .?'

'Joe.'

'Sorry, Joe.'

'Yes,' I said, blankly. A hot wave made its way up my legs. 'Everything's fine.'

'Because I'm scared you may be taking on too much with Grace's case and everything else you're doing. That you're –' he clasped his hands together – 'not really coping too well at work.'

My cheeks burned hotter. I sat on my hands so that he couldn't see they were trembling.

'What do you mean?' I said.

'Well, it's come to my attention that you can't, or won't, take the Tube and so have been late for visits.'

This was true, I had, but I'd always made up the time, stayed my full allotted hour with them.

'I don't like taking the Tube when I'm pregnant,' I said. 'I always make up the time on visits.'

Jeremy nodded then gave a big sigh.

'You're not going to like this, Robyn, but I think you're perhaps dedicating a bit too much time to Grace, at the expense of other patients. And the photography and so on – it's a good idea, but you know what she was like in hospital with her camera. I'm concerned it actually makes her more agitated. Maybe we need to have a meeting with Dr Manoor, look at her dosage?'

I felt deflated and annoyed. Were drugs always to be the only answer? Just pump 'em up to the eyeballs with antipsychotics, so that they can't think, they can't do anything?

Surely, doing things that made her happy would do her good? Things that helped her to feel part of society? If that was crossing 'personal boundaries', I wasn't sure I even wanted to do this job any more. It only made me more determined to do what Grace and I had planned to do when we'd written her care plan – to take her out taking photos. To get Grace behind the camera again. When I came back to the office and told Jeremy how well it had gone, he'd understand. He'd see why I did it.

Chapter Twenty-Seven

February 2009

Dear Lily
Today is the day that I know for sure what I want
to do with my life. In all the time I've been there
(this is my third week of a six-week training
placement at Cygnet Hospital), my patient, Claire
has never ventured out of bed or spoken. Like most
patients, she's suicidally depressed. She was so bad
this week, in fact, she's been on 'special observation',
which means she has to be within arm's length of a
member of staff at all times, because when left alone
previously, she's got out of bed only to hurl herself
repeatedly at the wall. She hasn't spoken to anyone
for three weeks. But tonight, when I was on watch
with her, she spoke. It was only to tell me that she
felt so bad she wanted to die, but she reached out
nonetheless. She dared to connect with another
human being. I can honestly say, that moment was

the most fulfilling I've ever had in my life. I know now that this is absolutely what I want to do.

Joe had agreed with me some time ago to come on the official photography day with Grace and me in Elephant and Castle. He liked photography but, more importantly, he liked Grace. Neither being a fan of smalltalk, or ceremony, they'd got on famously when they'd met, even if Grace had fired questions at him like she was my mother: 'So how much d'you get paid, then? Are you in this for the long term, mister? Not let my Robyn down?'

Joe liked to talk, Grace liked to talk. I'd thought it would be fun for Joe to come with us for Grace's first shoot in fifteen years, but he'd been annoying me this week, if I'm honest. He'd been cloying. He didn't say, he never said, but I could tell by the daily phone calls and the constant texts – *How you feeling? How's baby? What are you still doing at work at this time?* – that he was extra concerned about me, since discovering my secret Internet habit. While I was grateful he cared, I also resented, if I'm totally honest, this idea that he couldn't trust me to look after myself and our baby. So, I wasn't being a responsible mum and, according to Jeremy, I wasn't being a responsible CPN either. I felt like I had to prove myself. I was determined to make today a success. I should have known, however, when Joe and I picked up Grace from her flat that morning that things were sliding downhill fast for her. But maybe, because things were sliding quickly for me at that point, I didn't really notice, or that, in comparison, she didn't seem that bad. If there's any job that teaches

344

the term 'everything is relative', after all, working in mental health has got to be it.

I'd spoken to Kaye and Leon and Parv about my idea to take Grace out with her camera, and they all thought it was a good one, even if Jeremy didn't. Sometimes I wondered if Jeremy believed in recovery at all; whether he believed anyone could get better, or it was simply a case of tinkering with their medication from now until death. Sometimes I wondered if he – and not just him but all the bureaucrats in Kingsbridge Mental Heath Trust – was just a bit Münchausen by proxy about it all: he enjoyed his hero role too much to ever want to make the sick people in his care any better. Maybe that was cynical of me, but that's how it felt sometimes.

It was all going so well at first (although we all know what happens in stories that start like that). Grace seemed excited when we went to pick her up. She wanted us to stay at her door, however, while she got her camera and so on together.

'You can't come in,' she said, practically shutting the door in Joe's face. 'Don't let him into my flat, Robyn, it's disgusting in here.'

'Believe me, Grace,' Joe spoke through the crack in her door (behind it, we could hear her clattering around), 'nothing shocks me. Nothing.' I looked at him, so tall, at his intelligent, open face. I still found him beautiful, even when I was annoyed with him – and contemplated whether anything would really shock him.

When Grace finally emerged she looked like a different person. She had this swagger. She pointed the camera in Joe's face and took a shot and I had a glimpse of the

345

woman Grace used to be. And then she put the camera down and did her nervous little geisha shuffle across the scrubland, where kids were playing football in the sun – and she was gone again.

We found our way across the confusing maze of underground burrows that is the Elephant subway, and arrived at the market. Grace knew everyone, everyone knew Grace:

'All right, Gracie?'

I love a London market, full of life, full of colour. I was glad we'd chosen here for the job. A man, wearing a cap that said BLING, held out a diamond-encrusted watch in the palm of his hand. 'This'd cost ya easy two hundred nicker in Debenhams.' It glittered and flashed in the sun. The dark head of a man dipped and rose as he prayed on the prayer mat laid out behind his stall, on which stood shiny brogues in boxes. A couple in love – him wearing a kilt, her with turquoise hair and earrings that had stretched her lobes so that they hung like chewing gum – kissed in front of a stall selling large-size ladies' knickers. A man wearing a belt that said DEATH BEFORE DISHONOUR ate fried chicken from a box, and danced behind his stall to reggae. His colleague had a new pair of trainers – the new Converse All Stars. 'Brown leather, box-fresh,' he said. 'Delivered to the Oxford Street Branch only yesterday.'

'Doze are nice, man, nice . . .!' said his friend with the DEATH BEFORE DISHONOUR belt. I wondered if he knew what that meant.

'Can I take your photo, Ron?'

'Course you can, Gracie. Do I look pretty if I do this?' Ron was maybe fifty, but looked a decade older in the way that people from round here often do. He owned a stall that sold Hawaiian shirts and shorts, but didn't look like he'd been further than the Dartford Tunnel. When he smiled, all his teeth were yellow and several were missing and yet he had the bluest eyes you'd ever seen. 'I'd bet he was a hit down the Palace Bingo when he was a lad,' Joe said, as we stepped back while Grace composed the perfect portrait. The Palace Bingo stood pride of place at the top of the Elephant Shopping Centre. Grace, Yolanda and I had been there on a few occasions, on a rainy afternoon. Yolanda in her glittery hot pants and her Stetson.

Grace was clicking like a pro.

'That is beaudiful, Ron, beaudiful! You got the golden triangle right there!' Grace had explained to me once about the 'golden triangle' rule of photography: that if you looked at anything of natural beauty – flowers, butterfly wings, beautiful faces – they all had this 'golden triangle' within them, this natural symmetry.

'Look at you with yer golden triangle, Ron,' Grace said again, clicking away.

'Golden balls more like!' shouted the guy with the new trainers. The man on the stall next to him, selling Calvin Klein boxers and the like, laughed wheezily.

To look at Grace with her camera, you'd never think she was mentally ill and on the cusp of a crisis, but I knew the telltale signs. She was paranoid and making connections that weren't there. Putting two and two together and getting five, like a child might do. We went to a Polish café in the shopping precinct for lunch. I could see Grace eyeing up Joe suspiciously. She'd not looked at him like that on the previous time they'd met.

'Where d'you live then?' she said.

'Manchester, remember?' Joe smiled.

'Oh,' she said, going back to her plate, but I saw her face darken. She watched him like a hawk as he ate. I knew what was coming next. 'Did you know Larry Gates?' she said. 'He was from Manchester.' Grace had told me this once, in one of her detailed monologues about her past – he was a long-distance lorry driver from Manchester. He and her mum had met when he'd come to stay at the hotel.

'Manchester's a big old place, Grace,' I said. 'I doubt it.' I didn't want to get onto Larry Gates today. I didn't want to feed her paranoia. Today was about moving forward.

'Who's Larry Gates?' said Joe. I gave him a look that told him to drop it.

'He's a nasty piece of work,' said Grace. 'That's what he is, Joe. He did things to—'

'Grace. . .' I said gently. 'Let's not get into that at the moment, shall we? I don't want you to get yourself upset.'

She dug a fork into her Polish sausage. 'I'm gonna snap his neck if I ever see him again.' She said, and I winced. Perhaps it wasn't such a good idea to ask Joe to come too. Still, you could tell he worked with people who'd fallen through the gaps of society, because he didn't bat an eyelid.

Even though it was a connection she'd made up in her head, I could tell that the Manchester thing had thrown Grace a bit. We ate the rest of our lunch in silence, Grace eyeballing Joe, watching every lift of his fork to his mouth, every self-conscious clearing of his throat, every reach for the salt, and Joe doing his best to ignore it and make conversation – about Poland. Had I been to Poland? Would I like to go to Poland? Did I like this Polish sausage? I was looking at him and thinking how mind-blowing our story so far had been, how far we'd come, at the same time as about the flashback I'd had that morning, and the fact that I didn't know if I could do this any more. And I was angry with Joe. It's wrong, but I was, because I'd always known I couldn't do this, deep down, and yet he wouldn't have it. He trusted me and I now couldn't see it through.

Joe was amazing, he could have any girl he wanted and yet he wanted me, who was clearly too damaged to be able to give him that. And now the fallout was going to be huge. I was going to hurt him so badly, again, and this could have been prevented if I'd just not weakened, if I'd just stuck to my guns.

My mind might have been racing, but Grace seemed to recover herself for a while after lunch, completely absorbed in her photography. She still had all the charm of a professional and people were queuing up to have their picture taken. It was so good, for once, to see her in control of something. She taught Joe and I a few things about composition that day: the rule of thirds, F-stops and shutter speeds. It stopped us actually having to have a conversation with each other. In the afternoon, she and Joe went off, taking photos together for half an hour, while I made some work calls.

I was still on the phone when I saw Joe waving me over. There seemed to be a problem. Grace was standing in front of a stall that sold Bibles, religious pamphlets and books called things like *Living in the Light of Eternity* and *Come, Let's Teach the World About Jesus*. The woman in charge of the stall was a large black woman wearing traditional African robes and a blue turban. There was a small black-and-white TV on the front table of the stall, playing the film, *The Crucifixion*, with the scene of the actual crucifixion on a loop.

'I see she's going for a subtle approach,' deadpanned Joe. Grace was transfixed by the film; she wanted to take the stall owner's portrait in front of it, but the woman wasn't keen; she was having a heated debate with a man about God, while flicking her hand away at Grace like she was an annoying fly. 'Miss, miss,' Grace was saying brightly (slightly manically, but brightly), 'let me take your picture next to Jesus. Poor old Jesus on his cross, it'd cheer him up,' she added with dazzling understatement. But the woman was too busy ramming her thoughts about God down the man's throat. She was shouting. I could tell it was making Grace stressed.

'He needed to die to relieve the sin! We are born sinners,' she was yodelling, arms outstretched to Him Almighty. 'Accept God as your leader and saviour and he will forgive your sins.'

Grace was holding her camera up, ready to shoot. I tried to move her away, distract her, but she wouldn't have it, and I didn't want her to cause a scene. She caused a scene anyway: the woman finally stopped talking, turned to Grace and, in a rather un-Christian fashion and a very thick accent, snapped, 'Stop that! Stop that now, wo-man. You get away from my stall.'

I stepped forward. This was all we needed.

'The photos aren't to sell or go in a newspaper or anything,' I said. 'She's just practising. Could she just take your picture . . .?'

'No.' She was wagging her finger, talking very loudly now. 'No, I do not want my photo taken.' She made a whistling sound, as if to shoo Grace off like a dog. After everyone had been so nice and accommodating, Grace was taken aback. She might have made a little 'tsk' sound through her teeth – nothing more – but the woman in the turban started shouting about madness and sin and the devil. Grace shouted back even louder:

'You say all this about God forgiving our sins. You call yourself a Christian, darlin', but I think there are some sins that should not be forgiven. Is he going to forgive Larry his sins? My stepfather his sins? Do you wanna know what he did to me, that dirty bastard? And then he just queues up at the gates of fucking Paradise, does he? And it's all all right 'cause God will forgive him?'

I had my hands on Grace's shoulders, trying to move her gently away. 'Grace, stop it. Come on, you can't shout at people in a public place like that.'

'She's shouting at me!' she protested, and part of me agreed with the essence of what she'd said about Larry: I was thinking about how one terrible event, one evil act – not even a series of them like Grace had endured – could ruin your life forever.

'She blaspheme!' The woman's eyes were bulging out of her face as she jabbed a finger in Grace's direction. 'She blaspheme in the face of God. Have you no shame, woman? God have mercy on you!'

351

I wondered who was more mad, Grace or her.

'Oh, fuck off,' Grace said. Both Joe and I sort of made a lunge for Grace – an attempt to get her away from the drama as the next few seconds unfolded – but neither of us moved fast enough. Grace took an orange from a stall nearby, hurled it at the TV – at Christ on the Cross (thankfully, it narrowly missed and bounced off the TV set instead), and ran off. I ran after her – as fast as a woman with a twenty-four-week bump can run – but Joe was close behind. Turned out I couldn't run to save my life, anyway, because he caught up with me almost immediately. 'Robbie, stop,' he cried, grabbing me by the shoulder and swinging me around. It was the first time since that day outside the museum that I'd seen Joe look properly angry, livid actually. 'For God's sake. What are you doing, running after her? You're six months pregnant.'

I knew he was right, at the same time as feeling this overwhelming responsibility: Grace was in crisis, she needed me, the woman on the Bible stall was threatening to call the police. If the police were called, Grace would undoubtedly be sectioned. She'd end up in hospital. The very thing I could not let happen.

I tried to argue with him – 'I can't just let her run off, Joe, you don't understand—' but he cut in: 'No, *you* don't understand,' he shouted, and I stopped. 'You don't understand, Robyn.'

I stopped then, saw him as if for the first time. Oh, God. He looked so stressed, so pale.

'Look, sorry,' he said, more quietly this time. 'But please? Will you just sit down?' Before I could do anything, he'd gestured to the man on the fruit stall to

352

give up his seat, who brought it round for me. 'I'll deal with it,' Joe said.

The panic attack came on in the five minutes that Joe was gone talking to the woman who owned the Bible stall, presumably to make sure she didn't call the police. (I'd no idea how Joe knew how vital this was, but he did.) I suddenly felt that feeling of detachment again, like I was underwater, or walking along at night in the dark; the blood in my ears, my chest tight. By the time Joe came back, I was hyperventilating, my fists already curled in, shaking and sweating like someone in the grips of a fever. A small audience had gathered (talk about Grace, I didn't half know how to make a scene), and the man on the fruit stall had given me a brown paper bag to breathe into.

'Robyn?' Joe dropped to his knees in front of me. He looked waxen, poor bloke, terrified. 'What's wrong? What the hell's going on?'

I would have told him but I couldn't catch my breath enough to speak.

'Someone help me,' he called to the people behind. 'Someone help!' he shouted. 'My girlfriend's in labour! 'We need an ambulance, over here, please!'

I remembered another weakness of Joe's, as well as the impulsiveness: he wasn't always calm in a crisis.

'Joe, it's ok, I'm not . . .' If I could have got my breath, I could have talked to him.

'Where's Grace?' I managed to say.

'Fuck Grace, Robyn . . . Jesus!'

He could see that I needed to know about Grace.

'Look, Grace is okay, Robbie, okay?' He was kneeling

up, his hands either side of my thighs, as if to stop me keeling sideways. 'Grace is streetwise. She's hard as nails and from Elephant and Castle. You're the one we're all worried about – where's the pain?'

I didn't blame him for thinking I was in labour, because I was breathing like I was – or how they depict it in the soap operas, anyway: panting like a dog.

'There is no pain,' I managed.

'Can you feel the baby?' he said. 'We have to get you to the day assessment unit. Dr Love said any worries at all and we had to get you to the day assessment unit.'

'*Joe* . . .' All I could do was to hold my head in my hands, keep my eyes closed until the wave of terror passed. 'We don't need an ambulance. We don't need to go to the assessment unit.' For some reason, I couldn't bring myself to admit to Joe I was having a panic attack, it felt ridiculous.

'Are you mad? Of course you need to go to the day assessment unit.'

There was a small audience gathered round at this point and the fruit-stall owner, who was wearing a Moroccan hat, was saying something about his mate who had a cab firm. 'My friend, he take her to the hospital, I call him . . .'

Joe was all set to go, until I finally managed to spit it out: 'No, Joe, we don't need an ambulance. I'm having a panic attack.'

Joe stopped then.

'A panic attack?' he said, breathless. 'How do you know?'

'Because I get them all the time,' I said. 'Every day.'

*

354

The journey on the way home was in silence. Panic attacks always exhausted me, and I slept most of the last half of the journey on the bus. When we got home, the first thing I noticed when I opened the door was the smell of turps and then that voice, Butler's voice: *Sorry about the smell, I've been doing up some house on that executive estate.*

'Jesus, Joe. Will you tidy your decorating shit up after yourself?' I said.

I heard him take a breath. 'Robyn, please will you just talk to me?'

I wandered into the cool of the lounge and sat down on the sofa. I heard Joe drop keys on the kitchen table, pause; the flat was so quiet I heard his hand brush across the stubble on his face, then footsteps as he walked across the hard tiles of the kitchen floor.

He stood in the doorframe of the lounge. 'What's going on?' he asked. I looked up. He looked strange, unfamiliar. 'Because this isn't you.'

'I know.'

I felt this awful sense of this being the end of everything. All my prophecies coming true. I couldn't do this; I never could have done this. I'm not designed for love like this: real love, where you have to let go. But then this calm descended, this feeling of detachment. Joe was talking to me but his words were hollow wisps flying over my head. I could understand them, but they didn't make me feel anything.

'Why didn't you tell me about the panic attacks?' he said. 'I feel like there're things you're hiding from me . . . that you *have* hidden from me. Don't you feel you can talk to me?'

I was looking at his shoulders; he had such broad shoulders for his build. How come I'd never noticed how broad his shoulders were before? It felt like I was looking at a stranger.

'If I'd known, I could have done something, we could have talked, I could have helped.'

'I didn't want to worry you.' My voice sounded odd to me, unfamiliar.

'Worry me?' Joe looked genuinely bewildered. 'Robyn, I love you.'

I understood, too, the gravitas of these words, but they bounced off me like rain on a pavement.

'I want to know if something's bothering you. I want to know if you're so fucking scared, you're having panic attacks – course I do. Also, it's my baby in there, too.'

He gestured towards my bump, which had developed now, at twenty-four weeks, into a proper beach-ball bump – everyone said I looked like I was having a boy, even though I knew I wasn't – but it felt like an appendage rather than a part of me. Inside, I felt her move, oblivious to the seismic shifts she'd caused.

'How often have you been having them?' he asked.

'Every day. Several times a day – but not as bad as that one in the market. I know what they are now. I can usually control them more.'

'Is that why you won't take the Tube any more?'

'Yes, partly.'

'Have they got something to do with the intimacy thing – with what happens when we try to have sex?'

'Yes.'

His whole body kind of slumped against the door.

356

'But, darling, why didn't you tell me?'

'I thought they'd go away on their own.'

Joe was really frowning at me, like he didn't recognize me; like he didn't really know who I was any more. I didn't know who I was anymore.

'But what about the anxiety . . . the hyperventilating thing you were doing then in the market? I don't know, lack of oxygen.' It was the same lack of medical terminology he'd had in Dr Love's office, but this time I wasn't finding it endearing, I wasn't feeling anything. 'Couldn't it affect the baby? You have to look after yourself.'

'It doesn't always get to that point. Like I say, I can control them now.'

Control them? Who was I kidding? Nobody had to see I was having one, but that didn't mean I didn't regularly feel terrified.

I put my hands over my ears. I suddenly couldn't bear this any more. All this talking. 'Dr Love said stress had nothing to do with it happening again!' I shouted.

'No,' said Joe, he sounded angry now. 'He said it wouldn't cause it, but that it could contribute to it. He said that adrenaline could affect the labour, make the birth more difficult . . .'

I just wanted Joe to go. I wanted him to leave me alone.

'Oh, and that helps, does it?' I said. 'That makes me feel relaxed, Joe? I am worried all the time that it's going to happen again. That this baby is going to die too. And I know she was your baby too . . .'

'But I can handle it, though, Robyn,' he said. 'I'm hopeful. I'm all right. But why the hell are you running around, trying to help the unhelpable, trying to "save" Grace, doing extra work, when you really should be looking after yourself? Grace is making you worse, if you ask me, and what happened to the list? That promise we made that you'd stop thinking you could save everyone . . .?'

'Well, you should have made a promise not to go on at me all the time! I need space, Joe, you're suffocating me. Don't you see, you're making the panic attacks worse?'

He started back.

'Oh, God,' he said, this awful realization crossing his face. 'I'm sorry. I just care, I love you.'

'You won't . . .'

'What?'

'Look, Joe.' I suddenly felt so tired, so tired with all this trying. 'I love you, too – so much – but I can't do this, I'm so sorry.'

He looked at the ceiling and sort of laughed. 'Oh, God, not this again.'

'*Yes*, this again,' I said. 'I can't. I knew I couldn't. I should have listened to my instincts. I don't want you to have to deal with me, Joe. I don't want to be this basket case you have to look after – I spend enough time with mad people to know how draining they can be.'

'But what about me?' he said. His lip was quivering; he had to take a sharp breath to gather himself, to stop himself from crying. Joe, with his soul on his sleeve, his heart on his sleeve. 'What about what I want? What if I don't give a shit if you're a basket case? I still love you.'

You won't.

I sat up straight then; I was absolutely clear in my head on what needed to happen.

'I just think it's best if you just go,' I said. He was crying and yet I felt numb, I felt nothing. 'I think right now, I just need . . .'

'No,' he said, shaking his head. 'You're not doing this again. You're not pushing me away again, walking away when the going gets tough, or when there's commitment up for offer, because that's what I am willing to do, Robyn, to commit to you. I mean, seriously, what do I have to do to make you . . .? It's not fair, it's like I'm doing all the trusting, the hoping, and you're not meeting me halfway. Robyn, all this happened to me, too, you know, it didn't just happen to . . .'

'I was sixteen when you asked me to marry you!' I said, although of course I knew the age was not the problem. '*AND YOU'RE MAKING ME WORSE!*' I shouted. 'YOU'RE MAKING THE PANIC ATTACKS WORSE!' I was sobbing now. I knew that Joe was, had always been, the one person in my life who could save me, who could make me so happy – if I could let him. The one and only person I had ever loved and who I'd let love me. And yet I couldn't do it. I'd tried, and I'd failed.

He stared at me for a few moments, shocked, pale as bone. I stood up. He leaned against the door then, to let me pass.

'I have to go back to work,' I said, laying my cheek on his by means of an apology, even though I knew no words – *no words* – I could say anyway would ever be enough.

'Please, Robyn, please, don't, I'm worried about you . . .'

I walked right past him, then, and towards the front door.

'And I think you should go back to Manchester.'

Chapter Twenty-Eight

A week later

And then it was like the globe stopped shaking, slowed to a stop like a train coming into a platform. The world took on an entirely new colour: a kind of cool, greeny-blue; none of this blood-red. Calm.

I went swimming every morning before work, like we'd stipulated on the AA list. I ate well. I went to bed early, the sheets barely ruffled by the time I woke up.

The panic attacks as good as vanished.

And God, I missed Joe. I missed the physicality of him, his solidness, his gaze on me: that dark, deep gaze that you could see right inside of, right to the bottom of. But there was this blue calmness. It felt like I'd been emptied, cleaned out. Perhaps this was how depressives felt when the antidepressants kicked in – they described it like that to me sometimes: this sense of calm, but a numb calm. A welcome blankness.

Whatever, I knew I'd made the right decision. I only

had to listen to my heart and my breathing – slow and even – to know that. Maybe soon, I'd be able to take the Tube. It wasn't even a 'decision' really, anyway, because it was the only thing I *could* do, I realized that now. I was never going to have been able to be with Joe. He was always out of bounds for me. I'd tried to go against my instincts, my capabilities. I'd tried to swim against the current. That must never happen again.

Joe was so angry and I didn't blame him. He sent me emails, the first at 2 a.m. after he'd got back to Manchester that day when I'd told him to go, when I'd watched him pick up his keys and his bag and walk out of my flat, thinking my heart would break. 'I just don't understand why you're doing this again – pushing me away,' he wrote. 'If that's what you want, then fine, but it's not fine with me – don't ever think this is what *I* wanted. We could have been happy . . .'

Then one the next day: 'Sorry, I was horribly drunk. I'm just upset. I just wish you'd told me earlier how you were feeling. Maybe I could have helped.'

I wanted to email back and tell him everything – about what happened with Saul Butler down Friars Lanes, how it had ruined me, how when we tried to make love, all I saw was his face, how it was like the past was repeating itself. Most of all, I was desperate to tell him my secret. My dark, awful secret. But how could I ever, ever tell him that and what good would that do? It'd only hurt him more and I still wouldn't be able to be with him. No, I decided, he would thank me in the end.

Instead, I wrote a one-liner back, saying that I loved

him and I was so sorry and that we would talk because he was still this baby's father, but that I needed time.

Today it is Wednesday and I go to the swimming pool before work as usual. I love it at this time. Sometimes I am the only person in here and, during those sessions, I feel like I am a girl again, in an early-morning training session at Kilterdale pool, the milky sun streaming through the windows and onto the turquoise water.

And I am weightless; thinking of nothing but my stroke, my breathing; ploughing through the cool water, rhythmically, letting it carry me: stroke, stroke, breathe, stroke, stroke, breathe. Just water and breath. No blood in my ears, no thumping heart.

I do thirty lengths as usual and then I get out. My bump is big enough now to draw admiring looks from women in the changing room: 'Oooh, you're a lovely neat shape. How many weeks?'

'Twenty-five.'

'When's it due?'

'Early January.'

'Oh, gosh. I hope it holds off over Christmas!'

'Yes, me, too, otherwise it'll have to have two birthdays, like the Queen.'

There is girlish laughter. I still, astonishingly, seem to have retained my sense of humour in all of this mess – or maybe I'm just good at pretending.

'Well, you look fab,' says one of the women: short, dark, Jewish looks. 'I've got three boys and my husband says he fancies me most when I'm pregnant.'

'Yes, mine, too, actually,' I say. It just slides right out, so natural. 'Mine, too.'

I get to work. Jeremy is already in, gargling with the TCP, with his door wide open.

'Morning, Kingy,' he says. 'You're in bright and early.'

I've got several assessments to fill in, calls to make, paperwork to catch up on, and I am eager to do it, and to be seen by Jeremy doing it. I want him to know I am coping, I am doing the stuff I know to be important to him: the form-filling and other bureaucracy. I want him to know that I am dealing with clients other than Grace, that I am on top of my workload.

He walks past my desk, whistling, and puts a hand on my shoulder. 'Good to see you bright and early this morning,' he says. 'Good to have our Kingy back.'

Maybe Jeremy was right, I think. My concentration has been awry these last few weeks, I have been distracted; but this week, I feel as clear as the water in the swimming pool and Jezza is in an extra-good mood today, because he's got a meeting with the medical director about budgets and there's nothing Jezza likes more than a meeting about budgets.

The day rumbles along at an even pace. I do my paperwork, I do two visits – one to John Urwin, who's home now from his recent admission and still wearing his Dennis the Menace wig, and one to Levi. Levi seems to have found a new level recently. He's still working at Dulwich Sainsbury's, with all the 'mo-fo dull witches', but he is, he tells me, well on his way to raising enough money to go back to Nigeria to see his niece, who is five months now and sitting up. He shows me a picture: she is beautiful, like him. He is making plans for the future, which is a good sign.

Finally, in the afternoon, I speak to Grace. After the

364

incident at the market, I had to come clean at clinical, that the photography day hadn't exactly gone to plan. When I'd caught up with Grace the next day, after Joe had gone (I found her smoking dope outside her block of flats and she had calmed down), she'd promised me she did not want to be 'sent to the funny farm' and therefore from now on would be 'swallowing her pills like a good little mental patient'. She also said she was sorry, and she thanked me for being her friend.

So I go about my business: more paperwork, risk-assessment and stress-vulnerability models. So often, my job is about 'risk': Are they a risk to others? A risk to themselves? But I have assessed my own risk recently and decided that to be with Joe is too risky for me; maybe what I have always suspected is true, that what happened to me means I am essentially dysfunctional, that love is too risky for me – who knows? That I am destined to have relationships like the one I had with Andy. I just know that I am beginning to feel back where I was in March, before Joe's Facebook message drifted into my inbox as silently as snow, as invisible and transformative as a spell.

Kaye has been on visits all morning. At 2 p.m., she comes into the office, looking tired but in good humour. She's been to see Mrs Patel again, and was marooned for two hours, being force-fed onion bhajis. 'And how are you, my love?' she asks me. We're both standing in front of the big grey filing cabinets that line one of the walls, looking for notes. She stands back and surveys me. ''Cause you look a bit pale and tired, to tell you the truth.'

'Actually, Joe and I split up,' I say.

Kaye stops what she's doing, her mouth hanging open.

'But before you say anything,' I add, pulling out the file I need, 'I'm fine, it was the right decision. It was *my* decision.'

She puts one hand on her hip and with the other she grips the shelf, as if to settle herself in for the lecture, the big talk. I stand back a little. I don't want to discuss this now but her ice-blue eyes are full of questions, concern. 'But, I don't understand,' she says. 'When did this happen? Why didn't you tell me?'

'I'm telling you now,' I say, with a smile, but my body language is saying, *I don't want to talk about this now.*

'But, Kingy, what about the baby . . .?'

'Well, I know it's going to be hard.' I've been thinking this might save me in the end. I'll have so much to do as a single mother of a new baby, I won't have time to agonize over me and Joe and everything else. 'But I just couldn't go through with it.'

She's looking at me like I'm crackers. 'But why, sweetheart?'

I clutch the file tighter to my chest, like a barricade between her and me.

'It just wasn't right. The pregnancy was totally unplanned, so out of the blue. I didn't want to make a relationship just of circumstance.'

She's doesn't say anything, but I can tell her mind is working overtime. She is giving the look she reserves for her clients: concerned but one step removed, objective.

'So, there we are, maybe we could go and live in that hippy commune after all, eat biscuits and grow our armpit hair!' I say, trying to lighten things, but Kaye's not smiling.

366

She is giving me that look that Joe gave me, like she doesn't know who I am any more.

'Anyway, so I was just going to make a cup of tea,' I say, gesturing towards the door, where she's still hovering. 'Fancy a cuppa and a chocolate HobNob?'

She nods and I walk through to the small staff kitchen, glad to have got away. I put the kettle on, get two mugs out, put the teabags in, but, when I look up, Kaye is standing there, watching me.

'It's all right. I can make a cup of tea, you know. I'm not a total invalid just yet – give me a few weeks.'

'Sorry,' she says, making as if to go, but she doesn't actually move. 'Robyn . . .?' She never calls me Robyn. Ever.

'Yeah?'

'Are you sure you're all right?'

'Yeah, positive, honestly. It was the right decision, trust me. Go on, be off with yer,' I say, flapping her away, 'I'll bring it over.'

I fill up the tiny white kettle at the sink. A dolly's kettle, we always joke. They've cut so many budgets, we have to have a Barbie-doll-sized kettle. I look out at the gardens below. My bump is so big now it's hard to reach the sink properly and I have to stand side on, looking at the tall, silvery birch trees swaying in the breeze, the sun, pulsing through the leaves like the flash of a camera, blinding me momentarily, so I have to close my eyes.

The kettle seems to take ages. 'A watched kettle never boils,' my mum always used to say, and I can hear her voice, see her standing there in our big but eternally messy kitchen, hair up, reading glasses on, and I smile at the memory. And then, the kettle clicks to say it's boiled, clicking me out of my daydream, and steam plumes upwards, clouding the window. I pour the water into the mugs and rub at the glass, absent-mindedly. Then, I stop. Just for a fraction of a second, but he was there and it's enough to take my breath away, and I stumble back.

I learned once, in my training, that flashbacks are your body's way of telling you you are ready to remember, and suddenly, remember is all I do. The memories come at me like knives. But they are not the peripheries of what happened that evening down Friars Lanes, the scenes before and after that have played over in my mind so often. This is the main event and it's like refocusing a camera lens; sliding a prescription lens in front of your own, cloudy vision and seeing everything in all its full, awful clarity.

I am there. It is happening now: the way he smelled, that petrol-mixed-with-paint smell of the turps-covered cloths that I had no option but to lay my head on. The way I smelled – not of sex and intimacy, of how things should smell, but of a terrified, dry, invaded me. There is the gearstick, black and threatening as a gun, stuck into my right thigh, the sun-warmed, synthetic material of the van-seat covers that left a friction rash on the backs of my thighs for days. The way his huge, moon-pale stomach made a slapping sound as it hit my hard, clenched one; how my arms were flung back and my eyes squeezed shut, and my teeth jammed together. The flush of red where his throat met his chest when he was done. How much it hurt. The aching inside for days, like someone had put a vice inside me and slowly creaked me open. And I was being wrenched open now. I could feel it, as if someone had reached inside me and were trying to prise my hip bones apart.

'Robyn, oh, my God.'

And then there is a huge, thundering smash and Kaye is there, at the kitchen door, and I am standing in a sea of hot tea and broken crockery, shaking, sobbing.

'Are you hurt? Have you burned yourself? Oh, God, are you in pain?'

No, but I wish I was. Physical pain is so much simpler than this. If I could have drawn physical pain, it would be one straight black line; mental pain looked like those nests I'd seen in the treetops down Friars Lanes. I imagined they'd be brittle to the touch.

'What's wrong? What happened? Don't worry, we can clear this up.' And then she is treading with a crunch over the broken crockery, pushing it to the side like someone treading over the debris of an earthquake, and taking me in her arms.

'I can't tell you,' I say, folding, crumpling into her. 'I can't tell you.'

I did tell her. We went into the disabled loo, which is about the only private place in our offices, and I told her everything: about the panic attacks I'd been having, the anxiety, about losing Lily, about how all these events of my past seemed to be seeping into my present so that I couldn't tell which was which any more and, finally, Saul Butler, what he did to me, late that August, only three months after I'd got together with Joe; how I kept seeing his face, how I felt I must surely be going mad.

'He was eighteen, Kaye,' I said. Kaye was sitting on the toilet seat. I was sitting on the floor, my back against the wall. Somehow, it felt like I needed to be as close to the ground as possible.

'He probably didn't know what he was doing. I shouldn't have let it happen. I don't know if it was rape. I don't know, I'm confused. Joe told me something Saul had said to a friend of ours, that we had a thing . . .' I looked at Kaye, as if for answers. 'Maybe it's just how I construed it?'

Kaye was listening to me, she was crying, too. She leaned forward, reaching her hand out to mine.

'No, you were raped, sweetheart,' she said softly. 'He raped you. And I think you're probably suffering, in some way, from post-traumatic stress, and that this pregnancy has triggered everything that happened then.'

Funny, I'd forgotten my best friend was a trained counsellor and a psychiatric nurse. That I was a psychiatric nurse. You'd think I'd have seen it coming, wouldn't you? But it's strange, I knew things were bad but I just didn't put two and two together. It was like it happened to someone else.

'And, darling?' said Kaye. 'I think you have to tell Joe.'

'I think it'll help you. Also, Joe deserves to know, doesn't he? After everything you've been through together; why you can't be with him at the moment. He deserves for you to tell him the truth about everything.'

I nodded. I just wondered if he'd ever be ready for the 'everything'.

PART THREE

Chapter Twenty-Nine

Several days later

Dear Lily,
Well, I feel like I've come full circle. I had Joe, I lost Joe once, and it's happened again (something tells me we aren't meant to be). The only difference now is that I've told him everything. Not everything, not every single thing, because I decided at the end of the day – what good would that do him? But I told him about the rape. That's the first time I have ever written that down, by the way, but there it is, in black and white: I was raped, but I survived, and I have told two people now (three, if I count you) and that's a massive leap forward. I feel, despite everything, that a burden has been lifted. That at least I have finally told the truth about my life.

It didn't exactly go well with your dad but, then, how did I expect it to go? Telling him something like that? He was devastated and furious and I felt guilty that perhaps I'd told him for my benefit, not his.

What am I supposed to do, here in Manchester, now? he'd shouted down the phone. *Some bastard does this to you, which means you can't be with me, the father of your child. Some total bastard has fucked you up and I can't do anything about it? Who did this to you? I need to know.*

I was prepared for him to feel angry. After all, I have had sixteen years to deal with this, while this is news to him, and I was prepared for the fact that he was going to know who had done it but I told him I am never going to tell him that, a) because I need to pretend Butler doesn't exist for my own sanity because, once that's out, the whole of Kilterdale will know, and b) because if he knows, he will want to kill him. And we can't have me, a single mum, and the dad in prison, can we? Also, if he were to find out and confront Saul Butler, I fear it would open a dark place so big inside for me, that I don't know if I'd ever get out of there, if I'd ever recover.

The answer-machine messages Joe left over the next day or two were always the same: they started off reasonable, under the guise of enquiring how I was, then descended pretty quickly into anger and bitterness. Joe has never been able to hide his feelings, he's just not capable. So, 'How are you, darling? I'm thinking about you' turned, eventually, after some cursory smalltalk about what he'd been doing, into, 'If I ever find out which bastard did this to you . . .'

374

I did take a couple of his calls but had taken the agonizing decision not to now, at least for a while. The simple bare truth of the matter was, that I couldn't listen to it. I couldn't listen to his emotions, too. I didn't feel like I could say anything that would make him feel better anyway. No, I had to look after myself and the baby now. It would do Joe and I good to have some time apart.

And of course there were my patients: Grace, someone who needed me, someone to pour my energies into, even if I had the feeling that she – unbeknown to her – might have triggered some of this.

On the Saturday of the week after Joe had left, I stood hammering on her front door, as I had so many times before, only for there to be no answer.

I knocked again – 'Grace?' – and peered through the viewing hole, noticing as I did that the wreath wasn't hanging on the door as usual. This was odd. Maybe after several years, she'd finally understood that the laws of physics meant it was going to fall off every time she opened it. No, that would be far too logical for Grace, far too sane. 'Grace,' I called again, 'it's just . . .' As I said the word 'me', I realized that the door was actually unlocked; that you only need push it with a little force and it opened. The windows were open, so it was cold inside, the ever-present odour of cigarettes partially masked for once by fresh air, or as fresh as the air gets in Elephant and Castle. I called out her name again and waited, but there was no answer, so I walked into the lounge.

The scene that greeted me told me all I needed to know about why she hadn't wanted me to come and visit her at home recently. Grace had been busy, very busy indeed. Every wall of the downstairs of her flat was covered in writing: red felt tip in varying sizes and fonts, some curly and elegant, some jagged and angry. The wreath that Cecily had made as a child hung from the light fitting, photos of her were scattered on the floor, and the graffiti on the walls all said the same thing:

MUMMY, HELP ME. PLEASE SAVE ME.

I stood for a moment, considering what to do. Above all, I told myself, *remain calm*. She's done some crazy stuff before – crazier than this – and she's got on the straight and narrow again. At the same time, I knew the chances of Grace seriously flipping out were getting higher as the days went by and that the likelihood she was remaining compliant with her meds was very slim indeed. The anniversary of Cecily being taken from her was nearing, and on every other anniversary of the past five years, she'd been sectioned; so, really, her track record was poor. She was probably skipping around someone's back garden naked right now, God love her. But I wasn't going to give up on her now. We'd come so far. I'd leave her a note, then I'd go home. It was Saturday, she was bound to call soon.

I found a letter lying on the floor from Kingsbridge Mental Health Trust and on the back I scribbled a few words:

Grace, it's Robyn. It's about quarter-past two on Saturday and I've come over to check on you but you're not here. Grace, I'm really worried that you're unwell and distressed. Please call me. I've seen what you've done at home and I'm not cross, I'm just concerned.

*

I could hear the phone ringing even as I got to the bottom of the stairwell that leads up to my flat and ran up them as fast as I could, given the size of me, trampling all over Eva's bags, which had been reduced finally from mounds and mounds to a far more manageable pile with Joe's sweet talking over the last few weeks. I was desperate to get to the phone because I knew it could be Grace, or at least work calling to say they'd found Grace. But it was neither of them. It was Joe. It had gone to answerphone by the time I got in the door and he was leaving a message. He sounded odd.

'Hi, Robbie, it's me, it's Joseph, the father of your child in case you'd forgotten.' It wasn't odd he sounded, it was drunk.

'I know who it is,' he said darkly. 'I've worked it out. And I'm gonna fucking kill him. I am going over there right now, and I am gonna fucking finish him off . . .'

I picked up. This couldn't be any worse. 'Joe, listen to me.'

'It's Butler, isn't it? It's Butler who did this to you?'

I tried to stay calm but inside I was screaming. 'Joe, first of all you are really drunk . . .'

'I know it is, Robyn, so you might as well just admit it.'

I was concentrating on a little patch of wall that was no longer damp, that had been painted over, expertly, by Joe, weeks ago, when none of this was out in the open, when all that was still buried, my secret.

'I knew it,' he said. 'And I'm going to kill him. No, no!' He was talking at high volume, and melodramatically, as drunk people do. 'I am going to go round there and I am going to tie him up and torment him like he tormented you and then, when I'm finished with that, I am going to tie up his wife and see how it feels for him to watch someone hurt the person he loves.'

Joe couldn't tie up a fly, I knew that. I knew this was ridiculous, that it was the booze talking, but I couldn't be sure he wouldn't go round there at least. Passionate, impulsive Joe. Joe who would get an idea in his head and run with it. Who would chase after a gang of teenagers if they dissed his little brother. Especially with several beers inside him.

'Joe, you cannot go round there, do you hear me?'

'I have to, Robbie. Sorry, but I have to.'

'JOSEPH!' I shouted, more panicky this time. 'If you go round there, you will only make it worse for me. You will only drive me further away. What I need is to put it behind me, to forget it ever happened.'

'But I *can't* forget it ever happened!' he cried. 'I can't, Robbie, it's killing me.'

My mobile went off in my bag. I reached down and took it out. It was Grace. Oh God, what would I do now? I had to take this call, it could be my one chance to keep her from getting herself in serious trouble and ending up in hospital and ruining everything we'd worked at; but, if I let Joe go now, God knows what he'd do. I stood, paralysed. I wanted so badly to go to Joe, I couldn't bear for him to be upset, but he was miles away, in Kilterdale. Now it was my turn to trust him.

'Look, Joe,' I said, 'Please, can you do something for me? Stay where you are, or go to the beach or stand in the middle of a field and scream and shout if you want, just don't go to Butler's, okay? I'm begging you. Do you promise me?'

There was just the awful sound of him crying on the

other end of the line. Then, he hung up. I stood, holding the receiver, worried sick about him, but also thinking, *Please, Joe, please don't go round to Butler's.* This could be the worst, the very worst thing he could do.

I let my mobile ring another four times before I clicked 'Accept'.

'Hello? Grace?'

'I'm here, darlin'.'

She sounded remarkably sharp of mind, and yet gravelly, like she'd smoked her way through the world's reserves of cigarettes. 'I found it,' she said.

'Found what, Grace?' I walked out of my flat and stood on the landing, my mind was racing, going over the possibilities. Larry's grave? Her childhood home?

'Cecily's house,' she said, and my stomach lurched. Grace is under strict orders that if she goes anywhere near Cecily's house (her mother's house), then she could be sectioned, and this would mean hospital. Definitely. 'I've come to collect her and take her home.'

I took a deep breath: 'Okay, Grace . . .' I had to play this right, I had to play it calmly. We'd come so far, we couldn't screw it up now. 'You need to listen to me.'

'The voices are telling me, Robyn.'

'Telling you what?'

'To go and get her, that she needs her mum.'

'And where is the house, Grace?'

'Finchley,' she said. 'Finchley, darlin'. It's very nice around here; at least she's in a nice area, you know.'

She sounded quite high, but *Finchley?* I thought. This was close. This was good.

'Okay, I want you to stop there and wait for me. Okay?' I said, walking back into the flat and straight to

Google Maps. 'I know how powerful and terrifying those voices must be, but you must not listen to them. You must listen to my voice. Mine is the voice that is real and that cares about you. You must wait there and not move, until I get there. Promise me?'

'Okay,' she said. 'The voices are strong, though, Robyn. They're telling me you're just trying to trick me, to make me take medication.'

I looked down the stairwell, to the evening below. It was so clear, so soft and velvety, it didn't feel like the sort of night for all this to be happening.

'You have to trust me, Grace,' I said. 'That's all I ask. We've been on a journey together, you and I. Don't mess it all up now.'

And Joe? I had to trust him. It was *my* turn to trust *him*.

Chapter Thirty

It was late by the time I found the address. Grace's mother's road was a horseshoe-shaped cul-de-sac full of Identikit seventies semis; freshly laid tarmac and saplings planted equidistant. It was nothing like I imagined. Nothing like Grace.

Grace was standing in the road in front of her mother's house, which was white pebbledash with a strange attempt at clapboard on one side, painted red. The dark curtains were closed, thank goodness, so, hopefully, nobody had clocked that Grace was standing outside, although there was a little slither of light coming from one side of them, suggesting that someone was inside, watching television. Grace's flesh and blood leading another life, a life her mother knew nothing of.

It was almost dark now: the dome of sky above us was blue-black like a beetle, the only light being the moon, streaked with cloud, and the synthetic yellow glow of street lamps, dotted between the saplings. Grace stood under one, like a child on a spotlit stage. She looked lost and alone, and yet on the precipice of something; like she'd come to the edge of one world, and might leap into another. The scene evoked in me something familiar, some event lodged deep in my past – and then I realized, she looked like a woman in an Edward Hopper painting. I'd been to an exhibition once at the Tate Modern, alone, when I was new to London, and drunk on the feeling of freedom and escape. *Automat*, it was called: it showed a woman alone in a café, on a street corner – and I thought, if you could perfectly depict the state of things for Grace right now, tell the story of her life in just one painting, this would be it: there was Grace the child – she'd told me how when she was little and being abused, she'd often spend half the night like this, sitting outside the hotel in the dark; she felt safer there than inside – and also Grace the woman she became, who had suffered a break in her wiring at thirty, who lost the child who was separated from her now by only a green front door. I'd grown to care about Grace a lot and yet I realised now that Joe was right. That she'd exacerbated things for me. That I wasn't able to separate work and my personal life as much as I thought. That the history we shared was what drew me to her, but what had possibly reminded me of everything, too. Then it struck me: maybe it was Grace who'd caused the panic attacks more than anything, not Joe?

And yet it was too late for all that now. I was in too deep. Perhaps I couldn't save her, but I could help save her fledgling relationship with her daughter and make sure she didn't end up in hospital, and that was worth it, wasn't it? Because at the other side of that front door lay her future. 'As long as Cec is alive, Grace, there's always hope,' I'd said to her in the past few months. But I think I'd only believed it in theory. Now I saw it as a concrete fact.

Grace had her dainty chin tilted up towards that front door, as if listening to the gods. She probably was listening to the gods. I wondered what they were saying to her. Grace and I both heard voices, just mine came from inside and hers from outside of her. Wherever they came from, we both needed to learn to silence them.

I walked over quietly, so as not to startle her. She was still gazing up the driveway, at that green front door. 'Hello, Grace,' I said, gently touching her arm. 'It's a beautiful night, isn't it?'

Her eyes flickered towards me, so I knew she'd clocked me, but then drifted back to that place I knew she was: a place consumed by a need to see her daughter, to hold her and be close to her. But it couldn't be now and it couldn't be in the wrong way. If Grace was to go up to the front door, uninvited, it could ruin things between her and Cecily forever.

She took a deep breath and closed her eyes. Her whole body was trembling.

'It's time,' she said. She was muttering something, communicating with the voices inside her head. 'It's time, darlin'.'

'Time for what?' I said. The most important thing was to remain calm, I told myself. And I did feel calm. Strangely so. 'What are the voices telling you, Grace?'

A shadow moved from behind the curtains. I knew I had to get her away from here, but not in a way that frightened her, because if she screamed or ran, or made a commotion and they saw her here, she might never be able to see Cecily again. I didn't have to imagine how it might feel to not be able to see your daughter grow up.

'They're telling me to go and get her. That I have to go and get my Cec.'

Inside, the baby shifted. My stomach felt stretched and uncomfortable. I looked up at the sky, as if for strength. I could not screw this up.

'Grace, come and sit down with me,' I said. 'Look, there's a bench over there – you can have a smoke, we can have a chat?'

I tried to steer her gently with my arm but she pulled away.

'No,' she said. 'I've got to save my baby.'

'I know,' I said. 'I understand, more than anyone. But you have to listen to me. You have to ignore those voices and listen to mine, because mine's the one that's real. Please?' I said, putting my hand on her shoulder. She turned to me, gnawing at her nail, her thick brows furrowed. I could tell she at least *wanted* to believe me, even if her feet were rooted to the spot.

'Have you called 'em?' she said. We both knew she meant the police. 'No, I haven't and I'm not going to, as long as you promise to come with me and take your medication, okay?' I said, holding out my hand to her. 'Trust me, Grace, I only want the very best for you.'

Slowly, reluctantly, she took my hand and walked over to the bench with me. She huddled over – I thought she was going to sleep – collapsing into herself somehow; then I realized she was just trying to light her fag under her coat, or should I say poncho, because she was wearing

384

one of those plastic ponchos you wear in the rain. I wasn't sure how flammable it was.

She seemed to relax a little now she had nicotine in her veins, so I leaned forward to talk to her but, as I did, there was a sharp pain across my belly as the baby kneed me in some soft tissue with her pointy little elbow, her bony little foot.

'Grace, you can move on from the past, you know,' I said. She was blowing up smoke into the air, towards the moon that was a three-quarter moon, that looked as though it had been slid into the sky, like a record in its sleeve.

'You can have a relationship with your daughter, feel happiness again. Just imagine what that would feel like, to feel happy?'

Her eyes narrowed as she inhaled, as if she was thinking, *Not in my lifetime, darlin'*.

'Lots has gone wrong for you in your life but it doesn't mean it can't start to go right now,' I said. 'Not perfect, but more right. The past doesn't have to define you, Grace.'

And honestly, it was strange, because just like that, something slid into place in my mind, like finally working out a puzzle, a Rubik's Cube. The past didn't have to define me either, not if I didn't let it. I could choose to remember what I wanted and forget what I didn't. I remembered what Joe had said outside the Natural History Museum – I hadn't understood then. But now I did: 'It just becomes part of you . . .'

Not like a house you're carrying on your shoulder, but like something you can slip into your back pocket.

We both sat on the bench, Grace smoking, me leaning back, looking at the man in the moon with his slightly wan expression, his little sad frown, as if he was listening to us, apologizing for something that was about to happen.

I wanted to call the Recovery Centre, to see if I could get a bed for Grace. I'd heard about the centre some weeks back and decided, if ever Grace got to the point where I felt she was becoming unwell enough to be hospitalized, I wanted to get her in there. The Recovery Centre wasn't a hospital. It was a six-bedroomed house in North London, not even an NHS sign outside to give it away, and it did what it said on the tin. It helped people in the midst of an episode like Grace's to recover, rather than dose them up to the eyeballs. She'd get therapy and support but, crucially, be free to come and go as she pleased. She wouldn't be locked up.

I made sure Grace was sitting on a bench not in view of her mother's house, and left her, promising me she wouldn't move, as I tried to call the Recovery Centre. But just as I was punching in the numbers, another pain – much bigger, and so sudden this time it took my breath away, ripped through me, bending me double. I stayed there for a few seconds, chest on my knees, my mouth wide open, screaming silently. I didn't want to stress Grace out. But Grace had a third eye, a sixth sense.

'You all right, darlin'?' I could see her, through the gap in my knees, do her little geisha shuffle towards me. 'You all right . . .?' 'Yes I'm fine,' I said. But just as she got close, another pain shot through me, making me cry out.

'You're not all right, are you?'

There was no blood yet, but there would be. I knew. I just knew. 'Grace,' I said – she was rubbing my back,

386

patting it like a child might do if they were concerned about their mother – 'I think you're going to have to call me an ambulance.'

We heard the siren before we saw the ambulance, a wail that engulfed the quiet neighbourhood, shaking those saplings at their foundations, making curtains flutter – or that's how it felt, like it was ripping through the earth beneath my feet, on a path of destruction. Everything happening again, everything as I had feared.

Grace walked into the middle of the road as the ambulance neared, the ivory skirt of the wedding dress she always wore pearly in the lamplight. She was wearing the poncho over it, as well as the obligatory baseball cap and high-tops and, as the ambulance turned into the road and she ushered it to a parking spot – this nymph-like figure gesticulating in the drizzle – she could have been a car-park attendant at Glastonbury Festival.

The ambulance parked up and the wail subsided. Just the blue light remained, circling the cul-de-sac like a spaceship landing, like it was from some other world, a world I recognized, and it filled me with all kinds of dread. Two paramedics got out, just as another pain took me. One of them – tall, slim, greying hair, strode towards me.

'Hello, love.' He crouched down to my level. Closer up, he looked like Michael Palin, and this comforted me. Mum always fancied Michael Palin – she said he had kind, humorous eyes, and this man had kind, humorous eyes. I felt safe with him. I felt like Mum had sent a Michael Palin-lookalike here on purpose, to make this whole thing bearable, to let me know she was here, watching.

387

He asked my name and how pregnant I was, and told me his name was Glenn.

'So you've got pains?' said Glenn.

Grace, who had been fully involved until this point was now sitting at the other end of the bench, eyeballing Glenn suspiciously. Glenn looked at her, then back at me, as if for explanation, but I decided against telling him that my companion was paranoid and delusional, in the grips of psychosis.

'Can you tell me where the pain is?'

'In the stomach. Right across the stomach.'

'Have you had any kind of fall?'

'Not that I can remember, no.'

'And is the pain constant?' he said. 'Or does it come intermittently?'

'She's just got bellyache, haven't you, darlin? They're not contractions, you know . . . She ain't losing no baby on my watch.'

Even in the grips of agony, I was so grateful for Grace's note of confidence. At least someone was watching out for me.

'They may very well not be contractions,' said Glenn. 'It could be something as simple as constipation; it's very common in pregnant women and can be very painful.'

'Oh, yeah, I get terrible constipation,' said Grace.

Glenn looked at me, a flicker of a smile passing his lips.

'It's all the pills they have me on, wreak absolute mayhem with my bowels.'

Another pain wracked me, another and another, but there was no blood, I told myself, there was no blood yet.

'Right, shall we get you in the ambulance, love, get

you to hospital,' said Glenn, putting his arm around my back and leading me to the ambulance door. I stepped up the little ramp and, as I did so, looked back to see Grace, a figure in a white dress and a poncho, reaching out for me and, for a second, I had a flashback, so vivid I had to close my eyes and open them again to make sure it wasn't real: a dark, wet February afternoon, a navy-blue skirt plum-red with blood. The smell of hospitals as I get inside an ambulance, and then, looking back and there being Joe, sprinting out of school towards me, his chest heaving, his blazer blazing behind him. There's the yellow oblongs of the strip lights inside the school, his face sheet-white, reaching out to me like Grace was now, and this hollowness opening up inside me, because I knew; it was like a disconnect. Like a wire had been severed. I knew she was gone.

Did I have that same feeling now? I couldn't tell.

'Darlin', I wanna come with you,' Grace was crying from outside the ambulance. I wanted to tell her to keep quiet, that they couldn't know she was mad because I did want her with me, but Glenn didn't seem too concerned. I guessed he'd had much worse in his ambulance. Also, it was obvious. 'Sure, come in,' he said. 'You can hold her hand, you can calm her down.'

I was helped onto the red plastic bed by Glenn. The pains came in waves but in between I was fine, I could talk.

Grace asked if she could have a fag inside the ambulance.

Glenn said, 'You must be mad.

'D'you know that's my one regret in life – voting for Tony Blair. It's 'cause of him you can't have a damn ciggie anywhere.'

Myself, Glenn and the other paramedic laughed. I was glad Grace was here.

The wail sounded and we began to race through the dark streets. Grace was holding my hand. She'd found a stray bourbon biscuit in her pocket and was nibbling on it. Unbeknown to her, I was texting Kaye with my other hand, asking her to call the Recovery Centre.

'Cec is going to be all right, you know,' I said to Grace. 'You and Cec are going to be fine.' Secretly, I was thinking that whatever the outcome was of this, and I was preparing myself for the worst, at least it would have – in some inadequate way – done what I set out to do. It would have saved Grace, stopped her doing anything she might regret.

Grace pulled the blanket around me, and it was as she did that, that I felt the warm seep of something below. My heart stopped. For a few minutes, I said nothing. I couldn't bring myself to even say the words. I closed my eyes. I wanted to disappear.

Grace was asking Glenn about what certain equipment was for in the ambulance, how long he'd done the job, '. . . and 'ow much do they pay you, darlin'?' She added, 'I bet it's not as much as they should.' Then she turned to me, 'Oh, darlin',' she said, 'why you crying?'

I pulled her close so I could whisper in her ear. I thought if I didn't say it out loud, it might not be happening. 'I'm bleeding, Grace,' I said. 'I can feel it. I'm scared I'm going to lose the baby.'

She clasped my hand to her cheek right then. 'You ain't,' she said; she somehow knew she should whisper. 'You ain't, darlin'. Gracie won't let that happen.'

The ambulance careered around the streets, the siren

felt like it was coming from within me and, with every turn, I could feel another trickle. I was clenching my muscles, but I couldn't stop it.

'It's going to be okay, darlin'.' Grace was pushing back my hair from my face, a bit too hard but I didn't care.

'Gracie knows, you're going to be okay.' But I didn't believe her. I didn't.

I closed my eyes. I thought, *If it happens again, I'll never survive*. And all I wanted was blankness, the blankness of the swimming pool the other day, just the sound of water and my breath.

Chapter Thirty-One

'What's she like next to you?' Leah whispered, gesturing to the heavily pregnant woman to my right. She was forty-two, had constant hiccups, and was in here for blood pressure.

'She's all right,' I said. 'Always has hiccups, blows bubbles in her sleep.'

Leah made a face, sticking her tongue out like she'd just been made to swallow her own wee, and it made me laugh for the first time all day because it was so typically intolerant of my sister. Can you imagine the horror of having to share your space, the air that you breathe, with another human being in an NHS hospital? (Leah and Russ were private healthcare all the way.)

It was hard to believe we were from the same parents, sometimes, we were such polar opposites, Leah and I, but when she arrived, the only person close enough to come at visiting time, I was so pleased to see her. Friends are wonderful, but there's something comforting about your own flesh and blood. If Mum couldn't be here in my hour of need, having Leah was the next best thing. And she was here, just like Dad and even Denise were going to be here as soon as they could. Our relationships may not have always been perfect, or anywhere near perfect, but I had family in my life who cared about me and it was more than Grace had. I was one of the lucky ones.

I'd had a bleed and, although it had felt like it was pouring out of me, it was only a small one. The baby, they told me, was safe. When I'd heard the heartbeat, it felt nothing short of a miracle, and I'd cried so hard with relief.

Grace had shed a tear too. Then started saying how she needed to see her baby, her Cec. But Kaye turned up not long after; she'd found her a space at the Recovery Centre. 'It's like a four-star hotel,' she'd said to Grace. 'You'll love it there, you can have a massage there, acupuncture . . .'

I think the acupuncture's what sold it for Grace. 'A damn sight better than fucking jigsaws,' she'd said. By the skin of my teeth, I'd done what I'd promised: I'd kept her out of hospital and, hopefully, fingers crossed, she'd not ruined things with Cec.

Leah pulled a chair up, looked at me for a second, then leaned forward and kissed me. Totally out of character.

'Not been such a great road so far, this pregnancy, has it?' she said.

'Up and down, it's fair to say,' I agreed. 'It's kind of been like being on the best holiday of your life, knowing you've left the oven on.'

Leah frowned. 'That is such a Robyn analogy,' she said. 'You've always been strange, haven't you?'

'I thought it was quite good,' I said. 'It captured the bitter-sweetness perfectly.'

We watched the toing and froing of the ward for a bit, me having to remind Leah to stop staring at the woman blowing bubbles in her sleep.

'Dad's coming down to get me,' I said.

Leah rolled her eyes. 'Dadise, you mean. Because they are one person, you know Robyn.'

'She's not that bad,' I said. 'She's actually gone up in my estimation. She's actually been very supportive about this pregnancy. I feel like this baby will be her grandchild as much as Dad's, you know?'

Leah looked unconvinced. 'Really?'

'Yes, I think we should look at it like this: Mum's genes will always be around, she'll always be here, in some curve of the lip, her laugh, her hair, but I want my daughter to have a grandma, like we had a grandma, and Denise is *here*, Leah,' I said. 'She's actually *here*.'

Leah chewed the inside of her cheek.

'I just think we should accept her,' I said. 'She's never going to be Mum, but she makes Dad happy.'

'Mm, yeah,' she sighed. 'I guess so but, you know . . .'

I knew.

'Look, I think you need to try and forget the fact you knew they were together before Mum died. I think you need to get over it, Lee.'

After Leah had told me this at her house and Niamh had come down the stairs, interrupting us, we hadn't had time to discuss it.

'What? So it doesn't bother you?' she said.

I sighed. Leah's ability to hold a grudge had always

been better than mine, but also I just didn't see life as black and white as she did.

'Leah, I'm so grateful that you never told me, because I think it *would* have bothered me when I was younger, but not now, no. Now I understand that things are never that simple, are they?'

She shrugged.

'They're not though, are they?' I said. 'I think Dad felt like he lost Mum a long time before she actually died; he was her carer, not her husband, at the end, really. I see now how much you were hurting at the time, though, and why you couldn't handle it. Also, how much you protected me.'

'Well, I still sodded off and left you and Niamh, though, didn't I?'

'You were only nineteen. We were all hurting in our different ways,' I said.

'Yeah, but then you went through even worse after Mum, and I wasn't there.'

I realized, in that moment, that all I'd ever needed really was for her to explain it, acknowledge it. I felt this enormous release, I took her hand.

'Well, I survived, didn't I? And now there's a new baby.' I patted my bump. 'You can be there for her.'

I didn't say anything about Joe – or me and Joe – I would, but not now, I wanted to give this moment just to Leah. I felt like she'd probably waited long enough.

'Oh, I will, I definitely will,' said Leah. Then she said, 'I think I know what happened?' She said it as a question. 'I think I know about Lily and what you were trying to tell me in that nightclub, that night you came to see me in Brighton.'

I was so choked I could only nod.

She pulled her chair closer to me then, pulled the curtain around the bed and then pretty much lay on the bed with me, her arms around me. 'I'm sorry,' she said. 'I'm so, so sorry.'

Chapter Thirty-Two

The next day, safely back home, on the brightest day in September, Dad and Denise arrived at my flat just after lunch. Dad looked like he hadn't slept – he and Leah had been on the phone a long time, I knew that. He stood in my kitchen like a forlorn, lost sheep (and I thought I felt like the one who had just been hit by a train), while Denise wandered from room to room, having a nosy, muttering on to Dad about at least making his daughter a cup of tea. When she was out of the room, shouting to ask me what colour paint Joe had done the bathroom – was it white or duck-egg white? – Dad rocked forwards and backwards on his shoes, took three purposeful strides towards me, hesitated, then put his arms around me. 'I love you,' he said. It was the first time he'd told me he loved me since I was small; the first hug we'd had in years. Once I'd got over the shock, I was not about to let him go soon, so we stayed like that in my kitchen, while Denise pottered around, twittering on about how these flats are so much bigger when you get inside, finding her way around, sourcing tea and milk and biscuits, offering to carry my bags to the car, but never once demanding Dad's attention.

'Shall we go then?' I said, eventually, when we'd drunk our tea. 'Or Denise, maybe you'd little a little walk around Waterlow Park? It's a lovely day, there's a lake there.'

Denise coughed, like this might be hard for her but she was going to do it anyway. She was going to do it because she knew it to be the right thing.

'No, lovey, you're all right,' she said. 'I'm going to the Doll Factory in Hendon, it's not far . . . They do brilliant collectors' items. I've heard they've got some single-edition dolls on swings.'

Dad and I exchanged a smile.

'Oh, lovely, well, maybe Dad and I can go to the park then, and meet you back here when it's time to go?' I said.

'Oh, no,' she said, 'you don't understand. I'm not coming back with you for a couple of days. I'm staying with a friend. We're going to see the *Jersey Boys* tonight, then I'm stopping over . . .' She looked at Dad and he smiled at her. 'I thought I'd give you and your dad some time together.'

'Thank you, Denise,' I said. 'I really appreciate that.' And I did.

Dad and I decided to skip the park bit; I was looking forward to getting out of London. We took the last bits to the car, and Dad went back in to use the loo, so it was just Denise and me standing on the pavement, her in her tight jeans and her knee-length boots and her hair that didn't move, even though there was quite a breeze.

'I'm so glad everything was okay, love,' she said, giving me a hug. 'We can look forward now, eh? Not long now. And we'll have a new member of the family.'

'Yep,' I said. 'A new member of our family.'

So, here I am in the back of my dad's car on our way back to Kilterdale – to home. I can't remember it ever being the two of us on a long journey like this, let alone after Mum died. I don't think we've ever done this, in fact. It feels like such a treat, such a privilege.

The car is pristine, of course; it smells of pine freshener and leather and the latest Monday's valet clean. There's Dire Straits playing on the radio – we've already agreed this is quite funny – and Dad got me a blanket out of the boot, which I've got over my legs like some convalescing old lady, which is kind of how I feel. I sleep most of the way, my head resting on a cushion Dad also gave me out of the boot, but tells me not to mention that to Denise because, in retrospect, she wouldn't be very happy about bringing new cushions from their brand-new house into the car.

I doze, happily, in and out of consciousness for the first hour or so. When I open my eyes, I can see city lights, telegraph wires against a slate-grey sky, distant towns, housing estates, the M6 Toll and then, eventually, the countryside, the North of England, growing greener and hillier and craggy brown. Becoming more dramatic. Dad makes a point of turning off the music, to start talking to me, and it still takes me aback, like the drive through Friars Lanes all those weeks ago, when he'd asked me suddenly why I was going to Marion's funeral. He asks me what work have said and I tell him that, actually, I think they're glad to see the back of me for a bit, glad to grant me early maternity leave, since I've not been firing on all cylinders for quite some time now. I accept I need a break. Grace got a place in the recovery centre – it wasn't perfect – but it was a start, it was an improvement on hospital and she'd informed me by text that there were 'no bloody jigsaws.' There is silence, then he clears his throat and he says:

'I think a long break is just what you need, love,' said Dad, but then his voice actually cracks. 'It's very damaging, you know, to keep things to yourself for so long.'

I don't know what to say, so I just rest my chin on the back of his seat and smile at him through the mirror so that he knows how much that means to me, how grateful and relieved I am that this is out in the open. Also, I realize suddenly, that this is my moment, this is my time (in the car, where he can't walk off or announce he's going to the toilet or to read the paper) to tell him about Niamh, so I say:

'Actually, there's not just me who's been keeping secrets, Dad.'

'Mm? Why's that?' he says, changing lanes, momentarily distracted. 'Who else has been keeping secrets then?'

'Well, there's Neevy, too.'

'What *about* Niamh?'

Oh God, Oh God! 'Well, Dad, well . . .' My heart's thumping wildly – I didn't expect this. What if he freaks out? What if our newly formed closeness is smashed to pieces by his homophobia? His small-mindedness? I realize it wouldn't just be Niamh who would be crushed, but me too. I wouldn't be able to forgive him. Still, it's too late now. I've opened my mouth so I must carry on.

'She's gay,' I say simply, turning my head to the window, closing my eyes, as if ready for the blow of disappointment, the withdrawing, the stony silence. 'She and Mary are partners, they're lovers.'

But the stony silence doesn't come; what comes is laughter. My dad is actually laughing! And so I sit up to look and stare at him. And he says:

'I know.' He's shaking his head, coughing and laughing at the same time. 'Bloody hell, we may be old farts, Denise and I, but we're not *blind*!'

'So why didn't you say anything to me?!', I say in disbelief.

'Because we didn't know you knew, did we? We were waiting for you to say something!'

A few miles before we reach home, I feel I've slept as much as is humanly possible, and so I sit up on the back seat and get out the letter with the small, spidery handwriting; the same handwriting he had when he was sixteen. It had arrived at my flat while I was in hospital. I'd been imagining its soft thud on the doormat, whilst all hell was breaking loose.

Dear Robbie,
Before you start reading (I'm hoping you've at least read this far, that you haven't screwed this up and put it in the bin. Please don't. Please hear me out), this isn't one of those letters where I beg you to be with me.

I know you can't be with me, darling and, no matter how much it hurts, I understand. And I don't want you to feel bad. In fact, I only want you to feel free and calm, and to know that I will be okay

403

– I know you may find that hard to believe, but I will! You are about to give me a daughter, our daughter. Of course I'm going to be okay. I'm going to be brilliant. I am the luckiest man alive.

So, there will be no begging from me. I just wanted to write this letter because I wanted to talk to you, because I still have things to say. Things I want you to know:

I guessed about Saul – as you know. I put two and two together from things you'd said and certain looks and that time in bed when I'd mentioned his name and also I remembered about that night, Tony Middleton's party, all those years ago, about how you arrived and how you wanted immediately to leave. Why did I not ask you more questions then? Why did I not ask Butler if he knew what was wrong with you?

I won't lie to you – at first I DID want to kill him. I wanted to ram his stupid, thick ugly head against a wall. I wanted to break into his house and tie him up and terrorize him, and see how he liked it, to feel that scared; that violated and invaded.

It ate away at me. I couldn't stand that someone had done this to you, the only girl I have ever been in love with in this world and, more than that, I couldn't stand the fact that I had let this happen when I should have protected you.

So, Robyn, I went round there. I wasn't going to hurt him – I'd decided fairly early on this wasn't a good idea – but I just wanted to face him, head on. I wanted to have it out with him. I planned, maybe, I'd just give his car a good kicking.

I got there, though, and I couldn't do it, I didn't do it. I stood in front of his shit little house (where FYI, he doesn't live any more, because he's divorced now) and, I realized, there was no point having it out with him, that that wouldn't help you. That what you needed – as you said – was to move on from it, and me dragging it up from the past wouldn't help. So I walked away; but I can tell you that he has had his comeuppance, Robbie. His life is shit. He has criminal offences, his marriage broke up, he doesn't see his kids, he has had to move away somewhere far from Kilterdale, and live in a shitty little flat. Saul Butler isn't there any more, Robbie – he can't hurt you.

The other thing I know: I know that Lily might not have been mine. I worked that out, too. I hate to think how keeping that secret all these years must have torn you apart and I wish, God, I wish you'd have just told me, because I don't care, Robyn. I couldn't care less if she came from a stork or outer space or the moon. She WAS mine, is mine, because I loved her when she was a life inside you and I loved you. She was half you, so how could I not?

It absolutely kills me to think that for even a second in the past sixteen years you have thought that what happened to us – any of it – would change one molecule of the way I feel about you, that if and when I found out, I wouldn't want you. I love you, Robyn, and that means all of you – whatever happened, or may happen in the future.

That's all I wanted to say, that's all I wanted you

to know. Now just relax, that's all I want you to do. You aren't just going to be the most amazing mother in the world, you already are.

Joe x

I clutched the letter to my chest and I cried then, because I realised it wasn't Joe – it had never been Joe who caused me to get ill, to trigger the panic attacks, to fall apart – that, actually, of everyone in my life, Joe had been the one person who had always been there for me. He'd been the one constant person in my life. And I'd pushed him away. I'd sabotaged it. I'd *made myself* ill. Was it too late?

Chapter Thirty-Three

It was Denise in the end who masterminded the whole 'Going Through Mum's Things' afternoon. Dad was the one to actually tell us (only took him sixteen years) that there were six boxes filled with Mum's things that he'd kept in the loft of our old house and that we might like to go through them. But it was Denise whose idea it was to get us all together in Kilterdale and to make it an event of sorts.

None of us could believe, quite frankly, that Dad had had this stuff in the attic for so long and not thought to get it down for us. But then maybe he thought it would be too painful for us. Maybe he thought we weren't ready, or he wasn't ready. Maybe he just didn't think much at all, which is a far more likely scenario.

Leah said cynically at first that Denise probably got the ball rolling because she couldn't tolerate the mess Mum's boxes were making, cluttering up their spare room. (Dad and Denise have downsized fairly dramatically and their new place is more of a chalet than a house.)

But *I* think it was a nice idea, an olive branch to Leah in a way. Denise knew she'd come to Kilterdale if it was going to be about Mum, but that at the same time she'd get to spend time with her, to make a start on mending bridges. And that is what she wants to do, I think. I've watched Denise over the last few months and I think she wants nothing more than to be accepted by all three of us. I think she wants to be a grandmother to our children and I, for one, am going to let her, because as Leah said, they come as one anyway, so if you get one, you get the other. You get Dad, too!

So, on the weekend after I arrived in Kilterdale to convalesce, Leah and Niamh arrived by train to join me in going through our mother's things. I was feeling relaxed when I went to pick them up at the station, the kind of relaxed I used to feel as a fourteen/fifteen-year-old when I had nothing more important to worry about than what I was going to wear to the U16s Saturday disco.

I'd had a lovely week. Dad had waited on me hand and foot. The first night I was there, we went to Mr Fry's together, just me and him, and had fish and chips outside, with a can of Dr Pepper. We didn't talk much, but that to me meant more than any words he could have said.

Denise made tea and biscuits for us all on arrival. Leah and her had the first proper conversation they had had in sixteen years, about how biscuits definitely go soft if you put them in the tin without their original wrapper and how annoying people are who insist on doing that (and then they wonder why their Rich Tea last only a few days . . . unbelievable). After tea, all three of us went into the spare room, took the boxes down from their pile up against the wall and began to open them.

And that smell. Our mother. Released immediately into the room like a dove. She was there with us! Obsession by Calvin Klein mixed with Vosene shampoo, a heady, indescribable, inexplicable *eau-de-our-mother* and, underneath, just a faint whiff – it was only on certain items, like her old fake fur and one or two handbags – of Rothman's cigarettes.

One by one, we opened the boxes as if they were treasure-troves. Niamh and Leah sat on the floor and I perched on the single bed that sagged in the middle.

Denise mainly kept out of the way, intermittently offering us tea and bringing us snacks in ramekins. Dad put his head around the door now and again. 'Don't worry, I'm not staying, this is your thing,' he'd say each time. But then, inevitably, he'd get drawn in – when we brought out this and that item that triggered a memory – into telling us tales, filling in stories, providing more pieces of the jigsaw, so that we could make the whole.

There was a collection of tacky plates from foreign climes, with things like, HOT HOT HOTTIE IN LANZAROTE! on them. Mum and Dad had loved their beach holidays. There was a particularly tacky one from Crete, featuring a Greek tavern and a donkey. 'Yeah, that holiday was bloody brilliant.' Dad laughed when he saw it, hovering in the doorway. 'Your mother crashed the car on day one by driving on the wrong side of the road, meaning we had no other option than to daytime drink by the pool for ten whole days – no visiting ancient ruins, no wandering around shops.'

And of course, there were so many things we'd forgotten that came back to us when surrounded by her possessions; memories that had been tucked away in each of our heads but never shared until now. It made me feel rooted.

I brought out a plastic bag from one of the boxes; even that looked from another era, another time. It was a green 'St Michael's' bag. Nobody says St Michael's any more. Only M&S or Marks and Spencer's. In this bag were various items of clothing, among them the pink towelling playsuit that she wore to do the gardening from the very first ray of March sunshine to the last of October.

I held it up and gasped.

'Do you know what?' I said. 'This is what I imagine her wearing when I think of her.'

'God, that's so weird,' said Leah. 'Because so do I. That and the massive sunglasses.'

'Yes. The massive white-framed sunglasses!'

'Although, let's face it,' chipped in Niamh, 'half the time she used to sunbathe in her underwear. Even I remember *that* shame!' We all then remembered about the boiling-hot day, when Leah had brought home a couple of mates from school without ringing first, and Mum was making quiche Lorraine with Niamh in only her pants (Niamh, oddly was fully dressed).

'I have never been more mortified in my life,' said Leah, dryly.

'The worst thing was,' I chipped in, 'she wasn't even bothered – boobs out, belly out. She was like, "Well, we're all girls here . . .!"'

We were there for three hours; it felt like three hours with Mum. There were the clothes – so many beautiful clothes (and some horrors; in particular a 1970s bright

410

mustard polo neck and a couple of diamond-encrusted, shoulder-padded monstrosities). But there were also old calendars with her hospital appointments on, her and Dad's engagements, our school events . . . And then there was her handbag: a roomy tan bag from Dolcis, with her reading glasses and her purse and some stamps and her work badge that said LILLIAN KING: SENIOR MIDWIFE on it (I used to stand and watch her put that on before every shift); the old cheque books and progammes from the endless dance shows we were in, which Mum loved but Dad had to sit through. Just stuff from a life lived. An ordinary life lived by an extraordinary person.

I couldn't remember the last time we were all in Kilterdale, in one room together (must have been when Mum was alive), and that alone felt like a blanket of comfort around me, let alone our mother's possessions; pieces of her, fragments of the life she had lived, and we had shared. The life that only we knew. It felt like such a privilege.

I looked over at my sisters on the floor. They were fully involved in a heated debate over who should have a pair of our mother's snakeskin Saxone heels, and so I took my chance. I picked up the tan handbag so it was nestling against my bump, stuck my head in, and took a great lungful of that glorious Obsession/Vosene/Rothman's potion. My mum. The woman who gave birth to me. The reason I am here.

I was thinking of the letter she wrote to me before she died. She'd been hardly strong enough to hold the pen and had had to keep having breaks but, finally, she got it down:

'Of the three of you, I am least worried about you because I know you are going to be fine. I know you are strong.'

Right now was the first time in sixteen years that I actually believed her. But then, that's because I wasn't really strong back then; but I am now.

Chapter Thirty-Four

Several days later

Rising from the back of Kilterdale, as if keeping watch over the village, as if holding the people to its broad chest, is a hill, and at the brow of that hill is an ancient wood where, in a glade, Joe and I had an oak tree planted for Lily. I used to worry I'd regret that tree; that, as it grew – something Lily never got to do – I'd somehow resent it; but, actually, over the years, I've found it incredibly comforting to go there. Sometimes I just sit and think; sometimes I take the Sunday papers and, like today, a flask of tea. I like how, despite the huge, much older oaks that almost form a canopy now, in the fullness of October, our tree still finds its way to the light, to keep on growing.

I'm on my way there in my car – or I should say, *our* car – the little Renault 5 that stays in Dad and Denise's garage for all three of us to use, if ever we go back. This week, staying at their new house has been one of the nicest I've ever spent with them. Not a defensive swish through a beaded curtain in sight from Denise. I think she's thoroughly enjoyed her role as matron. Her relief to be finally out of the house that was my mother's is palpable; she has relaxed, Dad has relaxed. I imagine my mother – if she could see us all – has relaxed, too. I imagine she has been wondering, as I have, what took them so long.

Today, I am thirty weeks pregnant. I said those words to myself when I got up this morning. I opened the Velux window of the spare room – the sun was just climbing over the hills, and the trees of this wood were stacked in three neat rows, growing lighter in green as they neared the horizon. I stuck my head out. The air was so fresh, you could smell the sap rising, and I said, *Today you are thirty weeks pregnant.* Your baby has pretty much the same chances of survival if she was born now, as a baby that has gone full term. I felt like I'd shed a skin, stepped into another life, one without constant anxiety.

I can't say for sure what will happen to Joe and me in the future. Some days, I worry I have put him through too much – it's too late. Other days, I read his letter and I'm hopeful it's not. Whatever I think I always knew deep down, that he wouldn't reject me when he knew the truth. It was me who had to accept the truth and then to accept me. And now that I've done that, and I have told my sisters, that truth doesn't seem so dark and so terrible any more; it feels like it's melted, like snow beneath the sun.

What else do I know? I know that, whether or not Joe and I work out, I don't want him to be a weekend dad. I've been thinking about what he said to me that

414

night all those weeks ago, when he lay on my bed in London, about him wanting to be there for the hard bits, the difficult bits too, the discipline and the potty training, and I've decided I want that too. Of course I want that too! Whether that might be in the same house or separate ones, I want that.

I couldn't wait to come up here to Lily's tree. I suppose it's my way of saying, don't worry, you won't be forgotten, but also to mark the start of something, because for every day that Lily's tree grows now, hopefully, I will too, and I feel comforted by that, like Lily's still part of things.

I turn a corner, change gear to make the last climb of that hill. I feel oddly light, like when I reach the top, I might just carry on, take off into the sky, like a helium balloon. Everywhere is so verdant: the green sprouts from every crevice of the countryside, from in between the folds of the hilly fields I can see from up here, like the countryside is literally bursting at the seams. The road is narrow, because of the fat hedges at either side, and I feel like I almost have to breathe in, to hold in my bump – pretty enormous to me, although I am told there is still a way to go, that I won't believe how big I become! – to fit through.

I park at the little layby and get out, pausing to drink in the green smell and make the short walk through the woods to the glade and that tree, which is just over fifteen years old now, but still a baby compared to the others around it.

There's this convenient little tree-stump chair next to Lily's tree and I sit down on it, slightly breathless after about a fifty-metre walk from the car – I wonder what I am going to be like at thirty-seven weeks pregnant?

Thirty-eight, hopefully, thirty-nine? I know Joe has been up here on occasions, too, over the past fifteen years, even though we've hardly been in touch; I've liked to think of him sitting here, the sunlight dappling through the leaves. I've liked how the tree has connected us in some way; how, whatever happens to my and Joe's relationship, it still does.

I get out my flask of tea. From up here, I can see that skirt of Kilterdale, the white froth of bungalows, right up to the hem, and then the sea, silvery and endless. I feel different. I can't put my finger on how, at first, and then I realize that that twist in the gut I always got when I came back here to Kilterdale, the feeling that every single beautiful memory I have of this place was taken from me, is gone; that those memories are starting to filter back now. I'm getting my hometown back.

I unscrew the top off the flask, set it on the floor, and am just about to pour it in the cup I have attached, when I hear something, footsteps, a familiar bounding rhythm, and I know before I even turn around who it is. *Maybe one day, in the future, we can meet there.*

'Hello, I thought I'd find you here.' And then he's there. Joe, his hair falling over his eyes, wearing a green polo shirt, as fresh as the countryside, and I'm already smiling. 'I've got these,' he says, walking towards me, turning two fun-sized Mars bars from his jeans pockets. 'I've got the chocolate if you can provide the tea.'

'Now that's an offer I can't refuse,' I say, and I pour the tea as he sits down on the ground next to me, elbows resting on his knees, blowing the hair out of his face. That hair that he can't do anything with – I wonder if the baby will inherit that? He needs a haircut.

'Do you know how pregnant I am today?' I say as he unwraps the chocolate. 'I'm thirty weeks pregnant, which is more pregnant than I have ever been in my life.'

'I know,' he says, reaching up and taking the tea from me, squinting, smiling with the sun. 'I feel like we made it, don't you?'

And I do, I say, I do.

He puts the tea down and shifts up then, wrapping his arms around my knees, laying his head on my knees. It feels so good. We sit like that, the breeze blowing the leaves of Lily's tree gently, and I think how there are two choices in life: to continue to tell yourself the same old story, or to be constantly writing yourself a new one. To be right, or be happy, I suppose; and I believed, for the first time in years, in that moment, that I could be happy and that was all that mattered – that what Joe could give me was bigger, more powerful than what Butler could ever take away.

EPILOGUE

Christmas Day 2013

Dear Lily

I write to you from the arctic tundra of Kilterdale shore, where today I am to scatter my mother's – your grandma's ashes. (It's what she would have wanted – swimming on Christmas Day!)

It's a big day! I'm saying goodbye to her, I suppose, and I'm saying goodbye to you. Lily, this is to be the last letter I ever write to you, and therefore I need you to know certain things: I may be saying goodbye today, but will never forget you for as long as I live. I won't forget that you existed – if only as a life inside of me – or how losing you changed my life. I won't forget what you taught me. <u>That</u> will go on forever, inside of me.

Writing to you has been my saviour at so many times, the only place where I have been able to be a hundred per cent honest about my life, but also where I have been reminded how beautiful life is, how, even when the worst things imaginable happen, good things happen too. I have some amazing people in my life, Lily. Love continues to grow, and ultimately, I think, to win. That's what life, what losing you, has taught me. It's also taught me that although your past will always be part of your story, it's not all of you and you can't – *mustn't* – let it define your future.

And I have a future, I have one with Joe, your father and our new baby – a little girl, Megan Lillian Sawyer. She's beautiful and she will always, in some ways, remind us of you. But I have to move on, my love. This is why this letter will be the last, because I have to leave the past where it belongs. I have to let you go.

THE END

READING GROUP GUIDE

🕊 One of the themes in the book is about the way in which mental illness is not that far from all of us. Early on, Robyn says, 'Sometimes I wonder if we're not all a bit mad, it's just a question of when, not if, the lid comes off'. What do you think of that statement? Do you think Robyn is right?

🕊 Robyn pushes Joe away at first and she is quite conflicted: she loves him but he reminds her of her past. Why do you think he hangs in there for her? What is it about Joe's character and his life experience that means he can take it when other people might not?

🕊 Why do you think that Robyn cares so much about Grace and helping her to make a connection with Cecily, her daughter?

🕊 Why do you think Robyn writes to Lily over the years, even though she died? Is this some kind of cathartic process, and why?

🕊 The past comes back to haunt Robyn once Joe reappears on the scene and she becomes pregnant again. Do you think that the past defines us, or has to define us?

🕊 The relationship between Robyn and her two sisters, Leah and Niamh, improves greatly throughout the book. How and why does this happen?

🕊 At the end of the book, Robyn says, 'I realized that what Joe could give me was much bigger than what Saul Butler took away'. What does she mean by this?

A Q&A WITH KATY REGAN

1. What do you listen to when you're writing? Do you have a playlist?

I can't listen to music at all when I'm writing! I have to have silence and am finding it harder and harder to find cafés to write in that don't play music, which means that when I'm bored of writing at home, I usually go to my local library now. It's so boring you HAVE to write!

2. What do you do when you get writer's block?

Panic! I'm a dreadful panicker. Then I usually leave it for a day or two, because by that point I've fretted so much that there really is no point in pushing it. It's better to have a break and come back refreshed. Also, sometimes, if I am stuck on plotting, I might go and do something else like write a scene I do know how to do, or work some more on characterisation.

3. Have you always wanted to be a writer? Was it hard to get into?

I've always wanted to write for a living but didn't think people like me could do it for real! It just proves, though, that with a little bit of talent plus LOTS of hard work and bum-on-seat time, you can make it happen. I was a journalist, initially, for magazines like *Marie Claire* and the fiction sort of evolved from that, but it still wasn't easy by any means – even though I was already used to writing every day. I basically spent a year teaching myself with text books, reading loads and there was lots of trial and error.

4. What Top 5 tips would you give to an aspiring writer?

Turn off the internet, turn off your mobile phone, guard some time of your life to write every week, read loads and have a brilliant, original idea (not much then!).

5. Who is the first person you let read your books?

My brilliant agent, Lizzy.

6. Is there a message in your novels that you want readers to grasp?

They all have different ones I guess, but I like writing about things that are true to life and that people can relate to. I think, consciously or unconsciously, I write about connection and community – my biggest fear of all, is probably loneliness.